RUBEN

DEVOTED BROTHERS

BOOK TWO

SIÂN UPTON

Ruben
By Siân Upton

Wear your OUTCAST status like a perfectly worn in leather jacket—cozy, familiar, timeless.

Dear Reader,

I often describe my writing as *romance meets realism.* What does this mean? I put my characters through things some readers may find unsettling. Childhood trauma, medical situations, death, dysfunctional families, self-sabotage, etc. are liberally sprinkled in because I believe characters are more profound if they are relatable. Nobody has a perfect, drama free life; therefore, my characters don't either. So, while there are often dark themes or events in my stories, rest assured there will always be a happily ever after or happy for now. Real people experience plenty of amazing things too, so I can promise you will find humor, love, connection, and triumph alongside the crazy. And of course, some spice!

XOXO~ Siân

Chapter One

VINNY

Vinny slotted her key into the deadbolt and gave it a turn. The party she could hear on the other side of the door to what *should* feel like home had reached her ears before she'd killed the engine of her car. All she wanted to do was sleep, but her boyfriend obviously had other ideas for her homecoming.

Pushing the door open, Vinny walked in and froze as confusion momentarily set in. *Where is everybody? And where the hell is Jake?*

Peals of laughter immediately followed by an erotic moan answered all the thoughts racing through Vinny's mind. She slowly walked down the hall toward their bedroom. Along the way, she saw items of clothing strewn haphazardly. *How cliché.* Through the open door, she could see their owners... and Jake.

Vinny had wanted Jake's second chance to work out. He seemed to have matured in their years apart, but apparently not—or not for long, at least.

Why aren't I mad?

Blood coursed through her travel fatigued body with a shot of relief.

And.

She.

Smiled.

I'm free again. I'm free again! Fuck, I should have known better. Carys was right about him, and getting this stupid apartment with him so soon...

Vinny's mind raced while her feet moved almost languorously back down the hallway. From the hall closet, she pulled out the cases for the guitars she hadn't taken out on tour with her. She removed the instruments from their wall hooks, carefully tucking her babies away. She had enough clothing still packed from the tour to get by for now, so her focus was more professional in nature.

No way I'm letting him sell off my expensive equipment for his own benefit.

It took a few trips back down to her car, but she managed to put all the most expensive and critical items she didn't dare leave behind in her car within fifteen minutes, while Jake was still in the middle of his little orgy. As oddly as it was to not be bothered finding him so, she wasn't about to go count the number of tits and asses flashing around in there.

Besides...if memory served, he'd have a few of his bros in there too.

And while Vinny was a huge supporter of the LGBTQ+ community, she drew a line at it materializing in her home at the invitation of her boyfriend—who had sworn her *monogamy*. It wasn't who or even how many was with him, it was Jake himself.

Disingenuous. Senseless. Moronic *Jake.*

He'd just bit the hand that fed him, the lazy slob. Not once had he worked since they had met back up on tour. Vinny knew his money must be wearing thin by now, even with all the bills automated from her accounts because his credit score was fucking shit, and nobody would let him on the billing statements without astronomical down payments. She didn't blame the system—Jake had shown her his bank statements as he explained his financial "bad luck" story when they moved in together—she blamed herself for settling, all because she was financially secure enough for the both of them.

No matter. She'd call around tomorrow and remove her name from every service. The super loved her, so getting her name dropped from the lease should be a breeze, since Jake *was* on that. Of course, he'd be royally fucked when he was on his ass at the end of the month when rent came due and further ruined when they charged him for breaking the lease.

Oopsie.

Vinny didn't need to get angry. She didn't need to huff and puff and fret over her blockhead *ex.* He'd sink his own ship fine alone, while she was too far away to be bothered by his pathetic cries for help.

She walked through the apartment one more time, grabbing anything she'd missed before. Her phone began to vibrate in her back pocket. It was late for most people. Vinny's gut told her this was not a good call, as she balanced her things in one arm so she could answer the phone.

"Hello?"

"Vinny," Eric said, his voice harsh. Her stomach plummeted as it filled with apprehension.

"Hey, hang on," she said, scuttling herself outside and closing the door. "What's wrong?"

"Are you back?"

"Sure am. And free as a bird, so tell me what's up because you don't cry, and it's freaking me out, Eric." If anyone knew how to keep their cool, it was her best friend's husband.

"There was an accident. Carys is in the hospital."

"I'm on my way," she said, her footsteps heavy on the staircase as she raced her way back down. "Where am I going?"

"To the house," he said, as she slid into her car. "I'm headed home to clean up and relieve Ruben, but I want to be back before she wakes up."

"See you soon."

Eric hung up the phone without a goodbye as Vinny shifted her car into drive and navigated back out onto the street. Less than an hour ago, she'd been bone tired and wanting nothing more than sleep. Now her heart was breaking as she navigated back onto the freeway headed south toward Oceanside, where her best friend lived with her husband and daughter.

Holy shit, the baby. He didn't say anything about the baby. Does that mean it's okay? She's still pregnant? But if she's bad off enough for him to sound this miserable, there is no way…

Stop it, Lavender Blume! Focus! Get to the house. Focus on Maya so Eric can focus on Carys and the baby.

A world where Carys lost her baby was unacceptable. There would be no more entertaining the thought. The baby was alive, and by the time Vinny got a turn at the hospital, Carys would be sitting up in bed with the baby either safe in her belly or her arms.

It was the only reality. No other could exist.

Vinny commanded her phone to play her favorite Weezer album and promised herself she'd drive whatever speed necessary to arrive before it ended.

She made it before the last song could even play.

———

BEFORE COLLAPSING onto the guest bed, Vinny had set an alarm so she'd be sure to wake little Maya at the usual hour. She loved her goddaughter—Carys and Eric's surprise love baby—who to Vinny's sensibilities embodied the permanent honeymoon their marriage seemed to be. And that wasn't lip service, either. People wrote all sorts of frivolous nonsense trying to personify what her bestie had found in marriage.

It had come at a price, of course. Eric was a Marine. His job required him to go places Carys wasn't allowed to know about. Any day, he could come home to her with the news he had twenty-four hours to be on a plane to who knew where, for however long Uncle Sam deemed necessary.

Sometimes it weighed heavily on Carys. Vinny did her best to be around more often when Eric was deployed, but she was a musician. Her job was on the road mostly, although she was well past supporting herself with what she generated through her ArtBeat account.

She'd been one of the first hundred—literally, she knew its creator and had been invited to beta test it before it had fully launched—to start their account on the now wildly popular media site dedicated to artists of all sorts. There were musicians with larger followings than hers, but all of them were headliners. Vinny had the largest audience of any account on ArtBeat that was a free agent. The rest all had record deals and touring contracts and the other things that stripped your freedom faster than it could promise to deliver in gold.

Freedom was priceless.

And since she had it, her ArtBeat account was completely organic. She created all the content she wanted; however she wanted. There wasn't a single product she repped she didn't use and believe in. She was in complete control of her own image, *thank you very much.*

So, she had the *freedom* to scoop her favorite little lovie out of her bed at seven in the morning on far too little sleep after so much travel, take her to the potty with promises of chocolate chip pancakes if she made it in time, and then happily stumble down to the kitchen to fulfill her verbal contract. Maya was feisty this morning, but *Auntie Vinny* knew how to play her toddler games.

By the time Eric stumbled down the stairs and into the kitchen an hour later, Maya had consumed her body weight in flapjacks and was helping Vinny scoop the coffee grounds for a fresh pot. Eric's favorite mug was already down, and as soon as there was enough, Maya helped Vinny make her daddy's cup just right.

"Hey," she said when he appeared. Eric lost his control the moment their eyes locked, tears tracking down his face. Vinny set Maya down in her booster at the table with the last of her breakfast and took him into the living room. "Let's have it, Eric," she said soothingly as she pulled him down to the couch.

"She'd had a checkup for the baby. Just regular pregnancy wellness visits. We were on our way home, joking around about what to name the baby. She did a double take, said something about a shadow on the overpass up ahead, but I didn't think anything of it. Traffic was moving along well for once," he said, choking up. "Next thing I knew, I was waking up. The windshield was smashed in, there was so much *noise,* and it smelled like iron. When I called out to her I tasted the tang of blood in the air.

"It was everywhere. All over Carys's face, down her body. Puddling on the floorboard…"

"Take your time."

He nodded. "They had to take the baby out. He's in the

NICU. Her uterus was…they couldn't save it. Not and save *her.*"

"Do they think she will make it?" Vinny asked softly through her own tears.

"Yeah. It's going to be hard, but she made it through surgery. The doctor said if they could get the bleeding to stop, she'd more than likely recover." Vinny could tell his mind spiraled off then, somewhere dark and cruel given his change in expression. She had seen enough trauma in her own life to recognize he'd experienced the unimaginable and would likely relive it for some time.

"Thank you for calling me, Eric. I would have come no matter what. Even if I'd been on the other side of the world, I'd have come." Vinny squeezed his hand tightly, hoping her sleep deprived brain was making some sense at all to him. "You're my family too."

He nodded. "Yeah. Family."

"Okay," she said, withdrawing her hand and standing. "What do you need? Let's see. I'll go up and pack a small bag for Carys. Her favorite bathrobe, real underwear. We can put in a picture of Maya too. Maybe some toiletries. And we'll do up a bag for you too, Eric. We're going to be good here, so you can focus on our girl."

Eric stood and pulled her into a tight hug.

"Thanks, Vin."

He's in the NICU.

Carys and Eric had a son.

Please let him live. She can't lose her baby and her womb both, she mentally plead the universe. Her best friend was a natural mother and had been reborn when she'd found out she was pregnant the first time. Vinny watched her best friend go from determined college graduate to a wife and mother in the blink of an eye. It suited her.

Their spring break no strings attached week in Mexico had ended with Carys coming home with an unknown stowaway. Eric had pulled strings before leaving, begging her before they parted to reunite months later at the same resort after she'd finished her master's degree and he'd come back from a deployment. He paid for the room—a full week in a luxury suite—plus handed her cash for airfare, knowing college wasn't cheap and not wanting money to be the reason he didn't see her again.

Vinny pushed Carys to follow her heart while her mother had been a total bitch, claiming the return to Mexico was a waste of time. They had walked away with only each other's first names and a promise to return for each other with no hurt feelings if either didn't show.

Eric had been fashionably late, but more than made up for it when Carys shared she was carrying his baby. They'd returned to the states married, further angering Carys's mother. Eric had stepped in, demanding her mother apologize before she could see his wife or child again. He'd already passed all Vinny's tests, but in that moment, she accepted Eric as her new brother from another mother.

She loved Eric as much as she loved Carys and Maya. She loved their new baby boy too.

She obviously had not loved Jake because it wasn't until he called her about his eviction notice three weeks later he even crossed her mind.

Chapter Two

RUBEN

"But I need you," she whined. "All you ever do is spend time with *them.* What about *me?* I'm your wife, Ruben!"

"Carla, they were in a huge accident. They could have died. Slow is my best friend, and he needs my support right now. It doesn't mean I love you less," Ruben tried to reassure her.

"You promised me!"

"And I will keep my promise like always. You've never asked for input booking a trip before," he pointed out. "I always love our time together, whatever you plan."

Truthfully, any time he made a suggestion to Carla, she'd insist on doing the exact opposite. Once or twice, he'd used it to his advantage with a bit of reverse psychology. Ruben loved his wife, as high maintenance as she could be.

Or rather *was.*

He'd made a lot of sacrifices for Carla over the years so she would feel valued. Deep down, he believed she was insecure from the way her mother had treated her as more of an accessory than a person growing up. Her father was a respected Navy admiral and had been gone a lot while she was young. She was a classic military brat who hadn't been openly loved enough by either of her parents when it had mattered the most.

Ruben was happy to love her now and to fill that gap. He poured his all into his marriage with his on and off again college sweetheart turned bride, patiently believing she'd settle down with time and stop seeing his friends as competition.

Except this week.

Eric and Carys were doing well, and baby Brendon was as well as could be expected for a four and a half pound preemie. But Maya wasn't allowed in the hospital wing where her mother was recovering, and Eric—who he'd given the moniker Slow back in college—was trying to juggle his wife and son in the hospital while pretending he wasn't still healing from injuries of his own. Ruben took his role as godfather seriously, and he was determined to be there for Maya.

"Tell you what, babe. I'll see if there is room in the schedule for an extra day or two of leave to make it up to you," he said, pulling her back into his chest and wrapping his arms around her middle. He could tell she'd been fad dieting again by how bony she felt and fought back a cringe.

"Really?"

"Yes. I'll call the scheduling office while Maya is busy," he promised. She tensed at the reminder he'd be heading across the street for a few hours. "And when I get home," he added, dropping his head into the crook of her neck and nuzzling into her perfectly styled locks, "I'll make sure to put some extra work into making you happy as reward for sharing a little of my time this afternoon."

He didn't tell her he'd taken it upon himself to go over today, despite Carys's best friend temporarily moving in. It had been over two years, and he still hadn't met Vinny. Slow and Carys talked her up so much, Ruben wanted to go introduce himself. Maybe they could set up a regular schedule for helping out until Eric could bring Carys and the baby home.

Either way, he was curious. And since he'd wanted to rely on his gut impression of her, he'd resisted the urge to check out her ArtBeat account. Okay, fine. He'd snuck a peak, but he hadn't watched a single video. He'd given her account a quick scroll a few weeks before he proposed to Carla. She'd been so high strung since then; he didn't want his wife to think he was checking out another woman.

Man, could she get jealous.

Good thing he was a completely dedicated, one woman kind of man.

"Fine," she said, as if she was doing him a huge favor. "Hurry up and come back to me, baby."

He kissed her cheek tenderly before walking away.

Ruben was still sweaty from his morning run, so he took the stairs two at a time up to the master suite for a quick shower. Once he was out, he threw on shorts and a tee before twisting on the pipe cleaner bracelet Maya had made him the last time they were together.

Yes, pipe cleaners. You didn't earn the title of *Funcle* by doing boring shit. If his princess wanted to make pretties, Ruben was right there with her ready to model her creations.

He shoved his feet into his favorite sneakers and headed out the front door and across the street. Ruben found the door locked when he reached the Blackwood's porch. It was no trouble since he had his key in his pocket.

There weren't any cars in the driveway. *Did I miss them? Maybe Vinny took Maya to the park or out for groceries.* He glanced at his watch. It was naptime. Ruben knew from experience it was not a good time to brave the outside world with Maya.

With a shrug, he let himself in quietly, just in case. As the door latch caught, he heard an alarming and familiar sound from behind him and froze. His hand was still on the knob.

"Don't move."

Her voice was hard, without a trace of hesitation. He hadn't even set eyes on her yet, and he knew he'd find a woman dripping with confidence like an oversaturated sponge when he laid eyes on her.

"The gun isn't necessary," he said as calmly as he could.

"Hand's up, turn slowly."

Holy fucking…hell.

As he turned, Ruben's eyes drifted up to where she stood in the doorway between the living room and kitchen, across the room from the front door. Her feet were perfectly planted, her hands and arms properly supported and prepared to double tap his ass.

She flicked the safety off.

What the hell? Ruben felt a bead of sweat run down his spine.

"Would you mind putting the business end of your firearm away, please?" An interminably long stretch of silent tension followed.

"Just so we are clear, you *never* come walking in this house without warning again. I don't care if you are Santa Claus, I will end anyone or anything posing a threat to my family." Her thumb flipped the safety back on and she relaxed, casually stuffing the firearm into a hidden holster in the back of her ripped jeans. "Don't fuck with me, Ruben."

Rage flared through his body, fed by all the adrenaline he'd had to fight since he heard her chamber a bullet as he closed the door. "Are you fucking *kidding me?* You knew it was me?" He kept his voice low and walked halfway across the living room—not too close to little miss psycho, but close enough he wouldn't wake Maya talking at the bottom of the stairs.

"I knew you weren't *Eric,* which was more than enough."

You got a permit for that, little girl?" he clipped out. "That's not a toy. It shouldn't be anywhere near the princess."

She snorted. "Yes, I have my concealed carry license. A lady can't be too careful on the road alone these days. Eric knows about it, so your opinion is moot."

"You aimed it at my chest."

"And *you* walked into an otherwise silent and dark house that I know was locked, you idiot!" she hissed back. "All you had to do was give a soft knock first or *I don't know,* maybe wait at the door for me to let you in, instead of making yourself at home!"

"I *am* at home here! That's why I have my own key. The fuck is wrong with you?" he snarled back.

Vinny crossed her arms over her chest and staired at him. Her firm posture and hard glare coupled with an air of superiority and rightness in the moment further tensed his entire body, given he had done same as he had for years.

And Ruben hated it.

Her confidence, the way she held a damn firearm, not to mention her obvious dedication to keeping Maya safe—*from him*. Especially since Eric had said the cops thought the accident was caused by a gang initiation task. Everyone was running on adrenaline right now, but still.

Fuck.

He wanted to hate her so badly but was conflicted in the moment. The Marine in him knew he'd do the same to anyone who posed a threat to Maya. The way Eric talked about Vinny said a lot about her as a person, and if he was honest with himself, the scene he found himself cast in was completely within the scope of who his friends spoke of.

"I've had enough unpleasant surprises from men over the years," she said softly. "You can't begrudge me a little reassurance."

He couldn't, damn it.

"You chambered a round."

"As a warning."

"And flicked the safety off *after* you saw my face."

"I didn't recognize you at first."

"My picture is on the mantel!" he said, picking up one of the many frames beside him he featured in and waving it in front of himself.

"I couldn't see you from across the room. It's dark in here with the curtains drawn."

"I'm not a goddamn thug, Vinny!" he growled out. "Don't you ever pull that shit with me again."

"I can't promise anything unless you remember to *knock* or otherwise warn me you are on your way over," she said coolly.

It pissed him off.

Ruben had never needed to notify anyone he was coming over. Not since he and Eric met in college. They were fast friends and had been inseparable since, even when they had different bases. They'd meet up all sorts of places as often as they could. Eric had even gone home to Georgia with Ruben a few times for the holidays.

This wasn't Vinny's house to stipulate rules in. She had no power over Ruben. He set the picture back on the mantel and rubbed his face with his hands, trying to scrub away the disbelief. When he turned back to face her she was still in the same spot, leaning into the doorjamb like she owned the place.

It set Ruben off all over again. *Fuck her!*

"The key in my pocket is all the permission I need," he finally said. "I don't answer to you, and I don't owe you my timetable for being here."

"I live here. So, you damn well can tell me when you are on your way or *knock* when Eric isn't home." There wasn't a trace of apology to her. She'd pulled a gun on him and clearly wasn't sorry.

It shoved Ruben back into a place he'd fought hard to get out of.

"You could send a text, Ruben. I don't care if you are here, I just need to know who is walking in the door. It's basic safety."

"Right. I'll send you a friendly text so next time you can shoot down the big black guy before he gets all the way inside the house." His voice came out hard and accusing.

Vinny scowled, but her words remained calm and even. "I'd never shoot anyone without a valid reason. Race has nothing to do with it."

"You sure?" *Why am I egging her on?*

"Get out."

Her voice was soft, more kind than anything. But the firmness—that confidence of hers—it was still there in spades. It told Ruben she held all the cards, and to quit while he was ahead.

It hit him then, how different they were. Slow and Carys were constantly going on and on about how similar he was to this woman. Ruben couldn't see it at all. She was *cold.* How had this woman amassed such a huge following online?

He gnashed his teeth together as he walked backward to the door, his eyes trained on Vinny. He unlocked the door, opened it, and didn't turn away until it was firmly locked between them again.

What a fucking psycho.

Ruben strode across the street and into his house. He could hear his wife talking to her travel agent at the kitchen table and quietly went to his office before she saw him. He'd call scheduling now, and the next time he entered a room with a woman in it, she would be filled with gratitude.

Or at least he hoped so. Carla's mood all morning wasn't a great indicator she'd be in a better mood now or later.

Chapter Three

VINNY

Eric had cleared the storage area at the back of the rear garage years ago, so Vinny would have a place to set up a studio with all her instruments. Unbeknownst to her, all those years of reminding her she would always be welcome was more than a casual offer. She'd nearly cried when he took her to see it the week after Carys and Brendon were released from the hospital. When she was done *not* crying over how moved she was by the gesture, she squealed with delight before throwing her arms around his shoulders and hugging him tightly.

Since then, she'd gotten to work making it a space she could fully utilize. He'd beefed up the insulation and installed a wall unit to control the temperature, complete with a humidifier. She'd added some soundproofing and acoustic materials to the room, along with an area to edit her ArtBeat content without lugging her laptop around. Within a month, she had all sorts of LEDs and props installed.

The last time she'd had a dedicated place to rehearse and create whenever she liked was when she lived with her fellow musician father. Since then, any home she'd made was too temporary to put in the effort, and too restricting since it was out of an extra bedroom or her living room. The studio was her dream; and knowing Carys and Eric wanted her here badly enough to prepare it long before she was ready to settle into anything permanent made her feel valued and cherished.

She only wished things in the main house were progressing as well as her studio and apartment set up were. Carys was struggling. Vinny did her best to hide her anxiety from her friend, but she needn't bother. Carys was far too lost in her own head to notice the way it was affecting her family.

All of baby Brendon's firsts seemed bittersweet to Carys because without her permission, someone else's recklessness had made Brendon her last baby. The day a rock sailed over the six-foot fence on the overpass and into oncoming traffic —specifically through the windshield of Carys's car, which Eric was driving—she'd been robbed of her ability to create life ever again. Neither Eric or Vinny were stupid enough to point out they loved her with or without the ability to procreate, especially given she would have bled to death if they hadn't removed her womb. The emotional wound was still too raw, despite her scars healing up nicely otherwise.

Vinny spent most of her days in the house, helping keep Maya occupied while Carys did as much as she could muster the will to accomplish. It had been several months now, and she wasn't improving. If anything, she was slipping farther away from them. It was hard enough for Vinny and Eric to be patient, but Maya was two and a half and didn't understand why her mother was so sad all the time.

"She won't let me in," Eric told Vinny one afternoon. It was Saturday, and Carys was inside napping with the kids. Eric had come up to Vinny's apartment over the garage. Her heart broke, watching him sit helplessly on her sofa. "I try, but it's like she doesn't enjoy anything anymore. Not our family, or outings, or even sex. I don't know what to do to break this depression."

"I thought it would have broken by now too," Vinny admitted. "She's never been depressed a day of her life until now. The only time I see her smile at all is when she's with the kids, and even then it's forced."

"What do I do, Vin?"

"I'm not sure there *is* something you can do on your own. When is her next appointment?"

"Next week. They want to be sure the last of her internal injuries are clear."

"She's going to be pissed, but I think you need to tell the doctor about the depression when you go in. She needs to get into counseling and probably take some medication for a few months while she sorts her shit. She'd refuse to take medication while nursing, but since that didn't work out…"

Vinny didn't need to say more. Carys cried every day while she washed Brendon's bottles. They had both witnessed it.

Eric let out a frustrated sigh. "Yeah, you're right."

"I'll see if I can't get her to open up when we are alone too. We'll figure it out, Eric. Don't give up."

"I'll never give up on her," he said fiercely.

Her heart warmed and shattered all at once with his declaration. She knew exactly how he felt. Carys had been her best friend so long, she didn't have memories of a time before they met, and all Vinny's greatest hits involved Carys one way or another. "Me either."

After Eric went back downstairs to the main house, Vinny paced around, back and forth from her bedroom to the living room. It was an unusual apartment, and she loved everything about it. Half of it was above the two car garage attached to the house, where Carys and Eric parked their cars. The other half was over the two car garage in the rear of the house, with an enclosed breezeway between the two with windows on both sides to allow a cross breeze.

This hallway between the front and back of her apartment was situated just above and off the side of the pergola Eric had built over the back deck. He'd planted several California Honeysuckle at the base and trained them to climb up over the beams into a beautiful, fragrant canopy which was currently in full bloom. As Vinny passed the window during her fruitless circuit, she breathed in their delicate sweetness and willed it to inspire her.

No dice.

She went back to the rear of her apartment, where a back door opened straight ahead out onto a staircase and terminated in the garage below, plus a second door off to the side leading to her bedroom suite. Vinny veered left and flopped onto her queen-sized bed with a groan. *How am I going to help Carys if she won't tell anyone what's really going on inside her head?*

The sound of car doors slamming and females making complete idiots out of themselves forced Vinny back to the front of the house, so she could peek out her front window onto the street below where all the present drama was unfolding. She kept back a few feet where she wouldn't be noticed while she satisfied her curiosity.

There was a *pink Cadillac* in front of Ruben's house. Not a mouthwateringly stunning, well restored and preserved pale petal pink classic—a new model the color of Pepto Bismol. Its driver should sue her sunless tanning consultant for turning her persimmon orange instead of the tawny peach her soft, golden brown locks suggested would suit her. To make it all the more retina combusting, she was wearing an oddly cut chartreuse-green dress that made her look sickly. Her shoes made Vinny think of disco balls.

Carla was strutting down the front walk with her overnight bag, blowing kisses over her shoulder at Ruben—who she could barely see propped up in the front doorway from the chest down—like she was on a fucking runway instead of saying goodbye to her husband. The women came together with a flourish, Carla leaning in toward Vomit Salad Woman for air kisses. The trunk was popped, luggage stowed, and the two were off in a flash.

"What in the *haughty couture mess* did I just watch?" she mumbled to herself with amusement.

Her eyes went back to the porch without permission, taking in the man she'd come to loathe. Vinny had wanted Ruben to prove her wrong desperately. She *wanted* to like him. After their first meeting, things only got more awkward. She knew why she wasn't impressed with him, but it had stung when he'd accused her of being racist.

Ruben pulled his front door closed and took a seat on the top step of his porch. He was wearing shorts, and she could see some of his *polka dots,* as Maya called them. Vinny was sure if anyone else referred to Ruben's vitiligo like that it wouldn't end well, but Maya...she liked to color in Ruben's polka dots with her markers. More than once she'd seen him hustle home for a shower afterward.

Vinny had albinism. She understood more than most how different life could be when you had a melanin deficiency. She wondered what Ruben had looked like before. He was a beautiful, dark umber colored man. Not black as night, but close to it. He looked like he'd taste of bitter cacao if she licked him. Like the dark and white chocolate tuxedo mousse boxes she loved so much from her favorite restaurant.

Wait, what? I need to get laid. I'm comparing the enemy to deserts.

She watched as Ruben stood and walked the rest of the way down the steps and across the street to the Blackwood's door. They were home, so he didn't bother knocking—she'd have heard it from her hiding spot through the open window —and instead let himself in. He hadn't been back once while she was alone with the kids.

Not to apologize for the near panic attack she fought off when he silently let himself in like a damn cat burglar undaunted by the daylight.

And not to put it behind them and move on.

Instead of allowing disappointment, Vinny reminded herself of all the times Ruben had let her family down. He wasn't blameless. She'd been willing to try, but he obviously had decided otherwise. The sight of his emaciated wife escaping on another weekend away with friends didn't improve Vinny's opinion of either of them.

So, it was what it was, and while she knew it made Eric and Carys sad, Vinny wasn't about to crawl on her knees to get Ruben to try again.

His loss.

A wave of melancholy swept over her. Vinny's face scrunched with confusion. *Why would I feel melancholy?* She shook her head, grabbed her favorite guitar off the wall beside her, and took a seat on her couch. When emotions caught her off guard, she liked to let her body sort it out through chord progressions. As she strummed along, her gaze took in this side of her home.

It was open concept. The living room area was at the front, with an exterior door leading onto a lovely deck and down to the side drive that went to her garage at the back of the property. From the couch, the hall to her room was directly to her right, the front window to her left, the door nearly in front of her, and if she followed down the wall farther, she'd run into the half bath. Behind that was her pantry, tucked into the corner. The right-hand wall was her kitchen, and there was a nice eat in island in front of it with two stools.

Vinny loved every inch of it. It was strange, yet functional. The garage in the back fit both her beat up old van she hauled equipment in and her car. With the staircase inside, she didn't have to haul groceries up in the rain. And whoever decided to install the dumbwaiter was a damn hero. Small things she'd carry up fine, but sometimes in was nice to allow the fully contained system to ease the burden.

As the days passed, Vinny became more settled into her new life in Oceanside. She'd found local places to gig now and again. Her dad was only a few hours away by car. Helping her bestie heal was important to her too.

Everything felt good short of the tension coming off the house across the street.

Maybe this can work to my advantage…if drama didn't sell, soap operas and telenovelas wouldn't have the audience they do. Everyone loves someone else's drama, as they say.

Her fingers had found a familiar tune she'd learned by ear as a small child. She began to hum along, until her mind had fully formed what she wanted to convey. Then she set down her guitar and walked down the hall, descending the staircase into the garage and through the door into her studio. Fifteen minutes later, she was ready.

She'd turned the LED mood lighting into purple and red tones, programmed to fluctuate with the music while she played. There was a foot petal she could use to guide transitions. Her mic was on, the steady red light above the camera making her blood shiver with eagerness as it coursed through her.

"Welcome back to the studio, aficionados," she purred into the microphone while playing the classic guitar riff that had taken hold in her living room. "What do the *marvelous* Marvin Gaye, Zapp & Roger, and Amy Winehouse all have in common?...I'll tell you—*all* of them have recorded a version of this Motown Records classic, first released by Gladys Night and the Pips. *That's right.* Creedence Clearwater Revival was not the first nor the second artist to record the tune, although at over eleven minutes, theirs was arguably the longest. Here is 'I Heard it Through the Grapevine.'"

Chapter Four

RUBEN

"Hey there, princess!" he said, scooping Maya up. "Whatchu wanna do today?"

"Swing!" she said cheerfully, placing her little hands on his cheeks and squishing them as he spun her above his head.

"All right. Lead the way." Ruben set his goddaughter on her feet and followed her into the back yard. In the corner, Eric and Carys were sitting on the porch swing. Beside them, Brendon was sleeping in a portable bassinet thingy.

"Hey, Ruben. Surprised to see you here this weekend," Slow said casually.

Ruben shrugged. "The Missus is off on another adventure, so I'm bachelor-ing it up this weekend."

He didn't miss the glimmer of annoyance in his friend's expression. Carla was gone more than she was home lately, and Ruben was getting fed up with it too. She'd been distraught every time they spoke his last deployment, yet she wasn't available now any more than she'd been when he was gone. Carla was always busy with her friends, who were constantly treating her to these weekend getaways.

"It's good to see you," Carys said. He could hear the exhaustion in her words, same as he could the dark circles under her eyes and the vacant expression she so often wore since the accident. "Maya has been asking about you all morning."

"That true, princess?" he asked, giving his full attention to her. She beamed up at him, brighter than anything he'd ever known in his whole life.

"It's Funcle Ruben day!" Maya boasted, bouncing up and down.

"Sure is," he agreed. "Give me a minute to talk to your dad, and I'll come push you in your swing."

"Okay. I'll be watering my garden," she informed him, then did the most adorable about face before stomping off toward the garden hose.

"Future Marine, right there. How is she so articulate already? She isn't even three."

"Yeah, I think Vinny is giving her independence lessons." Slow laughed. "She asked for a guitar yesterday."

Ruben stilled at the mention of *her*.

"You okay?"

"Yeah, man." Ruben forced a smile. "Just got a lot on my mind."

"Anything I can help with?"

He shook his head. "No, just sorting leave plans with some other shit going on." *Namely your tenant, whose mere presence in the neighborhood drives me fucking insane.*

"Are you joining us for dinner?" Carys spoke up.

Ruben's eyes drifted toward the rear garage, where he could faintly hear music permeating from inside the space he'd helped Eric ready for Vinny years ago. He'd love to stay for dinner, but he knew it wasn't Carys cooking these days.

He wouldn't put it past Vinny to poison him. The rare times they'd crossed paths since their first meeting had been tense, and Ruben didn't feel like it was in the best interest of Carys's mental state to be around them together. She needed good vibes to help her recover.

"I was going to see if V12 wanted to go out," he lied. "Raincheck?"

"Sure," Carys agreed, turning back toward the yard and resuming the blank expression she'd had when he arrived.

Ruben and Slow shared a look of concern before he wandered down to the lawn after Maya, texting V12 as he did. If he at least extended the offer, he'd feel like less of an asshole for avoiding dinner with the Blackwoods.

When he was well past his tolerance for swing pushing, bubble blowing, and whatever else Maya convinced him to do, he asked her for permission to hold her baby brother. When Brendon had first come home, Maya had not adjusted well. Preemies take a lot of care, and Carys was still recovering from severe internal injuries she'd sustained in the accident. Maya had wanted to climb on her mother and be carried like usual, which hadn't been possible for the first few weeks Carys was home.

In the end, the only person Maya didn't turn on was Ruben. He'd spend time with his godson after Maya's bedtime, so she wouldn't see him with the baby until after she'd warmed up to her brother. Since then, he'd made a point of asking Maya if he could hold the baby, so she felt a little more control in her world.

He'd gotten the idea from a parenting blog, but he would deny it until his dying day. For Maya and Brendon though, Ruben would read up on all the kid advise.

When naptime rolled around, he kissed her sweet cheeks

before Slow hauled her away, Maya's eyes heavy from the hours of play they'd done. Ruben sat in a lounger with little Brendon sleeping on his chest, soaking up his namesake. He hadn't expected them to honor him when they named their son, and it was significant to Ruben—an honor, really.

"I think he's starting to favor me," he said in jest, peering over to where Carys still sat on the porch swing. She smiled softly as she focused on her son in his arms. "Maybe his first name should have been Ruben instead of his middle name."

"That would get confusing, given you are around so often," she finally engaged back. "And no offense, but I don't see it."

If Maya was the spitting image of her father, Brendon was Carys's clone. Ruben knew he was being ridiculous with his comment, but he'd gotten her to speak. He'd take the victory. Not for the first time, he wondered if she was aware how tuned out she was with the world around her since the accident.

Shortly after Slow returned to the back yard, Ruben ducked out. V12 had responded positively, but instead of going out, had offered to swing by for Ruben on his way to his cousin Enzo's cookout. He still needed to run to the store for a watermelon as contribution.

Enzo was good people. Sometimes V12—whose actual name was Zeke Vorderstrasse—would bring Enzo along to their parties too. He was a paramedic in one of the worst parts of San Diego and saw some rough shit on the daily. He'd gone the civilian route, while V12 had gone Army and used his medical prowess to save his fellow servicemen down range.

And he'd promised neither of their mothers would be there, which was always...well, *promising*. Those women bickered incessantly, unless they were on the same page.

Then they rolled through their victims with the force of a damn hurricane. The moment you thought you were safe, you'd realize it was only the eye of the storm lulling you into a false sense of safety—right before they finished you off.

Enzo and Zeke were close in age and career oriented. Their mothers wanted grandbabies. It made for some dramatic parties if they teamed up on their sons together. Not the good kind of dramatic, either. If they'd been men instead of mothers, Ruben would have thrown a punch a long time ago.

As it stood, he'd never met a sister duo more terrifying.

He felt for both his buddies.

Ruben's mother had been the light in their world. Her passing had been a heavy blow to his fourteen-year-old self, and he missed her relentlessly. He'd give anything to have five more minutes with her, even if she spent every second scolding him. Just a moment with both his parents, the way they were when he was little and didn't yet understand the complicated dance of adulthood and being poor.

He found the soul withering ferocity of Zeke and Enzo's mothers intimidating as hell, but mostly he was jealous. You only get one mom, and Ruben's was long gone.

"Hey, man." Ruben knuckled his buddy across the center console of his truck as he climbed in, then pulled the door closed and buckled his seat belt. "How goes?"

"Honestly, I'm just glad to see Enzo. Since he transferred all he fucking does is work," he said as he backed out of Ruben's driveway. "No Carla?"

"Nah. She and one of her old sorority friends decided to do some spa weekend thing at a winery," he said, careful to hide his frustration. It felt like she was avoiding Ruben, and it was starting to burn.

"Her loss is our gain," V12 said casually. "It's always good to have you around. You bring the goods?"

"Hell, yes. Got it right here," Ruben said with a grin, holding up his homemade pica seasoning specially blended for sprinkling on fruit. "I know better than to show around your family without my passport."

They laughed together, the casualness between them easing the strain Ruben had been feeling in his chest all day, first over Carla and then Carys. They shot the shit over life as they made their way to the grocer and then down to Enzo's place.

"She's still catatonic?" V12 said with concern.

"She may as well be. Slow agrees it's been going on too long. He told me today he's going to bring it up at her next follow up on Monday. Hopefully it goes well. Things aren't right with Carys like this. She's got that *lights are on, but nobody is home* vibe most of the time; present but not *present.* Even with her friend there, it's gotten well past the point for letting her sort it out on her own," Ruben confessed.

"Anything we can do for our brother?"

"Not at the moment. Let's see what he says after Monday though."

"What about you?"

"Me?"

"Things good when Carla *is* home?" he asked, not one to beat around the bush.

"Things are great. We've got a whole trip planned for this fall. She wanted to do something involving snow and was researching a ski lodge for this winter," Ruben said, a laugh barking out. "I told her it was a great idea, because I hate boats and beaches and anything else with heat and sand after so many trips down range."

"Liar." V12 chuckled.

"Man's gotta do what a man's gotta do, amigo. This man does *not* do snow." Ruben shuddered, causing his friend to laugh harder. "I was raised in Georgia, not Siberia. Besides, she doesn't want to ski. She wants to dress up in ski *attire* and look cute pretending to read a book at the lodge where everyone will see and admire her. If we're lounging, it better be alone and naked somewhere warm."

"So, what trip did you manipulate her into booking instead?"

"Jamaica and a cruise." Ruben's smile pulled so wide with pride, he couldn't help puffing up his chest a bit.

"You might like skiing," V12 argued.

"Maybe, with the right people. Carla is not an athlete. We wouldn't hit the slopes for me to find out. If I'm gonna risk freezing my dick off, it needs to at least be enjoyable. Nothing is worth facing her wrath because I left her alone to do something on my own while we are supposed to be spending time together." *Even if all she's doing is holding court in some fancy ass ski lodge.*

"They say opposites attract…"

"That they do."

"Shit," V12 said as he parked his truck across the street from Enzo's place.

"You *fucker,*" Ruben said with amusement. "I hope those are tamales your mother is carrying to the cookout she wasn't invited to."

Marisol Vorderstrasse was many things. Among them, she could make just about anything out of nothing. But her tamales had stolen Ruben's heart years ago at their first encounter. In fact, he'd hidden under a tree stuffing his face with them while she'd railed into her son in Spanish about not giving her grandbabies yet.

He was only twenty-eight at the time.

"Looks like she and Tía Yesenia carpooled. Enzo will be thrilled," he said dryly. "I'll get the melon."

By the time they got through the gate in the side yard, Enzo was already crimson over whatever the two women were scolding him about. "They didn't waste time."

"They never do," V12 said, putting the watermelon down near a cutting board on the picnic table before sauntering their way to save his cousin.

"Ezekiel Vorderstrasse! Why haven't you called me?" Marisol scolded her son.

"It's just Zeke, Mom. We've talked about this." He'd shortened his name when he joined the military for personal reasons, but Ruben hadn't a clue what they were. He suspected for similar reasons his cousin went by Enzo instead of Lorenzo.

"I don't care what you call yourself, I know what I put on your birth certificate. Don't argue with your mother," she said crossly.

"How are you, Tía?" He asked his aunt instead of engaging in the battle his mother was set to start.

"Why are you bringing a man? You're as bad as my son. Both of you need to marry already," Yesenia fired at him. Ruben had to give him credit. His friend didn't even flinch.

Jesus. They don't waste time getting to the point, do they?

"Thanks for having me, Enzo," Ruben casually cut in. "It's good to see you."

They clasped hands briefly as Enzo replied, "Good to see you, Ruben. How is the wife?"

"Good, thanks."

"How long are you married now?" Yesenia said, narrowing her eyes at Ruben.

Here we go. Into the bowels of hell.

"Couple years."

"Why didn't you bring your wife and children so we could spoil them?" she demanded.

"I'm sure my wife would love the attention, but we don't have children," he said carefully. Carla had no interest in kids.

The sisters gave each other a knowing glance before Yesenia leaned in and whisper yelled, "You shooting blanks? I know a tea that will fix you right up." She nodded firmly, like it was a done deal and she'd be dropping it by his house on her way home.

Enzo and V12 both groaned.

"Mom."

"Tía."

The scolding did nothing to dissuade the woman.

"Children are the fruit of life, boys," Marisol scolded the three of them in return.

Ruben took a deep breath in through his nose, letting out an overdramatic groan. "Are those tamales I smell?"

Marisol instantly perked up, switching her scowl to a bright smile as she preened. "Yes. I made them special."

"Man alive, I have *dreams* about your tamales, Missus Vorderstrasse," he drawled out, letting his southern upbringing slip out.

"You're a good boy," she said, patting his cheek. "You call me Marisol."

Another crisis averted by a well-placed compliment and a *bless your heart,* and the three men were finally free to stuff their faces on the opposite side of the yard from the motherly duo who were now dishing everyone up like they didn't have hands to do it themselves. They really were something. Ruben couldn't begin to imagine what it was like being raised by them.

"Sorry about that," Enzo said sheepishly between bites. "They don't have a filter of any sort between them."

"On the bright side," Ruben said with an overexuberant amount of pep, "If you ever fear you are facing impotency, you now know your mother has a tea that will *fix you right up.*"

Chapter Five

VINNY

"We're headed down range in four weeks." The tightness in Eric's jaw as he clipped out the words said more than the words themselves. He was not happy about this development.

Vinny's eyebrows shot to her hairline. "Oh, fuck. They couldn't replace you with someone else?"

"Unfortunately, not. The guy who was supposed to be going broke his leg doing some advanced level hike trying to empress his new girlfriend. *She* is advanced. He should have been on flat terrain, from what V12 told me. The guy is a complete klutz. I *am* the replacement."

"Nothing sexier than falling off a mountain," Vinny said with a snort. She'd seen men do some stupid shit to get laid—especially while touring—but nothing so drastic as that.

"Especially when you are aiming to empress someone who has hiked the entire Pacific Crest Trail—all 2,650 miles of it from Mexico to Canada."

Vinny pealed with laughter. "Idiot."

"Carys is going to lose it when I tell her." His shoulders slumped.

"I'm sorry, Eric. Thanks for the heads up though."

"I've seen your concealed firearm. No way I'm risking you accidentally shooting me when she starts screaming because you thought our house was under attack," he said with amusement.

"Smart man."

At least someone on this block appreciates a woman who knows how to defend herself and her home at all costs.

After Eric let himself out, Vinny fell back onto her couch with her guitar, strumming along as she thought about her conversation with Carys earlier in the day. There had been a lot of tears from both of them. Carys was devastated she hadn't hidden her misery as well as she thought. Vinny was relieved Carys had accepted she needed intervention and had already filled a prescription for an antidepressant her doctor gave her to try.

It was a positive step toward getting her best friend back.

Since Vinny wasn't planning on leaving Oceanside anytime soon, she decided she needed to put more thought into how she could best accomplish her goals. Now she knew Eric was leaving soon, she needed to reprioritize some of them. She should have asked if any of his friends were deploying with him. Mostly she wanted to be prepared to deal with Ruben's wife, but she liked Zeke too. If he was staying, he'd be a good person to reach out to if something came up. Especially with his medical training.

But mostly because of Ruben.

Who she absolutely hated.

She didn't care about Ruben. *Obviously.*

She cared about Eric. He was going to have one hell of a time being gone at the moment, and she knew having at least one of his closest friends there would be helpful. Ruben and Zeke often deployed at the same time as Eric, and he'd need someone he trusted to talk to about Carys.

As the song her fingers had chosen sunk in, Vinny smiled to herself. She was going to open mic night later in the evening, and she had an idea. Setting down the guitar, she grabbed her phone and opened a new message.

Vinny: Hey! You going tonight?

Tripp: Hell, yeah! You?

Vinny: Of course. You want to do some Taylor and King with me? I'm thinking acoustic.

Tripp: You're turning me on.

Tripp: The version of "You Got A Friend" we were toying with?

Vinny: That's the one. You wanna strum or plunk?

Tripp: Strum. My piano is rusty AF.

Tripp: Want me to come over? We can record it for your ArtBeat and get the groove right for the show.

Vinny: Now *I'm* turned on.

Vinny: See you soon.

————

"THIS IS SO EMBARRASSING, VIN." Carys's voice came out muffled, on account of her face being buried in her hands.

"It's me, Carys. Let it out. You know I won't judge you, whatever it is," she encouraged.

They'd already been sitting together for half an hour. The kids were both napping, and Carys had returned from her therapy session that afternoon insanely nervous. Once she decided to open up though, it all came flowing out in signature Carys word vomit.

"Uh...well. You see...everything is different. All the things I thought were solid aren't anymore, and I think the meds are helping all around, but antidepressants don't regrow body parts and I'm not really sure what to do, you know? I mean, what if Eric doesn't want me anymore? It's bad enough I can't get pregnant but now I'm struggling with the Big O and how do I tell him, Lavender? How do I tell him I'm still broken and I'll never heal? Because I'm so worried...what if it's the last straw and sex is ruined forever and...and he leaves me for a woman who can orgasm right? And give him more babies?"

Vinny blinked at Carys a few times before taking a deep breath. "Wow. Let's take this slowly, so I'm sure I interpreted you correctly. Sex is different now. Less fulfilling?" Carys nodded. "And you think there is an alternate reality where Eric would *ever* choose another woman over something you didn't have control over?"

"Don't tease me."

"I'm one hundred percent not teasing you. Carys, you didn't see him. Your man isn't right unless you are. I'm glad the pills are helping break the fog you've been in, and I'm so fucking proud of you for going to therapy. Don't stop. Because you still are under the impression you can lose that man, and I'm telling you, it's not possible."

"You still think so?" The fear radiating off Carys shredded Vinny's heart.

"I *know* so. Eric is yours and always will be. It has nothing to do with having babies. It never did. You forget I was there when you met. He hadn't touched you yet, remember? But he already looked at you the same way he has ever since. You are his sun, Carys. He *revolves* around you." *Like my dad did my mother,* she added in her head. It was how Vinny had known whatever was blooming between them was real; she'd seen it before.

Carys nodded. "Okay," she said softly. "I'll try to remember that."

"Now, the O's… I'm so sorry that's another struggle for you. Tell me about it."

"Are you sure?"

"Yup. Practice what you need to tell Eric tonight on me."

They spent the better part of an hour hashing everything out. There was so much happening she'd been holding back, and Vinny was grateful Carys had decided to communicate her new reality to her husband. She was also taking a slew of mental notes for later, so Vinny would have an easier time helping Carys while Eric was gone.

For the first time, Vinny was getting a true taste of her bestie's life—a short turnaround on a deployment and all the rushed prep that came along with it. Four weeks' notice was better than twenty-four hours, and it had given them time to lock in the care Carys needed before Eric's boots landed in another undisclosed location. The three weeks of meds were showing a marked improvement in Carys she knew Eric was also grateful for.

When the kids woke, Vinny helped get them up and out into the yard before heading to her studio. She'd been feeling unusually *folky* lately and wanted to set up two more songs for her ArtBeat before the mood passed. A lot of her posts were in the moment—things her life was currently breathing into her—but sometimes it was nice to simply play around a bit. Those videos often became her favorites and top performers, so she liked to keep a dozen or so on the shelf as fillers.

The duet she'd done with Tripp three weeks ago had gone viral. He was a talented vocalist and guitarist with his own following, and she wasn't surprised. A lot of her guests gave her account a boost, because she loved arranging well known songs into something fun and new. All the better if it featured other artists.

She sat down at her mixing board with a notepad and

scribbled some ideas. As her set list formed, she realized a lot of them were meant to be duets or could easily be made into one. Vinny tapped the eraser of her pencil against her pursed lips as she thought.

That's a good idea. I could do a whole series of duets. It would be fun to cover my full range and allow me to bring in a wider range of guest artists. Cross overs always boost across the board. Tripp said his account had a big jump from the last collab too.

It was the start of something interesting, promising. She'd just have to keep thinking on it. Ideally, she'd have a blueprint set before Eric left in a week.

———

VINNY SAT in the far back of Carys's new SUV in silence. It was comfortable even for an adult, and she'd been glad Carys had upgraded after her sedan was totaled in the accident. Naturally, she'd chosen a shade of blue closest to her favorite color, indigo. Carys's love for the color had even prompted Eric to design her a wedding ring set featuring tanzanite instead of the typical diamonds.

Yet another indication the man was perfect for Carys in every way.

Since Carys had come to Vinny with her bedroom concerns, the honeymoon glow had begun reviving between them. Vinny hated Eric was leaving *now,* when his marriage to Carys was finally beginning to resemble what it used to be. The altered state of her bestie since he'd gotten her help was reassuring though.

Vinny had zero doubt they would make it. She'd been around enough to hear the whispers about spouses who lost it during a deployment and left divorce papers and little else for their men return to. It was a fact of military life: it was a hard path many hadn't the spirit to stick out.

Her eyes flickered over at the back of Ruben's head on the middle bench as she thought about it. His wife might be the daughter of a respected Navy man, but she was not wife material of any sort—much less for an oft deployed Marine. Vinny didn't understand what he saw in her. Then again, *she* saw how his wife behaved when Ruben was gone, something he couldn't.

Today was a prime example of Carla's ridiculousness. She should be dropping off her husband like the other families were, not leaving him to tag along with the Blackwoods. *C is for Carla—it's also for cunt. I hate that woman.* Selfish women had no place in this emotionally complex world. How did a decorated, dedicated Marine like Ruben end up saddled to someone so unfit to be a military wife?

Vinny dropped her gaze before Ruben noticed her eyeing him. She didn't mind being relegated to the far back in the least. Vinny understood she shared the Blackwood children with Ruben, and if anything ever happened to Eric and Carys, she would share their upbringing with Ruben as co-godparents. It chafed her he hadn't put any effort into talking to her since they first met. Yes, she could have offered a truce herself. She didn't feel it was her job, and she wasn't going to make it easy on Ruben.

If he couldn't understand why it was up to him to make amends, it wasn't Vinny's place to spell it out for him. He was a smart man—well, outside his choice in women, obviously—and could very well work it out on his own. So instead of exploiting this moment to murmur something helpful in aiding a truce between them, Vinny turned her head to the window opposite where Ruben sat.

She would not look at him.

She would not speak to him, if she could help it.

Even as they unloaded their gear from the rear of the SUV upon arrival, Vinny kept her mouth shut and eyes diverted unless one of the Blackwoods were engaging with her, mostly little Maya. Vinny's roll today was to support Carys as she said goodbye to her husband for the next four months, *not* appease Ruben.

Then why do I want to fix whatever this thing is between us? He doesn't deserve it.

Chapter Six

RUBEN

"She's going to be good, man," Ruben said as they climbed aboard the transport.

"I know she will be. And she's got Vinny here now. Not sure what happened in LA, but I'm grateful for her. We would have been completely fucked since the accident without the two of you."

Ruben involuntarily grimaced. "Uh. Yeah. I'm happy for Carys she's here too."

Slow turned his face away from Ruben, but he still caught a hint of his trademark smile tugging on his face. He knew Carys and Slow were curious about why he and Vinny were so at odds, but truthfully Ruben wasn't even sure *he* knew why anymore. The more he thought about it, the more he realized Vinny wasn't the one who had crossed boundaries and slung insults.

And he despised the idea this could possibly be blown out of proportion because he was too stubborn to admit he'd put her in a rough situation.

"I like her new wheels," Ruben said, eager to keep the

subject somewhere more comfortable for him. "A proper tank to haul around precious cargo."

"Yeah, replacing her sedan with something beefier was the only way to go. That thing has more safety features than I can count," Slow said with a firm nod.

"And I see she chose blue."

"The closest shade to indigo she could get." Eric chuckled. "She likes what she likes."

"It suits her. And the ride was great heading over here."

"Are you okay, Ruben?" Slow turned to watch Ruben beside him as he—maybe intentionally—fumbled his seatbelt so he wouldn't have to face him head on. "You've been a little melancholy lately. And right now you are over focusing on Carys's new truck, which is also unlike you."

V12 dropped into the seat on the other side of Ruben, cutting off his only escape from Slow and this conversation. "This to do with the drama low key buzzing around the water cooler?" he asked quietly.

"It's just talk, man. You know how people get. Can't stand how miserable they are themselves, so they have to go start shit for others." Ruben's tone straddled a fine line between defensive and his usual joviality as he attempted to brush off the exact subject he did not want to examine. He'd heard bits and pieces in the office when others thought he was out of hearing; enough to make him uncomfortable with the inevitable conclusions his coworkers were most likely making about Ruben's personal life.

"You know your business better than I do," V12 offered. "But if I were you, I'd pay attention."

"What's that supposed to mean?" It came out more wary than Ruben wanted, but he couldn't help it. When Carla had refused to get out of bed and bring him in this morning herself, all the whispers he'd been dutifully ignoring had slammed into him like a brick wall. Doubt spiraled in his gut, giving him the worst case of emotional diarrhea imaginable. It was all he could do, holding back from letting the ugly shit inside him fly as his friend poked his emotional wounds.

V12 shrugged casually, like they were debating the best way to cook a steak. "I'm surrounded by women in medical. I hear a lot. And right now, the loosest lips in the building are in a position to know firsthand. You understand?"

"Perez is running her mouth," Ruben said with annoyance. This time, he didn't try to control his feelings on the matter. There was some nasty talk going on about his wife that he gave Perez sole credit for.

"Yeah."

"Why can't that woman get orders?" Slow said with irritation. Perez had minded her business since moving in next door, but all three of them knew she could be both petty and vindictive if she got the inkling. Losing Slow as her down range lover after he met Carys had been a volatile situation. They'd all been relieved when the mission had ended and they'd returned home, if for no other reason than Perez knew better than to expect anything on US soil.

"How is she as a neighbor?" Zeke asked.

"Quiet, actually. After the first six months, Carys finally stopped waiting for the other shoe to drop. The Browns say she's a model tenant. Clean, friendly, pays her rent on time. I hardly see her, even in passing," Slow admitted.

"I see her," Ruben all but sneered. "She's always attending the girls' weekends Carla likes to host. They drive together most of the time, so Perez will come help my wife pack before they head out."

She's a damn thorn in my side, constantly making digs when Carla is out of ear shot.

"Is she coming?" Slow asked.

"No, she is benched at the moment due to injury. Should make for an easier trip for all of us," V12 said.

Ruben was damn sure Perez would find ways to fuck him over without being down range with them. The way she and Carla had been acting since he got his marching orders was suspicious at best. It made ignoring the scuttlebutt a fuck ton harder. The next four months were going to be big. He could feel it in his bones.

The deep seated instinct was not accompanied by anticipation.

"How is your cousin?" Slow asked V12.

"Enzo?" V12 looked to Slow for confirmation. Eric nodded. "Good as can be expected. He's been moved to a station where they respond to a lot of dark shit. I think it's been harder on him than he wants to admit."

"Does he like being an EMT still?" Slow continued.

"Oh, yeah. He loves his job. I worry though, you know. I don't care how old we get; Enzo is still the same fool who thought any girl who let him carry her backpack was his girlfriend back in the day."

"Not you," Ruben chided. "V12 is too jaded to fall in love."

"I'm not jaded, I'm realistic. Love is a lot of hard work. It means choosing that person every single day, even when you aren't sure you like them at the moment. I've had my share of ladies, Ruben. I'm just not running into anything long-term with serious consideration." He paused and side eyed Eric around Ruben, one eyebrow popping up. "We can't all be as lucky as Slow, here."

"No," Ruben said with weighted finality. "We can't."

What Slow had found on the sandy beaches of Mexico with Carys—on an R and R Ruben had insisted on and then bailed out of the second Carla asked him to—was the stuff of dreams. He knew they'd had their fair share of bumps in the road, but even so, Ruben envied how solid they were. It wasn't the easy times that defined a couple, but the hard times. How you came through those rough patches spoke more to one's character than the moments you were allowed to simply exist peacefully.

Four months ago, when Carys and Brendon had almost died, not once had anyone who knew the couple thought it would be the last straw. The Blackwoods were strong; forged into steel hand in hand as they recreated their normal and accepted their losses. Here they were deploying so soon after so much trauma, and Ruben didn't doubt for a second Carys would be there for Slow when he came back.

He was nervous as hell Carla would not welcome him home with the same enthusiasm. While he could begrudgingly admit Vinny was a steady, helpful influence for Carys, his own wife didn't have a single friend he would call steady *or* helpful, much less both. Carla had Sonja Perez. Willful and sometimes cruel Perez, and a handful of her old college friends who hadn't married mega gazillionaires and moved away.

Slow had nothing to worry about from the seat beside Ruben as their plane barreled through the sky toward four months of pure hell. Ruben was well aware he, in contrast, had everything to lose.

And that gut feeling he kept ignoring whispered to Ruben it was already long gone—if he'd ever rightly had it to begin with.

As his team slowly dropped into sleep around him, Ruben did not. He sat awake in the silence staring straight ahead at nothing, contemplating where he was in his life. It certainly wasn't where he'd *expected* to be at thirty-three.

As a boy, he'd imagined weekends away with his wife

while his parents spoiled their children. The military hadn't even crossed his mind. Ruben had been a bit of a late bloomer, scrawny and weak compared to most of the other guys in his high school.

Then he'd run into a few ROTC guys his first few weeks on campus. They were college freshman, same as him, and some of them just as lean. Ruben was there on scholarships and grants he'd busted his ass for, his books and other expenses covered by the sacrifices his father had insisted on making. He was a first generation college student, eager to make his way in the world.

By the end of his first term, he'd been around to talk to all of the different ROTC leaders on campus. It had been difficult to decide at first, but his gut told him it was the right path. He could build his body and his mind, and there were scholarships available too. Add a guaranteed job when he graduated, and Ruben was sold.

That was when he met Eric Blackwood. The guy was chill as could be with a personality you couldn't help but envy. He thought things through—far better than Ruben ever did, at least—and seemed so confident in himself. Ruben admired the hell out of him. The day he saw Eric in military dress on the appropriate day, coolly strutting through campus in his Marine fatigues, Ruben knew.

He wanted to be with that guy.

He wanted to be a Marine.

From then on out, he and Eric were tight. They studied together, ate together and eventually roomed together. Eric had even gone home with Ruben a few times over break since he didn't have any strong connection to his own family.

When Ruben met Carla at a party toward the end of freshman year, it had been one of those moments you see yourself experiencing—a full out of body experience—as he did his best to play his best game. Ruben had charm and magnetism. In truth, he hadn't had to work that hard the night he met his now wife.

And until recently, he'd thought it was because Carla was as drawn to Ruben as he was to her. But hindsight is a bitch sometimes, and he was beginning to understand what Slow and his other brothers in arms—the truest friends a man could hope for—had known all along. He'd married a good time, not a steadfast woman he could build dreams with.

The signs were all there. Over the years, they had been broken up almost as often as they'd been together. But the pull...*fuck, the pull to be with her.* It felt so damn good, so *real.* Nothing should feel so addictively good if it isn't.

But then again, that's unerringly what pulls an addict in.

Ruben had been addicted to the high of Carla's attention. For a decade he chased her, always backing off and giving her the space she demanded when she demanded it. But she *always* came back to Ruben, and he happily took her back, eager for more. On for a year, off five months. On for seven months, off for five weeks. On for...

Well, it had been one hell of a ride, courting Carla. And he'd enjoyed every second with her. He *still* enjoyed the precious moments with his wife when she granted him the time of day. There was the rub. Carla prioritized her friends and whatever she did for fun over Ruben nine times out of ten.

When he'd told her he would be deployed for the vacation she'd planned for them, Carla hadn't even been sad. Ruben had promised they could postpone it for when he returned, and he still wanted nothing more than to lounge on the beach with her and make love. He was ready for the fight she usually offered, whining over his priorities and how they never included her.

He had not been prepared for her apathy. Not only was she unfazed by their cancelled alone time, but she'd also decided on the spot she'd take Sonja instead. *Sonja fucking Perez.* Ruben's surprise quickly morphed into anger, followed by disappointment.

Carla didn't care if he was there at all, so long as she got what *she* wanted. The harsh realization had left a deep laceration inside him; not fatal, but certainly painful. Silent and unseen by others.

Ruben had firmly believed he was a *one life, one wife* type of man. When he got home, he'd suggest marriage counseling and regular dates where none of her friends "coincidentally" showed at the same restaurant and joined them. He would insist they lay out a five year plan for their life together, so they knew what the other expected and had something to build on.

It was a solid plan.

If they survived this deployment.

All I want is to fall asleep on this damn plane peacefully, knowing what I'm leaving behind will still be there when I get home. At this rate, do I want it to still be there when I get back? I've never quit something I've committed to in my life. How will I start now, with something so sacred as my marriage? This can't be it. I have to fight for us.

Chapter Seven

VINNY

A week before Eric left, Vinny had gone skipping through her favorite naughty store with the same glee Maya had when you gave her ice cream. Carys hadn't told her what exactly she and Eric had done to help bring her more satisfaction in the bedroom before he left, but it was moot anyway. Deployment was a bitch, and this one was poorly timed for her friend's recovery.

Ba ba ba bamp ba ba!

Never fear! Vinny is here!

Well...sort of. At least Carys wouldn't be without options letting off her sexual frustration. Besides, if you weren't bold enough to kink shop for your suffering bestie, could you even *call* yourself their bestie? Vinny sure as hell didn't think so.

She'd filled four baskets—one for herself and several for Carys—before asking the manager for help with reading material. She didn't know if Carys would actually read a book all about getting herself off, but knowing she'd stumble on an *adult textbook* as she dug her way through made Vinny deviously happy.

Especially with a title like *Masturbation for Dummies*.

Shortly after they returned home from the airfield, Vinny went up to her room for the black bags she's stored in her closet where Carys wouldn't see them if she ventured to come up—it wouldn't have done any good to ruin the surprise, after all. With the same giddiness she'd had while making the purchase, she took the bags into the main house, where she knew Carys would be in her room.

It was the perfect place to ambush her with toys she would never want her children to see.

"What the hell is that?" Carys asked as Vinny stormed into her room with *three* black plastic shopping bags.

"It's your new kit," she said enthusiastically.

"My what?"

"We are going to figure out how to get your motor running again!" she announced, lifting the bags up and giving them a little shake.

"What did you do, Vin?" The absolute mortification on Carys's face was priceless. *You'd think by her reaction we hadn't spent the better part of our teens and twenties describing our romantic and sexual exploits for each other in detail.*

"Now that you are feeling better and more communicative, I decided it's time to bestow all the wisdom I have gained as a single musician on the road with a strict no fraternization policy." Carys gave her a stern glare. "Most of the time, anyway."

"I don't care what you do when you are lonely on tour buses, I am *not* getting a sex-ed class from you, Lavender."

"Ew, no. My gate only swings one way, and it's definitely into the pasture of dicks." She set the bags down on Carys's bed before emptying them into one glorious heap in the middle. "I got you a little of everything, so you can decide for yourself. Feel free to ask questions, but there will be zero in person tutorials. Even I have limits."

Carys smirked with disbelief.

"What's this?" Vinny asked suddenly, picking up the giftbox from Carys's pillow.

"I don't know," Carys said, waving her hand at the shiny foil in Vinny's hands. "As you can see, I haven't unwrapped it yet."

"What do you *think* it is?" she asked, wiggling her eyebrows.

"No clue. Now put it down. I'm saving it for later."

Spoil sport.

Vinny dropped it back onto the bed and moved on to the mass of packaging she'd spread out. "Well, what do you think?"

Carys picked up something from the top of the heap. "What the hell is a Taco Tickler?"

"Oooh! That's a good one. I have high hopes that will work out for you. I've replaced mine—"

"Do not start telling me how often you have to replace your sex toys, Vin!"

"*Fine.*" She pouted. "But for the record, you will want to pair it with this," she added, snatching up her favorite brand of tingly lube and tossing it Carys's way before making her escape.

She'll thank me later.

———

"HEY, do you mind if I add a few things around the apartment?"

"It's your apartment, Vin. You know we don't care what you

do so long as it isn't trashed. Besides, what could be more damaging than all those guitars you decoratively hung across the back wall of the living room?" Carys smiled and shook her head.

Ha. Like she wasn't drooling all over the 1972 Stratocaster Dad gave me last Christmas.

"Okay, well if you hear noise on the roof, it's just me running lines," Vinny warned.

"Lines, huh? I don't advise snorting coke off my roof. Might not go well with asphalt."

"You're a dork," Vinny said with a laugh. "That would be *doing* lines. I'll see you later."

"You only have permission for rock and roll on this property!" Carys shouted at her backside. "Leave the sex and drugs for the road!"

"I'd have to meet someone to have sex!" she called back over her shoulder before the back door closed behind her.

As much as she would love to end her current dry streak and put away her own toys for the real deal, things needed doing around here. Vinny took her role in Carys's life seriously, even more so because Eric was gone and she'd promised him she'd keep an eye out.

Which was why she was hauling the extension ladder across the backyard. Vinny hated ladders, but she wasn't freaking Spiderman. Since she lacked the ability to securely web sling herself safely across the roof, she'd have to deal with the unnerving feeling of an extension ladder stretched to its bouncy max. So up the ladder she went, the end of a rope looped around one arm as she climbed. Once she was safely up and her butt planted on shingles, she carefully used the rope to hoist up her bucket.

It would take a few hours, but it would be well worth it. After weeks of research, Vinny had gotten Eric's approval before ordering security cameras. They had decided together where the best places to put them were, and Eric had insisted on sharing the expense, since more of them covered the main house than Vinny's apartment. She wasn't sure if he'd actually told *Carys* what the plan was, but the cameras had arrived and it was perfect weather to risk breaking her neck.

She'd already set up several around her own abode—both internally and externally—so she knew how to do it. The trick was doing it two stories off the ground. Once she had her wires ran and protected, it was more or less plug and play. She could control the system from the console in her living room, or through the handy app on her phone.

Eric too had downloaded the app. The first external camera on the main house would face the back yard, so he could see Maya running around. He hadn't asked for it, but she knew he missed playing with the kids when he was away, and it would bring him joy to see their antics.

Soon as her wires were run.

They had debated a wireless system, but the thought of climbing back up to change batteries hadn't appealed to either of them. Of course, they had also anticipated Eric being here to help set up the system, so the whole wire running adventure had seemed less daunting when they'd made the call. Now her partner in crime stopping wasn't here to lend a hand, it was a bit more daunting.

"Just get it over with," she muttered to herself. "You've helped run wires on stage rigging. This is nothing."

Besides, she wanted it set up before Carys's gathering next Saturday. After three years in Oceanside, she'd finally met other wives with young children she felt a connection with. It was a solid deadline, and Vinny would enjoy the party so much more if she wasn't constantly eyeing the places she had yet to mount cameras.

Get it done and get out of the sun. It's too warm to be in pants and long sleeves.

Her resolve firmly in place again, Vinny adjusted her oversized sunglasses, made sure her wide brimmed sun hat was secure enough to stay if a breeze came up off the ocean, and got to work. When she lowered her bucket to the ground several hours later, she did so with immense satisfaction. The worst part of the job had gone smoothly, and all that was left were the cameras she'd need to mount under the eaves.

She rewarded herself with a shower before slipping into her favorite pair of old Levi's and going down to her garage. The Camaro needed new door seals. Like always, Vinny's body bubbled with happiness as she opened the garage door and got to work. She loved her car.

When she was around twelve, her father had found the poor thing collecting dust in a garage. It wasn't a common year due to production disruptions, so he'd been surprised the owner answered in the affirmative when he inquired after the car two weeks after he'd first found the ad.

But Quincy Blume was not afraid of what it's late availability might indicate of the condition of the car. He was looking for something to teach Vinny on—both repairing and driving—and while a pony car wasn't the approach most fathers would take when purchasing for their only daughter, he wanted every second she spent on the road to be an experience.

Which meant an American classic. The Camaro wasn't known for its visibility while driving, but the name was slang for *friend.* Being the artist he was, her father loved the idea of sending her down the road with a comrade. He'd settled on the car and waited until the right one appeared before pouncing.

Vinny's car had been purchased while they were on the

road. She could hardly remember the day, only that when she'd fallen asleep they were in Florida, and when she woke, they were crossing into Tennessee. Somewhere between the two, her father had stopped long enough to purchase her 1972 Camaro RS, load it onto the trailer attached to their touring van, and get back on the road.

It hadn't been much to look at back then. The paint was in bad shape, but there wasn't any serious damage or decay. The engine turned over but sounded like an unstable sawmill. Over the following three years, every moment her father wasn't on tour they spent together turning wrench in his garage.

By the time she had her learners permit, the car was running beautifully. One of her father's friends had given her a deal on her custom paint job. Vinny had helped with all the prep work to help cut down further on costs. She took her driving test three months later, her baby freshly cleaned and polished to shine in the California sun.

Vinny was lucky, as far as sight went. Some people with albinism were legally blind.

Most people understood melanin was what pigmented your skin, but few realized how important it was in other aspects of life—like *vision.* Melanin is a crucial part of healthy sight as well as eye color. Because she lacked melanin, her eyes were more sensitive to light than normal eyes, a condition called photophobia. It's absence also allowed her eyes to look anywhere from pale green or blue to a lovely shade of violet, which was rather fitting given her name was Lavender.

She needed contacts or glasses but could see well enough to do what everyone else could with the correction. What she would likely fail to escape as she aged, were cataracts. She didn't need her sight to be an amazing musician, but it *was* necessary for driving.

Lavender Blume loved her father all the more for making sure she would enjoy her freedom on the road. There was no guarantee she would or would not have issues down the line with her sight, and she protected her eyes and skin best she could, but nothing in life was guaranteed for anyone.

When Vinny lay on her deathbed, nobody would ever be able say she hadn't lived life to its fullest; and that was sincerely all she could ask for as she took her last breath.

Chapter Eight

VINNY

Carys's luncheon play date was a success. Marcy, Hailey, and Lexi were all low key and fun loving women. Vinny had enjoyed chasing around the kids and playing songs for them on her guitar while their mothers relaxed.

As they were discussing how everyone met their husbands, Vinny saw the moment Carys hesitated. She'd tried saying they had met in Mexico and leave it at that, but Vinny didn't let it slide. Just because the first spouses she'd met had been judgy bitches over her elopement didn't mean all of them were. Carys wouldn't know where she stood here unless she was honest.

There was no shame in how Carys and Eric had met and wed. People eloped all the time. Reality shows featuring complete strangers meeting at the altar were a thing too. There was nothing for her friend to be nervous about; a truth Vinny reflected on with smug satisfaction later in the evening because her suspicions had been correct: not one of these women cared she'd married fast.

When it was time for everyone to leave, Lexi came in from loading her things with an axe to grind. Carla had also hosted friends for the day. Knowing through observation and experience nobody across the street would be nice about sharing streetside parking, Vinny had helped move everyone's vehicles into the driveway, so they wouldn't have to fight leaving when Carla's friends inevitably parked too close, blocking them in.

Vinny had seen it before and knew their MO…she hadn't expected Lexi to come in angry over the parking situation.

"Seriously?" Vinny huffed. "They blocked the *driveway?*" She strode off around the back side of the house and up the long drive from the back yard. Sure enough, two hoity toity bitch mobiles were perfectly positioned to keep anyone from leaving.

One of them was a familiar pink Cadillac.

Pretentious, useless, stuffy bitches with their status symbols. They wouldn't know a quality car if it ran them over and left grill marks imprinted on their faces.

She walked across the street, tamping down on her fury as she came to a halt at the front door. Inside, she could hear laughing. *Ooooohs* came through muffled, the tone decidedly that of those who think they are being naughty.

Carla opened up after the fourth time Vinny set to pounding with her full fist. "What do *you* want?" she sneered. "I'm entertaining here."

The sound of tittering came through from the living room to the doorway, a breathy female voice asking, "How many speed settings did you say?"

Oh, joy. It's a yuppy sex toy party. God forbid they be seen at the "store" browsing like a commoner. They might be seen carrying a black bag into their mansions and give the neighbors the impression they have needs other than cashmere sheets and Rodeo Drive duds.

"Sorry to disrupt the fun," she forced out cordially while

suppressing an eye roll. "Our guests have littles to get home, and some of *your* guests have blocked the driveway. Could they please take a moment to move their cars?"

"Sounds like a *them* problem," Carla said offhandedly. "I'm certainly not spoiling all the fun here because of some snot nosed brats."

"And you feel confident speaking for your friends on this?" Vinny asked, continuing to hide her desire to rip the woman's extensions out.

"Yes," she snarled. "Don't ever knock on my door again! Just *float away* like a good little ghost, Casper. You aren't wanted here."

Carla slammed the door in Vinny's face. She pivoted on her heel and abruptly marched back to Carys's house, mumbling all the way.

"Casper," she spit out. "Real original. Never heard that one before. Stupid hussy," Vinny fumed, reaching for her phone.

"Don't worry ladies," Vinny said with smile as she passed through the front door. They were all clustered at the front window, watching her exchange from a safe distance. "We deal with this sort of thing in the music industry all the time. I'll have you all free in a jiffy."

She plowed through the house and into the back yard, going straight into her music studio where she couldn't be overheard, and dialed out. It rang twice before his soothing voice answered.

"Vinny, my little blossom," Groove crooned. "Tell me this means we are making more art together. Or are you finally accepting my dinner invite?"

"Possibly, still a *no,* and I need a favor."

"Are you okay?" he asked, dropping the smooth talk and immediately switching to his fix-it tone.

"Yep, just got some spoiled hussies blocking the buses in the drive. You know anyone who knows anyone on shift today?"

"My cousin's boyfriend works for Oceanside PD. Give me the address; I'll text you when it's done," he said, all business. "Nobody fucks with our Vinny."

She laughed with relief. "Thanks. I tried being nice, but the neighbor across the street is a nightmare."

"It's nothing. Call anytime," he insisted.

After he hung up, she waited for Groove to text her before rejoining the others inside the house. Groove was the owner of Groove's Club and Karaoke Bar, where she frequently went for open mic night. He was fun, but not someone you wanted to fuck with—or anyone he considered a friend. Groove had been trying to woo her since she first stepped foot in his establishment years ago while in town visiting but was always respectful when she repeated she still wasn't interested. You didn't find many gentlemen on the music circuit, and he was a rare one.

Within half an hour of Groove's affirmative message, the police had come by to issue parking tickets to the two luxury cars blocking the driveway, a tow truck pulling in just as the officer was leaving. Vinny smirked smugly as the tow truck driver did nothing to stop the equipment from scratching the shit out of Pinkie's freshly polished wheels.

"You fight dirty," Marcy said. "I like it."

———

Ruben

"I'm sorry, baby. I wish I could make it better for you."

"My friends don't feel safe visiting anymore!" Carla

seethed. "The hostile environment on this street is so bad, Megan had to schedule an emergency counseling session before she felt safe to drive!"

Megan—pronounced ME-gan—was one of Ruben's least favorite of Carla's clique. The fact she had a counselor who would take "emergency calls" over suburban house party trauma was as foreseeable as it was ridiculous. Ruben's neighbors were quiet, respectable people. He couldn't fathom whatever had gotten his wife's panties in a wad.

For all he knew, it was because he had the nerve to interrupt her day with a phone call. She had been less than encouraging since he left, always too busy and rarely someplace she thought was *appropriate* to video chat so he could actually see her. Not that she ever told him where she was, so who knew? Maybe she'd been in the mud room at her favorite spa every time.

After another fifteen minutes of shrieking at him without saying anything useful or illuminating, Carla made her excuses why she couldn't talk anymore and hung up without so much as a good bye. No "I love you," or "stay safe," or even a paltry "I miss you."

Ruben's anxiety burned in his gut, sending him outside to pace off the bad energy he'd been desperate to shake since before he left home. At this rate, V12 would have to treat him for a fucking ulcer. As he wandered around, he saw Slow sitting off to the side and made tracks in his direction.

"Man, what the hell is going on back home?" Ruben said, dropping onto the seat across from Slow. "Carla is losing her shit right now."

"Carys said things have been going well," he answered with a shrug. "She even had some people over last weekend."

"So did Carla, but she said 'the bitches across the street

ruined her whole vibe,' whatever the hell that means," he said, using air quotes and mimicking her angry tone.

"Did you ask her to clarify?"

"Of course I did."

"But she wouldn't?"

"She said she was too distraught to go into details."

"Ruben. You know Carys didn't start anything with Carla. She hates unnecessary confrontation. So does Vinny."

"I don't know, man. It's been a month, and she's already on a bender. I hope it blows over before we get back."

"Vinny said things went smoothly too, so I don't know what Carla is on about. Sorry."

"Why do you look like someone egged your grandma's house?" Zeke asked, sitting down next to Slow as he observed Ruben's frustrated posture across the table.

"I *wish* it was something you could fix with a damn hose, man." Ruben shook his head. "I don't want to talk about it. Tell us about you."

"I had the privilege of doing the inventory today," he answered dryly. "Exciting stuff."

"I had to reprimand a cocky little fucker out here on his first tour," Slow added. "I hope you are stocked on all the critical items, because at the rate this kid is going, you will be patching him up soon."

"Let me know, I'll give him *my* first timer out to make this tour hell as his personal nurse," Zeke said, grinning from ear to ear.

"You got plans for your down day, V12?" Ruben asked. Listening to them talk about difficult charges only reminded him why he needed a Zantac. He wasn't sure if his issue was worse or better being thousands of miles away from her. *At least Slow and V12 can pull rank and end their bullshit quick. There is no rank in marriage.*

"Nah. I'll probably talk to Enzo, go to the gym, maybe read a book. Not much to do out here, but the solace of my bunk will be nice. I'll be lucky to get another day off before we go home," he said.

Slow and Ruben nodded knowingly. Deployment was fucking exhausting.

"What about you, Slow? Got plans after your shift ends tonight?" Ruben pressed.

"I'm hitting the rack early so I can wake up for some quality time with my wife," he said, the slow smile that partially earned his nickname growing into a wicked look of sexual self-satisfaction. "Figured it was time I surprised her."

"I do not want to know," Zeke said, standing. "That smile says dirty things."

Slow laughed as V12 made his escape.

"Do you want me to talk to Vinny and Carys again? Ask something specific?" Slow asked when V12 was out of ear shot.

Ruben contemplated the offer. "No. It won't change anything."

Nothing will change for the better, so long as I'm here. The only chance I have is to get her away from her friends, and that's not happening anytime soon.

The real question wasn't if he needed to know more about the situation back home. It was whether or not Ruben wanted to do anything about it. He was bone tired of fighting for something alone. He knew through and through Carys was not the problem.

But Carla?

The damage control never seemed to catch up with the state of their marriage, stateside or deployed.

Chapter Nine

RUBEN

"Hey, Dad. How are things?" Ruben couldn't help the smile he felt whenever he caught his dad on the phone. They had always been tight knit but losing his mother had driven them even closer together.

"Nothing new here, and nothing for you to worry about, son." Abner "Abe" Holt was a live wire with a dodgy heart and a lifetime of digging his heels in under his belt. He had raised Ruben to be a good southern boy and was not impressed Ruben had worked as hard as he had to lose the majority of his drawl in college. Aside from that crime, he was the most supportive parent Ruben could imagine, even if his pig headedness over his health added to Ruben's developing ulcer.

"It's my job to worry. You're my father and I love you," he said firmly.

"I'm the parent. You just keep your head in the game and get home safe, you hear? No more of your meddling in my affairs," Abe insisted.

"Will you please take pity on your son and give me an update on your healthcare issues, Dad? You know I can't turn off the worrying over you anymore than you can for me. Knowing helps," he added, hoping it would sway him to talk.

"Well, I did talk to the caseworker they assigned me. It's getting sorted."

In other words, the paperwork is collecting dust some-where on a desk belonging to someone who is likely out of town or on maternity leave, and he hasn't bothered following up.

Ruben let out an exacerbated sigh. "Dad—"

"Don't you start on me, boy. I've been taking care of myself for longer than you've been breathing," he barked, cutting Ruben off.

"Do you at least have enough of your medications? I know how you feel about me covering the cost for a few months, but you need to take it, Dad."

"I'll be fine."

"You're completely out now, aren't you?" Abe's silence confirmed Ruben's worry. "Would you at least call your cardiologist and explain? See if they have samples to get you by? They might even have a patient advocate who can press the Medi-whatever people to fix your paperwork faster."

"It'll get fixed when it gets fixed, son," he said stub-bornly. "Now, tell me something about you. They feeding you good over there?"

"Yeah, Dad. Three squares," he answered with resigna-tion. This was how it typically went. He'd call his dad, they'd dance around his healthcare conundrum, then he'd get shut out.

Abe was all the family Ruben had left. He didn't under-stand why his father refused to let him help. It was an *honor* to be in a position to help him, after everything his father had done to make sure he made it into college and on to a better life than he'd been able to achieve for himself.

It was an honor to do everything he could for his father in his mother's stead.

"Well now, that's good. Growing boys need to eat."

Ruben quirked a small smile, temporarily pulled from the frustrations and fears his father's medication issues brought on. "I'll be thirty-three soon."

"Still a boy, son."

"Guess that makes you a cave man," he chided.

"Don't disrespect your elders, son; we raised you better'n that," Abe shot back with equal parts amusement and affection. "It's bad enough you talk like a Yank."

"Yes, sir," he answered, allowing his natural southern drawl to take over.

"That's better."

They didn't talk about Carla or California. His father didn't like those subjects. Instead, they spoke of *safe* topics, like the weather and whatever had been on the six o'clock news the evening before. By the time they finished covering current events and his father insisted Ruben get some rest instead of worrying over him, there was only one thought prominent in Ruben's mind.

He needed to go home to Georgia.

———

Vinny

"Was that the neighbor's car?" Vinny said once they were all buckled, and Carys was pulling out of the parking lot.

"Looked like it to me," Carys said quietly.

"Why would Eric's old boss be getting into a car with Sonja Perez?" she thought out loud. Perez was a medic. She didn't work under Greer, but he was still her superior and their paths crossed at work.

They were leaving the children's holiday party on the installation after spending the day there with their new friends, minding each other's children and losing several rounds of the cake walk. It had been a good time, right up until the end when Greer had been making friendly with Carys across the room. It had seemed innocent enough at first, until Marcy informed them he had a wide open marriage and was a total dog out of uniform.

The warning had immediately put Vinny's hackles up, but Carys seemed unsure. Eric always spoke well of his former boss, and Vinny knew it was hard for her to reconcile her husband's opinions with a friend she also had no reason to doubt. Vinny had no such hesitation. Greer had been too far away for her to see him crisply, but she saw his body language loud and clear.

Marcy was right. She'd bet her classic '72 Stratocaster on it.

Carys said something weak about his car possibly being in the shop and needing a ride, but Vinny could tell she wasn't convinced either. A guy like him would need a rental, given his position. The higher you climbed, the more important it was you could report in quickly if there was an emergency.

Vinny saw red—flags, lights, she was pretty sure a Minion had taken over her internal alarm system and something was on fire—thinking of all the odd things she'd been noticing on her security feeds when she scanned over them. It wasn't Greer alone who had her on high alert. Sonja and Carla were up to something. More than once she'd seen Sonja crossing to or from the Holt's house to her own as she was coming home from a late gig. They were too quiet all day, and suspiciously sneaky at night.

She didn't need perfect vision to see what was under her nose. Those bitches were shady as fuck, and Vinny was going to be monitoring the situation closely.

After the kids were settled, Vinny went upstairs to her apartment. She should have been getting in an afternoon nap since she had a performance ahead of her, but she couldn't shake the bad feeling in her gut after their brush with Greer. Instead, she found herself in her living room with her curtains drawn for privacy and her laptop hooked into the ninety-eight inch TV mounted to the wall. The massive unit had been a splurge she could well afford; one which helped her see things she'd miss on a smaller screen.

She didn't miss anything on this beauty. Rewinding the recordings back, she ran through all the motion flags she'd gotten since the first day, this time looking for consistencies within the oddities. She jotted down notes as she went. Dates, time stamps, plate numbers and car descriptions. Anything that might be telling.

By the time her alarm went off, she was confident what she was seeing wasn't a coincidence. Since Eric left, a car had been coming by late and leaving insanely early more and more frequently. It parked in different locations on the block, trying to blend in if Vinny were to guess. Dozens of times, she'd captured the driver parking somewhere on the block, always headed back to one of two places.

"Gotcha," she said, freezing an image of Greer on the screen. "What are the three of you up to?"

If she didn't get ready soon, she'd be late for her set. Vinny didn't want to put Groove in a tight spot—he was a good man and a solid friend—so she reluctantly shut off the TV and unplugged her laptop. She'd need it tonight.

But before she hopped into the shower, she set the system to recognize Greer's car and alert her with a custom tone every time he came into view. She'd figure this out one way or another, and the less Carys knew, the better. Her bestie had enough going on, trying to accept and relearn her own body.

Vinny hopped in the shower, letting the heat release some of the tension in her back and shoulders from spending her nap hunched over a laptop instead. Her mind raced, throwing out theories faster than she could pick her guitar. It was like the old Tri-bond game they played on the radio every day when she was growing up, listeners calling in, hoping they were the first to say the correct answer and win a prize.

Greer, Sonja, and Carla: What do these three things have in common?

"You okay?" Groove asked.

"Yeah, why?" Vinny answered.

"You don't seem as focused as usual."

"I'm fine," she said a little defensively.

"Lavender," Tripp purred in her ear, coming up from behind her. He kissed her cheek before stepping around to face her. His brows instantly pulled in, his jaw ticking. "What's wrong, baby?"

"Nothing is wrong," she repeated with gusto. "And you know how I feel about being called *baby*. Did Silla make it?"

"She did. So did her cousin," Tripp said, waggling his brows suggestively. He'd been trying to get those two into bed with him for years. Vinny didn't have the heart to explain why it would never happen.

"Is Jae singing too?" Vinny asked.

"I am!" Jae squealed, running toward Vinny with her arms open. She practically shoved Tripp out of the way as she grabbed hold of Vinny for an intense hug. "I missed you so much!"

Vinny relaxed into her friend, realizing how much she reciprocated the affection. "Me too," she admitted.

Before Jae let go, she felt Silla join from behind her. "Vinny sandwich!"

She laughed. "Hi, Silla."

"Ugh. So fucking hot," Tripp moaned beside them, earning himself a resounding eye roll from the other four.

If he's not in music mode, the man only thinks with his southern head.

"Now the reunion is out of the way," Groove began, "Is the line up still the same? You know I like to warn the sound and light guys early as possible."

"We'll just need the extra spot ready in Jae's usual place," Silla assured him. "The rest of the set up will be fine."

Groove nodded before walking away to talk to his in house technicians.

"Did you have a good visit with your grandparents?" Vinny asked when the girls let go. She didn't miss the sad eyes they gave each other before Silla spoke up.

"It was good, but hard. They are the last of our family left in South Korea but refuse to immigrate. We worry about them being so far away," she admitted. "But we did get to make kimchi the traditional way with our *halmeoni.*"

"And I forgot how much fun the markets are," Jae added. "Nothing in America compares. Although *hal-abeoji* had a little too much fun teasing us. He wants to know when we will take over the K-pop scene from the states," she said with an eyeroll, although her smile warmed as she spoke.

"And he teased us for letting our hangul skills slip. It's all we speak at home!" Silla laughed. "He's cantankerous like that."

"I'm glad it was a good trip," Vinny said.

"Sooo…" Silla drawled out. "Did you *really* move to Oceanside?"

"I did. It's been…seven months? Something like that."

"Do you like it? I thought you would tour until you died," Jae teased.

"Actually, I love it. I get to see my bestie and her kids regularly. I *do* love the road, but I was feeling majorly drained at the end of the last tour. I don't know how deep my roots will go, but it was time to put some down and see what will grow." Vinny was surprised with how strongly she felt her admission.

And even more surprised with the ease it put her mind in, given the current situation. For once, Vinny had time. She didn't have to do anything rash. Staying meant she didn't have to bolster Carys up for her impending absence. She could be steady for the first time in over a decade, by her bestie's side through thick and thin.

"Come on, let's go to the practice room and run through the harmonies on the Camila Cabello track we're covering," she said, her heart full of optimism.

Chapter Ten

VINNY

After a fun afternoon at the beach with the kids, Carys had decided to run into the commissary—the military grocery store—while Vinny worked on her laptop in the SUV with the sleeping kiddos. She'd been so engrossed with her work it took her a moment to recognize why the hairs all over her body were standing on end. When she looked up, Greer was standing in front of her, staring. He gave her a heated leer, licking his lips, then climbed into his vehicle and drove away.

Shortly after, Carys came out with her bags, silently loading them into the back of her SUV before putting the cart in the corral. She still looked distracted when she climbed into the driver seat beside Vinny.

"You okay, Carys?"

"Hmm? Oh. Yeah, I just…saw someone in the store who caught me off guard."

"His name wouldn't happen to be Greer, would it?"

Carys glanced over at her in surprise. "How did you know?"

"He was parked in front of us. He waved at me as he climbed into his tiny dick mobile and *winked*. With *smolder*.

It was disgusting." Vinny fought back the bile creeping up her throat. She really hated that man. Her stroll through the surveillance feed had solidified her poor opinion of him.

"He offered to come over and *help out,"* Carys admitted, her voice soft and tone clear on what exactly he meant. "And was clear he'd be happy to service us both."

"What a pig. Are you going to tell Eric?"

"No," she said quickly.

"Why not?"

"He doesn't need that on his mind while he's out facing god knows what, Vinny. I'll tell him when he gets home, but not before. Besides, I heard Greer is leaving soon. I'm not interested in creating drama."

Vinny crossed her arms over her chest. "I think that's a mistake, Carys. But I won't say anything…so long as he doesn't ask me directly. I won't full on lie to Eric. I respect him too much."

"I know, Vin. Thank you."

Back at the house, Vinny helped put away the groceries before she wandered out to her garage. "Hey there, baby," she crooned to her car. "Your new brakes will be here soon, and then we can take that joy ride."

She patted the hood before walking around to the door of her studio. If she couldn't punch Commander Cuckold in the cock, she needed to pound out some of her aggression on her drum set.

———

VINNY MADE her special chocolate caramel custard cake— aptly named Better Than Sex Cake—for their next gathering. They sat around Carys's table while the littles crashed in the living room with a movie after expending all their crazy in the back yard most of the afternoon. Vinny preened as Marcy, Hailey, and Lexi made obscene sounds as they stuffed their faces with her confection.

She loved these women. It was the first time Vinny had felt accepted outside of the music scene. Her not being a military spouse didn't matter to them. The fact Marcy in particular didn't trust Greer only made Vinny love them more. If they had been around the past three years, she would have stressed a lot less over Carys and Maya when Eric was gone.

They talked about kids and families while they suggestively licked their flatware clean, laughing merrily. After they'd cleared out and Carys had put Maya and Brendon to bed, she and Vinny flopped back on the couch to enjoy their lingering sugar high.

"They're shacking up," Vinny said outright when Greer came up. She'd seen him on the surveillance cavorting with Sonja enough to leave her with zero doubts. She suspected Carla was involved somehow but wasn't sure how deep.

"Probably. Kind of pisses me off he had the nerve to say what he did to me regarding both of *us* when he is obviously spending time with *her.*" Carys would have sounded jealous to someone else, but Vinny knew her comment came with a hefty dose of disgust.

"Pig," Vinny muttered.

"I'm glad Eric will be home in a few weeks."

"Me too. Maybe Ruben will get his skanky wife in check." Another thing Vinny had picked up on several days ago...a small box of laundry soap on the upstairs window ledge, where Eric had told her Ruben's guest room was. She'd heard plenty of talk traveling with the USO, but a quick text to a Navy friend confirmed what she thought she remembered.

It had started with Army wives long ago, and signified

their door was open while their man was on duty or away. It was the equivalent of mounting a red light in the middle of suburbia, letting passing men clued into the symbolism know there were legs open for business inside.

Vinny didn't have an issue with open marriages, but everything she knew said Ruben didn't think he was in one. *That* she had a problem with, even if she wasn't Ruben's biggest fan.

"That's pretty strong talk, Vin."

"Truth is truth. She's not an honest woman, no matter how much Ruben spent on her wedding ring."

"You know something I don't?"

"Yes."

"Care to elaborate?"

"No."

"Vinny, you aren't going to take whatever it is out on Ruben are you? That's not fair. He can't help what she does while he's gone."

She wasn't upset with Ruben because of what his wife did when he was away. She was upset about the things *he* did—or often didn't do—while he was home. Her list of grievances was three years in the making, and she wasn't about to spell it out to Carys. Her heart was too soft, her affections for Ruben too strong to see the cold hard facts.

So, she did what she always did after a good stew in her head over things better left unsaid. She changed the subject.

"Let's talk about your reunion," Vinny said.

"It's the same as always," Carys said with a shrug. "We'll go get him and come home."

"Nope."

"What do you mean *no?* We can't just skip town!"

"Of course you can. I'm here, and the kids will be fine. Find a romantic something somewhere and book two nights."

"You're crazy. One, maybe. Two?" She shook her head.

"Carys, listen to me," Vinny said, turning sideways on the couch so she could face Carys straight on. "You have done so well these past three months without him. You made friends finally, and I know the counseling has helped a ton. Go spend a couple nights with your husband alone and show him how okay you really are. You need this. Eric needs this. The kids will be fine with me."

"Are you sure?"

"Let me put this another way. One of us should be getting fucked senseless. It's obviously *not* going to be me. I *demand* it be you."

Carys laughed. "Blunt as ever."

"I love you. Go spend some time bonding with your husband. In fact... I think you should consider a second honeymoon for your next anniversary. Brendon will be over a year old, and Maya will be in preschool by then part time. You should bring it up with Eric while you are hydrating between fucks."

"You really are impossible."

"The last time I demanded you travel, you met Eric. Obviously my intuition is better than yours," Vinny crowed.

"And thank god he is who he is, because that could have ended with me scraping by as a single mother with my own mom barking up my tree to find a *nice guy* who will forgive my transgressions," Carys huffed, rolling her eyes.

"Does it upset you she never came around or apologized?" Vinny had wondered how Carys felt about her mother's abandonment after she eloped, but it wasn't something you just came out and asked out of the blue.

"Sometimes," Carys admitted. "She's my *mom.* It would absolutely decimate me if Maya or Brendon disappeared from my life. Especially if there was something I could do to make amends. I'd be swallowing my pride and doling out whatever apology they needed."

"Honestly? It surprised me she never called. It's not like you changed your phone number. Even my dad is disappointed in her," Vinny admitted. She knew her father still regularly checked in with the woman, but she had grown more and more distant. Reconciliation wasn't promising.

"There is only one Quincy Blume, and I'm lucky to have him as a surrogate parent. And you too, Vin. I guess in the end, I know exactly who my family is," she said warmly.

"Even if it hurts sometimes," Vinny said with feeling, grasping Carys's hand and giving it a firm squeeze.

"Especially when it hurts."

That night, the alerts on Vinny's phone were driving her insane. It was a Tuesday. There was no reason for so many cars to be driving by at this hour of the night. Finally, she gave up sleeping and went to her living room, switching on the TV and changing the input to a grid of the security coverage.

Holy shit.

Is that…yup.

The disbelief emerged from her body in a psychotic sounding, babbling giggle. It was all too good to be true. There was no way she was going to be able to sleep now, with so much going on. She silenced the surveillance alarms on her app for the next few hours, made popcorn, and settled in for the show.

Carys was right. Military life could be *wild.*

She was so grateful she was used to staying up late performing. Vinny didn't want to miss the show outside.

Chapter Eleven

RUBEN

"What the fuck is going on?" Slow barked.

"What's up, man?" Ruben asked beside him. They were in the chow hall, shoveling down breakfast.

"Another of those random sexts. This one says, 'It won't be long now. I can make you feel so much better than she can'," he read aloud with disgust.

"Who the fuck is trying to get between you and Carys?" Ruben said angrily. "That is *bullshit.*"

"I don't know. They keep coming from randomly assigned numbers. They aren't traceable, and as soon as I block one, the same shit comes through from a different number. I asked if there is anything I can do, but since there haven't been any threats or talk of criminal activity, there are no legal grounds to have any of them traced back to whoever registered them." Slow paused to shovel more food into his mouth before continuing. "I don't want this getting back to Carys. She's finally acting like herself again."

"Then tell her," Ruben said with a shrug. "Send her the screenshots so she sees you aren't replying, and make sure she knows how pissed you are. Whoever it is obviously knows you are gone right now and returning home soon. No way this isn't going to follow you, Slow."

Eric clenched and unclenched his jaw several times before replying, "You're right. It's better she hears it from me. I don't want this to set us back."

"I'd lose my shit if someone gave my wife the impression I was unfaithful," Ruben continued. "That is not cool."

"I'll tell her about it after my shift ends tonight. No point dumping it on her when I'm not even able to answer her questions."

"And the queen of Oceanside will demand answers," Ruben said with a grin.

"That she will. In this case, she deserves every answer I can assure her with."

They chatted about a fellow Marine whose wife had almost pulled a Dear John under pressure from her family. Carys and her new friends had stepped in, convincing Bella to hold faith in Javier and their marriage long enough for him to return from deployment.

"How our women wait around for us, man. They're the ones who deserve a medal. What pushed Bella over the edge?"

"She found out she was pregnant again right after we left," Eric said. "They had only meant to have two kids, and it sounds like she's still struggling with their two young boys. When she asked her mother for advice, the old bat saw her opportunity and pounced while Bella was vulnerable."

"Javier didn't know about the baby at all?"

"I'm not sure. He didn't say, and I didn't think to ask. Either way, he sure as hell knows now. Bella's mother was outside their home with a moving truck, Ruben. She absolutely meant to drag his family away and let him come home to dust bunnies and the old sleeper sofa in his office, and little else. It sounds like she's been making backhanded comments since they were married, but he never put much stock in them before."

"What did Bella decide?"

"She decided to fly back with her mother for a visit instead. Marcy is next door and will be watching her home. From the shrieking in the background of the call, I'd say Bella's mother wasn't happy her plan was spoiled," Eric said, his mouth hitching up on one side in amusement.

"Damn. Javi is a good man. I'm glad the ladies got word to him through you, but still. What a mess." Ruben's heart pinched behind his sternum uncomfortably, a phantom pain of sympathy for his brother in arms. Javier positively doted on his wife and their two boys. Her mother must have laid it on thick to convince her otherwise, even if she was unexpectedly pregnant again and worried about how her husband would take the news.

"Letting it down easy on a friend is a bad damn day," Eric said. "But I'm happy Carys finally has the kind of friends who will rally the way they did, making sure another family stands a chance. And as shit as it was to be the bearer of difficult tidings, at least I was able to reassure Javier his wife and children are in good hands. He was devastated Bella hadn't thought she could talk to him directly."

"And fucking furious with his mother-in-law, I'm sure," Ruben said. "The fucking *nerve.*" He shook his head.

"Goes without saying. I can empathize with him there. After he called his wife, we sat down and had a good talk about family. He was surprised when I told him Carys's mother had cut ties when we eloped, and I think the realization she survived it fine gave him some hope and clarity. They don't have to put up with the meddling hag."

"I can't imagine a mother not being kind and supportive,

man. My mom was my biggest cheerleader. Like Carys is," he added.

"I married a damn good woman. Loyal to a fault and a heart of gold. The way she delivered the news to *me,"* Eric said, laughing. "I almost said 'Yes, ma'am' at the end of her directive. She was all business. Find Javier, tell it to him straight, and get his ass a working phone to call his wife with."

"I'd say I'm surprised, but I'm not. She's always been inclusive. Sometimes I wish Carla was more…inviting," Ruben said. They had cleared their trays and were walking back to their quarters now.

"Inviting? She's constantly bragging about her parties and girls' weekends," Eric said with a shake of his head. "That's not the same as taking people in who need it. She's usually with the same crowd. I think the word you are looking for is *nurturing.* Carla isn't one to go out of her way unless she can see what she will get out of it for herself."

"That's not right either," Ruben said snappishly. He knew Slow didn't mean it unkindly, and he hadn't spoken cruelly. It just didn't sit right on top of his inner turmoil. "She likes to have a tight bond with a few people is all. Quality over quantity."

"How many people were at your wedding again? And how many did *you* invite?" Eric reminded him gently.

Ruben sighed before admitting, "Around five hundred. I maybe knew a hundred of them, and most of those through her, unless they were my military brothers."

"I'm not trying to be an asshole, Ruben. This is my observation of her over the years. There is room for all types of people in the world and I don't care how Carla chooses her friends. It's how she treats those she decides are beneath her I have a hard time with; especially since it feels weaponized and divisive. You're like a brother to me, military or not—black, white, or polka dot." He gave Ruben a playful elbow jab, reminding him of Maya's description of his vitiligo.

"Funny, Slow. That joke gets better every time someone tells it. Fucking polka dot..." he muttered. Everyone knew the only one who got away with saying he had polka dots was the princess.

"My point is *you* don't treat people the same as she does. It's hard for me to understand why you would tolerate that trait in a partner. But she's your wife, and I'm not going to be a dick about it."

Sometimes Ruben thought Slow's silence on the matter might be worse. Would he have done things differently if he'd invited Eric to share his thoughts on their relationship before he got in this deep?

"I wish they got along, but I can't make Carla change her mind. She follows her first impressions, you know?" It was a lame excuse, and Ruben knew it. It felt like a lie, and he hated dishonesty.

"Yeah," Eric said with a controlled neutral tone and expression. "You can't tell someone not to trust their gut instincts."

"All I know is, I'm over this fucking sand box," Ruben said as they approached their quarters. "I'm using all my reintegration leave to hole up with my woman."

"Amen, brother."

After they parted ways, Ruben lay back on his bunk and pulled out his phone. No new messages from Carla, but Carys had sent an adorable video of Maya. She was spinning in the dress he'd had shipped to her for Christmas, showing off her twirl while saying in her little singsong way, "I love my Funcle Ruben!" over and over, until she collapsed into giggles.

It eased his heart. Ruben missed his godchildren as much as he missed his own bed. Both were an integral part of what he associated with *home.* They always cheered him up, and he appreciated Carys sharing these moments with him while he was away. It helped more than he cared to admit.

Exiting the thread, he pulled up his chat with Carla. He'd sent her at least one message every day, telling her how much he loved and missed her. She hadn't replied in over a week. Same for phone and video calls. He knew she was okay because her credit cards were still being used in all the usual places. He figured if something bad had happened, there would either be no charges, or crazy ones places Carla wouldn't be caught dead.

It hurt so fucking much.

Was he the next to get a Dear John?

As he was standing up to leave for his shift, the phone dinged in his hand.

Dad: I was able to get some samples from the doctor. You can stop fretting now.

Ruben: Your paperwork should have been fixed weeks ago, Dad. I'm glad you talked to your doctor, but please go to county health and ask what the holdup is. I love you.

Dad: I can take care of myself, son.

"Then fucking *do it,"* he said out loud, his frustration getting the better of him as he typed out something completely different.

Ruben: I love you, Dad. Please let me know what they say.

Ruben: My shift starts in ten, I have to go. I'll call this weekend.

Chapter Twelve

VINNY

Silla and Jae had planned out some seriously tight beats to thread through the remix they would be melding for an upcoming ArtBeat collab. They were planning to go live from Groove's club. Tripp was helping with the cameras, making sure they hit all the right angles at the perfect time with an assist from the club's staff. They'd been going over it all day, and Vinny hadn't been this fired up in months. Maybe even years.

She loved those women. When Jae picked up an instrument, her whole demeanor changed. The charge in the room went electric right along with her. Silla behind the mic shone bright enough to illuminate anyone within a mile radius in the middle of a blackout, converting her cousin's energy into pure, radiating light. Vinny felt like she played and sang her best when they took the stage together.

The show was tonight, and she didn't know how she was going to settle down enough to nap before. *I really need to work on this dry patch,* she thought for the millionth time. Including the time she'd been on tour before she came home to her cheating ex, it had been way too long since she lost herself under someone else's body.

Vinny was cruising home in her baby, enjoying the way her body and the car melded together in perfect synchronization. If she could find a man she gelled with the way she did her Camaro, she'd be set for life. If only men were as easy to diagnose and tune up as her car was.

Pulling into the drive, Vinny noticed Carys pacing in the back yard. *That's not a good sign.* Carys beelined her way over as Vinny backed into the garage, vibrating with agitation as she waited for Vinny to cut the engine.

"I know that look," Vinny said as she closed her car door. "Who's fucking with you?"

"No idea!" she seethed.

Vinny glanced over Carys's shoulder toward the fence line in time to catch a peeping tom ducking out of view. "Let's go up to my place. I'll turn on the monitors so we can hear the kids while they nap."

Carys followed Vinny up the back stairs in her garage. As soon as they were inside and Vinny was sure the windows were closed, they collapsed on the couch in the same way they had as kids, preparing to vent all their woes.

"Let's hear it," Vinny said after she had made sure both monitors were on.

"Someone is sending dirty messages to Eric!"

Vinny's jaw dropped. "Someone he's deployed with?"

She shook he head. "The messages keep alluding to him coming home soon, so I think it's someone here." She thrust out her unlocked phone, the first of Eric's screen shots open. "Just swipe through. They started over a month ago, and they are getting more aggressive. He was hoping he wouldn't have to say anything, and it would go away on its own, but I think he's worried about our safety at this point."

If that were the case, he would have said something to me, she thought to herself as she scanned the messages. *I'm betting he's worried whoever this is will make a move before he gets home, trying to drive a wedge between them. When will these hussies respect what Eric and Carys obviously have together?*

Vinny felt her cheeks flushing with anger. She handed back Carys's phone, her mind already working out who she knew with the ability to track this fucker down. "He doesn't have to worry about our safety. Nobody is touching any of us. I'll talk to him about it, but this is still not acceptable."

"I don't want all this shit, Vin! *What is wrong with people?* When did marriage stop being sacred?" She let out a growl of frustration and collapsed back into the corner of Vinny's new sofa. "I like this couch better."

Vinny rolled her eyes. "Easily distracted. Look, whatever or whoever is out there, we're a team. Nothing is going to happen because I'm here, and I'm not going to let anything happen. You know I'm always watching out."

"Yeah, what's with that? Not that I'm not grateful to know the neighbor is shacking up with Eric's old boss on the sly. Or that Carla has visitors at odd hours—I don't even know how to approach poor Ruben about that. You have been very busy around here."

"I take my role as your bestie and the kids' godmother seriously. You are finally getting your glow back, Carys. Nobody is fucking that up on my watch." Her words came out with a sharp intensity that made Carys visibly shiver.

"I love you, Vin."

"Same. Will you forward those texts to me?"

"Why?"

"See if I can find the source."

"Eric asked. They aren't dangerous, so there isn't anything they can legally do."

Vinny smirked. "That doesn't mean it can't be done."

"Legally, right?" she asked suspiciously.

"I promise you; I won't do anything stupid that could land my ass in jail and ruin the weekend of reunifying sex that is due you soon as Eric's boots hit the California sands."

"That's not really the same thing, but whatever. He's not happy about this any more than I am, so I'm not asking for additional clarification," Carys said as she tapped away at her phone screen. "There you go. Have at it."

"Thanks. Hey, don't forget I'm going to open mic night tonight. I'll be home late, so don't worry."

"Right, I forgot. Thanks for reminding me. What's on your list for tonight?"

"I made nice with the manager. He's going to let me do a couple I had in mind and record them. I'm going to use the best ones on my ArtBeat account to help promote a big event they have coming up. Tyler is giving me a special code to offer my subscribers if they purchase their tickets through a specific link you can only get through my lists," she said smugly. Tyler was Groove's legal name, but people rarely used it. She honestly wasn't sure what made her say it just now.

"Oh?"

"I get a cut of the ticket sales I generate, and he gets free advertising. If it goes well, we are both hoping to partner again in the future."

"Sounds like you are putting down some serious roots, Vin. I thought once Eric got back you'd be itching for a tour."

"Eh. I don't know. I love the road, but right now it doesn't feel right. Dad is looking into a short-term thing in Nashville I might join him on, but that's way out. I only agreed to go if it didn't ruin the vacation I'm going to make Eric take you on."

Carys laughed, the anger and hurt she'd felt twenty minutes ago melting with Vinny's antics. "I don't have to leave Oceanside to get laid."

"No, but you can both get laid and sleep if you leave. Trust me, you need *both.*"

"Yeah, yeah. Thanks for listening, Vinny. I don't know why this made me so angry. I know Eric is never going to cheat."

"It doesn't matter. A threat to your marriage is still a threat. Frankly, I think you should have told him about Greer."

Carys shook her head. "Maybe when he gets home. I'm not out and about enough for it to become an issue, and he wouldn't dare show up at the house. Eric doesn't need the extra worry distracting him from staying safe and coming home in one piece."

"Pot, kettle," Vinny deadpanned, holding up her phone with the forwarded sexts on her screen. "I know you want to believe it's different, but it's not. You should be the one to tell him, Carys. If joining your friend circle has taught me anything, rumors run wild through this community."

Carys excused herself a few minutes later, leaving out the front door so she could go look for a hidden pineapple. Vinny laughed after the door closed, glad Carys was able to find a bit of humor in the situation. She wasn't one to share such intimate details of her marital state, and Vinny knew these texts were a big deal to her.

Looking at the messages again, Vinny took note of the different numbers. Whoever it was might have covered their tracks, but only from legal channels. She copied the numbers off each into a new message before sending them to Tripp.

Vinny: Can you work your magic on these?

Tripp: Who are they?

Vinny: Pretty sure it's all one person, and they are fucking with my friend. If I knew who it was, I wouldn't need your help.

Tripp: *Touchy.* But I get it. This the friend you live with?

Vinny: Yeah.

Vinny: She's pretty upset about it. The messages that came from them are addressing her husband in a way neither of them is comfortable with.

No way was she forwarding the messages themselves. Tripp was handy, but he was also a talker. Especially when he was drinking, which he would for sure be doing later on. Better to leave him in the dark since he'd violate Carys's privacy the second the whiskey hit his blood stream.

Tripp: I'm on it, but this isn't my thing. I need to phone a friend, and he's a bit of a sloth.

Vinny groaned. She didn't like the idea of a delay on this, but she didn't know anyone else she could ask for help either.

Vinny: As long as he can do it, I can wait.

Tripp: You looked so fucking sexy up there at rehearsals today.

Tripp: Can't wait to see you guys tonight. The live is going to be wicked.

That was all Tripp's way of saying he'd be happy to fuck the high out of her when the show was over. As sexy as he was, Tripp wasn't Vinny's type. She wasn't interested in a relationship with him, and she knew he'd try to use a good night of debauchery as a reason to be exclusive. They had undeniable chemistry while performing but allowing it to flow into something deeper would cost Vinny her freedom.

It was too high a cost for the intimacy she desperately craved.

Something had changed inside Vinny. She wasn't sure if it was turning twenty-nine, Jake's bullshit, or Carys's accident. Maybe it was everything. All she knew was she longed for more. She'd chased the high for most of her twenties.

It would be nice to enter her thirties with a sense of stability.

An incoming text broke her out of her introspection.

Groove: What are you doing after your set?

Jesus, what is with these guys tonight?

Vinny: Going home to my cozy bed to sleep.

Hopefully. If the neighbors aren't putting on another show.

Groove: Dinner after? Your set, not the whole evening. We can toast the collab between the club and your ArtBeat. I have a good feeling about us.

Us. These men. They are killing me. Have I gotten so bad they can smell my sexual desperation like a damn perfume? Eu Desperation la Lavender...

Vinny: I'll think about it. There is a lot going on at home, and I want to make sure my bestie is good if I'm out late.

It was a stupid excuse. Carys had been fine for weeks now and was more or less back to her pre-accident self. But Vinny didn't like not having an out, and it was girl code. They had covered for each other since boys went from nasty to intriguing back in middle school.

Plus, if things went sideways with Groove, it would mess up everything they were building together. This was business, and she wasn't comfortable banging someone she had a work contract with.

Chapter Thirteen

He stared at his phone screen. Two responses in the last month. It was time for Ruben to admit to himself his marriage was a sham. Loving partners didn't ghost you while you were fucking *deployed*.

He wasn't sure what stage of grief he was in at this point —or if he'd even begun to grieve—but Ruben knew he was going to be okay. He'd wanted to tell Carla the good news on leaving for home early, but he wasn't going to beg. Instead, he'd gone and talked to his commander about the situation with his father and made all the necessary plans. His father would welcome him with open arms.

His wife wouldn't even know he'd stopped on the way home.

All Ruben had ever wanted he'd pinned on the wrong woman.

Like a lovesick idiot.

He was in the common area right now, tired of being cooped up in his rack or with other guys who hadn't used proper laundry soap in months. None of that fancy shit here. All your clothes got boiled to death and dried in the sun.

Forget the fabric softener too. At least in this area they could all spread out a bit, get some much-needed space.

Across the way, he could see Slow on a video call with he assumed Carys. *That's what a man should look like when he's talking to his wife. Not stressed over whether she'll even answer.*

After he hung up, Ruben walked over, dropping onto the bench beside him. "You look like you are ten years younger from before that call."

"I *feel* a decade younger."

"She's doing well then?"

"Better than well. I can't believe how far she's come. I owe Vinny bigtime for making sure she had the time to work through her trauma," Eric said humbly.

"Doesn't free rent cover it?" Ruben quipped. He couldn't help himself. It had been almost eight months, and he still hadn't let go of what happened when they met. Something about it...

Eric looked sideways curiously. "She *doesn't* have free rent. Vinny wouldn't hear of it. She's helping with the kids and keeping Carys sane, but she's helping in other ways too. And she made it clear babysitting wasn't how she was paying for her part of the power bill."

"Right," he clipped out. *Saint Vinny.*

"Fuck, Ruben. *What happened when you met her?* I cannot for the life of me understand the bad blood between you two."

"Doesn't matter, man. We don't get along, and that's all there is to it. It's not like we run into each other much, anyway. It took *years* to meet her at all," he said pointedly. "Just drop it, Slow."

Eric held up his hands in surrender before dropping them

back into his lap. "You still going to Georgia on the way home?"

"Yeah. I managed to get a leave in route approved, so once we hit US soil, I'll be breaking off from the group."

"You want me to be bring the heavy shit back with me?"

"Nah, I got it. Thanks, though. I just need to get home to my dad."

"How is Abe doing?"

"No fucking clue. He keeps going on with his 'I'm the parent, son' bullshit. He was spacing out his heart medicine at first, but I think he's completely out now, and they still haven't fixed his medical shit. If nothing else, I'm hoping I can at least get him a supply and put my credit card on file. Maybe get the prescription transferred to an online pharmacy so its delivered and he can't do fuck all about it," Ruben bit out. "I can't lose my dad. Mom went too soon for no fucking reason, and I can't let the system fail him too."

Ruben stopped talking, choked up by the helplessness he felt.

"You need anything at all, you tell me. I mean it."

"Thanks. I have it set to be in Georgia five days, then fly back to Oceanside. I'll still be a few days earlier than they originally said getting home, so I'm looking forward to surprising Carla. She mentioned seeing her dad about the time you get back anyway, so I'll let her have a moment with him while I take care of *my* dad, and then I'll be able to give her what she deserves."

Ruben didn't mention he wasn't quite sure *what* his wife deserved at this point. Part of him still wanted to sweep her away on an exotic vacation before dragging her off to marriage counseling. This felt like quitting, damn it. But mostly, he felt abandoned. What was the point in fighting for something that couldn't give you what you needed in life?

"Sounds like a solid plan," Slow said with a nod. "I can't fucking wait to get out of this hellhole."

"No kidding," Ruben snickered. "This shit is getting old. I'm due to PCS. There is an opening across the hall from you. Think I'll pull a Slow and apply for it. Try to PCS in place like you did and stick around a few more years in a non-deployable roll."

Slow patted Ruben on the shoulder before he stood. "I have shit to do. Apply for the position, Ruben. Sometimes the grass *is* greener on the other side."

He watched as his friend strutted away.

Greener on the other side of the base.

Maybe on the other side of divorce papers?

Hell, who knows what fertile pastures I'll find myself in when I'm free of all this shit.

His racing thoughts only further drove home the need to see his father. It wasn't healthy to pin your worth on what you could offer others—he knew that—but right now Ruben felt like if he could just do this one thing for his dad, he'd be ready to do something for himself.

———

RUBEN BACKED his rental car into the driveway. The guy at the counter had been surprised when he asked for the most basic model and refused an upgrade. If he'd asked Ruben one more time if he was sure, he might have lost it.

He put the car in park, casually glancing up and down the street as he climbed out of the driver seat and retrieved his belongings. Yes. He was fucking sure. He'd paid for the insurance–he wasn't a complete idiot—but this neighborhood had fallen deeper and deeper into disrepair since he'd moved away. A flashy car with all the bells and whistles was a sitting duck and future paperwork nightmare.

Ruben did enough paperwork.

As he made his way up the cracked front walk, weeds making their homes in the gaps, he heard the door open from halfway down toward the front stoop. Ruben looked up, locked eyes with his father, and felt his whole being sigh with relief.

"Hey, Dad."

"What are you doing here, son?" Abe asked, holding the old door open for him—it's paint long faded where it hadn't peeled off along with the strips of veneer it had once adorned. He scowled as he spoke, but his tone was gentle, laced with gratitude and bewilderment. "Get on in."

Ruben dropped his gear on the thread bare carpet that was older than he was and turned to face his father. "Hi." He opened his arms and stepped into his father's reciprocating stance, holding on for as long as he could. None of that three pat on the back bro code shit here.

Real men know how to give a handshake, son. But they know how to love too. That's a strength too many have lost, regardless of gender. Hold tight to the ones who matter, you hear?

He choked back a sob as his mother's voice permeated his mind, the memory nearly toppling him. Abe squeezed Ruben harder, stabilizing him though Ruben towered over him a good two inches. It wasn't the strength he'd had when Ruben was a boy, or even the last time he'd been home. But it was all he needed to put his pieces back together.

When they finally parted, Abe gestured toward the flabby old couch. It too was a relic from his childhood. "Have a seat. Hungry? Thirsty? I haven't been to the store this week but we can scrounge something up."

"Thanks, Dad. I'm good though." He'd been too nervous to eat much since he landed stateside, and Ruben thought he might throw up if he tried to put anything inside the roiling barrel of acid impersonating his stomach. Besides, he knew exactly where his father was getting groceries these days. It wasn't a store with a produce section.

"You look good, Ruben." Abe sat down in the old sinking recliner he'd had as long as the couch Ruben was perched on. Beneath him he felt the old coils complain and he hoped like hell he didn't fall through.

"Nah. It's just been a while. Nobody looks good the first week back from the sand box," he joked. "Tell me about home, Dad. I've been missing all this," he said, letting the lie slide smooth as ever.

He hated this town.

This was where his parents had settled down and raised him. Ruben had fond memories here. But it was also the place his mother needlessly suffered until she died from a treatable condition. He was bitter, and he didn't care. Across from him, he could see the way his father's breathing wasn't as deep and steady as it should be. His skin had a sickly pallor—which said something given his dark complexion—and his eyes were bloodshot.

Ruben despised this place with good reason. If he didn't convince his father to leave soon, it would claim him too—if not the shit healthcare skewed to leave its most vulnerable citizens swept under the rug, then the drive by shootings he'd read about online. He'd never tell his father, but Ruben knew it all, even though Abe glossed over the decay of his surroundings when he asked how things were.

He kept this all to himself while he sat across from his father. Ruben loved and respected this man like nobody else and he wasn't about to do what needed done by force. There was a dignified way to approach the issues Ruben was most keen to address. Anything else would only be met with push back and resentment. He would not hurt his father's pride if he could avoid it.

So Ruben listened.

Not as much to the same stories about the same people his father always told him, but to the atmosphere around him. Ruben noted how long it took his father to become winded from talking in his slow, southern way. He noticed the obvious presence of the gangs who had moved into the area as they strutted down the sidewalk out front. He heard the sound of the toilet running upstairs and the sink dripping in the kitchen. He could smell the rot left behind from the infestation of too many things to count. The clear evidence his father wasn't as "fine" as Abe would like him to believe.

Ruben watched and listened, and he made his plans.

Abner Holt would *not* die alone in this shit hole if his son had anything to say about it.

Chapter Fourteen

RUBEN

Ruben stared at his computer screen in complete disgust. He'd taken the time to email his father's cardiologist the day after he'd gotten into town, detailing everything he had observed the first twelve hours with his father. V12 had been nice enough to go over some things with Ruben before they flew back, covering little details some might think were simple aging, but to a trained medic were red flags.

And there were so damn many red flags.

He had texted his friend before sending the email, making sure he had all the appropriate details covered before clicking send. Now he sat in front of the reply, seething over the man's incompetence. Beside him, his cell phone rang.

"Hey. You get it?" he asked.

"This guy is a fucking moron," V12 barked.

"Yup."

"Abe needs a new doctor. This asshole is going to kill him."

"Yeah, well…this asshole is the only guy approved for Medicaid in the area. He'd have to get a special referral to see the next closest, and since he doesn't drive anymore, it isn't a viable option long-term. He's completely dependent on things being walking distance or a drop off location on the local senior transport circuit." Ruben spoke low, knowing the paper-thin walls would not save him from being overheard once his father turned off the shower.

"Shit. Sucks he can't drive."

"Never said he *can't*. He doesn't. After his last car crapped out, he gave up. Said it was too much money and work to maintain," Ruben said in frustration. "His driver license is still valid."

Although with his heart issues, I wonder if the Georgia DDS would have revoked it if they had been notified?

He heard V12 blow out a breath over the line. "Is he still refusing to leave?"

"Adamantly."

"Is it just living with you? I don't mean that in a snarky way, but what if he stayed with me?" V12 suggested.

"Nope. Won't leave the memories of my mother behind, and he swears he'll hate California. Too many yuppies," Ruben said with a snort. "He's never been west of the Mississippi."

"Sometimes things have to get worse before they get better."

"You better knock on that wooden head of yours before you bring the sky down on us all," Ruben drawled. "You know better than to put that shit out there."

V12 laughed. "I see you found your southern slur."

"Fuck off," Ruben said good naturedly. "Hey, you seen the queen yet?"

"Nope. Saw the kids though. Vinny sent Carys and Eric off for a few days to reconnect. We had a lovely dinner the other night. She made pork tenderloin with grilled pineapple," he said with a laugh. "Carys still isn't over the bubble we burst on the fruit. Vinny said she still points out every pineapple they see when they go out together."

Ruben laughed along, perfectly imagining Carys doing just that. Ever since they had explained to her pineapples were the sign for swingers, she'd been on the lookout for them everywhere she went. Resuming the practice was a good sign for her recovering mental health and reinforced her playfulness as of late when she sent him funny memes and videos of the kids to cheer him while down range.

"I can't wait to see them all," he mused.

"Even Vinny?"

"Don't push it, man."

"Come on, Ruben. She's a damn peach. I don't understand."

"Which is your burden to bear, my friend. I gotta go."

"Yeah, all right. But one day we'll get it out of you."

———

ABE SAT across the table from Ruben silently stewing. It was ridiculous, yet understandable. Ruben had quietly put his foot down the only way he knew how to get results, and it had not impressed his old man.

He had finally pressed Abe into going down to the appropriate office for a lovely sit in the waiting room until someone with half a clue dug up the paperwork on his father's medical care and agreed to see them. Ruben had worn one of his favorite shirts, which made it obvious he was a Marine.

Just in case the haircut and physique didn't give him away.

And to be fair, he *was* freshly back from deployment. It's not like he had a closet full of civilian attire to pick over.

To make it worse, the guy tasked with his father's file graduated school with Ruben, though he couldn't remember his name. He'd seen the shirt and done what so many did, asking him how long he'd been in, thanked him for his service, and attempted to shoot the shit. And boy did he shit.

Right in his proverbial pants.

Ruben was many things. He was not a show pony or a liar. When whats-his-face asked where he racked and stacked these days, he calmly stated he was a major. The man blanched, his face filled with shock and embarrassment. Ruben was used to it, but it was still bullshit.

He'd been in the top ten percent of his graduating class and harassed mercilessly by the reigning dickwads every second he wasn't safely seated next to a teacher. The poor scholarship kid with big dreams and no gumption. Never mind most of those guys were still in this shit hole town, working dead end jobs while their beer guts grew so big they couldn't reach their own cocks to rub one off.

None of those past tribulations mattered to Abner Holt. The moment he uttered the word *major* Ruben knew he was in hot water. His father was proud of him, but in this setting, he viewed it as bragging. He may as well have challenged the guy to a dick measuring contest as far as his father's old-fashioned notions of politeness went.

It didn't matter the man had asked a direct question and been given a direct answer. Abner would have Ruben sugar coat it so as not to ruffle feathers. Ruben refused to lower himself back into the filth he'd crawled out of by pretending he'd accomplished less than he had in life. There would be no middle ground on this between them.

In the end, they had walked out of the office with Abner's

paperwork sorted, which was all Ruben cared about. He'd already called the pharmacy to see how long it takes the system to update. They would have Abe's prescriptions ready by tomorrow afternoon.

And with any luck, taking them consistently again would improve all the symptoms Ruben couldn't help mentally tallying every time he looked at his dad. Assuming he was still allowed to sleep in his old room when they got back to the house, given how angry Abe was with Ruben right now.

"I didn't raise you to treat others like that," he said again as he glared at Ruben over the rim of his decaf coffee.

"We aren't going to see eye to eye on this, Dad. You think I used my job and rank to push an agenda. I think if someone is sticking their nose where it doesn't belong looking for a juicy tidbit to provide at the next poker night, you should give them what they want. He asked what I do and my title, and I gave them to him in a calm and direct manner."

"You weren't like this before," he dug in. "My boy was a quiet, respectable young man when he left my home."

"And now I am a less quiet, far more confident man who believes respect is earned. I wasn't cruel, Dad. Facts are facts. Not to mention the quiet young man you sent into the world was terrified he'd get picked on in college same he was in high school." Ruben took a moment to let that sink in. "I like the man I am now, Dad. I have a strong mind and a strong body and *confidence.* But I'm not cruel. Being a Marine taught me to combine all the good you instilled into a shell strong enough to enforce those lessons with strength and kindness."

"You're lost is what you are," he insisted. "I don't care how big your biceps are. And don't think you can butter me up by treating me to lunch."

Give me something, Mom. How do I get through to him?

———

"WHAT ARE you doing in there, boy?"

"Fixing the leak in your faucet," Ruben answered with a grunt as he gave the wrench a final turn. "That should do it."

"It's too fancy," Abe insisted. "What did you do to my old faucet? I want it back."

"This is the same style you had before, it's just new. The old one couldn't be salvaged," he explained as he climbed out from under the kitchen sink and began putting everything away.

It's literally the base model of faucets. You can't get any less fancy *than this thing.*

"Good to go," he said when he was finished putting the cleaning supplies back and closing the cabinet doors. "Give her a test drive."

Abe reluctantly reached out and lifted the handle. Where the old one was so crusted you had to fight it in every direction, the new one was smooth as pudding. "It'll do, I guess."

"The part for the toilet will be in tomorrow. I'll fix it before I fly home," he said.

"What's wrong with the toilet?"

"It's constantly running, Dad."

"All you have to do is jiggle the handle, son. No need to waste money on that."

"Well, now you won't have to jiggle the handle to ensure your water bill isn't sky high."

"Don't get smart with me," he huffed in warning. "I'm still the parent, son."

Oh, believe me. I know. Like you'll ever let me forget it.

"I need a shower first, but how do you feel about grilled chicken for dinner?" he asked instead of taking the bait.

"I don't have any chicken."

"I bought some."

"When?"

"While you were in talking with your doctor yesterday," Ruben admitted. "A few other things too."

He'd stocked the freezer and pantry with easy to prepare foods that would be heart healthy. It wasn't a long-term solution, but it would get his dad by for a few months at least. Assuming he didn't get a stick up his ass and donate the whole lot to the local food bank in protest because *he's the parent.*

"Well since it's already here, I guess that would be fine. I'm going to sit in my chair."

It wasn't fine. Ruben spent an hour preparing one of his favorite dishes he'd learned to make from Carys, only for his father to eye it suspiciously. He didn't like the fresh vegetables. They tasted better with the tang of the can, he'd said. Ruben didn't tell him it "wasn't salty enough" because he'd skipped the salt completely, given Abe was supposed to be on a heart healthy low sodium diet.

The longer he stayed, the more he seemed to muck things up between him and his dad. Ruben had hoped to broach the topic of Abe moving closer again after a few days, but kept his trap shut instead. If this was how his dad reacted to basic maintenance and a proper meal being supplied, there was no way they would be on speaking terms when he left if he brought up California.

Ruben would have to take heart in the progress he *had* made. His father was back on his meds, the plumbing issues had been resolved, and his bloodwork had come back better than Ruben had expected. *Small miracles,* he reminded himself. *Sometimes you have to take the win, no matter how small.*

Then he missed his flight home after a slashed tire on his rental car held him back four hours waiting for it to be repaired.

He really, *sincerely* hated his hometown.

Chapter Fifteen

RUBEN

The red eye he'd managed to snag a seat on back to California had been quiet. Normally Ruben would pass out immediately, often while the plane was still taxiing to the runway. The tenuous emotions he'd left in Georgia had prevented him from finding rest. Ruben had never felt such tension with his father before, and Abe hadn't made it easy on him.

Still, he didn't regret how things had played out. In addition to straightening out his healthcare mess and making some minor home repairs, Ruben had installed a security door in from of the flimsy, peeling front entry for his father. It wasn't much, but it was something. The day he left, Abe had finally yielded on an Advanced Directive and Durable Power of Attorney.

The first spelled out Abe's wishes should he need emergency treatment. The second allowed Ruben to legally make choices for him if he was unable to do so himself. Ruben was well aware his dad made him sweat out those forms as punishment for *flashing his rank* in the Medicaid office. He was relieved it was done and regretted nothing.

Now if only their hug goodbye had felt more like their one in greeting, instead of a silent truce.

When the plane landed, Ruben hauled himself out to the baggage claim. He collected all his things and trudged his way to the USO. The stress and night flight had taken its toll on his hygiene, and he didn't want to go home smelling of stale travel air and excessive BO. He needed coffee and a shower. After a ten minute wait for the doors to open, the morning volunteers welcomed Ruben with cheery smiles, directing him where to store his luggage and getting him checked in.

There were some things you learned not to take for granted. One of them was the USO. Military life could shovel plenty of shit sandwiches your way, but not once had Ruben walked out of a USO feeling worse. Especially not one with showers. If he was going to take a stand with his wife, Ruben knew he'd feel a whole lot better doing it clean and caffeinated.

By the time he was cleaned up and in fresh clothing, the morning's coffee was ready for his travel mug. Ruben stuffed himself with whatever they offered him gratefully while he waited for his ride share to pull up out front. On the way out, he stuffed a Benji in the donation box with a heartfelt smile of gratitude.

The advantage to driving away from the city in the morning…most traffic was gridlocked in the opposite direction. Ruben sipped his coffee in the backseat of the car, fighting off the sleep he'd missed out on. Familiar scenery flew by as a local classic rock station played quietly. The driver was blissfully silent, aside from occasionally drumming his fingers on the steering wheel along with the music.

A little after eight in the morning, the car turned up Ruben's street. Would it be a welcome surprise? Would she even be home? Carla hadn't contacted him in almost three weeks, and he hadn't bothered telling her he was in Georgia. Something in his gut told him telling her about his stop over was the wrong move, even though his fool heart fought his instinct on the decision.

His gut had won.

As the car came to a stop at the end of his driveway, it was obvious his gut was correct. Ruben unloaded his things and sent the driver on his way with a wave of appreciation. Then he turned to the giant black monstrosity posing as a truck in his drive.

Ruben wasn't a violent man, but things were definitely about to get ugly. He hauled his shit toward the front door with confident strides, reminding himself along the way all the times he'd made excuses for Carla's behaviors. How she treated his friends. All the times she came home smelling like cologne swearing she'd only been out dancing. The long weekends away with her "girls."

He unlocked his door, dropped his things silently on the living room floor, then strode up the stairs with purpose. Unmistakable sounds echoed down the hall from his open bedroom door. Ruben walked into the room quietly, picking up the interloper's belongings and setting them in a convenient pile on the dresser by the door.

They didn't even notice him.

Until Ruben yanked the pasty ginger railing his wife off her mid thrust.

That got their attention.

Carla screamed, scrambling to cover herself as her lover brayed like the jackass he was. "Hi, honey! I'm home!" Ruben said in a cheery tone, right before he turned and threw the man out the door into the hallway. "Move it!" he barked, picking up the pile he'd set on the dresser as he followed the naked man scrambling toward his front door.

"I didn't know!" he yelled, stumbling on the bottom step.

"Sure, you didn't," Ruben said with the same false cheer he'd used to announce himself.

As Pasty and his limp dick scrambled down the front porch, Ruben kindly returned his belongings, one at a time. He'd played baseball as a kid and was happy to see he could still hit the broad side of a wife fucker's back as he chucked first his pants and shoes—the second with a satisfying thud and grunt upon impact—followed by his phone and keys. Pasty hissed as the keys struck him in the temple. He'd had the misfortune of thinking it was safe to turn for his shit right as Ruben fast pitched them his way.

I really should consider joining an adult league. That was satisfying.

Staring the man down, Ruben said in an even, low voice, "If I ever see you again, you are going to find out the kind of tactics a Marine learns to endure if he's ever taken hostage." He pointed toward the demasculinized truck and growled out, "Get the fuck off my property before I make this worse for you."

Pasty's entire body flushed red, which clashed horribly with his carrot orange hair, as he scrambled after his belongings. He fumbled his keys several times before managing to find the unlock button on his key fob, lunging at his door and jumping in as fast as he could. The truck roared to life before pealing out of the driveway.

Ruben's satisfaction was short lived.

His problems were not yet dispatched.

He pulled out his phone, pacing his front walk to manage his adrenaline while he taped away on the screen, ordering another

Uber. This one was set to take his cheating wife back to her daddy's house. It would cost a pretty penny, but Ruben knew it was the best investment he'd made since he met the bitch.

He took a few deep breaths, releasing some of his pent-up aggression before determinedly turning back to his house. Ruben strode back to the bedroom like a panther, knowing his intended prey would be stupidly waiting for him right where he left her. Why wouldn't she? He had proven time and again over the past near thirteen years he was her lap dog, eagerly begging for a scrap of attention or affection.

When he stepped inside, she was nervously posed at the foot of the bed. She'd put on one of her lacy slip things—a new one, given he didn't recognize it—with her little fluffy toed heeled "slippers" and one of those Japanese robe things. Her eyes were wide, tears slowly tracking down her cheeks while her nose glowed red in the middle of her exquisite face. For the first time, Ruben didn't see her beauty.

Ruben only saw the ugliness she hid behind her carefully maintained façade.

He turned to the closet, pulling her weekender suitcase down from the shelf and returning to the bedroom. He plopped it down unceremoniously beside her, jerking open the zipper before returning to her closet.

"Wh-what are you doing? Ruben?"

"Packing for you."

"I don't understand," she sniffled. "Are we going somewhere?"

He almost laughed. *Now she wants to go somewhere together. Cute.*

"You are moving out," he said firmly.

"What? No! Ruben this is our home!"

"Not according to the deed it's not. The house is in *my* name. Not yours. Therefore, this is *my* house, and since you are no longer welcome here, you will be vacating the premises immediately."

Her jaw fell open in disbelief, the innocent act falling as her expression morphed into hatred. "You can't do that to me!" she screamed. *"I'm your wife!"*

"Yep. An error in judgment I will be contacting JAG about this afternoon. Expect to hear from my divorce attorney soon." He maintained his straightforward tone as he hauled an armful of her belongings out of the closet and stuffed them into the suitcase. Next he pitched a few pairs of shoes in, then slapped it closed and began zipping it up.

"Wait, I need undergarments!" she cried.

"Why? You obviously don't wear them much," he said coolly. "Think of it as a time saving measure, expediting the next dick you decide you desperately need inside you."

"You don't have to be mean," she huffed, crossing her arms over her chest.

"I'm not mean; I'm realistic," he countered, picking up the case and walking out of the bedroom.

"I'm not leaving you!" she called after him.

Without a word, he spun back to Carla, grabbing her wrist before continuing his brisk pace back downstairs and to the driveway. Carla attempted to pull him to a stop—then to slow him down—to no avail. The tension coursing through Ruben finally broke as he set down her suitcase outside.

"Stop making a damn show of yourself, Carla. For once in your life, *own who and what you are,"* he barked out.

"I'm your wife!" she wailed, trying to drop to her knees. Ruben caught her upper arm in his hand, yanking her back up before her knees ever touched the ground.

"You aren't my anything anymore. I'm done."

"This is because of *them,* isn't it?" she spit out. "You went away with your stupid friends who are jealous, and they talked shit about me until you caved, didn't they? You are so *weak!*" She stomped her prissy little foot. Ruben was unmoved. He knew what she was doing.

"You make it sound like I was on a fucking luxury vacation. I was *deployed.* Contrary to whatever you think, we don't have time to fuck around in each other's lives while we are watching each other's backs for enemy fire. Not *once* have my brothers said a word against you, Carla. Not when we got back together and broke up over and over. Not even when you purposely made it impossible for Slow to stand up as my best man—"

"He could have chosen you! I only said *no kids!*" she interrupted.

"Because you *knew* he wouldn't leave his family at home! You want to talk about jealousy, Carla? You were so jealous of Carys and Maya, you couldn't stand the idea of them drawing attention away from you on your wedding day. I know you made your bridesmaids wear styles that made them feel frumpy on purpose too, so you'd stand out more. You are the most vain, shallow person I have ever met. Everything and everyone is competition to you... I don't know what I ever saw in you," he fumed.

"Puh-lease," she snarked back. "If he was *really* your friend, he would have been there."

"No, Carla. Real men choose their *families.* He belongs with Carys and Maya, even if he wishes he could be with me. You didn't give him the option to bring his family, so for him, there was no choice. You took away *my* family on what should have been the most important day of my life, and like a fucking idiot, I let you!" he bellowed.

"You know, I did you a favor saying yes. I mean, *look at me, Ruben.*" Carla waved her arm down her body. "I could have anyone, but I took pity on you. Even after you came home that summer from your boy time messed up, I still fucked you."

Ruben's jaw clenched so hard he vaguely registered the feeling of his ears popping. *"'Boy time,'* Carla? It's called *OTS* and it's fucking hell. Day after day of getting the shit kicked out of you, until you know how to be a god damned Marine. Again, *not a fucking vacation!"*

"Whatever. You left a catch and came back blotchy and defective. The point is, I can do better."

"I don't think you can, Carla. Not in the ways that matter. You—"

"I'm a fucking *goddess,* Ruben! You are nothing! A mottled piece of trash! I can't believe you think I could ever lo—"

"Look, *witchy woman!* That's about enough out of you!" Vinny growled out as she stomped her way toward them from the middle of the street. She was wearing an old pair of jeans, streaked with black stains, whisps of her long hair that had escaped her braid flying around her face.

Ruben froze, his body homed in on her like a heat seeking missile, as she launched herself toward Carla. Vinny pulled to a stop toe to toe with her, still holding a few inches height on Carla in her battered old sneakers.

Where the hell did she come from?

"I know all about you and your exploits, little desperado. You took it to the limit, but the fast lane is closed up ahead for you. The only heartache tonight will be yours because we've wasted enough time around here on you," Vinny went on.

Holy shit. How many Eagles references can a person cram into one speech?

Ruben stared at Vinny, slightly askance. Was she seriously defending him? Vinny was the anti-Carla; with her messy hair and grease-streaked face, staring down her scantily clad, frilly target with a confidence that almost had Ruben taking a step back.

She was *fierce*.

This was the woman he'd heard so much of from his friends, the warrior who would do anything for those she cared about. Which begged the question, *why is she out here defending me? We aren't even friendly, much less actual friends.*

"Who the fuck do you think you are, *freak?*" Carla's voice was aimed low, her gaze shooting darts like she could double tap Vinny with her imaginary mind powers. "I thought your kind was allergic to sunlight. Shouldn't you be safely tucked into your coffin by now?"

"You aren't very original, but that's to be expected from a self-serving hoe. I mean first *Casper,* and now you are referring to me as a vamp?" Vinny clicked her tongue before tsking Carla. "Maybe if you exercised your brain as much as you do your cunt, you could do some *real* verbal damage."

Whoaaaaa.

The sound of a car stopping at the end of the drive pulled Ruben out of his stupor. While Carla and Vinny glared at each other, Ruben quickly loaded Carla's suitcase into the trunk of the car and confirmed with the driver, handing him his last fifty in tip, knowing it wasn't enough for the long drive he'd be spending with her.

"Carla," he called out quietly, motioning for her to get into the car. Ruben watched the car leave, using the time to collect himself before turning back toward Vinny.

She was standing there perfectly erect, spine straight and proud with her arms defiantly crossed over her chest. The adrenaline rush he'd been coasting on since arriving home crashed, leaving him exhausted and confused.

"Lavender," he began, but that's all he got out before she launched herself at him.

"Don't." She shoved her finger into his sternum, surprising him again with her strength. "You don't get to say a damned thing. Not after what you've recklessly done around here."

"That's a little harsh, don't you think?" he said softly, taking a step back from where her finger was still digging into his chest.

"You were given the *gift* of the babies still peacefully sleeping across the street in their beds, same as I was. Time and again you have missed out because you *chose to marry that harpy piece of shit* instead of realizing what gifts you already possessed. They deserve better. Eric and Carys deserve better. I didn't step in for *you;* I stepped in for my *family.* A family that adores you and would never want to see you treated the way you have let her treat you.

"They won't do something about it because they love you too much to try and influence your life like that. I have no such qualms," she said. "Get your shit together, Ben. I'm done tolerating your stupidity and managing the following damage control."

"Lavender, please…" he said softly, but she'd already spun away, stomping her way back across the road and down her personal stretch of the driveway.

Ruben stood there on his drive, empty and exhausted, wondering what she'd meant by "damage control."

Chapter Sixteen

VINNY

Vinny finished double checking her work before sliding out from under her baby. The only advantage to the pissing match she'd launched herself into an hour ago was she'd just set up for an oil change and by the time she came back, the pan was full of the near black sludge which used to be oil. Throwing herself into the blissful process of auto maintenance also helped her shed the last of the aggression she'd hurtled toward the neighbors.

All she could think as she overheard them arguing in the driveway was *the kids don't need to hear this*. Before she knew what she was doing, she was toe to toe with the town bicycle. It felt good to tell Carla what a piece of shit she was.

Less so Ruben. *Why did I call him Ben? And why didn't it feel good to finally tell* him *off too?* She was confused by the whole altercation.

That night was the last of her agreed performances at Groove's club. She'd been rearranging classic tracks for weeks in preparation. Tonight, they were covering the Eagles. Vinny had even convinced her dad to help out with the intro to "Seven Bridges Road" as a surprise for Carys.

Jae had pushed for a Diane Warren mash up, which was proving to be a touch tricky. By choosing a songwriter instead of an artist, they had opened themselves to virtually every genre of music. Celine Dion, Genuine, Dione Warwick, The Pointer Sisters, Trisha Yearwood, Uncle Cracker...she was a legend for a reason. The trick was pulling from Warren's catalog in a way that both covered her versatility and blended into something interesting and believable. It was coming along, but Vinny still wasn't happy with it.

Tripp had been distracted lately too. It was like everyone was stuck in a creative block at the same time. Usually they would feed off each other, breaking through each other's blocks and cranking out their best work in the process. Instead, there was a weird vibe holding them in a creative stasis.

After she'd cleaned up her garage and showered, Vinny flopped down onto her couch with her favorite guitar and tried to strum out the last of her emotions. There was too much happening all at once, and she didn't know how to see through it all clearly. Eric was home, sure. It was good to have him back, and Vinny loved seeing Carys and the kids curled up in a Blackwood family dogpile on the back lawn with him.

It was all the rest of it...Greer and Perez were still a nagging presence on the block, and Vinny didn't trust either of them. Consulting her Navy friend had illuminated a lot of things too. Greer had offered Eric a fast track to his next rank. Given what Eric did and how long he *should* be at his current rank, her friend assured her the only way Greer could make good on that promise was to push him hard.

More deployments, TDYs, responsibility...all the things that would have Eric home a minimal amount while he worked himself to the bone. Eric had chosen to focus on his family and be the kind of father he wished he'd had—his words, and Vinny loved him for it—but given Greer's recent behavior, Vinny suspected his motives toward getting him promoted faster were less for Eric's benefit so much as his own.

Greer was looking for a way to get Eric out of the way so he could seduce Carys. Given what Carys related to Vinny of their grocery store conversation, the man was brazen. Her instincts told her Greer was not a man who took no for an answer. He was used to getting his way. The only silver lining, Greer was due to leave in a few months while Eric had taken another job adjacent to what he was already doing here at Camp Pendleton, extending his time here another three years.

"You gonna play that thing, or just hold it?"

Vinny's gaze swung to her front door, a smile stretching her cheeks wide. "Dad! You came early!"

"I thought I'd join the family for dinner before we went off to make music." Quincy Blume was easily the coolest dad ever to walk the earth. Nobody could convince Vinny or Carys otherwise, and she suspected her father knew it.

"They'll love that," she said, setting down her guitar so she could get a hug. "Eric is home."

"I heard. Best time to drop in." Vinny clung to her father tightly, breathing in the familiar smell of his after shave and leather jacket. "Hey. You okay, Lavender?"

"Yeah," she said. "It's just been intense around here lately. And I'm blocked."

"Ah. That'll do it," he said with understanding. "Do you want to talk about it?"

Vinny pulled back enough to meet her father's gaze as she said, "You know what? I do. It probably won't help my block, but all the other stuff could use another pair of eyes."

They curled up on the couch and Vinny filled her father in on all the things weighing on her mind. She even went so far as to show him some of the security footage she'd flagged and taken notes on. At the end of it, she felt much better.

"I don't have the answers for you, but I think you are on the right track, Vin," he said.

"That's good to hear. I feel like I'm losing my mind," she admitted.

"Are you feeling cooped up?"

"No, actually. It's the opposite. I feel an immense sense of freedom here. I love being near the family. The beach is close by if I need to go have a moment to take in the tranquility of the water and let everything else drift away with the tide. I've always been half packed, you know? It's nice having things put away instead of tripping on all my gear."

Quincy chuckled. "It is nice to have something you can rely on. A place that is all yours."

"This apartment is quirky, like me. It feels right."

"It suits you. And the studio space has been a boon to *my* storage space," he chided.

"Do you think I'm being too stubborn? I'm not trying to be, but I'm genuinely upset about all the drama happening around here. These people...I guess after all the things I experienced touring I expected a well-kept street in suburbia would be less like *Desperate Housewives* and more like... I don't know."

"I think you need to marinate in your feelings until you understand *why* you feel the way you do. There is nothing wrong with protecting yourself, both physically and emotionally. I'll stay local the next few months or so, but the job in Nashville starts in late July. I'd still love for you to join me if that's what you feel you need when it's time to head out. If not, we still have until then, and I'm going to miss the hell out of you, Lavender."

"Thanks, Dad."

The question is, which feelings do I marinate in first?

————

THE EAGLES MASH up was everything Vinny had hoped for. Groove had been wanting to expand his business for some time, and with all the buzz generated with the combined ArtBeat attention from Vinny and her friends, he was close to making his dream of a second location possible.

She was still blocked. Vinny would disappear into her studio for hours, but nothing was happening. She'd been stuck before, but this was different. There was absolutely *nothing* in her head. Not a fun beat, or a plucky riff. She'd stopped humming random ditties until lyrics poured out of her so fast, she could only capture them all by recording it first.

It was like someone had switched off her soul, and it was beginning to freak her out.

A week and change after Carla was unceremoniously dethroned as the neighborhood's resident madame, Eric and Carys hosted their welcome home cook out. Ruben had been over most of the week, helping Eric build a new play structure in time for the party. Vinny kept herself hidden for the most part unless she was collecting their water bottles to be refilled. Then she made an effort to ask if they were happy with their progress and to offer a hand anytime.

Carys had been threatening to serve nothing but pineapple —her last welcome home bash the guys had explained it's roll in finding swingers in the wild—and while not *everything* was made with it, she did find plenty of interesting ways to incorporate it. Vinny had giggled over Carys's plans with her before washing up to help her bestie make all her pineapple infused dreams a reality.

Marcy and Hailey had made it with their families, and Marcy's neighbors too. Bella had struggled with the last deployment, almost allowing her mother to convince her she'd be better off leaving her husband and moving back with her parents to raise their kids. Marcy had stepped in, and since then, Bella had been a regular fixture in the group chat.

Vinny liked her, though she thought Bella needed to work on her backbone. This was the first time she and her husband, Javier, had joined the rest of the group for an event. Javi knew the guys and fit right in. Bella had looked nervous at first, but the sight of her boys playing with Marcy's son Mason had put her at ease, and they'd had a good time after that.

Without her permission, Vinny found herself pulled toward Ruben all night. She didn't approach him or even greet him. She didn't even know what she *would* say were she to attempt a conversation. Like her creative block, she found the unwanted pull toward enemy number one to be increasingly unsettling as the party wore on.

Ruben continued to avoid Vinny too. All afternoon and evening, they managed to steer clear of each other. Vinny was relieved, and…not. *Why do I feel like I need to say something to him?*

It was so *stupid.*

She thought about what her father had said, about sitting in her feelings until she understood her whys. Maybe that's all it was—she had been in a funk for weeks now and was earnestly lacking clarity in her life—but something told her it was more than that. Since the only thing that didn't feel broken was her instincts, she decided to let them guide her until something important happened.

And it did, four days after the cookout via text.

Tripp: Good news.

Vinny: You've been approved for a personality transplant?

Tripp: Hush or I'll make you earn it.

Vinny: Did your sloth finish?!

Tripp: He did.

Tripp: All the numbers were generated and linked to the same email account. He's pretty sure the email is a throw away established solely for the purpose of setting up the numbers. The name on it was bogus.

Vinny's heart plummeted.

Vinny: Tripp. You said you have good news. This sounds like a dead end.

Tripp: Oh, it would be. If it were me. But my friend followed all the tiny digital breadcrumbs right back to her IP address and even managed to get into her computer.

Tripp: Her name is Sonja Perez.

Tripp: And the files he sent me are fucking WILD.

He followed the last message with a cluster of links, all to the same website.

Vinny: Why are you sending me links to what is obviously something porn and/or escort related?

Tripp: Trust me. You want to see this.

Vinny: I really don't.

Tripp: Damn it, Vinny. Have a little faith. CLICK THE LINK.

Vinny: If I get a virus, you are replacing anything it fucks up.

Tripp: Fine, just open the link already!

Swallowing back her unease, Vinny took a leap of faith

today was the day Tripp was using his upper head. She clicked the first link.

"Holy…"

Her eyes scanned over what she was sure should have been private access information unavailable to anyone other than the website curators. One after another, she scanned through them all, her mouth hanging open in disbelief.

Sonja and Carla were co-hosting an exclusive sex site catering to a clientele eager to get off on… Well, she wasn't exactly sure what just yet, but some of her security camera footage made a lot more sense now. She needed a bigger screen to properly understand what she was looking at.

Vinny: Your friend was worth the wait! What's his price?

Tripp: Don't you worry about that. He said what he found was payment enough.

Eeeew.

Chapter Seventeen

RUBEN

After shipping his wife off to her father, Ruben's adrenaline had crashed hard. As soon as he went back inside, he'd collapsed on his couch, dead to the world for the following six hours. When he woke, he was hollow and numb.

Had she ever loved him at all?

Did I really love her, or just the idea of her?

Slow's words from down range rang through his mind. He'd been testy at the time because he didn't want it to be true. Now it was hard not to agree with his friend's assessment. Carla was not a nurturing person and treated others like dirt if she didn't deem them worthy.

He didn't know how to process being her charity case.

When his vitiligo came to life during training, it had been a shock. The doctors told him it could be brought on by stress, but he'd read after he got home that usually happened later in life. It was what it was. He'd been treated to slow the spread, and it had eventually stopped. At the end of the day, it was cosmetic.

Ruben was still Ruben. His vitiligo didn't stop him from being a good man or a good Marine. Most of it was covered by his clothing anyway. It had reached as high as his earlobe on one side but mostly affected his torso and limbs. He generally only remembered it when he was dressing these days. For Ruben, it was more like a tattoo. Yes, it was there. He saw it. But it wasn't an unpleasant thing that made him cringe away.

It just *was*.

And until the morning of her abrupt departure, he'd had no idea his partner found him wanting for it.

He'd thought about unpacking next, but the idea of mixing his gear in with her frivolities made his stomach twist. Ruben used to love the contrast between Carla's tasteful wardrobe and his rough and tumble badassery—as if he was *her* Marine alone. Her protector.

Instead, he grabbed the keys to his truck and went out to the garage. If he was busy, he'd be distracted from what all this really meant for him. Ruben desperately needed to ignore the magnitude of the morning's events a little longer.

The battery was dead.

Fuck. She couldn't bother to start it once a week? Seriously?

He sent Slow a text and took out his jumper cables. Soon enough, Carys's SUV was in his drive, nose to nose with the hood popped. The men worked silently, connecting the cables and bringing Ruben's truck back to life. When they were finished, Slow gave him a casual fist bump, a knowing expression on his face.

"You know, don't you?" Ruben finally asked.

"Saw the whole thing," he admitted. "Proud of you, Ruben. That was a hard thing you did."

"Yeah."

"Do you need company?"

"No, man. You go enjoy the little prince and princess. I've got this."

Slow gave a subtle nod of acknowledgment before climbing back into his wife's rig, backing it back across the street into his own garage, and disappearing as the door rolled down. Ruben appreciated his buddy, but now wasn't the time to accept his help.

He climbed into the cab of his truck for the first time in four months, the familiarity assuring him not all had gone to shit in his world. A man and his truck. It was as solid a relationship as anyone could hope for. So long as he took care of Hank, Hank would continue to take care of Ruben.

Yes, he'd named his truck Hank.

It seemed like a trusty name when it came to him, even if it did elicit flashbacks to old King of the Hill episodes now and then. In hindsight, Carla's hatred toward the practice of a man naming his chariot should have been a major red flag.

Hank was a friend to Ruben.

It was a machine to Carla, same as he apparently had been.

After thirty minutes of driving around, Ruben headed toward the local moving supply store. When Hank's bed was full of boxes and packing material, he headed home. He would start on the ground floor and work his way up. It was as sound a plan as any. There wouldn't be much left by the time he was done, given he'd allowed Carla to pick most of the furniture and décor when they married.

At the time, it seemed logical. She was home all day. He generally wasn't. What did he care what was on the walls, so long as the couch was worthy of a nap? But as he packed away the Williams Sonoma exclusive—and exceptionally frilly—dishes she'd chosen on their wedding registry, he realized how much of his life he'd allowed her to control.

There was nothing practical about Carla's dishes. They looked like they belonged in a whimsical English tea house, not as the primary plates you would eat with every day. And since Carla rarely prepared food herself and had most of her parties catered, they were more of a decoration anyway. A practical item made *impractical* with frivolity.

He packed the entire kitchen the first night before scarfing down a pizza he'd had delivered and crashing on the couch again. The next morning, he woke with a kink in his neck. The first light of day was faintly beginning to penetrate the night, but he was wide awake.

A few painkillers and a hot shower later, he had the living room packed up. It was barely eight in the morning. Ruben celebrated by posting the barely used couch set Carla had insisted on for sale. It was a garish shade of burgundy he'd never have picked himself and given it hadn't passed the sleeping test last night, he was happy to be rid of it.

After he ate lunch, he accepted a cash offer for the couches and helped load them up, feeling a sense of relief as they disappeared from his life. He went over to Slow's that afternoon with a spring in his step. Not of the Tigger variety, but...*lighter.* He even caught himself smiling a few times as he worked with Slow on the kids' new play structure.

The following week was the same from day to day. Ruben woke and cleared another room of Carla's influence, packing what fit in boxes and preparing the rest to either be returned to her safely or immediately put it up for sale on the local buy/sell/trade pages. Every item removed from sight brought him closer to the next step.

Whatever that step was. Ruben wasn't completely sure what came after evicting your spouse, but he'd figure it out. Surely the divorce paper's he'd had served would force the matter to a head.

Finally, it was time to do the master suite. He'd barely looked at the room since returning, opting to take a bunch of his things out of his drawers and keep them elsewhere so he didn't have to acknowledge the bed he'd found his wife fucking another man in—their marital bed. She hadn't even had the decency to use the spare room.

The only thing he'd done was strip the bedding and stuff it into black yard debris bags, so he couldn't smell the evidence of her deceit. They'd gone out in the trash immediately. He would never use any of the bedding in this house again. Ruben had also stuffed in the custom monogrammed towels she'd ordered. It was the classic *his* and *hers,* but on the towels marked *his,* the word was marked out with *hers* written off to the side.

Because in Carla's world, everything was about her.

How the hell did I ignore so many red flags for so long? Fuck.

After the master, he'd taken a week off. For one, his reintegration leave was over. Ruben had applied for the job across the hall from Slow the moment he logged into his work computer before quietly going about his day. It had been difficult to pretend he didn't hear the whispers, but so was the nature of any group—there would always be gossip.

And while his return to work on Monday had slowed him down because he wasn't home *to* clear things out all day, there was something else bothering him that had nothing to do with his house and everything to do with the fierce little rocker chick who simultaneously lit the world with her presence and made him feel like he was crashing her party.

The whole week he'd been helping Slow build the new play structure, she'd been nothing but nice. Their water bottles were kept full, and she often brought them back with snacks. Ruben was included in her generosity, but he knew it was by default. When she stayed long enough to ask how the work was going, the conversation was directed toward his friend. She hadn't so much as looked at Ruben that he saw.

And it bothered him.

Lavender Blume was not kind to him. She wasn't rude either. What perturbed him was her indifference. The cool way she accepted his presence and treated him like anyone else, but without actually looking at him or engaging in any way. She made it clear he was below her in all the ways that mattered with her dismissal.

Ruben was rattled.

Slow's cookout the previous Saturday had been amazing. The food, company, atmosphere…it was everything you knew to expect when you went to the Blackwood's home for any occasion. Except in the past, Rubin and Vinny had always been two ships passing in the night. For once, they were both present.

How can I be drawn to her when she makes me so fucking crazy? I don't even like her, past what she's done for my friends. There is no logical reason for me to want *her to see me in a better light.*

If it were anyone else, Ruben would have shrugged his shoulders and let it pass. He couldn't do that with *her.* Not only because she was around all the time now, but because his friends wouldn't let up on him about it. They wanted to know what had happened and had all but demanded he spill his guts.

It made him angry. He didn't want to talk about meeting Lavender. He didn't want to *remember* meeting Lavender. For one thing, he couldn't decide if he'd been in the right or not. Some days it was obvious he was—he had a damn key to the house, for fucks sake—but when she'd stepped close enough, he remembered how tightly her body had been wound, ready to spring the moment he was clearly identified as a threat.

She'd been protecting Maya.

Ruben couldn't hate her for that.

After a week of debating his own guilt in the back of his mind, Ruben decided it was time to tackle the last room in the house. He'd left the spare room for last, knowing Carla had spent a lot of time in there doing whatever it was she did. Her computer was in there, set up as an office neatly tucked under the window facing the front of the house. On the opposite wall sat the bed. It was a bit tight, but it worked, and she'd been oddly pleased with how it all fit together.

Carla had left the door locked. In fact, she'd had the lock changed out—he couldn't imagine her using a tool herself—to one requiring a key to open. Having already been all over the house, Ruben knew he'd have found a random key by now. So where was the key? He wasn't interested in the expense of a locksmith.

It was Saturday, so he was free to dig around. For three hours, that's exactly what he did. There wasn't a key anywhere he couldn't explain, and he was starting to take it personal. *I'm thinking like* me. *I need to think like Carla...or at least like a woman.* He sure as hell wasn't about to call *her,* but there was one woman he knew he could count on for advice.

Ruben took out his phone and sent a message.

Ruben: If you wanted to make it difficult to find something—let's say you locked it up for safekeeping—and you didn't want anyone to open it, how would you hide the key?

Carys: What, like a jewelry box or something?

Ruben: Yes.

Carys: Do I want Eric or Vinny to know about it?

Ruben: Does it matter?

Carys: Of course it does. If it's something I might want to send them after, it will change my logic in finding a good hidey-hole.

Fuck, why didn't I think of that? Of course, the fucking key wasn't sitting in a random drawer!

Ruben: Then, no. Nobody is ever to see it. Even if they see the item and ask about it being locked, it needs hidden so well even Slow won't find the key.

Carys: I'm intrigued…but in that case, I would put the key somewhere super easy, where it would be easy enough to grab, but not a place they would think had significance to me.

Ruben: Good to know.

Ruben: You're kinda scary, dear queen.

Carys: Nah. Just don't make me mad. *winky face*

Chapter Eighteen

VINNY

She came around the block in time to see Ruben locking the front door with his key and moving to sit on the Blackwood's front porch step. If she'd returned from her walk from the other direction, she might have been able to duck up her driveway without being noticed. But she hadn't, and now she had to walk past the front of the house.

Ruben looked…despondent. *With a touch of pure shock,* she mentally added as she drew closer and therefore could better take him in. His posture smacked of a rejected teen, his spine curved over his legs and his forearms crossed, elbows supported on his knees. Except he wasn't all gangly, given he was very much a *man.*

"They aren't home today," she said as she strolled up the sidewalk, taking a sharp right up the front walk and stopping just below where he sat on the top step. "Carys woke this morning with the crazy notion stroller pushing through a theme park all day would be fun."

"Ah. Carys didn't say anything when I was texting her earlier," he said morosely, lifting one hand to rub the side of his head.

"Did you need something?" She didn't have to be Ruben's biggest fan to be nice. He was important to her family, and since they were absent, Vinny thought nothing of stepping in.

"I was hoping to talk to Eric," he answered, looking down where he was now rubbing his hands together between his knees. "But I guess it can wait."

"I'm not your biggest fan," Vinny said gently as she joined him on the top step, leaving a good foot between them as she sat. "But I absolutely detest your wife. Given you had the good sense to boot her out, I'm willing to be a proxy."

"A *proxy?*"

"Fine," she huffed, "A *friend.* Just this once."

"How noble of you," he deadpanned.

"You have no idea," she answered in all seriousness. "I suggest you consider my offer."

"I don't think it's wise to talk out here. It isn't private." His eyes quickly darted over to the Brown's house, and Vinny understood immediately.

"I've already ordered Chinese. Care to join me?" If he ate all her cashew chicken she would take her revenge with his chopsticks. But he looked so damn sad, and she knew she wouldn't get any sleep if she sent him home. *Damn conscience. Completely overrated.*

"I don't know," he said carefully, side eyeing her with a hint of playfulness. "Did you get any barbequed pork?"

She pulled away, fainting offense. "Are leprechauns Irish?"

"Lead the way," he said standing, one arm extended forward in invitation for her to direct their path.

Vinny silently got to her feet and walked across the yard and driveway to the steps leading up to her little deck and front door. It was a strange sensation, knowing he was right behind her. She didn't loathe it nearly as much as she believed she should. *Must be the kicked puppy vibe he's rocking. I still don't like him.*

She unlocked the door and swung it wide, stepping aside so she could lock up behind him. "Make yourself at home," she said casually. "Do you need anything?"

"No, thank you." She watched as he took in her space, his gaze tracking across her guitar wall directly across from the door. "Wow. This is…different. I haven't been up here in a long time. Did you paint?"

"Yeah, it was all white. White wall, white trim, white ceiling. Not really a big deal usually, given I'm renting. But the owner is a friend, and when I explained I don't like blending into the walls so well I disappear, he told me I could do whatever I like."

Ruben's laugh started as a low rumble in his chest that worked into something akin to the jolliest hyena imaginable. "Did you *really* just crack a joke on yourself?"

"I'm lacking melanin, not a personality," she retorted dryly. "Besides, I like to laugh."

They stood there awkwardly for a few moments, still rooted to the floor by the door. Vinny grew nervous enough to break away, directing him to have a seat. He strolled over to her couch and made himself comfortable. "Oh. Now *this* is a nice sofa. A man could sleep like a baby here."

An unsolicited giggle escaped her before she could stop it. "Spent a lot of time sleeping on the couch, have you?"

"Only lately," he confessed. Vinny immediately sobered, looking away. "Hey, don't do that."

"Do what?"

"Clam up like that. I was sleeping on the couch by choice, Lavender. I don't want or need your pity. Besides, I've graduated to an air bed," he added lightly.

"That doesn't sound much better," she admitted.

"My neck disagrees."

"I've slept on a lot of couches. My neck and I had a lot of disagreements the following day. Especially when I was trying to look cool on stage with half my normal range of motion," she conceded. Couch surfing was something she was definitely too old for.

"It's about as fun riding bitch in a convoy. You got all the gear strapped on including a helmet, and the guy driving needs you to look over your shoulder to check what's doin'. Fucking agony."

You got me beat there," she said with a nod. "Tour buses and stages are roomier than one of those rigs you and Eric roll around in, packed in like sardines."

"It's not a competition, but if it was, you would win." Ruben grinned at her as he settled back deeper into her couch. "I think you haul more than your fair share of amps and shit around."

"My equipment is lighter than your gear," she countered. "And I don't carry it all at one time."

"Ah, but I *train* to haul my gear."

"Hauling it around since I was six *was* my training. Don't be an ass." She mean mugged him playfully. He grinned back.

The comfort between them was so disarming to her, she broke it without thinking, grasping for the tension she was more accustomed to when Ruben was around. Wordlessly, Vinny turned her body abruptly toward her kitchen space, as if she were a marionette whose novice puppeteer was struggling to keep her strings from tangling.

She pulled down two glasses and filled them with ice water, setting them on the eat in bar. Paper plates quickly joined them, along with a roll of paper towels. A knock at the door saved her from finding more busy work to keep her focus away from whatever temporary truce had developed with her nemesis.

Okay, nemesis is a strong word. But she still didn't like him, and she didn't want to.

Vinny thanked the delivery girl and handed her a tip, locking up behind her and hauling the food over to the place settings she'd set. Ruben was already there, waiting.

"How can I help?"

She shook her head. "It's fine."

"I crashed your dinner, Lavender. Let me help," he said gently.

Vinny hesitated before handing over the takeout bag. "Okay."

She took the seat on his left, her usual spot when she didn't eat on the couch. Although she'd done so less often since she treated herself to the new one. The last thing she wanted was to damage or stain her couch.

"So," she began once he'd set out and opened the containers. "What had you moping on the steps?"

"I do not *mope.* If anything, I was flummoxed." Ruben handed her the chow mien noodles. As she accepted them with a nod, he continued. "I've been trying to pack up and sell off everything from my marriage. Today I opened the last room, after spending five hours looking for the key."

She paused mid scoop to stare over at him. *"Five hours?"*

"Yeah," he said quietly. "The door wasn't locked when I left. It was a normal bedroom doorknob. She replaced it with an external style lock that requires a key to get in."

"This wouldn't happen to be the room over the garage, would it?"

"How did you know?" His voice came out strangled, a mixture of surprise and wariness.

"How much did Eric tell you about what I've been doing here?" she asked in reply.

"Just that you are helping with the kids, making sure Carys has the time she needs to focus on all the healing she has to do since the accident."

"You know they confirmed it was a gang initiation thing, right? The brick going over the overpass that almost…" Even now, Vinny didn't like to think about it, much less say it aloud. *The brick that almost killed my family, almost left Maya an orphan.* She involuntarily shuddered, the hairs on her arms standing on end.

"Yes, I know." He sounded as affected as she was, but Vinny kept her eyes on her plate.

"We were worried *almost* wouldn't be good enough for them. Before he left, Eric and I researched discrete security systems you can install yourself. I spent a lot of time setting it all up around the time you guys left. Nothing has happened so far, but we both felt better knowing if it *did,* the cameras might be able to help catch whoever it was."

She wasn't being precisely accurate. Plenty had happened, it just wasn't gang related.

"Okay, what does that…*fuck.* You could see what she was doing through the window, couldn't you?"

"Sort of. Not enough for detail, but enough to have a lot of questions. She usually had the sheers closed, if not the curtains too. But some things were meant to be seen," she said.

"Such as?"

"The detergent box on the windowsill."

Ruben's chopsticks froze in the air. "What else?" he forced out through his tight jaw.

"It's hard to explain, but I can show you if you think you can handle it." She looked over at him cautiously. He was staring at her, his expression contorted with too many emotions for her to identify. Vinny realized how little she truly knew him, but mostly *of* him. She didn't like not being able to read someone she was talking to. "I don't mean you *couldn't,* Ben. It might be hard watch. But if you sincerely want to know, I'll show you anything you want. Even the things I haven't told Eric and Carys yet."

"You're keeping secrets?"

"No, it just hasn't been the right time. Look at them, right back in their honeymoon phase, like the accident hadn't happened. He doesn't talk about it, but I saw the way he looked at her after. Eric would never leave Carys, but he had resigned himself to being married to a shell of the woman he loved."

Ruben nodded. "Yeah, he was really fucking worried he'd lost her. If not their connection, possibly even all of her, if she woke up one day and decided she couldn't handle this life anymore."

"Did you doubt her?" Vinny asked curiously.

"The queen of Oceanside? *Pfft.*" He shook his head. "Not for a second. But in his shoes, I can't say I wouldn't have been just as worried. The day Slow met Carys he was reborn a new man. A *better* man."

Something dark flitted across his face. He turned away, scowling down at his plate while poking a piece of his pork.

"Carys too," she said softly. "She found herself when she found him."

They both halfheartedly pretended to eat for a few more minutes before Ruben broke the silence. "Okay. I need to see it."

"You sure?"

"Yeah, man. I need to know what happened so I'm not

dreading any new unpleasant surprises coming out of nowhere."

She nodded. "Okay. Although I think you could resolve your issue easier by buying a new mattress. Air beds are torture, even if it is better than the ugly couch I saw you help haul out to the highest bidder."

Chapter Nineteen

RUBEN

"What do you want to see?" Vinny asked as she hooked her laptop into the biggest TV Ruben had ever seen without a projector.

"All of it? I don't know."

"Why don't I show you the things I noted around *your* house, and if you want to view more, we'll keep going?" she suggested.

More than around my house? What the fuck else has been going on while we were away? Ruben had a strong suspicion he could guess at the cast of tonight's "show" all too easily, given Lavender's words.

"Okay. It's a starting place, at least."

"This is day one, from the first set of feeds I connected. One of them is under the eave above my front window, so it spans our driveway across to yours, and the window directly across from here," she said, indicating her large front window with a nod of her head. Her hands flew over her keyboard. A few seconds later, the screen mirrored onto the TV where she'd already opened the video recordings. "Hand me that green notebook, will you?"

Ruben looked over to her little side table. On top was the notebook. Wide ruled. *I always preferred college ruled,* he reminisced. Ruben had figured he'd spend less on paper if he could fit more onto each sheet. Better still, when he'd finally been able to afford a laptop and rarely had a reason to use paper at all.

The randomness of his internal monologue struck him as he handed over the notebook, a state of alarm breaching his consciousness when he also realized he wondered *why*—as in, *why* did Lavender Blume prefer wide ruled to college ruled paper? Had it been the inverse of himself, and she'd had money to burn on extra paper? Or had there been a special on notebooks and wide ruled was all that was left? Ruben understood the phrase *beggars can't be choosers* intimately. Did she?

He shook his head and focused on the TV. It did not escape him Vinny had sat herself as far as possible from him without moving to where the screen was out of her line of sight. *Friend by proxy. She isn't doing any of this for me. I'm the enemy of her enemy,* not *her ally. Stop being curious about who she is under the ripped jeans and...shit, I think she's wearing a legit classic Pink Floyd tour shirt. How the hell did she get ahold of that?*

"Here," she said, using her mouse to indicate the screen. "You see it?"

"Yeah," he said on a sigh. "Hard to miss the bright orange fucking box."

"Subtlety doesn't appear to be her strong suit," Vinny agreed.

The laundry detergent. Ruben looked at the date and time stamp on the video. It was two days after he'd left. *Two days.* She'd opened their marital bed to third parties the second he was well and gone. Somewhere next to the emptiness he'd been nursing inside, Ruben felt a flicker of anger.

"There is plenty of footage with little to see clearly because the sheers are drawn, but look here," she continued, moving to a clip a few weeks later. "She hadn't closed the sheers or the curtains first, so I was able to get this."

Carla was on the TV, clear as day, turning on the neon sign hung over the top of the guest bed. She was wearing navy-blue lingerie with a thin, sheer robe over the top. It wasn't a set he'd ever seen her in, but he recognized it from earlier today. It had been hanging in the closet with dozens of other things he'd need gloves to clear out.

In scrawling cursive, the sign read *When he's away, it's time to play...*

"I'm not sure what the sign is for, but it was still there when I opened the door earlier today."

Vinny made a strange noise, somewhere between gargling and humming. Ruben looked over at her. She was staring at him, chewing her bottom lip, her face contorted in thought. He had no idea how to read her. It further unnerved him.

"What?" he finally snapped, breaking her silent stare-off.

"I don't know. Maybe nothing. Let's keep going."

For the next few hours, Vinny showed Ruben clips of everything he'd dreaded since he walked in on his wife with a lover—and some things worse than he had imagined. The anger building inside was beginning to edge out the numbness.

How could Carla do this? To anyone? How long? Did it start before we married? Was I a meal ticket the whole time? Something to fill her boredom and bed with. I'm not even a person to her. I was a sick and twisted plaything.

"Ben," Vinny said, nudging him. He'd zoned off. "Ben, get up."

"Huh?" he looked up at her, dazed.

"Up," she commanded gently. Ruben stood, taking a step away. Vinny flipped a lever and the entire couch rotated into a bed.

"Woah." Ruben watched as she pulled a sheet over it with practiced ease, finishing it off with a haphazardly tossed pillow and blanket.

"You've been lost for the last half hour at least. It's late. Get some sleep."

"I could—"

"Nope. I don't trust you to make it down the stairs in your condition. Lay down, Ben." She stood there with her arms crossed, looking him down expectantly, though he was easily half a foot taller than her. Only one other woman had ever made him feel small in that particular way, and it sure as hell hadn't been his wife. Ruben toed his shoes off, tucked them under the coffee table, and did as he was told.

"Oh, fuck," he groaned. "You've ruined my airbed."

Couches that became beds should *not* feel this luxurious. She quirked a slight smile at him before dropping her arms and making for the hallway to the only bedroom. "Goodnight, Ben."

"Night, Lavender."

———

Vinny

It was some of the worst sleep she'd ever had…including a few questionable hostels she'd resorted to on the road. Except it wasn't phantom bedbugs and lice she felt crawling over and beneath her skin. It was something far worse.

She'd taken pity on *him*.

As many times as she told herself it simply wasn't true, *it was.* Yes, she'd learned a lot about Cunty Carla's machinations by showing her estranged husband the evidence of her infidelity. Ruben's reactions were all real, from shock right down to resignation and confirmation. Seeing him as he processed so many emotions made it harder to cling to her hatred.

Part of her wished he'd hogged her cashew chicken after all, so she'd have had a reason to kick him out before the video montage ever began. But he hadn't. Ruben had made a point to serve her as much as she wanted of everything before a morsel touched his plate.

Asshole.

Why couldn't he have left things alone, where it was easy to hate him properly?

When she finally gave up on sleep, she tiptoed down the hall back to the living room. He was sleeping peacefully, and shirtless. It was the most she'd seen of his skin. Even in the soft glow of the nightlights she had for her own safety, Vinny could tell that he'd been lucky like her.

Lucky his melanin issues hadn't been worst case scenario, but easy to live with. More or less easy to *hide.* He likely didn't get a whole lot of staring and double takes, or other forms of unwanted attention. An ugly green monster she refused to name reared up, and Vinny quickly made like a burglar through the night, escaping down the back stairs and into the comfort of her studio.

She could forget everything and anything—at least for a little while—when she was in her studio. Vinny lost herself in needlessly reviewing her ArtBeat schedule. Posts that had been satisfactory before were suddenly lacking. They could be punchier, more vivid. For four hours, she threw herself into adding a little something extra…only to realize she'd changed close to nothing.

This is his fault. What was I thinking? Friend by proxy… I need sleep!

A wave of anger drug her back into the sea of her familiar distrust and repugnance toward Ruben. She glanced at her phone, noting the dawn was breaking any moment, if not already. Daybreak was as good a time as any to retake her territory.

Vinny got up from her computer abruptly, leaving the studio and silently making her way back to her living room. She glowered down at *him,* letting the tides of past transgressions wash over her. *He doesn't belong here. He isn't worthy. I don't care if Eric thinks he's a good guy. Maybe at work he is, but this isn't Camp Pendleton.*

Right.

My turf, not his.

She went to the kitchen and pulled the spray bottle out she used on her plants. As quietly as she could, she took ice out of her freezer, pleased the machine made smaller chunks that would fit inside the skinny neck of the bottle. Then she filled it halfway at the kitchen tap, letting the water slowly flow in so as not to alert him.

Through the top of her curtains, she could see the light of dawn. *Yep. Past his welcome.* She screwed the spray head onto the bottle and walked back over to Ruben, who was still obliviously sleeping in past his welcome.

"Ben," she said softly. "*Be-ennnn,* time to go."

His nose twitched.

"Ruben Holt, get out!" she whisper yelled.

He rolled from his side to his back, one arm going over his head, his other hand resting on his abs right above…*look away, Lavender! His package is not that interesting. Even if it is the most impressive morning wood you've ever seen... Focus.*

"Ben," she said in her regular voice. Three times was fair, in Vinny's eyes. She'd tried to be nice about it. Now he needed to get the hell out. With the smile of a devious crocodile, she lifted her icy weapon, made sure it was on stream, took aim, and let him have it.

"What the fuck!" he yelled, bolting upright, his hands up in an attempt to block her attack. "Lavender, stop!"

"Oh, good! You're up," she chirped sweetly, ending her assault.

"Man, what is *wrong* with you!" It was obviously rhetorical and not meant to be question. She could tell by the way his brown eyes homed in on her like the weapons he probably used all the time.

Or at least that was how Vinny liked to imagine their deployments. What did she know?

"I tried calling your name," she said with an innocent shrug. "You didn't respond."

"So you decided to spray me down with *ice water* like a fucking cat who refused to get out of the Christmas tree? You're a fucking psycho!" he yelled as he got to his feet. "You could have shaken my shoulder or something."

"Eeeew. No way. I'm not gonna touch you," she said, wrinkling her nose in distaste.

Ruben grabbed his shirt off the coffee table and yanked it over his head. He didn't seem to notice it was inside out and backward, but Vinny did. It made her ecstatic she'd thrown him off so well. Next came his shoes.

"I don't have cooties, Lavender."

"Maybe. Maybe not. Either way, it's a new day!" she singsonged. "Proxy is over. Get out."

He froze. "You woke me because it's *dawn?*" This time

she could read him completely…disgust and indignation, with a chaser of outrage.

"Yes."

"Was this planned?" he asked, his voice dripping with accusation. "Let me over, have me stay the night, then take it out on me in the morning?"

"That's absurd," she said, rolling her eyes. "Given that much time, I could have thought up something *waaaay* better than a little cold shower."

"You are seriously looney. I don't know how Eric puts up with you," Ruben spat out as he walked toward the door. "Thanks for nothing, Lavender."

He grabbed the door knob and wrenched it open, his arm tight with rage. Vinny waited for it—the slam. Carys would hear it and send Eric to check on her. She could tell him in all honesty it was Ruben who'd done it. Instead, he paused.

Ruben looked back at her, his expression stern and jaw as tight as the rest of him. He shook his head slightly, then quietly pulled the door shut behind him.

All her pleasure melted with the soft snick of the door.

"Damn it." *He took all the thunder out of the finale.* "I'm going to bed," she said to the empty room.

But instead of walking back to her room, she found herself flopping down where Ruben had been, his heat still present and pillow damp around the area his head had been resting. *I'll just curl up here. I'm so tired, and this is closer than my bed. It has nothing to do with the way it smells like him.*

Chapter Twenty

RUBEN

Slow laughed so hard, Ruben watched as the tears he *wasn't* fighting ran down his friend's face. He'd gone back across the street after the hour he knew the kids ate breakfast, hoping a sit down in the office with his best friend would help let off the frustration he felt toward a certain white haired heathen living over Slow's garage.

Instead, he got laughed at.

Heartily.

"Are you serious, man?"

"Sorry," Slow said, wiping his eyes. "Ice water. Sounds like Vin."

Ruben *hated* that nickname. It wasn't enough she had a nickname everyone seemed to love—one as eccentric as its proprietor—Slow had taken up his wife's habit of shortening it further. While "Vinny" felt whimsical and fun, "Vin" felt intimate. And if anything pissed harder in his Wheaties than Vinny right now, it was the reminder she had an *intimate* relationship with Ruben's family.

They loved her, damn it. Even if he wanted to, Ruben couldn't be rid of her unless he was willing to lose the Blackwoods. Since there was no way he was quitting on Slow and the gang, he was as stuck with Vinny as she was with Ruben. *At least the mutual forced proximity hurts the psycho as much as it hurts me.*

"Can we focus on the video, please?"

Slow sobered slightly. "Right. The security footage. You want a copy of it? I know Carla hasn't made contact, but I doubt it will last. She's too flashy for an amicable ending."

"No kidding," Ruben said, shaking his head. "I can't believe what she's been up to behind my back. It makes me wonder…"

"Go on."

"It makes me wonder if all those weekends I spent alone were her way of being with other men while I was home," he admitted. "Or more."

"More? What is *more* than covering her tracks with weekends away with her friends?"

"They always came to get her, man. She *did* go with friends. That's what I mean by more. How much of it was innocent, and how much of it was a cover? She would send me pictures sometimes and I could tell they were sharing a room. So how many people are involved?" Ruben didn't say the last bit bothering him—that his wife hadn't once shown interest in an extra body in the bedroom. He was a monogamous man, but for his wife he would have at least considered it. So, why didn't she ask him?

"You think she was off having orgies at these resorts?"

"I don't know. Maybe."

"Have you considered calling some of the more recent ones and asking if they had security footage that might give you a head count?" Slow suggested.

"No, I never would have thought it was necessary. And I'm willing to bet a lot of them don't keep footage going back that far. I could check the credit card statements and call around though. Maybe I'm wrong."

"But you aren't going to, are you?" Slow said gently.

"Would *you* want to call around asking hotels to release security footage of your wife banging other people?" Ruben couldn't even say *other men,* because he strongly suspected Carla hadn't cared so long as she was satisfied with the results. "Not that Carys would ever put you in my position."

"You're right, she wouldn't. I'm sorry Carla did this to you, Ruben. You deserve better." Ruben knew his friend well enough to read between the lines: Slow wasn't shocked in the least by what Ruben had found, but he was upset Ruben was now fully aware and suffering for it.

"I'm not asking *her* for anything," Ruben responded.

"Ice water aside, was she genuinely that bad?" Slow mused.

No, damn it. Which just makes it worse. Hot, cold. Hot, cold. The woman has a faulty gauge somewhere in her head.

"It wasn't amazing, but what was I gonna do?" Ruben didn't like lying, and he technically wasn't. His evening with Vinny hadn't been amazing…but it had been surprisingly *okay.* Until his rude awakening at dawn, he might have believed they would eventually reconcile. Maybe not be friends—he was too terrified of her to attempt real friendship —but at least be *friendly.*

"Go home to your airbed and wait for me to get home, apparently," Eric chided.

"It wasn't…she was…" Ruben let out a frustrated grunt. "Look, it was all fine, man. I found the *proxy* bullshit a little condescending, but then we settled in and she was completely open sharing the footage and notes she has." *Well, mostly open. She did hint there was more happening on the block than just my house.* He thought about mentioning it to Slow but bit his tongue. If he didn't know, Carys probably had a hand in it. Ruben wasn't going to step on the Blackwood's toes, so to speak. "I don't fucking understand."

"The only person who comes close is Carys, and maybe Q." Slow shrugged. "She's just Vinny."

"Who is Q?"

"Her dad, Quincy. He goes by Q."

"Ah. Maya's *Papa Q.* "

"The one and only."

"I thought she'd gotten the name of a pizza place wrong when she said her Papa Q was coming for dinner," Ruben admitted. Slow laughed. "What?"

"You *would* think it was food related."

"Hey! Maya loves food. It wasn't a far out idea," Ruben defended.

"Relax. You know I don't mean it callously."

He did. Ruben nodded.

"There was some stuff in the spare room I didn't tell your live in demon," he said. Ruben needed to get back on topic.

"Like what?"

"Cameras. Webcams. All connected to a new looking computer I don't recognize."

"Add the neon sign over the bed and…"

"Yeah." Ruben sighed. "It doesn't look good. My divorce attorney will love it, but if this shit gets around…I can't get a nickname like this, man."

"You won't," Slow said firmly. "I'll see to it. Besides, with any luck, you'll move over and be with me. New building, new people. If we can settle this before the switch, we can probably avoid at least some of the rumors and drama."

Like hell "we" will. I certainly won't. Carla's friends are fucking vultures, and I'm fresh carrion for them to pick apart.

"Thanks, man." He wasn't going to argue over this one.

Neither of them had control over the situation. "Don't take this the wrong way, but next time, I'm calling Zeke."

Slow's trademark smile spread wide. "He'd have laughed in your face too, Ruben."

Probably.

"Yeah, but it would have been over the phone. I had to watch you wipe away *tears,* jackass." Ruben said drolly as he stood from where he'd been leaning against the desk and offered a fist. Slow met it with his own. "You still crashing our training this week?" he asked as he headed out of the office and toward the front door, Slow following to see him out.

"Yeah, I don't know what's up Greer's ass. He keeps asking to borrow me, and since he and my new CO are buddies, I keep getting sent over. It's getting annoying, given I still have my *actual* job to do. I made the switch to spend *more* time with my family, not less." The irritation in Slow's voice gave Ruben pause. Slow didn't get frustrated often, so whatever was happening was obviously getting out of hand.

"I don't understand why he's doing it at all. No offense, but the rest of the team is there, plus your replacement. We don't need you there," Ruben stated plainly. "Not that we don't like having you around."

"Yeah, I need to talk to the boss man. It's not sustainable," Slow said.

They stepped out onto the front porch together.

"Thanks for the talk," Ruben said. "And if it comes to it, I'll let you know if I need some of the footage to give to my lawyer."

They nodded their goodbyes and Ruben walked back to his house. There was still a lot of work to be done on Carla's creepy sex dungeon. He had no doubts that's what it was given the tools and toys he'd found in there.

The thought made bile rise in his throat.

————

THE FOLLOWING WEEK WAS CALM. So was the week after that. Ruben had forced himself to pack up all Carla's kink into boxes and pile them up in the dining room with the rest of her crap. All except for the sign, which had an unfortunate accident in the garage when his hammer smashed it to bits.

It was the craziest thing.

Ruben had never had a problem keeping his hammer from aggressively pummeling the ground over and over before in his life.

In the evenings, he heard the sound of Vinny's vehicle coming and going. He knew she was down jamming with her friends at Groove's club. He'd watched the kids one night while Eric and Carys surprised her by showing up for one of her bigger sets. Ruben didn't see Vinny, nor did he seek her out.

As far as he was concerned, the woman was insane. *Good riddance.*

After a few weeks, he got his dad to answer the phone. Things had been tense between them, but once Ruben texted Abe he split with Carla, he came around. It was a relief to hear him talk on the phone. Abe sounded less winded now, although not necessarily great—but better than he'd been when Ruben was there a month ago. Ruben hoped it meant he'd gotten back on his meds before real trouble could come calling.

Work was crazy. The position he'd applied for in the same unit as Slow closed. He was in the "hurry up and wait" stage of receiving orders. Ruben was running around, staying busy, trying not to get his hopes up. Greer was downright shitty these days, and nobody seemed to know why. It added extra stress to his days Ruben didn't need, especially since he got the impression a lot of Greer's attitude was aimed at either himself or Slow.

Nothing made sense.

And the longer he went without hearing from Carla, the more keyed up Ruben became. He'd agreed to lease a car instead of purchasing it—which he preferred since your money went toward *owning* something—when Carla had gone out looking for her dream car. Ruben took it back to the dealership on his lunch break soon as they had a buyer for it, which kept him from having to pay to break the lease early.

He'd really thought things over, and decided the webcam and computer set up would stay. Everything else was gone or packed away, and after almost a month of silence, Ruben finally scheduled a company to take Carla's shit to her father's house, same as he'd done when he kicked her out.

It was a huge relief, having his home back. Empty as it was, there wasn't a trace of Carla anywhere. Ruben had called in a company to thoroughly deep clean the entire house, and now there wasn't even a smidge of her perfume lingering to catch him off guard. Not even in the closets.

The money he'd made off the items he'd sold were sitting in his lock box at Slow's house. On the off chance Carla got inside and started fucking around while he was at work, Ruben figured the wad of cash he'd amassed would be her first lift if she had her way. He'd returned her car, sold the majority of the larger furnishings, and sent what was left back to her. The cash and his air bed were about all he had left.

She could have the airbed.

He'd already ordered a swanky new mattress be delivered the next week.

Ruben had convinced himself if he cleansed his home of everything related to his soon to be ex, things would settle back into what they once were. He'd see the Blackwoods all the time—and to be fair, he did—and the rest would fall in place. The papers he'd served her with would come back signed and that would be that.

After six weeks on his own, he'd truly begun to settle into his misconception. Ruben should have known better. He should have anticipated Carla was merely pausing for dramatic effect. And he should have seen her approaching in the admiral's car from a mile away.

He *should* have.

But denial is a powerful thing, right up until it's ripped away. Like a blindfold suddenly removed, the reappearance of his ex near blinded Ruben. There was the blissful peace of willful ignorance, and then there was the retina searing pain of reality glaring down at him while Carla looked over her father's shoulder with a satisfied smirk.

In the driveway.

On a Saturday.

While most of the neighbors were outside enjoying a lovely day.

"I have been patient with you, Holt. I did hope you would come to your senses," the admiral sternly scolded Ruben like a child. "My kitten deserves better than this treatment."

"Sir," Ruben answered respectfully, if not a touch gruffly. He'd been caught off guard, mowing the lawn when his father-in-law and wife arrived in a shiny silver luxury something or other. One minute he was alone, the next, he turned to find the most fearsome man on the planet staring him down. "I'm not sure I understand what you are referring to."

"First you sent my daughter home to me practically naked," he barked out. "Then, those *ridiculous* divorce papers

—as if I would *ever* let her sign anything worded to make her out to be a monster—and then you sent all her belongings along as well. A real man faces his problems, Holt."

It had been this way with the admiral from the beginning. *Holt.* Not Ruben, or son, or anything else showing a level of respect or relation. The admiral treated Ruben like one of the seamen on his ships; a lower ranking man lucky enough to serve under his liege.

"Sir, it pains me to have anything less than kind words to say about Carla. I've always seen the best in her. As it turns out, it was to my own detriment. The terms my attorney outlined are fair. I came home from deployment to find my wife in bed with another man. Since serving her, I have discovered he wasn't the only one by a long shot. I don't want drama. I just want her out of my life," Ruben said. He managed to keep his cool, barely.

Carla's father could make his life and career hell for a long time with his connections, and Ruben was well aware of it. He'd overheard guys at work joke he'd married her for the career boost, though it wasn't the truth. Ruben had believed in their love. If he wasn't careful, this man's blind love for his *kitten* would sink Ruben's ship before it left port. The fact he was a Marine and the admiral was Navy meant nothing.

The admiral was not a man you fucked with.

"And what about the baby?" he snarled under his breath.

Ruben blinked back in shock. "I'm sorry, the *what?*"

"You heard me."

"Sir, with all due respect, I haven't been intimate with her in…almost seven months." Not that he hadn't tried. The last month he'd been home, Carla hadn't *been available* once. "If she is pregnant—which I doubt given her adamancy she never wants children—it most certainly is not mine, nor is it my responsibility."

"Daddy, he's *lying,"* Carla whined from behind his shoulder, her hand on her abdomen for dramatic affect.

It was then Ruben registered how many neighbors were making a show of *not* watching the three of them. Her father couldn't see Carla's gesture, but the whole street did.

"I know, kitten. Let me handle this," he said without looking back, his gaze burning a hole between Ruben's eyes as his lips pulled into a snarl. "Apologize at once for the damage you are doing to my daughter."

Ruben took a deep breath in, closing his eyes. He didn't have a lot of options here, but one thing was for sure: if he didn't manage to put his foot down right now, he might not ever fully get out from under either of their thumbs. He let out his breath on a five count. "Sir, I—"

"Eddie? Eddie!" A familiar laughter floated across the street. "It's really you!"

Ruben watched with disbelief as Vinny—apparently unaware of the audience or anyone else remotely nearby— launched herself into the admiral's arms in a bone cracking hug.

It was the first time Ruben ever saw the man truly *smile.*
What the fuck?

Chapter Twenty-One

VINNY

For weeks, she'd been working herself to the bone. When she wasn't working, she was swiping through potential dates left and right. Some she met online; most she met at Groove's club. None of them had tempted her enough to let her guard down—much less her panties—but Vinny was having fun and meeting some interesting people along the way.

She was still blocked.

No matter how hard she tried, nothing came to her.

Her ArtBeat account wasn't affected since she used it mostly to do covers and share her musical knowledge. Plus, the work at the club combined with all the guest spots she'd been doing with her friends had filled what could have been a lot of dead space. Her income was steady, her life was clipping along at a fast enough pace, and her baby was running like the well-oiled machine she was.

All hail American classic pony cars.

It was a beautiful Saturday, and Vinny had decided to go wander down the beach with her favorite six string for a few hours. It hadn't helped her creative block, but it had allowed

Vinny to release some tension. Every day, she felt it building and building. It was *too calm* lately.

She could hear the reverb of a future shoe dropping, and it was making her antsy as hell.

As she cruised back home, she thought about the three-month stint in Nashville her dad kept hinting at her to take with him. Vinny was beginning to think her father was right. She needed to break her patterns if she wanted out of this dead zone.

I should just take it. It won't be like touring, more of an extended vacay gigging with Dad. It felt right. She should call him.

Vinny's concentration was shattered by a familiar silver car—not her style, of course, but beautiful in its own way—parked perfectly on the near side of Ruben's driveway. On the other side, she could see the torso of the man himself, and her heart raced with anticipation.

She pulled her car back to her garage, parking as carefully as she usually did, but with more impatient hope than she'd had in longer than she could recall. The last time she saw her favorite Navy friend had been the end of her USO tour, several years ago. They spoke often, usually over text, but it wasn't the same thing.

Dad will be so jealous, she thought giddily as she hoofed it down the driveway to the street. The car was still there, and beside it was the man of the hour.

"Eddie? Eddie!" Vinny felt her laughter project out, pure joy melodiously rushing to greet him before her legs could get the rest of her there. "It's really you!"

He turned to her, surprise drawing out a genuine smile she knew was from pleasure. His arms opened just in time to catch her. Vinny squeezed Eddie with all she had, taking in the feel of him. "It's been too long," she murmured.

"Hello, little blossom," he said into her hair. They pulled away enough to see each other, but no farther.

"What are you doing in Oceanside? I thought you had a family emergency you were sorting out."

"That's why I'm here," he said, scowling to his right. It was then Vinny noticed Ruben—it *was* his driveway after all —standing beside them, his jaw slack with shock.

"You've *got* to be kidding me!" Carla fumed from behind Eddie. *"This is the girl you won't shut up about?"*

Oh.

Fuck.

"Miss Lavender Blume, this is my daughter, Carla," Eddie said stiffly. "And her estranged husband."

"We've met," she said, her face flushing. *This is…wow… I'm going to have to tell him.*

Carla let out an unladylike kitten sized growl from where her feet were planted. If Vinny had to guess, she knew the jig was up.

But Ruben didn't. Vinny looked over at him thoughtfully, noting his wide eyes and tight posture. Part of her liked it. Seeing him uncomfortable and off his game gave her a thrill. The other part hated Carla enough to give Ruben the win. She knew nothing he said would register with Eddie. Vinny, on the other hand, wouldn't have to try hard to sway him.

"Have you been here long?" she asked, turning her attention back to Eddie.

"Only a few minutes. We were just getting down to business."

Vinny had seen the admiral conduct business before. What he meant was he had just begun to make verbal mincemeat out of Ruben. That would upset Maya, and Vinny couldn't have that. *Yup. I'm doing this for the kids. Only the kids.*

"I think I can be of service," she said softly. "Will you join me across the street for a moment? I'd like a private word if that's okay."

Eddie nodded his agreement and followed her across the street to Eric and Carys's drive. When they turned to face each other, he didn't hesitate. "What's this about, blossom?"

"Eddie, this is going to hurt and I'm truly sorry for it. So, I'm going to let you work it out as gently as I can."

"I can take it."

No, he can't. Not where his "kitten" is concerned.

"This driveway we are standing in, it belongs to my friends I live with," she said pointing down first. Then she pointed up. "That window is *my* window, to my apartment. This is Eric and Carys's house. You might have heard Ruben call him Slow."

"He's mentioned him," Eddie said with a nod.

"Eddie. The things I've been asking you about, the neighbor I've had issues with...is the house *directly* across the street from me. And while I would love to roast Ruben, he hasn't been the one causing problems. Especially when most of them happened while he and Eric were deployed." *Please don't make me say this outright.* "You understand what I'm saying?"

She watched him carefully. Realization dawned in his expression, followed by fury. "If it were anyone else...I wouldn't believe them."

"I'm sorry, Eddie. I know you love her with your whole heart."

"I was a fool for too long," he said. "Letting her mother raise her. Selfish bitch," he muttered.

Vinny quirked a smile. *That's the man I know.* "If it will help, I listened to all your advice, Eddie. The locks and cameras, all of it. I can prove the woman I've asked advice over is your daughter."

"No. I believe you," he said firmly. "Carla Jean!" he barked out as he strode back across the street. "Show me the picture again."

Carla's smile displayed the wolf in sheep's clothing she was. "Of course, Daddy." Carla pulled her phone and tapped the screen before handing it over to her father.

"I only have one thing I need to clear up with you," he snarled at Ruben. "Is this *you* leaving a woman's apartment at the break of day?"

Fucking Sonja Perez.

"Eddie," Vinny said, placing her hand on his arm. "Look at the picture and then look across the street."

He did. "You, blossom? You wouldn't get in bed with a married man!"

"And I didn't. I can prove that too." She looked at him— only him—and pleaded with her eyes. *Please understand. I do not want Ruben to know there is a camera in my living room. I need you to remember.*

Eddie put his hands on his hips and turned back to Ruben, who had yet to speak since her arrival. "You are damned lucky this woman is here to vouch for you, Holt."

Ruben gave the slightest of nods before looking at Vinny with bewilderment.

"Carla, get the papers out of the car."

"But Daddy—"

"I said get the papers out of the car, Carla Jean."

Carla didn't dare huff this time. When Eddie meant business, it was the worst thing you could do, and she obviously knew it. She went to the passenger side of the car and pulled out a brown manilla envelope. Then she came back around and handed it to her father, though her gaze was hatefully fixed on Vinny. Eddie removed the paperwork from inside, pulled a pen out of his pocket, and spread it out on the hood of his car.

"Come sign the papers, Carla."

"What? No! Daddy, this isn't fair," she wailed, her lower lip jutting out and her eyes going wide, tears pooling immediately.

And the Oscar goes to...

In a low voice Vinny could barely hear, Eddie leaned into Carla and said, "You have embarrassed me enough for a *lifetime* today. Sign the damned papers and get in the car, or you can find someone else's roof to lick your wounds under."

With a dramatic flourish, Carla took the pen from Eddie's hand and scribbled her name everywhere he pointed out. Vinny watched silently as Eddie went through the paperwork a second time, making sure all the "sign here" flags in Carla's designated color were properly handled. In complete contrast to his daughter, Eddie shoved the paperwork back into the folder with zero fuss and handed it to Ruben with a slight nod.

"Thank you, sir," he managed to squeak out as he took the envelope from Eddie. "Appreciate it."

Eddie looked at Ruben thoughtfully. "I'm sorry, Ruben. I should have taken the time to get to know you."

Ruben's eyes widened a little more, hitting cartoonish dimensions. "That's the first time you've ever called me by my first name."

"I'm sorry for that too." Eddie turned to Vinny. "Well, blossom. Next time we meet, let's have it be under better circumstances."

"Agreed," she said softly, stepping in for a quick goodbye hug. "Drive safe, Eddie."

He nodded to Vinny, a small smile gracing his humbled

face. He'd come to defend his daughter's honor and instead learned she had none to speak of. It had hurt Vinny to be the one to deliver the lesson to such a good man. "Get in the car, Carla."

As Eddie opened the driver side door, climbed in, and started the car, Carla went around behind the car instead of the shorter route around the front, shoulder checking Vinny as she went by. *"Grub,"* she hissed. "You'll pay for this."

Vinny didn't show anything, though she felt the sting of the insult land deep inside. She kept her expression more or less neutral, stepping closer to Ruben where she wasn't in Eddie's way as he backed down the driveway. Carla was sulking in the passenger seat, but Vinny kept her focus on her friend. She gave a little finger wave to Eddie that he returned before shifting into drive and disappearing down the street.

"Lavender—"

"Don't," she said firmly, holding her hand up but keeping her gaze on the road. "Just don't, Ben. This doesn't change anything."

"Are you kidding me? It changes *everything,* Lavender!"

"Not for me, it doesn't." She spun on her heel and strode away, escaping as fast as she could to her garage.

"Lavender!" he called after her. Before she disappeared around the side of the house, she heard him murmur, "Thank you."

Goosebumps erupted over her body, infuriating Vinny.

I will not be moved by him.

She went through the garage straight to her studio, locking the door behind her. Vinny sat down at her keyboard and began to plunk out a tune. It rolled into another, and another. Soft, slow, plucky, fast, heavy, happy, furious—she played until her fingers hurt, but still nothing came. Vinny moved to her drum kit. *Nothing.* The base. The guitar.

Mandolin. Banjo. *Whole lotta nothing. Why can't I shake this block?*

Composing was the only think that set her free and she couldn't do it, damn it.

Vinny gave up. She shut down the studio and went up to shower, flopping onto her bed afterward with a loud groan. A knock came at her bedroom door. *Carys.*

"Just a second!" she shouted, rolling toward her closet. Vinny hopped into her shorts and tank, then went to open her door. "Oh! Hi, Eric. Real glad I put clothes on."

He quirked a brow up, a slow smile pulling the opposite side of his face into a lopsided grin. "Me too. You got a few minutes?"

Vinny pretended to think, placing a finger over her lips as she looked at him questioningly. "I suppose I do for you. Why don't we go sit down on the couch?" she suggested.

Eric nodded before wandering down the hall to her living room, where he unceremoniously flopped down. "You okay?"

"Why wouldn't I be?"

"You were in your studio for five hours, wailing away on more instruments than I can count."

Oh. She shrugged. "I'm blocked."

Eric took her in, sitting across from her on the couch, cool and calm. As she was beginning to squirm under his scrutiny, he said, "Ever wonder if there is a *reason* for the block?"

"Of course there's a reason," she said with a snort. "I just don't know what it is."

Eric looked like he thought *he* knew what her block was.

Vinny didn't like it.

"Okay. Well, I wanted to tell you I'd like to accept your offer to watch the kids while Carys and I go back to the resort in Mexico for our anniversary. I got lucky and scooped up a cancelation," he said with a wicked grin.

"Of course you did," she said with an eye roll. That was how he'd gotten the extravagant honeymoon suite the last time, when he begged Carys to come back after his deployment and her graduation. And lucky it was, since Carys had left Mexico only to find out she was pregnant with Maya.

"The dates aren't exact, but it's a good time to go down there. Before it's too hot."

"You mean too hot to have sex in the beach cabanas without sweating so badly you slide off the satin sheets into the sand," Vinny said sagely.

"That too."

Vinny hesitated. "Will you be good by the end of July? I'm thinking of leaving with my dad."

"Ah, the Nashville thing?" She nodded. "Yeah, we'll be good. Maya will start pre-k this fall, so that should give Carys a little break."

"Okay, then," Vinny said, some of the tension bleeding off her body.

"Soooo," Eric began, glancing toward her window.

"Don't ask."

"Oh, come on! What did you say to the admiral?"

"I said *don't* ask."

"Fine, but you should know…I'm impressed. And grateful. Ruben showed me the divorce papers. He couldn't have gotten it done so fast without you."

"I have a gig to get to," Vinny said, rising to her feet. "Catch you later?"

"Uh huh. One of these days, Vin. I'll learn your secrets." Eric laughed as he stood, then departed out her front door.

When Hell freezes over, Eric.

Chapter Twenty-Two

RUBEN

"Well?" he asked as Slow came back into the house.

He shrugged his shoulders. "Man, seriously?"

"She didn't want to talk about it. In fact, she kicked me out when I pushed."

"Seriously?" he parroted himself.

"I'm sure she'll go down to Groove's club later, but I know for a fact she doesn't have a gig tonight like she claimed," he said with a grin.

"Why are you happy?" Ruben asked incredulously. *Could this day get any fucking stranger?*

"She's got a block." Slow shrugged. "Looks to be a bad one, given she's had it for months."

"A creative block?"

"Yup."

"And this is relevant how?"

"My wife has a hypothesis she won't share with me yet," Slow mused. "Now I've got one of my own. We'll see who is closer sooner or later."

"What are you talking about, man? All I wanted to know was what she said to the admiral!" Ruben must have hit his head because his brain was scrambled. Nothing Slow was saying made sense, and the man *always* made sense. Er go, it was obviously a deficit with Ruben.

"She isn't going to tell me. Sorry, Ruben. I did express gratitude for whatever it was before she politely evicted me."

"So that's it? The freaking *pain in my ass* managed to get Carla's hooks cleanly out of me and her dad off my back, and I just have to accept it?" He stared at Slow, who looked all too relaxed in his fancy leather desk chair. "I don't like it."

"That's the southern in you," Slow said with a drawl offensively close to the one Ruben had worked so hard to hide. "Not all ladies want a dinner out of a man. Vinny hates Carla as much as the rest of us. Cutting her off at the knees was reward enough. She doesn't want any of your nonsense."

"It's called *appreciation.* For fucks sake, I would like to bury the proverbial hatchet somewhere other than in each other!"

"You like her." It was a confident statement. Ruben instantly scowled at Slow. "It's okay to admit it."

"She's a damn psycho. I do *not* like her. Especially not the way you are implying," he insisted. "I've met cactus more huggable than that woman," he said, pointing diagonally in the direction of Vinny's apartment.

"I believe you mean either *cacti* or *cactuses,* both plural. I don't think it would be all that shocking to find a singular *cactus* without a few spikes. The Christmas variety come to mind."

"You're getting off on this aren't you?" Ruben said flatly. The glint in Slow's eyes confirmed his suspicion. "Damn nerds. You and Carys both."

Slow's grin grew broader. "You ready to tell me what happened when you met Vinny?"

Ruben glared at him.

Outside the office there was a shriek, followed by the magical purity only found in the giggles of little girls. "Funcle Ruben!" Maya shouted between giggles.

"One day, you'll tell me," Slow egged him on as Ruben opened the office door.

"Don't count on it, man."

Ruben ignored the sound of Slow chuckling behind him as he stalked into the kitchen, ready to be his princess's tickle monster.

———

OBLIGATION. That's what he couldn't shake. Ruben felt obligated to do Vinny a solid after she swooped in and made his divorce a reality. *Can't pay if she won't accept payment. Or maybe I can call the dinner she split a few weeks back as early payment...fuck. That doesn't work given* she *paid.*

"How the hell am I drawn to someone who also completely *repulses* me?" he said aloud. He was laying on his airbed, alone. Ruben still hadn't moved it into his actual bedroom. He was sleeping in the equally empty living room, which totally makes sense. You can't place a bed in a room with other things in the way.

Or at least that was how Ruben rationalized it to himself.

When he wasn't talking out loud in the dark to an absolute *nonentity.* But maybe the ideas would flow more freely if he worked it out verbally. It seemed worth a shot...from half court, but a *shot.*

His thoughts trailed off to his divorce papers. Ruben had sat down on the next to last step of the staircase, feet on the floor, and read through them twice. Carla really had signed, dated, and initialed in all the right places. On the third pass, he'd taken out a pen and signed all of his lines too. He would drop them with his lawyer first thing Monday morning.

Because of Lavender.

Ruben shook his head. She didn't want his gratitude. Hell, she'd made it clear she didn't want a single thing to do with him. Ruben had royally fucked up her first impression of him. Truthfully, his gut told him it would have been an uphill battle either way because she had already decided to be weary of him.

The vicious cycle in his head was disrupted by the rumble of her vehicle creeping up the block. Ruben checked his phone. *The hell is she doing out this late? The clubs shut down hours ago.*

"Yaaaargph. Not my fucking problem. Let the little heathen get into trouble. Ain't nothin' good doin' this late at night," he said to himself with all the firmness and superiority he did not feel inside. "I am not going to worry about her."

But he wasn't going to sleep, either. Ruben got out of bed and went out onto his back patio, taking in the cool night air, the proximity to the Pacific tingling his senses. He'd made a lot of changes lately, but none of them truly felt like progress. If anything, moving on without his wife still stung with failure, of moving backward.

Ruben looked out over the yard. Like Slow, he'd been lucky his home was on a fairly deep lot. Except where Slow had the second garage in the back—not thinking about the tenant who used it, of course, or how late she'd parked there this evening—Ruben had a blank slate. There were a few mature trees far enough away to keep his foundation safe, but little to no landscaping otherwise. Maybe he should do something about that.

Suddenly he saw it. The answer to all his worries. *Build it and they will come. I need a space for Dad.* He padded to the garage after a tape measure and headed back into the yard, this time out onto the grass. He stared at the external wall to his dining room. He could do it. There was plenty of side yard. Ruben was pretty sure he could do it without giving up the window too.

Two hours later, the sun was cresting the sky and Ruben had staked out a rough footprint to what he wanted to create for Abe. *I will build this, and he will finally come to California. This will work, damn it.*

Chapter Twenty-Three

VINNY

"Hey, baby! Whatchu doin' hur t'night?" Tripp slurred happily.

Vinny winced at the way he called her baby. *Again.* "Isn't it a little early for you to be this...plastered?"

Tripp sobered enough to confess, "Jae and Silla shot me down again."

"And you think getting trashed is going to impress them into changing their minds?" she deadpanned.

"Damn. Should have thought of that. Oops," he said, before spinning back to the bar and tossing back another shot of vodka. Vinny rolled her eyes. Tripp was an idiot when he was skunked. A happy one, but still an idiot.

"Where is Groove?" she asked loudly.

"'Sss offish," he said with a nod toward Groove's door across the bar, almost falling off his stool with the motion. Vinny righted him before wiggling her way through the crowd to the back hallway.

The last door on the right wore a plaque that read *manager* on it in gold script. She knocked firmly but not obnoxiously. "Tyler?"

"Come," he called out.

Vinny opened the door enough to slip in, buttoning it up tight again from the inside. She could still feel the pulse of the music, but it was pretty well muffled in here. "Hey, Tyler."

"Hey, Vinny. Thought you had the night off?" he said, craning his neck to glance at the schedule.

"I do," she said with a halfhearted one shoulder shrug. "I got bored. How is it going out there?"

"Eh. I like live nights better. This DJ is giving me a damn migraine."

"Too much synthesizing," she agreed with a small smile. "He needs to fix the treble too."

"I've always liked live music better, but business is business. Unless you want to get up there one night and spin?" Tyler looked at her suggestively, and not for the first time.

Their contracts had ended. Right now, they were back in the friend zone. Vinny hadn't ever thought of pursuing anything else with Tyler, but maybe…it could be fun. He wasn't her usual type, but those hadn't panned out well. Maybe she needed to try something new.

Maybe she needed to try Tyler.

He wasn't her typical musician, though he owned a club and had another under construction. He was *steady,* and not prone to moving around constantly. Tyler was good looking too, though a little harder around the edges than she was used to. Vinny supposed he needed to be a bit of a tight ass at work if he wasn't going to get taken advantage of by the staff.

I wonder if he has a softer side. I've never seen him outside the club unless he was making connections in the business elsewhere. Who is Tyler at home? The beach? Does he ride in the front row on a coaster, or look as green getting in his seat as he does stumbling out at the end?

Maybe this was why she was blocked. Vinny hadn't written anything since shortly after moving here. She shook the thought from her head. Sex wasn't the answer to everything.

"I'm taking my dad up on the Nashville gig," she said.

"Figured you would. Best of both worlds. You get a break from here, but you don't have to be on a bus with a bunch of pigs," Tyler joked.

"They aren't *all* pigs," she said.

"Your dad doesn't count, Vin."

"Hey!"

Tyler's answering chuckle was infectious. Vinny finally left the door where she'd been leaning and headed over to the black leather sofa on the adjacent wall. Tyler got up from his desk and moved to join her.

"Something bothering you?" he asked seriously.

"Just can't shake this damn block," she said. But that wasn't what was really bothering her, and she knew it.

Carys still refused to tell Eric about Greer coming on to her and attempting to include Vinny when she didn't take him up on the offer solo. Vinny still caught him sneaking into Sonja's next door in the middle of the night too. Everything about it made Vinny uncomfortable. She didn't want to get in the middle of their marriage, but Vinny sincerely didn't like keeping this from Eric.

The whole situation was chafing her. There was *more* to this. She could feel it as true as her heartbeat.

"Want to go get lost for a while? I'll keep you safe out there."

"You hate dancing."

Tyler shrugged. "I wouldn't hate dancing with *you.*" His voice came out lower, laced with his primal cravings.

Vinny looked up to find him studying her intently. Her nipples hardened, and she knew he'd seen her reaction by the way his nostrils flared.

What harm could there be in getting lost in him for a night?

"Yeah," she croaked back. "Yes. Dance with me, Tyler."

Wordlessly, Tyler took Vinny by the hand and led her out to the dance floor. They moved together for hours, occasionally taking breaks to hydrate. Tyler would check in with his staff, and soon as he got the all clear, he'd take her right back to the dance floor. True to his word, he stayed by her side. Given the growing bulge he was grinding into her, she wasn't sure he could do much of anything without using her to block his arousal.

By the time the club closed down, Vinny was high on adrenaline and pheromones. Tyler hadn't been drinking because he was the boss. Vinny hadn't because there was no way she was Ubering home and leaving her baby in downtown overnight. Whatever she was feeling toward him was purely driven by her natural reaction to their bodies grinding together for hours on end.

They had gotten a cab for Tripp long ago, and as the last of the patrons stumbled out into the night, Vinny realized the throbbing in her core was still going strong…even without the pulsing music. She sat on the edge of the stage, completely at home, while Tyler locked up after the last of the staff left.

"I have to finish counting out the deposits before I can go. Will you keep me company?" His voice was rich, promising sins so sweet she wouldn't mind the trip to hell she'd be signing up for if she stayed. Vinny watched him stalk across the empty room, a predator after his prey.

Her panties weren't gonna make it under his smoldering gaze. He moved like sex, talked like sex, and she was pretty sure what was straining behind his fly was going to make for ah-mazing sex. *Yes, please. Come gobble me up.*

Before she could answer, he was standing between her thighs, his hands around her waist. The stage was tall, but so was Tyler. Tall enough to lean into her neck for a taste. The feel of his tongue was exquisite, the coolness of his breath over her warm, dewy skin sending shivers down her spine. Her nipples had been hard most of the night, and they ached to know what it would be like for him to repeat his tease against her pebbled mounds.

"Or maybe I'll devour you right here." He let out a feral growl as he nipped at her collar bone, moving one hand up from her waist to cup her breast and pinching her nipple through the thin fabric of her tank and bra. She moaned.

"I'll go with you," she said through her panting.

Tyler pulled her forward roughly, his hands grabbing her ass firmly as he lifted her from the stage. Vinny circled her legs tightly around his waist, grinding into him. *Shit. He's either huge, or I've been alone too long.*

Her arms were around his shoulders, hands messing his hair as he carried her back to his office, grinding his erection against her sex the entire way. Vinny took his mouth with hers, nipping and teasing his lips until he opened up, devouring her. Dominating her.

"Fuck, Vinny. I've wanted you for so fucking long," he said, breaking their kiss in order to set her down on the leather couch in his office. "All this professional bullshit has been killing me."

"Count the deposits up, Tyler." Vinny threw one leg over the arm of the couch, spreading herself wide. The possessive growl that came up from his chest as he looked down at her made her feel powerful. If her panties hadn't been soaked before, they sure as hell were now.

"Don't move," he ordered.

"I wouldn't dream of it." She batted her eyelashes innocently.

After another rough kiss, he forced himself to sit down at his desk and finish his work. His fingers flew so fast over the ten key as he double checked the staff's work. Tyler didn't even look at the keys. His fingers knew precisely what to do as his other hand trailed down the columns on the deposit slips, keeping his place. He used a machine to count the cash one last time before signing off and shoving it all in his safe.

"Impressive," she said as he prowled toward her, nodding toward his desk as she watched his approach with anticipation.

"Oh, it's *impressive.* I promise you that." She'd love to throw back a snarky retort along the lines of *I've heard that one before,* but she'd felt him grinding against her enough to know Tyler had the right to be so confident. "We're going to my place."

"My car—" he silenced her with a finger over her lips, a tender touch contradicting the way the rest of his body tensed with his hunger.

"I live over the club," he murmured. "Your car is safe, baby."

Ignore it. Don't let it kill the moment. It's just a stupid pet name.

"Okay."

Tyler pulled her to her feet before crushing his mouth over hers. Vinny's body surged with renewed heat, boiling her annoyance over the name right out of her system. He led her through a side door she had assumed was a bathroom. Instead, there was a softly lit stairwell leading up. Tyler paused to pull the door closed before hefting Vinny up like she weighed nothing. Again, she wrapped her body around his, grinding against him as he took the stairs two at a time.

They made their way through the door at the top in a blur, Vinny's body quivering with anticipation in his arms. She wanted the release. She was *desperate* for it. Tyler took her over to a huge four poster bed on one side of what was— upon a quick glance—a fairly large studio apartment. All the while, they were nipping, kissing, *claiming* each other as they went.

He was hot. Stronger than she had anticipated too, carrying her around like he was. Nobody had *ever* carried her up a set of stairs before. Vinny yanked at his shirt buttons, unconcerned whether they yielded or flew off. She needed to see the body beneath.

The sinew of Tyler's muscles and the way the veins showed prominently... She moaned as the shirt fell away, revealing everything she'd hoped to see. He was a master-piece. Her mouth watered to see the rest of him, and she scrambled for his belt.

"My turn," he said gruffly, stilling her hands with one of his own. Vinny paused, looking up into Tyler's eyes. He let go of her hands and grabbed the hem of her tank, pulling it off. One of his large hands grabbed her ass, pulling her against his erection as he ground it against her sex. The other grasped her breast, firmly squeezing it through the film of mesh she was wearing as a bra. "A perfect palm full," he said, squeezing.

"Oh, god." Vinny's voice came out husky, heavy with need. She rotated her hips against Tyler's own motion, begging with her body what words had failed to do. *Take me. God, take me!*

He guided her down to the edge of the mattress, next to a

nightstand. Vinny's hands immediately went back to his belt. If she didn't see what she'd been grinding against all night right fucking now, she was going to die…

"Don't you worry, baby. I'm going to take care of you," Tyler groaned as her deft fingers worked quickly over his fly before jerking down all of the layers of fabric in her way.

Vinny froze, eyes bugging, as the biggest cock she'd ever seen sprang from his pants and nearly brained her. She silently cursed herself for blinking first and showing the thing fear in the process. Her eyes went down to her wrist and back up to Tyler's dick. She was pretty sure his cock was thicker. And *long.* Taking him could very well break her, because he was hung like an actual horse.

The horse might be jealous.

"Uhhhh…"

"I get that a lot," he said, not bothering to hide his pride.

She didn't blame him.

"I'll work you so good baby, you'll be ready for me. Promise."

"I don't think—" She was cut off by the sound of a *jug* of lube landing on the nightstand beside him. It had a pump, and it looked…industrial. *No wonder the table has a cabinet instead of drawers. It's where he hides the condiment bar sized necessities.*

"I know how to make a woman feel good, Vin. Don't worry, you can take me."

A slight buzzing in Vinny's ears pulled her further out of the moment. She was hesitant, and not because she thought Tyler couldn't deliver.

It was Vinny.

She wanted this night; but *only* this. Tyler's words from earlier flooded her mind, pushing back the tides of her arousal long enough for her to come to her senses.

"No," she said.

Tyler smiled. "I understand."

"I don't think you do, because you are misunderstanding me," she said, taking her eyes off the danger long enough to meet Tyler's gaze. *"No,* I don't want to. I'm sure you could spend a few hours—or weeks—loosening me up with your buffet of lube and it would probably end up being the best sex of my life, but *no."*

He looked…confused. She focused back on the Graboid —this thing was straight out of the Tremors movies—before it tried eating her face.

"Tyler…this is some Guinness World Records level dick I'm staring down. I feel like I should offer a sacrifice or something for even being in its presence. But I'm not willing to *be* the sacrifice—or sacrifice our friendship. This is too much for me."

She looked back up at him. His face had softened, and she found something she hadn't expected.

Respect.

"You're right. Women don't say no to me. If anything, they see me as a challenge. But that's not you. I wish you would take a chance on me, Vinny. I meant what I said. I've wanted you a long time. And maybe *he's* a monster," he said gesturing one hand at his still hard cock, "but I'm not."

"I know you aren't," she said softly. "If you were, we wouldn't be having this conversation."

They both dressed themselves wordlessly. As they did, something niggled at Vinny's conscience.

"Tyler?"

"Hmm?"

"Do you ever…feel used by them?"

He let out a heavy sigh beside her, and Vinny looked up to meet his eyes. "I know I am."

"I get that."

"I'm sorry you do."

"I'm sorry too. For both of us."

"This isn't how I saw the night ending," he said, a sad little smile quirking on one side.

"But at least you know I respect us both enough to be honest," she said. "Friends?"

He turned to face her fully, gently cradling her face in his massive hands. His thumbs swept delicately over her cheeks before he leaned in and kissed her with a tenderness and passion that made Vinny's entire body tingle. She felt cherished.

"Friends," he said after he ended the kiss. "And if you ever want more, all you have to do is say so. You don't even need to ask."

"Thank you."

Vinny wasn't sure what exactly she was thanking Tyler for. Understanding, perhaps? He walked her down to her car, not leaving until she was safely inside with the engine going. On the way home, she thought about it some more.

She knew what it meant to be a notch on a bedpost: *the freak of nature notch.* For her, it was her albinism. She'd had several men pursue her hard, only to disappear the moment she let them in. It hurt. But for once, she realized how easily women would do the same.

Women used Tyler, their own notch denoting the special night they had spent with a *freak,* completely disregarding Tyler as a man. No, he was just a good dick to ride, bragging rights for a future girls' night out.

Why did love have to be so hard? Why did people have to be so cruel? And when she finally found a man she gravitated toward who actually understood what it felt to be the victim of such a thing, *why couldn't I choose him the way he chose me? Tyler would have put me on a pedestal and worshipped at my feet if I had let him.*

Because she'd gone to Tyler for a good time, damn it. Vinny wouldn't do that to him when he obviously had been hoping for a lot more than she was willing to offer.

Chapter Twenty-Four

RUBEN

"You're insane." Slow looked at the stakes and string Ruben had planted all over his yard earlier in the day.

After he'd been content with his start, Ruben had crashed out on his air mattress for a good five hours before wandering over for Sunday brunch with his people. After Slow helped Carys put the kids down for naps, he'd asked him over to take a look.

"Wow. Thanks, man."

"Ruben...you know how some guys get a rebound relationship? This is your rebound project. Abe has told *me* he will die in the house your mother made into a home. I don't see how this is anything more than busywork. *Expensive* busywork," Slow amended.

"I told you how things are going, man. He can't stay alone much longer. Between his health and the way the neighborhood is falling apart around him, it's not *safe*. I can create what he needs here, Slow. He can have safety, healthcare, good things to eat, and still have some independence," Ruben said.

"I'm not saying your heart is in the wrong place."

"Then what are you saying, man?"

"You *know* what I'm saying. Abe isn't going to leave Georgia unless it's in an urn," Slow said matter of fact like, but not unkindly.

"It won't be easy," Ruben admitted.

"I think you need to sit on this. Make sure you really want to do it."

"I slept on it like a baby," Ruben said. "I'm sure. I already texted the guy that helped you with your income suite asking for an estimate."

Slow shook his head. "If you're sure."

"He's my *dad.* I know you aren't close to yours, but think of it like this: what if it was me?" Ruben postulated. "What if a bullet caught me down range or something?"

"It's not the same thing, but I see what you are getting at. You know I'd do anything within my power to help you," Slow said dryly. "Let's see what the contractor says and revisit the discussion then. He set you an appointment already?"

"Yeah, after work tomorrow."

"Okay, then. When he gives you the figures, bring them over and we can talk some more. I think *I* need to think on this one."

Ruben was disappointed Slow wasn't on board, but he understood too. He didn't know if he was going to be moving soon or not and starting a big project like this when he was due for a reassignment was kind of…well, *idiotic.* Hopefully he got word back on the move across Pendleton soon and maybe then Slow would be more on board.

Maybe.

"Can't you just get laid like everyone else going through a divorce?" Slow said glibly.

Ruben smiled at that. "Nah, gotta be all original around

here." As he said it, he bounced on the balls of his feet and shook a fist in the air. "Who needs women?"

"Me," Slow answered immediately. "And with another forty-seven minutes of nap time, I'm off to find mine. Excuse me."

Slow waggled his brows at Ruben before turning away. He walked up the patio steps and into the house, making his way back to his own home.

"I see how it is here," Ruben groused. Then called after his friend as he too went back inside, "nobody likes a braggard, Slow!"

His buddy laughed. "It isn't bragging if it's the truth."

The front door closed behind him, leaving Ruben alone again with his thoughts. He couldn't tell his father what he was up to, but he'd like to hear his voice. Tell him Carla had signed the papers too.

Now *that* was news Abner Holt would want to know.

————

Vinny

She watched as Ruben crossed the street with Eric, frustration and annoyance coming to the forefront. Vinny needed to talk to Eric, and she'd been waiting for Ruben to leave for hours. She heard a noise…and realized she was growling.

Okay, need to break in Taco Tickler the Third after I finally catch Eric. Growling, Lavender? You aren't an animal.

To her relief, Eric didn't stay long. Vinny ran out her front door as soon as Eric stepped down off Ruben's front porch and called him over. "Hey!"

Eric stopped at the end of his driveway, his gaze bouncing back and forth between Vinny and the front door.

"You can nail your wife later. Come talk with me," she deadpanned. She watched Eric's slow smile grow as he heeded her command, walking up the steps to her deck and coming to a halt before her.

"It's as if you can read my thoughts."

"You're a man. It isn't hard." Eric feigned offense. Vinny rolled her eyes. "Come on in."

"What's troubling you?" Eric asked as they settled down on her couch together, each taking an end and turning enough to mostly face each other.

"I talked to Hailey's husband this morning when I was running errands," she started. "You know Samson."

Eric nodded. "I do."

"He said something to me that has my hackles up."

"Was he inappropriate with you?" Eric asked gruffly. His body immediately tensed, ready to act.

"No," she quickly said. "Nothing like that. He's still the amazing, dedicated, *monogamous* man who followed his wife around your yard like a puppy dog the last two cookouts."

Eric relaxed slightly. "Sorry. With Carla…"

"I know, it has all of us prepping for treachery from every which way. Which brings me to the *real* concern. Sam was saying Greer pulled strings and is rumored to be staying here at Pendleton in a new capacity. You know, like you did." Vinny wanted to throw up. She'd told Carys she wouldn't tell Eric first, but ignorance was *not* bliss if the man was staying.

"Yeah, I'm about ninety-eight percent sure it's true," Eric said with irritation.

Interesting... "I thought you and Greer were tight?"

"I didn't have issues working under him before, but he's been a thorn since I moved over. It's like he won't let up in me, ever since I told him I wasn't interested in advancing to the next rank early," Eric admitted.

Those pesky Minions with their alarms started up in Vinny's brain again. "Like what?"

Eric shrugged. "I told him I wanted to spend time with my family, not double down to impress the higher ups. He knows that's why I made the lateral move across base, out of the deployments for now."

"But when something happened, he still requested you specifically, didn't he? The last tour, even with Carys a mess."

"Yeah. He did. I'm going to tell you something my wife doesn't know, and doesn't *need* to know," Eric said with a firm look. Vinny nodded. "I did some digging while I was down range. The guy I replaced was injured, but I wasn't the only option to replace him. Greer *insisted* it be me."

"And now he's not leaving…"

"And now he's not leaving," Eric repeated with a nod.

"Fuck. Okay, this is how shit is happening. I'm going to show you some things and you are going to ask a lot of fucking questions. *All* the questions, Eric. Do not hold back," Vinny said as she turned to her laptop and plugged it into her TV.

"What are you showing me?"

"That's an excellent question," Vinny said with a punch of false cheer. "We are going to take a tour of some of the nighttime footage from while you were away."

"Does my wife know about this footage?"

"Some of it."

"Am I going to be *happy* about what I see?"

"Not a chance in hell."

"And I'm seeing it months after returning because?"

"I promised not to show it unless you *asked* first."

"Promised Carys."

"Yup."

"Vinny," Eric said cordially. "I've been thinking about all our mutual concerns before I left. What with the gang issues and the accident, I'd feel better if you would show me any and all footage you found *worrisome* from my time down range, please."

Vinny looked up at him with a genuine smile. "Well, since you asked so nicely."

Sorry, bestie. I've got a bad feeling about this. Greer staying changes everything.

Vinny cued up some of the earliest examples of the "worrisome" footage she felt Eric should know about. "This is Sonja and Carla," she said. The clip showed Sonja entering the Holt's home late and leaving several hours later before anyone was awake to see her.

"Ruben mentioned she was a pain in his ass. What's she doing?" Eric asked.

"Coming and going at odd hours, mostly. But it gets better." Vinny moved on, showing Eric extended versions of a lot of the things she'd shown Ruben, and so much more. "This one is from a few nights before you got back," she said as she cued up the clip. There wasn't any sound, but there didn't need to be.

On the screen, you could see everything. She'd already shown Eric clips involving Greer coming and going, but this one was different. He had Sonja pinned to the side of her house, on the inside the fence to the Brown's back yard. They were up against the side where Sonja lived, and not where they would easily disturb her landlords on the other side of the main house.

Greer was taking Sonja, her back against the siding and legs wrapped around him. At the edge of the frame another person came up from behind, but not fully in view yet.

"Who is that?" Eric asked.

Vinny shook her head. "Just watch."

Greer slowed to a stop, and Sonja dropped her legs. Then she turned, palms to the wall and her ass presented toward Greer. He immediately took up behind her, his hips thrusting into her. The third person came fully into view, dropped to her knees, and climbed under Sonja, using her hands to prompt Sonja's thighs wider so she could join in.

Sonja's back arched, her head flying back, her mouth in an O of pure bliss. The third person—clearly a woman—held onto one of Sonja's hips while she enjoyed a meal, her other hand caressing Sonja's hip before striking. Sonja convulsed on the screen, Greer's body ruthlessly pounding into her chasing his own release. When he finally stopped rutting into her, he kissed up and down her spine while their third continued to clean up their mess, eating out Sonja before moving to lick Greer clean as well.

When she pulled back, her face was in full view of the camera.

"What the...does he know?" Eric asked, his voice conveying his shock.

"No. I didn't think it was helpful to show Ruben footage of his *wife* sucking his boss's cock clean." Vinny said quietly. "I showed him a lot, but not this."

"Good. He'd go after Greer and fuck up his whole life in the process."

The video ended and Vinny turned off the screen. "Yeah. That's about what I figured. Eric..."

He turned to her, his shock morphing into wariness. "No, Vin. Don't tell me there's more."

"Okay, I won't tell you. I'll *show* you." Vinny opened up the links Tripp had given her, scooting herself and her laptop close enough to show Eric. "This is a subscription-based website. Did Ruben tell you about the freaking sex room she had locked up?"

"Yeah, he showed me pictures."

"Well, I think I know what she was doing with the computer and cameras." They scrolled through the site, Vinny pointing out the things she found most relevant, but keeping the video files buttoned up. "It's obvious she is running a live feed regularly, even now. But this is beyond her. *Someone* set this all up and funded it. Carla is an attention whore—pun intended—but she isn't the type to put this much effort or forethought into a scheme.

"This isn't as simple as an exclusive porn site. I asked a friend to help out, and one of *his* friends followed the trail of phone numbers that were sexting you down range back to Sonja's computer, Eric. This website was also there, and she and Carla are the main admins."

His head jerked back like she'd slapped him. *"What?"*

"I think this was all part of a master plan," she murmured, as if softening her voice would soften the blow. "I don't think Sonja ever got over you. I think she moved next door because she's an opportunist. She saw the accident and the way Carys fell apart afterward as her way back in. I don't know if she had anything to do with Greer sending you instead of someone else, but they are definitely in on it together."

"That doesn't make sense," Eric said. "If I *were* to lose my ever loving mind and leave or cheat on my wife, Greer would lose his play thing assuming Perez got her way."

"No, he'd just trade her for another."

"Who?"

"Carys. He hit on her in the commissary the day after the children's Christmas party. When she didn't leap at the chance, he tried sweetening the pot by suggesting I join them." She felt her hands go clammy as she spoke, bile

creeping up her throat. "Greer is a taker, Eric. And he didn't get what he wanted. I don't know what all he said to Carys, but I bet she knows important details and doesn't realize it. She was hoping she could avoid the guy until he left."

He let out a heavy sigh, closing his eyes for a minute as he took it all in. "She wouldn't want me to be upset about someone I have respected in the past."

"That's pretty much what she said."

"Do you know who the ringleader is? The person financing this website?"

"No, but if you want, I can ask my friend to ask his friend to do a little more digging."

Eric opened his eyes and looked at Vinny. The sadness and worry contorting his face made her heart hurt. "Yeah. I think we need to know as much as we possibly can. I hate it, but yeah."

"Okay. Just...please don't go too hard on Carys. Her intentions were good, even if she was being a hypocrite." Vinny had scolded Carys so many times, for not coming clean with Eric after he shared the sexts he'd gotten while down range.

"She's going to be the death of me one day," he said dryly. "But it's still better than living without her."

Ugh. Stupid perma-honeymoon phase. Vinny rolled her eyes. "Eeesh. Go home."

Chapter Twenty-Five

RUBEN

Several months later...

Heart attack. *But he's been on his meds...there is no way. No way...*

"Sir? Are you still there?" snapped the woman.

"Yeah, sorry." Ruben's voice came out wrong, disjointed. "Yes. How is he?"

"Lucky. He was at the store when it happened, and EMS got to him quickly. If he'd been home alone, this would be a very different phone call," she said gently this time. "Abner is stable, but we need to know how you want to proceed with your father's recovery, Mister Holt."

Fuck.

"I don't know just yet. I'm in the military. I need to ask for emergency leave so I can fly out. Do you need an answer right now?" he asked.

"No. He'll be here in the hospital a few days longer. But sooner is better so we can start reaching out on Abner's behalf."

"Right. I'll call back tomorrow, if that's okay? And I'd

like to talk to the doctor at their earliest opportunity. I have questions."

The nurse spoke to Ruben a little longer, making sure he had the right number to call back when he decided what to do about his dad, and promptly hung up. Ruben sat on his couch with the phone still to his ear, stunned. *My dad had a heart attack.*

If he hadn't been at the store, he'd be dead right now at home, with nobody the wiser. Ruben bolted up off the couch and down the hall, flying through the open door in time to hang his head over the toilet as he heaved. By the time he was back on his feet, his resolve had solidified again.

Enough was enough.

He was bringing home his father, willing or not.

———

"I'LL JUST BE A MINUTE," he told the driver, who'd agreed to make a stop for him to drop off his bags before taking him to the hospital where his dad was still under observation. Ruben got out of the rideshare car and walked up to the front of his father's house, key at the ready to get in, drop his shit in his old room, and get out.

He was not mentally up to snuff, or he might have realized the danger before it saw him coming. The safety door he'd installed was unlocked, making Ruben scowl. His dad had promised to use the damn thing. When he realized he could see though the heavy grate *into the house* he understood the full scope of the matter. Ruben looked again at the lock and this time saw where it was scratched from being picked.

Someone had noted Abner's long absence and broken in. Ruben's stomach tightened, his anger taking his blood pressure through the roof with it as he yanked the useless deterrent open and stomped inside. The place was a mess, but what got him the worst was the *smell.* The old sofa had been torn apart and used as a latrine. Gagging, Ruben took long strides down the hall to get away…

And was nearly done in with the old metal bat he used to take to the park every day after school.

Ruben's sense of danger and preservation kicked in fast enough for him to yank his head back in time, but his right foot was another matter. The bat swung hard and fast, right down onto the top with full force. The sound of metal connecting as bone shattered was sickening, but nowhere near as awful as the sound of the tweaker who came shrieking out of his dad's room on the other end of it.

He was little, but high as a fucking kite. The man lunged at Ruben, who had stumbled back into the wall but remained vertical. With the wall as support and his weight all on his left foot, it was a challenge. His combat training kicked in, and Ruben managed to disarm the crazed man.

He waved the bat around confidently toward the intruder, who had stumbled back up the hall past him in the process. The man yowled like a feral cat, to which Ruben immediately let out a roar so loud, he surprised himself. It also freaked out the druggie—who turned and ran out the wide open front door—which worked out fine for Ruben.

There was no way in hell he was leaving *anything* in this house.

He hobbled back out to the street, where the driver was looking nervously around, clearly on the verge of bolting. "Hang on!" Ruben yelled as he came down the walk. "I'm coming."

Ruben got back in the car without bothering to lock up. The damage was done.

"You okay?" the driver asked, wasting no time gunning it down the block as soon as Ruben closed the car door.

"Nope. But we're headed to the hospital anyway. Just pull on around to the emergency entrance instead, please."

———

"HE'S BEING IMPOSSIBLE," Ruben said into the phone. "I have a broken fucking foot, the house has been desecrated, and he wants to go *home,* instead of to the safe and secure hotel I booked us with a room service option."

"At least you don't need surgery," Slow said. "Hell, Abe didn't either. You have to count the wins, brother."

"That's not all," Ruben said bitterly. "He refuses to fly back with me."

"Okay…"

"He's never flown, and he says he never wants to."

"Sounds about right."

"Eric. I can't drive like this."

"You could take the bus," he mused.

"Don't even suggest it to him, man. I'm serious." Ruben let out a groan, resignation washing over him.

There was no way to keep his father from returning to the dilapidated Hell house. Ruben had paid handsomely to have the couch hauled off and the place cleaned, but the neighborhood had gone to hell. It wasn't safe. It hadn't been for a long time, and his dad was being headstrong over nostalgia.

"No plane, no bus, I'm guessing no train," Eric said, pausing long enough for Ruben to grunt his affirmation. "That leaves automobile. Give me a few hours, Ruben. I might have a solution."

"What solution? Slow?"

"Go put your foot up," he said with a snicker, and hung up.

Ruben stood up, got his crutches under himself, and began to hobble back down to his dad's hospital room from the waiting room just down the hall. It had been four days since Abner's heart attack, and two since the junkie assaulted Ruben.

His foot hurt.

He was cranky.

And his dad was a damn nightmare to deal with.

"What's with the sour puss?" Abe asked as Ruben propelled himself into the room.

"Just trying to sort shit out is all," he said, wincing at the way his southern drawl seemed to grow deeper every second back in this hell hole.

"How we getting home?"

"Dad," Ruben said.

"I'm going *home,* boy. With or without you."

"Would you please reconsider?" he begged. "The hotel will be a much better place for both of us to convalesce."

"No. Home." Abe leveled a look at Ruben that brooked no arguments.

But he still tried. "I got attacked by an intruder when I tried dropping off my bag. It's not safe."

"Should be fine now. You said you ran him off."

"That doesn't mean it's safe *now.* I got lucky." If he could call a broken foot lucky. It was better than dead at any rate, and Ruben hadn't been back since. He saw no reason to tempt fate. The hospital had heard what happened and kindly let Ruben sleep in the vacant bed in Abe's shared room instead of making him use one of those terrible roll-away cots. At least he'd slept somewhat comfortably last night.

"Why don't *you* stay at the hotel then, and I'll go home on my own."

Ruben about lost it then, but bit back his scathing commentary just in time. *He's lost his damn mind if he thinks I'm dropping him off in his condition at that house and leaving him there alone.*

He was distracted by the buzz of his phone vibrating in his pocket. "Hold that thought."

Slow: What's the address?

Ruben sent it to him.

Ruben: Please tell me this means you are flying out on a red eye, renting a car, and driving us all back tomorrow…

Slow: You aren't going to like it, but I can get you home.

Slow: Tonight is Vinny's last gig in Nashville. They trailered her car out there behind her van, so her and Q both had a set of wheels.

Ruben: So, Q is coming to get us in the van?

Slow: No, it's full of their gear. He's going to drive it back himself.

Ruben: NO.

Slow: You got a better idea, slugger?

Ruben: Cute. Slugger. Ha ha, man.

Ruben: I am not riding in a car over 2000 miles with the heathen. NO MEANS NO.

Slow: Still waiting on your way better idea…

Fucking hell. Damn it!

Ruben didn't have *any* ideas, and Slow knew it. He thunked his head back into the wall behind the chair, letting out a frustrated growl.

"What's got you riled up now?" his dad barked.

"Nothing," he lied. "We got wheels to California. Car arrives in the morning. We'll need to decide what you want to take with tonight and either store or donate the rest," he said.

Or more likely send it to the dump. Who knows how bad the rest of the house was damaged.

Ruben: I really hate this idea.

Ruben: What time do we need to be ready by?

Slow: *grin*

Slow: I knew you'd come around.

Slow: I'll text her your number so she can keep you updated. Tell Abe the family can't wait to meet him.

"What car? Who is coming? I'm not getting in some death trap bottle rocket mobile," Abe said.

"It's a…" *Huh. I've heard her vehicle, but I haven't actually seen her driving it. I don't know if it even* is *a car.* "Don't worry about it, Dad. You'll be nice and comfortable, I'm sure. Slow wouldn't have it any other way, and he's the one who organized it for us."

"Eric is a good boy," Abe said fondly. "I never thought I'd get to meet his family."

"Well, he said they can't wait to meet you too." Ruben looked over at his dad, taking in his relaxed posture and hint of a smile. Abe had mostly been a grouch since Ruben got there, even though he'd gotten attacked for his efforts in showing up at all. "You're going to love it, Dad. I've got a nice place, and Carys will be right across the street if you need company or a cup of sugar or something."

"Calm down, son. I don't suspect I'll like it much, but I agreed to go…at least until I'm recovered enough to come home."

Ruben didn't have the heart to contradict his father on that one. Abe would return over Ruben's dead body.

Chapter Twenty-Six

VINNY

"You've lost your damn mind, Eric. You want me to drive them home in my *car?* I can't even find a car seat that fits well in the back for Maya! Ruben's gotta be six feet."

"I know I'm asking a lot, Vin. Abe refuses to fly, and Ruben got attacked. He can't drive in his condition."

"What condition?" she snapped. Vinny was in no mood to coddle anyone, much less Ruben. If he needed help wiping his own ass, he was on his own.

"There was a squatter in the house when he got there. Guy nailed him in the foot with a baseball bat," Eric said.

"Oh, for fucks…that man has the *worst* preservation skills!" Vinny took a few seconds to fume before she spoke again. "Fine. But he has to ride in the back seat."

Eric let out a laugh so hearty, Vinny softened a touch, a grin of her own breaking free.

"Beggars can't be choosers. Besides, you'll love Abe. *And* you will make it home faster if you aren't stuck stopping at every weird roadside attraction that catches Quincy's fancy."

True enough. I can safely say the world's largest ball of twine is underwhelming at best.

"Just send me the address," she said, then promptly hung up.

———

THE CLOSER SHE got to the address Eric had sent, the more her nerves jangled like a set of chimes in a hurricane. Vinny could see traces of the charm that had once graced the neighborhood, but she could also see the seediness that had crept over it with time, robbing the inhabitants of anything resembling tranquility.

This is where he grew up?

She passed a field with a leaning section of fence, the lawn brown even in the early morning light. A baseball diamond. Vinny wondered if anyone was brave enough to still play there…unless it was some sort of neighborhood gang potluck. Her phone sang out from the dashboard, startling her back into focus.

The voice was set to "boy band." Normally it amused her, but on this road, it made her feel foolish. Joy didn't exist here. No way she was leaving her baby outside alone either. They better be ready. If not, she'd drive back a few miles to the tempting coffee drive thru she'd passed and wait in a near*ish* Target parking lot—where there were cameras and she wouldn't be waiting to be shanked—for Ruben to text they were ready.

As she pulled up at the curb of a dilapidated little house she guessed was once red, Vinny fought the urge to cut and run. Every instinct in her body told her to get the hell out with her life while she could. Fuck Ruben. He'd figure it out.

Thank god I did a fluids and tire check before leaving

Nashville. I am not waiting around here long enough to do anything maintenance related.

He must have been waiting at the front window. No sooner did Vinny set the parking brake, she saw Ruben hobbling out on crutches. Knowing his foot had been broken was different from *seeing* it. He was always so lively, with a perpetual bounce in his step affirming the energy his strong body struggled to contain.

He was not bouncing now.

Ruben looked weary, both mentally and physically.

Against her better judgment, Vinny stepped out of the car. She didn't go far—in fact, she settled herself right against the door. She wouldn't make Ruben lean down to talk through her window, but she wasn't leaving her baby either.

"He's been fighting me all night," Ruben said by way of greeting. "I'm sorry, Lavender. I don't think he's going to leave. I'm in no condition to force him, and I sure as hell can't leave him here alone."

Damn it. I do not want to be here for this. Vinny took in his body language, the defeat and frustration rolling off him heavy enough to stifle her. *Fuck it. I'm not letting Eric down,* she told herself. *Time to turn up the charm.*

"Guard my baby with your life or you will wish you had," she said firmly, enjoying the way it caught him off guard. She smirked—she couldn't help it—before sauntering up the walkway like she owned the place. "Mr. Holt," she called through the open doorway. "My name is Lavender. I'm here to escort you on a tour of the southern states."

Before she'd finished her speech, a man emerged from a back hallway. He was picking his way across the ancient carpet with carful experience, avoiding all the hazards from where it had piled up over the years from neglect. He had a small suitcase and nothing else.

"Miss Blume," he said with more southern charm than all the would be lovers she'd encountered her three months in Nashville. "It's a pleasure."

"Eric has told me all about you, Abe. No flirting, now. I know you'll break my heart if I let you," she said, laying on her own charm. She couldn't remember the last time she smiled so wide. Abe was a charmer for sure.

"Oh, you call me Abner, sweet thing." He gave her a wink and walked right out the door toward her baby, with a pep in his step she hadn't expected in a man who'd recently had a heart attack.

"Abner it is," she said, easily catching up to him. "This is a full service experience, Abner. You go get seated shotgun. I'll stow the luggage. Maybe I'll even let Ben ride inside."

He laughed as he handed her the old case. "Oh, I like you. See you in the car, Vinny."

She opened the trunk and placed his things inside next to her tote with emergency gear and extra fluids. Old cars had old car issues, but nobody had touched her baby except Vinny and her father since they picked it up. She *was* the mechanic, and she could fix anything so long as she was prepared.

Vinny leaned around the hood and called out to Ruben, "What else? You won't have much room in back for stuff. You have a bag, Ben?"

He was staring at her in shock, wide eyed and jaw flapping in the breeze.

Vinny scowled. "What?"

"How did you do that?"

"Do what?"

"Get him to *leave* like that."

"I didn't do a thing," she said. "You watched him stroll out on his own steam and determination."

He continued to stare at her until she quirked a brow at

him. "Right," he finally responded, straightening up over his crutches. "I'll grab my things. Just give me a minute."

She watched with amusement as he swung himself back up the walkway and into the house. He came back out half a minute later with a backpack and nothing else. *Men. It's completely unfair how light they can travel.* He closed the door and made his way back to the curb.

"Take out what you need," she advised. "Phone charger, that sort of thing."

Ruben patted his pocket. "Got it."

"Let's get out of here," she murmured, a hint of trepidation laced in her tone. He nodded in response as he tucked his crutches and took off his backpack. Vinny stuffed in in the trunk, locked it up, and quickly moved to her door. "I'll help you."

Once again, Ruben decided to do the most idiotic of things and *froze* when he reached the open door. "Ben. Get in the damn car. So help me, I will leave your ass here." Her words came out low enough only he would hear her, but they had the effect of a lightening strike. Ruben nearly threw himself into the back of the car, pulling his crutches in along with him.

Vinny pushed her seat back—it was going to be a long trip, hauling him in and out of the back of a coupe—and wasted no time sliding into her seat. Just as her door was about to latch, it was yanked back. Vinny didn't hesitate.

The would be car jacker had a knife, but Vinny had her gun. Wordlessly, she drew it out in a flash, her aim true. The guy was *rough.* Wild eyes, his whole person covered in filth. He probably hadn't had a real meal in days.

He would *not* be financing his next one with her Camaro.

One look at the instrument aimed at his center, and the guy held his hands up and backed away until he was out of sight. Vinny closed and locked the door, dropped her piece in her lap, and put the car in drive. She kept her cool, easily navigating the car back toward the part of town where people wouldn't see her as a meal ticket.

It's okay. You were ready. Nobody took advantage of you.

No matter what she told herself, Vinny knew she needed to find an outlet for her adrenaline before it was too late. She'd been in some crazy situations in her life, but *never* on her own. Abner was recovering from a heart attack. Ruben had a busted foot and was sardined into her back seat. Neither was capable of much at the moment.

The weight of what she'd taken on hit her like a bullet train. A familiar red and white sign caught her attention, and she carefully navigated her way into the parking lot, finding a spot under a tree. With a smile she was sure looked more manic than genuine, she turned to Abner.

"I just need a few things," she said warmly. "Do you want any snacks or drinks, Abner?"

"I'm good, Vinny. Thank you." His easy smile was a monkey wrench in the gears of her mind.

Did I imagine what happened? Was I so paranoid by the condition of the neighborhood that I invented a knife wielding whacko? Why hasn't Abner said anything about it?

Nobody had said a word in the eight minutes it took her to get from the dumpy little house to the Target parking lot. Not. A. Word.

She didn't trust her voice, so instead, she nodded. Her trembling fingers grasped the doorhandle and she pushed it open, grabbed her purse—her firearm was already tucked inside it—and exited the car. She'd go inside the store, walk a couple laps, grab some random shit, and everything would be okay. Abner didn't need to know driving through his neighborhood had nearly caused her to have an aneurysm from fear.

Vinny was stepping up to the front door when the sound of her name caused her to jump.

"Lavender! Slow down, woman." She spun to find Ruben swinging across the blacktop fast as he could on his crutches. "Come here," he said, nodding off to the side. There was a decorative pillar, and behind it a tidy little corner. "There."

She forced her trembling body after him, her legs uncooperative rubber with a mind of their own. Ruben backed into the corner and leaned into it for support, propping the crutches on the walls on either side of him, and opened his arms. Vinny collapsed into him, muffling the sound of her sobs in the firm plane of his chest as her hands grasped his soft T-shirt. Ruben's arms pulled her in close.

"You are damn terrifying," he murmured into her crown. "But I know right now you just *feel* terrified. Let it out, Lavender. All of it."

And the flood gates opened.

Chapter Twenty-Seven

RUBEN

He didn't know how long they stood there, tucked into the corner next to the entrance of a Target that hadn't existed back when he'd lived there. Ruben held her close to his body until the shakes subsided from her adrenaline crash.

"You've never done that before, have you? With someone who was a real danger," he asked softly when her breathing began to normalize. She shook her head against his chest. "I know what it means to aim a firearm at a stranger…and to pull the trigger. I can tell you I did not handle my first time as well as you just did."

"Don't lie to make me feel better," she blubbered, her face turned sideways enough she wasn't talking directly into his torso.

"I'm not. Ask Eric. The first time we deployed, I was way too cocky for my own good. That lasted about a week. We went out on patrol and took enemy fire. It was the first time I lifted my weapon to a living target." Ruben had spent a lot of time in counseling after his first deployment. He hadn't once regretted becoming a Marine, but there were serious draw-backs from time to time. Then he admitted something to her nobody else knew. Not even Slow. "I pissed myself, Lavender."

She tipped her face up then, and he could see the doubt swirling in her azure eyes. He'd noticed how they changed color before. They looked—well, *lavender*—most of the time, but depending on the light, her eyes shifted to a stunning blue sometimes, or an emerald green.

"You don't believe me?"

"Not for a second."

"You should. I ain't got a reason to lie," he drawled. "I grew up in that house, Lavender. It wasn't so bad back then, like it is now. But it was never the *good* side of town. I thought I was prepared for real war because I came from a rough area. Turns out, I wasn't."

Ruben watched her watch him, her thoughts and emotions flitting across her face like a film that had been patched together with too many random clips in short order to tell a whole story to anyone observing. But he caught the gist. Vinny was at war with herself right now, trying to decide too many things at one time with her emotions sending sound reason into a separate tailspin.

How to keep her dignity in front of him, for one. She was still weary. For the first time, he thought maybe it wasn't really about *him.* Maybe he'd been arrogant, and there was a whole lot more backstory in play he wasn't privy to.

He'd have to ask her later, when she was less vulnerable and able to decide whether she wanted to tell him. For now, he was happy to see her more herself. He let go of her slowly —reluctantly—and reached for his crutches. "What do you need inside?"

"Snacks. Drinks. I don't have pillows to prop your foot up with. I was hoping they still had a few of the ones they put out as dorm room specials, even though it's past back to school season."

His brows went up. "You were going in to buy me pillows?"

"It's not exactly spacious back there and we have twenty-three hundred miles of road ahead of us." She shrugged. "That's a long way to go cramped up with a broken foot."

"Thank you, Lavender." *For everything.* "I think it's best if you push the cart," he said, jerking his head toward the door.

For once, she didn't try to argue or send him away. Vinny stepped out of his reach, pausing long enough for him to position his crutches, before quietly strolling toward the entrance. Fifteen minutes later, they exited with a few bags, the smaller of which he insisted on carrying since they didn't keep him from using the crutches correctly. She'd tried to pay, but he'd beat her to it. Ruben was smart enough to know she wouldn't take gas money, and putting long miles on a classic car was going to rack up maintenance costs.

He was paying for his own damn pillows and snacks.

The errand had been laconic, but not unpleasant. Vinny had asked Ruben for his input on granola bars and beverages with as few words as possible but seemed genuine in her interest. There were no eye rolls or sarcastic mutterings when he added his favorites to the cart, and she even thanked Ruben for pulling down a jug of water from the top shelf for her.

When they returned to the car, he couldn't help himself. "So, a Camaro?"

"You against Camaros?" she asked in her usually saucy tone.

"Nah. We had one once. Not as nice as yours. It was my

mom's baby." He didn't like to talk about his mom, but this was different.

She drives a Camaro like Mom's. The mystery as to why his father had leaped into the front seat without a fuss was solved. They had dreamed of fixing up his mother's car, but she'd died before they had the chance. It had sat in the garage while she slowly succumbed to her pain.

"She wasn't this pretty when we got her," Vinny said, patting the top affectionately. "Dad and I fixed her up. It took nearly all the money I scratched up from age seven to fifteen, but I paid for her paint job myself."

"She's a beauty," he said.

Ruben wasn't looking at the car. Luckily, Vinny was and missed how he couldn't turn away from her in this moment.

Vinny cleared the emotion from her throat. "I had the air mattress pad thing custom made a few years ago, in case I ever broke down somewhere I'd be stuck a long time. I hope it helps. And it has old school lap belts in the back, so even turned sideways with your foot propped, you can buckle up."

Ruben watched her open her door and hold the back of her seat foreword so he could back his tall frame into the car. By the time he had himself tucked back and belted in, she had his pillows out of the plastic.

"Lift," she commanded. Soon as his right leg was reasonably clear, she tucked both pillows underneath for him. "You set? Need your phone plugged in or something?"

"Nah, I'm good." Even if he needed something, he wouldn't have asked. Ruben was too busy chewing over everything he *thought* he knew about Lavender Blume.

"Did you find everything you need?" his dad asked Vinny as she buckled up.

"We did. You're snack bitch, Abner. I hope you understand how serious a job you accepted when you claimed your seat," she said. All traces of her earlier upset were smoothed over, though Ruben had a feeling they were still simmering below her seemingly calm surface.

"Happy to help," Abe replied. Ruben rolled his eyes over the flirtatious tone of voice he'd used, his words dripping as syrupy sweet as the southern sweet tea he shouldn't be drinking in his condition.

They were on the interstate in short order. Ruben relaxed into the bed she'd made up, surprised how comfortable it was for such a tight space. Vinny had put her own pillows in the corner for him to lean back on and he could smell her shampoo on them—lavender. For the first time since he'd gotten the call from nurse cranky pants informing him his dad was hospitalized, Ruben felt like he could relax.

———

Vinny

"That didn't take long," she mused, confirming in her rear view mirror the sound from the back seat was the soft snores of the man she'd managed to cram into the tight space. "He's out like a light."

"Boy has always been an easy sleeper," Abner said. "You got him spoiled back there with all those pillows."

Vinny giggled. "Not sure I agree with you, but at least he's not making a fuss."

"He allows you call him Ben," Abner said with a touch more seriousness. "Nobody calls him that anymore."

"Anymore?"

"Not since his mother passed."

Vinny thought on what Abner said. Calling him Ben had been a spur of the moment reflex, bubbling out one day when she was trying to annoy him. It hadn't seemed to faze Ruben, but she'd kept at it. Now it was like breathing…*natural.*

"He said earlier she had a car like mine, a Camaro. I've never heard him talk about his mom before. I've heard a lot about *you,* both from him and Eric. Not his mom." Well… mostly Eric, but Vinny had overheard Ruben talking to Eric about Abner, so she decided it counted.

"Ruben hardly took the time to grieve her properly. The pair of 'em were *thick as thieves* as the saying goes. He didn't take her passing well, and he was furious when I sold her car to help pay for his schoolbooks. She was so proud of him," he said warmly, and Vinny knew Abner wasn't seeing the Georgia countryside out the window anymore by the way he spoke. "She would have sold everything we had if it meant he had what he needed for college. He was always smart. Way too good for what little we had to give."

"She sounds like she was a wonderful woman," Vinny said. "How on earth he ended up with the town bicycle after being raised by a mom like that…I don't understand, Abner."

"Oh, that's easy. You got real love you got something to lose, and Ruben, he doesn't think he'd survive it twice," he said with surety. "Like I said, he never healed from losing his mother."

"That's…" *Sad. So incredibly sad.*

"Yes," he said, as if he'd heard her thoughts. "It is."

"You know what, Abner? I think you gave him an exceptional childhood. Maybe you didn't have a lot of *things,* but it sounds like he didn't lack on the important stuff." She sighed, thinking of her own mother. "Sounds to me like Ruben had everything he needed."

"Bless you, girl. Bless you." Abner's voice rasped with emotion.

She reached across the center console and took Abner's

hand without taking her eyes off the road and gave it a firm squeeze. Abner answered with equal pressure, and they stayed that way—hands clasped in solidarity—until Vinny needed her hand back.

"We need music. What's your poison?"

"Surprise me."

Vinny smirked as she hit the voice activation button on her stereo. "Start joyride playlist two," she commanded.

A moment later, the familiar intro began.

"Woo! You're playing hard ball," Abner said. "'Slow Ride.' Uh!"

Vinny laughed. "I love what I love."

She began tapping out the beat on her steering wheel and harmonizing. Beside her, Abner made puttering sounds along with the beat. By the time they reached the second verse, the last of the morning's tension left her body.

It was just Vinny, her new "roadie," and her baby.

They stopped for an early lunch a couple hours later. Ruben didn't stir. Vinny decided he probably needed the sleep more than the pit stop, parked in the shade, and cracked the windows like he was a Labrador while she and Abner went into the small sandwich shop she'd discovered on a previous tour through the area.

Sandwiches were something she hardly ate at home, but on the road, they hit the spot. It was one of life's mysteries. Who was Vinny to challenge it? There was infinite possibility in a sandwich. Since he was sleeping, Vinny decided to custom create something *special* for Ruben. Abner watched with amusement as she directed the staff member.

Back at the car, she turned the engine so the AC could do its job—and not melt Ruben, who was still sleeping—while she led Abner through a few movements in the shade beside the car. She had to slow down while she taught him, but Abner was a quick study.

"What are we doing?" he asked halfway through.

"Simple motions that help move the blood and loosen everything else. We are going to be sitting a lot over the next five or so days. It's important we keep limber," she explained. "I like to take walks before I settle in for the evening too. I'd love some company."

"This your way of tricking me into exercising?" he said with dry amusement.

"No tricks. I'm actively trying to prevent either of us from developing blood clots. I'm not striving for a stroke before I hit thirty," she said. "I've seen enough 'sudden' illness on tour to take care of myself."

"Smart and a looker," Abner said.

"Flatterer." But Vinny noticed Abner taking her instruction more seriously afterward, and it made her happy. There wasn't much point in dragging him across the country if he was going to relapse along the way, given the point was to help him improve his quality of life.

They were back on the road, sandwiches in hand, and Ruben none the wiser. Abner asked questions about her Camaro that were surprising in their complexity. He didn't seem overly interested in other classic cars they passed when she pointed them out, but he had an inordinate propensity to dig into the nitty gritty of the ride he was coasting along in.

"What's that?" he asked, pointing out faint script most people missed.

"It's her name, of course. Every sweet ride needs a name."

"It's a good one."

"Thank you."

"There a story to it?"

"Well...shouldn't there be?" She shrugged, a nervous laugh bubbling up. She could tell him the obvious answer, but she had a feeling Abner would know it was a half-truth, and the thought made her uncomfortable.

"You don't have to tell me, honey. That's your business. Pay no mind to an old man," he insisted.

They finished their sandwiches in companionable silence, her playlist keeping the mood upbeat. "Sweet Home Alabama" blared through her system as they crossed the Alabama state line. She couldn't have planned it better. Abner hooted beside her with glee.

"What a ride," he said, affectionately running his hand down his door and patting the dashboard.

Vinny swelled with pride.

Chapter Twenty-Eight

RUBEN

The flicker of sunlight through the thinning autumn trees permeated Ruben's eyelids, dragging him out of a deep sleep. It gave him the same peaceful, warm greeting he'd felt coming to in his hammock—or one of Slow's, depending on whose back yard he accidentally sacked out in. The hum of a strong motor was next to register, followed by the sound of his parents crooning along to a familiar old song.

That's not right. Dad doesn't sing anymore.

The scent of lavender registered, along with a heavy throbbing in his right foot. Ruben's hazy nostalgia broke as the pain seeped in. His mother was long gone. His foot had been smashed by a junkie with his own baseball bat. And Lavender…

She was singing.

With his dad.

"I see you stirring back there, Butterfinger," Vinny singsonged toward him as the bridge to Pink Floyd's Comfortably Numb registered in his brain.

Of course the pain killers stopped doing their job in time for this *song.* The song was about various forms of sedation

—primarily through the high of playing music—and the irony was not lost on Ruben.

"You calling me sweet, Lavender?" His voice held the roughness of sleep still, but his eyes were alert now.

"Hell no," she said with a snort. "Nutty, maybe. You know how it came to be called a Butterfinger, Ben?"

His dad chuckled in front of him, amused by Vinny's ribbing. "No, but I got a feeling you're about to tell me."

"It's from baseball."

"Surprise, surprise. Thank you, Lavender." He groaned as he shifted his weight and his foot throbbed harder, a pain shooting up through his ankle along with it. "Are we nearing a stop at all? I need my meds." The little paper pharmacy bag he'd wrapped them in landed in his lap. Ruben blinked down at them.

"I got them out of your bag at the last stop. Figured you'd need them sooner or later," she said.

"Uh. Thanks." He checked his watch. "Shit, did I really sleep *four hours?*"

"Closer to five. We took a few breaks. We got you a sandwich if you are hungry. Next stop is Birmingham. Should be there in fifteen," she said.

Ruben's stomach growled at the mention of food. He was supposed to eat with the pain pills too. "Sandwich sounds amazing, thank you."

"Son," Abe said, handing an unfamiliar bag back to him over his shoulder.

Ruben murmured his thanks and pulled the wrapped sub out of the paper bag. It smelled…interesting. *Must be a local shop special or something.* He unfolded the end of the paper without giving it much thought and took a huge bite.

Then promptly choked.

Vinny and Abe immediately let out a laugh; hers soft and his low. They had played him.

"What the hell is on this thing?" he asked after forcing the first bite down.

"A little of everything," Vinny said innocently.

"Uh huh. Like school glue? You make it yourself?"

"No, she gave the lovely fella at the shop great direction in how to build it. I watched," his dad said. "What's wrong, son? Don't you like it?"

It was disgusting, be he wasn't going to tell them that. "It was unexpected," he answered diplomatically. "Seriously, what's on it?"

"I told you, a little of everything. Meat, cheese, peanut butter, Dijon…it's a specialty shop, Ben. You name it, they have it. Watch out for the jalapeños."

"You went all out," he said dryly before taking another bite. Now that he anticipated it, Ruben decided it wasn't so bad. He put back half the sub before stopping to wash down his medicine with half a bottle of water. The city limits of Birmingham were coming into sight as he crumpled the empty wrapper and napkins up and stuffed them back in the paper sack for disposal.

If she thought a mystery sandwich was going to throw him, she severely underestimated what was passed off as edible down range. Ruben had stomached far worse. Besides, the peanut butter did a fine job of balancing the jalapeños. He'd give it a six out of ten: oddly interesting, but still edible. It might have made a seven if it hadn't had tuna salad mounds hidden here and there.

Vinny took an exit with various truck stops lined up on either side of the overpass. "Time for a stretch," she said as she killed the engine off to the side where there were plenty of vacant spaces. "Ready Abner?"

"Sure am," he boasted.

What in the Twilight Zone did I sleep through?

Vinny got out slowly, stretching her arms up before turning back to hold her seat for Ruben. "Come on, Short Stop."

"It's going to be baseball jokes all the way home, isn't it?"

"I'm not a huge fan. I'll probably run out of material by the time we reach Arizona," she teased as he wiggled himself toward freedom.

"Goody." He took her proffered hand and pulled himself to a standing position stiffly. *"Fuck."*

"Looks like you need to stretch with us."

"On a broken foot?"

"We'll modify. Now go on in. Soon as you guys get back, I'll follow."

"You can go first," Ruben offered.

"I've been out of my seat twice already. I can wait," she insisted. "Don't pee on my car, Ben."

He rolled his eyes before turning toward the building. Once he got going on his crutches, Ruben realized how badly he *did* need the bathroom. By the time he got into the men's room, his dad—whose own need had motivated him to hot foot it inside before Ruben could scoot out of the backseat—was at the sink washing his hands.

"Why haven't you ever told me what a delight that girl is?" he chastised as Ruben stepped up to the urinal.

"Can you wait until I'm buttoned up to accost me?" he quipped.

Abe did, but not by much. As soon as Ruben got to the sinks where Abe was waiting, he piped up again. "Well?"

"Because she's *not* a delight. She's a pain in my ass. We

don't get along and likely never will," he said, scrubbing his hands more aggressively than necessary.

"Why not? What did you do?" Abe accused.

"Me? Nah, Dad. She… Look, sometimes people just don't gel."

He couldn't tell his dad about the day he met Vinny. There would be too many questions, like why it took two years to meet her in the first place, and Ruben was exhausted. He'd say something he shouldn't and land himself in hotter water than he was already in, if the set of Abe's jaw was any indication.

"Hmm." It came out a hybrid growl—a *thoughtful* growl —ala Clint Eastwood.

"Dad. Please. This isn't the time."

"Fine."

Abe held the doors for Ruben as they silently went back to the car.

———

"LET'S GO! BEN!"

Ruben startled awake. He'd been having a nightmare.

"Ben!"

"Yeah," he called back. "I'm up."

"Hardly," she said with a snort, her voice coming nearer with her footsteps. Vinny came to a halt in the doorway of the room he'd been given to sleep in by her extremely hetero friend last night, given the way the guy's eyes followed her everywhere. Her spunky scowl turned worrisome the second she laid eyes on him. "You okay?"

"Fine."

She studied him shrewdly before closing the door and

moving to sit next to him on the bed. "Liar," she said softly. "You're clammy."

"I haven't been sleeping well," he said.

"That wouldn't make you clammy."

"It's okay, Lavender. I'm *fine.*"

"Mick has breakfast ready. Do you need help?"

Ah, yes. Mick from Memphis. A successful drummer.

"I'm not sure I'm hungry," he lied. Honestly, he didn't want to sit across the table from Mick and Vinny while their host coasted his hands all over her.

"Tough. No food, no meds. You aren't throwing up in my baby."

Ruben let out a groan. Despite the pillows and cushion, he'd been feeling claustrophobic by the time they pulled in for the night. There was little air movement in the back of the car, given they didn't put vents in the back seat in the good ole days, and it was going to be stifling back there. The only thing going his way was the season. October wasn't nearly as miserable in the south as say August. But it was still hot.

"Come on," she prompted. "We pushed a little harder than I would have liked yesterday. More stops, less driving today. I have a friend in Norman we can stay with tonight."

"Norman?"

"Yeah, Oklahoma. It's a little south of Oklahoma City," she said. "You sure you don't need a hand?"

"I'm good, Lavender. Thanks."

She nodded her head before getting up and leaving the room, closing the door behind her. Ruben let out a heavy sigh. He didn't know what was worse: Vinny's scorn or her kindness. Aside from some playful ribbing, she'd mostly ignored him yesterday in favor of becoming Abe's new favorite person. He hadn't seen his dad so animated in a long time, not to mention he didn't fight her the way he did Ruben.

Vinny said stretch, Abe did it.

Vinny said drink all your water before the next stop, Abe did it.

If Ruben so much as suggested the things Vinny kindly insisted of his father, there would be hell to pay.

And that dream…he was back in California, coming home to Carla. They weren't alone, and Ruben wasn't given a choice on what the evening's activities looked like. If the dream had stayed NC17, he might have been able to shudder through it and say it was from going so long with only his hand to make love to. Instead, it had warped into a kind of vividly domestic hell akin to the wars he'd managed to survive.

It was a jumbled mess, honestly. The images blurred as soon as he woke, but the chill they left behind was as real as the stabbing pain in his broken foot.

Get up. You are acting ungrateful.

Ruben forced himself to his feet and hobbled across the hall to the small bathroom on one crutch. He carefully showered, relieved there was a grippy mat in the tub. He used a trash bag and waterproof medical tape to keep his casted foot dry while he efficiently took care of business. Freshly washed and dressed, he felt more himself. By the time he made it down the hall to where everyone was laughing in the kitchen, he even felt ready to watch their host make an ass of himself drooling over Vinny.

"He lives!" Mick cheered as Ruben entered the room.

"Hey, man. Thanks for having us. Appreciate it," he said. Ruben might not like Mick overly much, but he *did* appreciate his hospitality.

"Anything for Vin," he said, leering over her. He was not so subtly looking down her tank. "It's always a pleasure."

"Here, here," Abe joined, lifting his mug of black coffee in solidarity. "She's a fine one."

Vinny subtly bit the inside of her lower lip and looked down, her alabaster complexion instantly flushing under their praise. "You guys…"

"It's all true, baby," Mick said easily, leaning down to kiss her cheek.

Ruben didn't miss the way she wrinkled her nose at his use of the common endearment.

"She's a pistol," Ruben said, "that's for certain."

Mick laughed as he turned back to the stove. "Have a seat," he called over his shoulder. No sooner did Ruben settle down next to his dad, Mick had a coffee and plate ready for him. Ruben blinked down in surprise. "Eggs benny with browns and fresh fruit."

"Wow. Beats the free continental at the Holiday Inn," Ruben joked.

"His dad is a world-renowned chef at a five-star restaurant here in town," Vinny supplied.

"Can't grow up under his roof and not learn the basics," Mick said with a nod. He was already back at the stove.

Basics? Since when is freaking hollandaise from scratch basic? Ruben took a bite and hated how loudly he groaned. "Damn, that's good."

"Thanks."

Vinny was quick to help clear and load the dishes into Mick's dishwasher as soon as possible, filling up their travel mugs and bottles with coffee and water while she caught up with her friend. Ruben felt useless. Between his foot and lack of musical talent, there wasn't much he felt he could offer the conversation or the workload.

It was frustrating as hell.

He was at least able to pack up his own backpack and

strip the comfortable double bed he'd been provided in an effort to pull his own weight. Back at the car, Vinny had everything well in hand. She was standing in the side yard next to Mick and Abe, the duo doing a series of motions together in preparation for the next stretch of road while their pervy host admired Vinny's body as she moved.

Ruben plopped his bag in the open trunk, tossed his necessities into the driver seat, and joined them. Fifteen minutes later, they said goodbye to Mick—who had no qualms cupping Vinny's ass with the whole world watching —and got back in the car.

They were nearly back on the freeway before Ruben noticed the little fan fastened onto his dad's headrest, blowing a steady stream of air into his corner. "What's this?" he asked.

"Oh, it's a rechargeable fan. I found it this morning when I was reorganizing the trunk. Figured you'd be more comfortable back there if you weren't suffocating," Vinny said lightly.

This shit. How do I handle this? Every time she has historically done something nice for me, I have paid for it in the end. The video footage, standing up to Carla when I came home, keeping the admiral from slaughtering me when he showed up...

He finally broke the uncomfortably long silence that had built while he pondered over what airflow would cost him in the long run. "Yeah. Thanks."

Chapter Twenty-Nine

VINNY

Vinny had forgotten how *handsy* Mick was. In a big group it was easier to avoid the contact, but in a more intimate setting like his own home, it had been hard to convince him it would be inappropriate for her to "sleep" in his bed, much less keep his paws to himself. She had shamelessly used her recovering travel companions as logical reasons she needed to be on the other side of the house where the rest of the guest bedrooms were.

Damn percussionists. It's like a prerequisite or something, being just a little bit extra in the confidence of their own swagger.

He'd been covertly strange about Ruben too. Mick had been far more appropriate when Ruben was out of the room, but anytime he was around, it felt like Mick was marking his territory—like a dog peeing on a tree, and about as comfortable considering she was the tree. Vinny was glad Ruben hadn't gotten weird about it. She knew he'd noticed and hadn't found it...*oh, hell. I can't read the man's mind. He didn't like it, but he didn't go feral over it either.*

It had been a relief to climb back into her car and drive away. Or at least it *had* been, until Ruben noticed the fan she'd added. Now she was just *pissed.* He had thanked her, but he hadn't sounded genuine in the least. Vinny was embarrassed she'd gone to the trouble of running out at midnight—she'd thought about it while her racing mind was refusing to go to sleep, not this morning like she'd told him—to bring it in for charging.

She was trying her best to be nice to someone she didn't like and didn't want to help, and he was being an ass. If it weren't for Abner, she wouldn't have gone out of her way at all. Now she had the enemy's smell on her pillows, distracting her from sleep after he'd spent the day propped up on them.

"We're jumping a few decades, Abner. I hope you don't mind," Vinny said, hitting her 90's metal playlist.

"Your wheels, your rules," he said jovially beside her. Vinny gave him credit for not flinching when Metallica blared through the speakers. Her mood today wasn't anything like yesterday, and there was no way she could sit through The Rolling Stones and Co. in her present mindset.

Just get to Oklahoma.

———

THEY MADE IT. Collette was as wonderfully welcoming and eccentric as always. Vinny's pillows smelled even more like Ruben than yesterday. It was a disaster.

Day three would end in Albuquerque. It was a longer day of driving, like the first one had been. If her brain wasn't completely scrambled she'd probably be in a better mood. Abner was as wonderful as he'd been since he first climbed into her baby.

But Ruben—the fact he was breathing at all further irritated Vinny. *Asshole.*

If Mick had been strange with Vinny, Collette had been worse over Ruben. Every time Vinny turned around, she caught him stepping out of Collette's touch. The only person who hadn't begun to wear on Vinny's nerves was Abner.

They were just outside Amarillo, Texas when Ruben spoke up for the first time since they'd hit the road that morning. "Do you mind if we make a side trip?"

"To where?" she asked.

"A store south of town. A friend was telling me about—"

"The interstate runs through the north of Amarillo, and we have more miles to cover today. If it was closer to the route it'd be fine, but I don't feel like going out of the way will be wise," she said coolly.

"Oh. That's okay. It was just a thought." He didn't say it with any sort of inflection to make her take it wrong, but... *isn't that sus all on its own? First he asks for a damn side quest like we don't have anywhere to be, then acts like it's no big deal when I tell him no? Pfft. Passive aggressive bullshit.*

Nothing with Ruben was ever easy. Why should a cross country drive be any different?

When they arrived at the Airbnb she'd booked, he piped up again. "This is cute. Who lives here?"

"We do, for tonight."

"No friends in Albuquerque?"

"They moved up to Santa Fe, which is too far north this particular trip," she said tersely.

She could feel his gaze on her as she got out of the car. Vinny held her seat back to make it easier for Ruben to climb out like usual, but she didn't offer a hand or look at him.

As he slid out with the expertise of a man who was way

too familiar with her car, he called out, "What sound's good to eat Dad? I can see what delivers."

"Oh, I'm not picky."

"Vegan it is," he teased jovially.

"Son," Abner barked out, but he had no bite.

Vinny ground her teeth.

"You okay?" he asked softly as he tucked his crutches under his arms beside her.

"Just tired," she snapped, still looking off into the distance.

"Did I do something wrong?"

He's putting on a show for Abner, she told herself. *Don't fall for it.*

When she didn't answer he took the hint and moved off. Vinny grabbed her pillows out of the back and headed to the front door, eager to unlock it and get her baby parked safely inside the garage. By the time she was back inside, Abner and Ruben were already done selecting dinner.

"What's my portion?" she asked quietly as she came into the room.

"I got it," he said.

Before she could make a fuss, Abner piped up with, "Have you ever seen such a thing, Vinny? You can pick your supper from just about anywhere, and someone will bring it right to you!"

She smiled at him. "It's pretty neat."

"It's the darndest thing," he agreed.

Vinny swallowed the vitriol poised on her tongue and nodded. No matter how much she wanted to verbally level Ruben out, Abner didn't deserve to be party to it.

"You sure you're okay? I can tell you when the food arrives if you want to go rest." Ruben studied her with concern—*fake, obviously*—while she twiddled her keys in her hand and tried not to notice.

"That's a pretty good idea, actually. I think I'll go float around in the giant soaking tub in the master." *Anything to get away from you right now is a good plan.*

"Okay," he said, giving her a gentle smile. "I'll knock when the food arrives."

Vinny nodded her head and carried her things off with her. Even from under her arm, she could smell him on her pillows, stronger than yesterday. *Ugh. I'm never going to sleep with him in my face like this. Might as well use the shitty pillows provided in the room.* She closed the door behind her and locked it before dumping the offending mounds onto the floor with a huff. Her other possessions she positioned with more care.

Her body protested as she rolled her shoulders back, attempting to rectify her posture. The achiness from hours semi-slouched behind the steering wheel flared with every step toward the en suite bathroom. Once the water was flowing hot, she stopped the drain and went back to her bags. She would need her toiletries, and she still had some of the bath salts she'd bought while wandering around Nashville one afternoon before work. This seemed like the perfect occasion to use a scoop or two.

Once Vinny was clean, she tried some of her favorite visualization tricks. No matter what she attempted to conjure, her thoughts were interrupted by rich, dark brown eyes that shimmered with life—amusement, playfulness, empathy, kindness, frustration, confusion, even anger at times. It was all there in vivid hues, ruining the peaceful brushstrokes she was trying to create of willow branches dancing in the breeze at dusk, long before she could add the whimsical fireflies that mesmerized her inner consciousness into much-needed tranquility. Over and over, Vinny tried to discard the images from her rearview mirror—the man whose presence had sent her off kilter—and claim some sense of ease.

She lay in the giant tub well past the knock on her door. Her aches enjoyed it, but she was pretty sure she'd only set her frustrations to simmer into a dull anger. Even through two closed doors, Ruben's presence in the house had managed to disrupt her personal time. Vinny quickly dressed in sleep shorts and a tank before padding out to the living room.

"Even natural, you're a beauty, Miss Blume," Abner called as she approached the table. Ruben was bent over a takeout container and glanced up as he spoke, doing a double take. She watched as he shook his head slightly and dropped his eyes back into the container.

Doesn't look like your son agrees, she thought. "What do you mean, Abner?"

"You don't have the stuff on your eyes." He swished a finger up and down in front of one eye as he spoke.

Vinny blinked. "Oh! Mascara. Yeah, I washed it off. I don't wear much makeup anyway, but I do tend to wear mascara and a light brow pencil most of the time."

"You're lovely," he reiterated. "Won't you join us? Ruben made me get some low sodium nonsense, but he got you the good stuff."

"The good stuff, huh?" She forced herself to sit down across from them instead of bolting to her room. She *was* hungry.

"These are for you," Ruben said, sliding takeout boxes her way.

"Thanks."

Chinese takeout. Ruben had remembered all the things she'd ordered the night she had shared with him. A lump rose in Vinny's throat as she poked at her cashew chicken with the complimentary chop sticks. It was too much. What was she supposed to do? Why did he order this?

"Everything okay?" he asked from across the table.

"Yeah," she lied. "I'm just road weary." Vinny forced herself to eat half of her food before shoving the rest in the fridge to eat cold at breakfast, said a hasty goodnight, and went to bed.

———

"LOOK AT THIS," Vinny said softly to Ruben, holding her tablet out. It was barely five in the morning, still dark out. She'd heard him get up and decided to be proactive.

"Why are you showing me flights leaving out of the Sunport this morning?" he asked in confusion.

"Well, you could be home by lunch. I'm sure Carys would be willing to pick you up at the airport. No more back seat." Even in her own ears, it sounded weak.

"Lavender," he said, his tone dropping half an octave while simultaneously causing her body to erupt in goose-bumps and her nipples to harden. *What the hell?* "Why are you showing me flights out of the Sunport? I won't leave my dad, and he won't get on a plane. You know both those details. It's why we're here in the first place."

She stuffed her apprehension aside. "You're just so crunched—"

"Stop." He looked up at her with hard eyes. "What did I do wrong?"

"Nothing."

"Then why are you trying to get rid of me? I have tried to be kind. I have helped as much as you'll let me get away with. *What did I do wrong for you to try to dump me at the airport on your way out of town?"* The genuine hurt in

Ruben's voice sent a wave of shame skittering through Vinny. The frustration in his expression was the final straw, snapping her resolve in half.

Vinny swiped her tablet back and turned to go. "Forget it."

His hand wrapped around her wrist firmly. "Don't. Why do you… Please, Lavender. Tell me."

"Ben. Let me go," she rasped out. The warmth and pressure of his flesh against hers lifted and she immediately fled back to her room, locking the door behind her.

Vinny climbed back in bed hoping she might get a few hours of sleep, but the pillows provided had been shittier than usual. She'd switched back to her own and was now surrounded by his scent. At least she wouldn't have a kink in her neck to contend with the next two days of driving.

I hate him.

Chapter Thirty

RUBEN

She tried to get rid of me. Ruben sat at the table in shock, staring at Vinny's closed bedroom door across the open floor-plan living room space from where he sat at the dining room table. It *hurt*.

He knew she'd been getting progressively testier the longer they were on the road and had kept his trap shut so he didn't add to whatever was upsetting her. But she'd seemed fine with his dad, talking and singing and bringing out a side of Abe Ruben had thought long gone. He'd been enjoying the trip from the back seat, especially now he had some airflow via the rechargeable fan Vinny had dug out for him. He didn't mind being stuffed in the back at all, truth be told.

Vinny obviously felt differently. *What did I do wrong?*

Ruben made himself scarce after starting the coffee pot. He took his mug full and leftovers to his room and polished them off before taking a shower and repacking his bag. He could hear Vinny laughing in the kitchen over something his dad had said. Anger pierced through him. How could she be so kind to a stranger, yet so harsh with him?

He'd known, hadn't he? From the start, all the nice things

she'd done had put Ruben on edge. Nothing was ever without consequence with Vinny, no good deed unpunished. Not when Ruben was the one going about his day in the least offensive way he knew how.

Meanwhile, she gets to flirt with *Mick* and prance around in her barely there pajama shorts and tank, her pale pink nipples showing through just enough to drive him insane. Not because he wanted *her,* he was a *man.* One who had recently ended a two-plus-year long marriage with a woman who spread her legs more with others in that time than she had with her husband. It had been a long fucking time, damn it. He was only human, with needs like any other.

And his father was right; Vinny was beautiful. At least on the outside. She was still the same whacko who woke him with an ice water spritz last spring on the inside.

It's not me, it's her.

How are we going to make it two more days crammed in a car together?

Before the Tilt-A-Whirl in his head fully careened out of control, the familiar sound of his father's knuckles wrapping on the door pushed Ruben into action. He cleared his trash and put his coffee cup in the dishwasher before going back to the bedroom for his bag and second crutch.

Ten minutes later, they were flying back down Interstate 40, bound for Kingman, Arizona. Tomorrow evening they would make it back to Oceanside. He was ready to be home. To settle in and show his father he could be comfortable and *safe.*

He was clever enough to know *he* wasn't safe until he was home as well. Not until he understood what drove the heathen currently in control of his life via the car she wielded with precision as it barreled along at eighty miles an hour.

"You've been awfully quiet back there," Abe said as he walked beside Ruben toward the men's room. It was their first road break, a combination truck stop and casino with enough cameras around for Vinny to feel comfortable leaving her car unattended to cut the time they weren't in motion.

"There isn't anything to say," he said with a shrug, doing his best to play off the tension he'd felt since he woke.

"Son, I'm not blind."

"Never said you were."

"What did you do to that poor woman? She's terrified of you."

Ruben stopped. His whole circuitry crackled like someone had stuck a paper clip in one of his outlets. But he'd heard it, loud and clear. Turning his head to his dad, he said, *"She's terrified of me?* You got this backward."

Abe shook his head. "I don't."

"Dad. She's a fucking terror. I'm a thousand percent sure she hasn't snapped my neck in my sleep because of you— scratch that, she only *came* because of you. If it had been me alone, she probably would have cackled all the way home with her dad. I have tried to make peace, but she's not interested."

"Because she sees you as a threat," he insisted, seemingly disregarding Ruben's declaration.

"How am *I* a threat to *her?*"

"When you figure it out, you'll stop being a threat."

"That doesn't make sense. Knowing her weakness, in the eyes of someone like her, means I know exactly how to hurt her worse."

Abe shook his head. "We both know you aren't the type, son. You figure it out, and then you prove her wrong—over and over and over again if you have to. She'll be worth it."

Ruben snorted. "Worth what, exactly? Other than losing my place as number one on her shoot to kill wall."

His father gave him a knowing smile, filled with humor and challenge and *love.* It made Ruben's blood run cold. *What am I missing?*

"Time will tell, son. Come on, now. It's rude to keep a lady waiting."

Lady. Ha. Ha ha! Right.

———

KINGMAN WAS ANOTHER STRATEGIC STOP, if Ruben was guessing. Vinny had friends there too, an older couple this time whom he guessed were closer to her dad's age. They treated her like a long-lost member of the family, and she reciprocated. It put her in a good enough mood to not twist the knife she'd landed in his back that morning for the duration of their stay.

Abe and Vinny had spent most of the evening dancing their aches away—a fair substitute for their stretches, according to her—down in the sizable study where the Holdens had the biggest record collection Ruben had ever seen. He'd had to sit out, given his foot, and leisurely did stretches of his own off to the side while listening to the conversation around him.

But nobody likes being the spare tire, Ruben included. He did his best to help with the dishes before wandering off to his shared bedroom while the rest went back to the study. When his father came in a few hours later, Ruben was rolled away from him on his twin sized mattress, pretending to be asleep.

His last thoughts before he drifted off to oblivion were a simple prayer. *Please let her be in a good mood tomorrow.*

Ruben didn't know how much more of her indifference he could take. When shoving him off hadn't worked, she'd doubled down on attending to Abe while solidly blocking out Ruben's existence, aside from holding her seat so he could get in and out of the back seat easier.

He suspected the gesture was in deference to her upholstery, not his injury.

Day five started off well. The Holdens made them a feast, shoving a picnic lunch at Vinny as they loaded up. There were actual tears in her eyes as she said goodbye to them. He was all but convinced she was a vessel of darkness, and the display made Ruben uncomfortable.

Instead of watching, he'd scooched himself into the back seat best he could. As his eyes roamed everywhere but the emotional scene outside the windows, he saw it for the first time. Across the top of the dash, so well done you'd have to be looking to see it, were the words *Lavender's Joy.*

His flesh ribbed as the hairs stood on end. *It's not possible.*

Before he could put too much thought into it, the passenger door opened and his father slid into place. "Lovely couple," he said after shutting the door.

"Yeah." His response was automatic, his mind still chewing over the name of the car he'd spent the last four days riding in.

"Ahh," Abe said, noticing where Ruben's eyes were focused. "You finally noticed."

"Hard to see from back here. I'm guessing you picked up on it immediately."

"I did."

"Is it?"

"It is."

"That's why you got in without a fuss. You knew who she was the second she pulled up outside, didn't you?"

"Of course I did." The humor in his voice was an ice pick in Ruben's heart.

"Why?" he croaked. "You've had chances to tell me. Why didn't you?"

"Would you have gotten in the car if you knew it was your mother's?"

No. Not a chance in hell. Ruben had begged his father not to sell the car. After several months of his turning down offers, it was a slap in the face to come home and find the garage door open, the inside hollow where it had once held his mother's pride and joy.

"Ruben. It's just a car. *You* are her legacy. I don't regret selling. And look at what the Blumes did to it," he said, waving his arm around. "We couldn't have done it justice. *This* is what your mother dreamed it would become, and it *has.* Don't you see?"

He shook his head dumbly.

"She's with us right now, boy. I can feel her," he said with grit, placing a fist over his heart. Ruben looked up to find tears streaking down his father's cheeks.

How do I argue with that?

By the time Vinny finished her long goodbyes and got in, Abe was his jovial self again, and Ruben was propped up in the back with nothing but time to think over a confounding pile of clues. Factoring in time changes and breaks, it was still their shortest day, and they were pulling into Oceanside by three in the afternoon.

In Joy Holt's Camaro.

Lavender's Joy.

Was his mother part of that equation, or was it a coincidence? There was only one way to find out. Ruben had a strong feeling he'd only get one crack at Vinny's vault of horrors. He needed to be prepared.

And he needed to catch her off guard.

Vinny pulled up into Ruben's driveway but didn't shut off the engine. Once out, Ruben unlocked the front door while she opened her trunk for their luggage. He barely had his father inside and the door closed before she'd reversed back across the street to her own sanctuary.

"Welcome home, Dad. I've got something to show you," he said nervously. For now, Ruben had to put Vinny out of his mind.

Abe grunted suspiciously. "You haul me out here to get my money to pay for this house?" He was kidding. Mostly. Ruben hoped so, at least. *His monthly assistance wouldn't cover the mortgage.*

"I know you think I'm taking advantage of your heart attack, but I've been wanting you close for a long time." He held out his arm, "It's this way."

"What is?"

"Your personal space."

"You can't buy me off with a makeshift bedroom, son. I belong in…" Abe's tongue froze the same time his feet did, taking in the space Ruben had spent his summer building for him with help from Slow and his contractor friend.

"You belong *here,* Dad. I don't want to take away your independence; I want to give it back. This is all yours. If you lock me out, I'm out," he said. "Was kinda hoping you'd like it enough to stick around, but I can't force you."

Ruben watched nervously as his father looked around the decently sized studio apartment. It had a new bed—something he knew his father had never owned—off to one side behind a privacy wall. On the visible side of the wall was a TV with a sitting area. Off to the right was a small kitchen with a two burner stove and camper sized fridge. The table was arranged next to the window, where he could enjoy the yard outside. Behind the kitchen was a bathroom and closet.

It wasn't a lot, but it was enough for a man who had fit everything he deemed worth saving into a medium sized suitcase. Ruben had done his best to keep it simple, knowing it would hurt his father's feelings to go top of the line on anything.

"Everything can be exchanged if you hate it. I was going for comfort and practicality…" he trailed off awkwardly. Abe showed nothing, and it made Ruben nervous.

Finally, he said, "You've been busy." Abe nodded before adding, "I suppose it will do."

Internally, Ruben collapsed with relief. Externally, he said, "Nah, just a little weekend fun. I'll let you get settled in, Dad."

Chapter Thirty-One

VINNY

She collapsed onto her bed with relief. Vinny had survived five days in a car with Ruben Holt. Her baby needed an oil change and fluid check, but she'd made it. *Hell of a way to end more than three months away from home.*

Nashville had been fun, but it hadn't given her what she had needed most. Vinny was still as blocked as she'd been when she left California. All she'd managed to accomplish out there was night after night of performing when what she'd craved most was to play on the beach with Maya and Brendon. Every video call with the kids had been agony.

She had missed her family here in Oceanside.

After a quarter hour, Vinny got up and took a quick shower before heading back down to her garage. Joy came first—her baby. She didn't know the full story behind her car, other than the previous owner's name was Joy. She'd died a few years before her dad found the car and bought it from the woman's husband.

Vinny liked to think it was fate. Her middle name was Joy. Now her car was named Joy too, like it's previous owner. She always thought about her when she was working on her baby. *What was she like? I bet she had a big personality. Did she have kids? Why didn't any of them want to keep her car and fix it up themselves?*

The answers weren't so important as the process of remembering the former owner. She liked to think it came to her for a reason, and that was okay with Vinny. Maybe someday she'd come full circle with her automotive benefactor and have the opportunity to show them they'd made the right choice when they sold the car to her father.

This time, as she did her checks and noted what needed tended to, Abner came to mind. He'd enjoyed the entirety of their five-day drive. The way he'd run his hands over the interior absentmindedly, like he was trying to memorize every detail, told her so. He'd caught the subtle lettering of the car's name right away too. He might be getting up there in years, but Abner was intelligent as he was kind.

She was almost through draining the oil pan when she heard the side door open and close. Footsteps drew close before stopping right beside her. "Almost set," she called out. "Give me a few minutes to get the new filter and pan back on."

Vinny was so focused on the job; it caught her off guard when she rolled out from underneath on her mechanics board and found someone other than Eric or Carys standing in her haven. She scowled up at him. "Why are you here, Ben?"

"I came to talk to you."

"No."

But he didn't *move.* He just stood there like he had her number and wasn't going to stop calling until she answered. It was unnerving as hell. She popped up off the floor, determined to show him he couldn't rattle her. Vinny grabbed the fresh oil for her car and went back to work, ignoring him.

Ruben didn't leave.

She checked the rest of her fluids before moving on to tire pressure. Her air filter looked good. Windshield wiper fluid and water, both good.

Still, Ruben stood in the same place watching her.

"Shouldn't you get off your foot?" she snapped.

"Why, Lavender. I didn't know you cared. I'll just go sit on the stairs until you're ready to talk," he said, carefully gimping over and plopping down. He settled back on his elbows and nodded at her with a kindly, "Please. Finish. I'm in no rush."

"Where are your crutches?" she demanded, placing her hands on her hips.

"Propped outside the door."

Vinny continued to scowl at him. *Why is he really here?*

"You go on," he said. "I'll just think out loud while you finish up, and when you're ready to join the conversation you can tell me how close I came in accuracy."

"Accuracy in *what?"*

"The real reason you *think* you hate me."

"I do hate you! Every fiber of my being *loathes* you!" she shouted, completely losing her cool. "You're an *idiot,* Ben! How could you possibly think I like anything about you after all you've done?"

His brows went up, his right hand landing on his chest as he innocently proclaimed, "Me? I haven't had the opportunity—"

"Stop lying!" she shrieked. Her insides tossed and rolled painfully. Wrong. Everything was wrong. *Make him leave; how do I make him leave?* "All you do is hurt the people around you, Ben. God, it's all I know for sure about you! You drug Eric off to Mexico and *bailed on him."*

"I think that turned out rather well for him. He might not

have met Carys otherwise," he said nonchalantly, leaning back on the stairs again.

Vinny ignored his interruption. "I probably could have gotten over it, but it wasn't exactly a one off. You raced back here to that piece of trash and married her, even when her jealous power trip cost you your best friend—your *family*—standing beside you. Do you have any idea how much it hurt Eric to miss your wedding?" she fumed. "All you have done is bring discord into their lives."

"I can see why you feel that way," he said calmly. It only made her angrier.

"You bailed out on trips and cookouts and all the precious things that make life worthwhile to make *her* happy, even knowing she was doing it on purpose in order to drive a wedge between you and the family."

"Yes," he said simply.

"You don't get it," she cried, a sob breaking free. "That's *my family.* And you hurt them, over and over. Every time, they forgave you and moved on. Well, I'm not going to forgive for you! You don't deserve it."

This time, he only nodded. Vinny screamed—threw her head back and let everything she'd been holding inside come out in a sustained wail made more impressive by the strength she'd built in her core from a lifetime of singing.

"You inconsiderate *asshole.* You came in when it was dark. I couldn't see you. You were in the shadows by the door, across the whole fucking living room, *and I couldn't see you.* A fucking gang member tried taking out my best friend, I was there watching her child while she fought for her life in the hospital, *and you just let yourself into her house.* Do you have any idea how terrifying that was? All I could think was 'don't let them get Maya too,' because if Brendon and Carys didn't make it, all I would have left of my best friend was her little girl."

"You were right. I should have knocked."

"You accused me of being racist!" she snarled back.

"You took the safety off after I told you it was me."

"Because I couldn't see you, Ben! I'm near sighted. It was dark. Maya was asleep upstairs. You were too far away for me to see you, and you were standing at the base of the staircase that goes right up to her room!"

"I'm sorry, Lavender." His voice was barely a whisper, but it slammed into Vinny's chest with the power of a locomotive.

"No! You don't get to be *sorry. Sorry* doesn't fix it!" Vinny began whirling about in the tight space between the back of her car and the workbench at the back wall, balling and releasing her fists. *Don't let him see you shaking. That's what he wants. He wants you weak.* She wrapped her anger around her like a security blanket and turned back to him with renewed energy.

Ruben was standing now, taking careful steps in her direction. *Fuck.* With the bay doors closed, there wasn't anywhere she could go from where she was pacing. "I was angry you aimed at me. I was furious when you took the safety off. I knew you would do it and I lashed out. I made it about something else because I was ashamed of myself, Lavender. From the moment I pulled my key out that day, I did everything wrong."

"Stop moving!" Her anger was shifting to panic. She didn't trust what he'd do when he got within reach, and Vinny didn't want to find out. "I said stop!"

He did, leaning slightly onto her workbench to take the weight off his broken foot. "It's okay if you hate me, Lavender. I hate myself. I chased Carla for a long damn time. She wasn't ever going to change, never be a good person. I hate the things I let her do. I hate the things I let her manipulate *me* into doing. But do you know what I hate most, Lavender?"

Ruben stepped in close, and Vinny realized she literally had her back to a wall, in the rear corner of her garage. He had surprised her with his confession, and now she was trapped. Panic set her heart skittering arrhythmically.

"I don't care," she said weakly. He continued like she hadn't spoken at all, same as she'd done to him when she released her anger minutes ago.

"More than anything else, I *hate* I left Mexico when she asked me to—because I know if I had stayed I would have met you. And if I had met you, I can't help believing I wouldn't have run to her again." Ruben's hand stroked her cheek gently, his gaze taking in her face as he continued speaking in the same gentle whisper. "I would never hurt you, but you didn't know that. It was my fault. All the things you said, they were true. I stopped being the friend Slow deserves the moment I pulled Carla back into my life. She's gone now, and I know you don't want my gratitude for the part you played in all that, but you have it anyway."

"You need to go," she said hoarsely. "You'll never convince me. Just go." His hand slowly dropped from her cheek, and she hated the way she missed the warmth of his touch against her skin.

"I'm sorry, Lavender. I'm going to keep telling you, keep *showing* you, until you believe me."

"I don't need another Jenny Moore!" she yelled. "Get out, Ben!"

He took a step back, a small smile forming on his face. "So that's who hurt you."

For a man with a broken foot, he disappeared remarkably

fast. Or maybe it was Vinny, frozen inside the memory that cursed name had pulled her into. Either way, she was sitting on the floor in the corner where he'd left her when Carys found her later.

"Come on," she said. "Let's get you upstairs. I think you need a margarita."

"I don't think Tequila can fix me," Vinny said through her tears.

"Of course not, but it's a place to start." Carys insisted.

"What's wrong with me, Carys? When did I get so mean and jaded?"

Carys cocked her head sideways, a crooked grin Vinny had known her whole life taking form, and an eyebrow popping up with it. It was Carys's *are you kidding me right now* face. "I don't think you are either of those things," she said. "We are all formed from our experiences, and yours haven't all been as flowery as your hippy name would suggest."

Vinny let out a snort of laughter. "My parents weren't even hippies."

"Makes it funnier," Carys countered. "Come on. I think we need to have a long talk as soon as the blender is switched off."

Chapter Thirty-Two

RUBEN

"Who is Jenny Moore?" he asked, stumbling through the back door with his crutches in his hurry to enter the Black-wood's house. "Oh, and uh… We're back."

Eric laughed from his seat at the kitchen table.

"Not sure why you're laughing, I won the bet!" Carys chirped. "Have a seat, Ruben. Sounds like you finally cracked that nut you've been struggling with."

"Yeah, apparently all I had to do was be silent and let her boil over. Guess ole Teddy was on to something good when he said speak softly and carry a big stick—or in my case, crutches." He grinned, but it was halfhearted at best.

"That's not…it's political in nature…forget it. This is Carys's territory," Eric digressed.

Watching Vinny fall to pieces had taken a lot out of Ruben. The whole time, he had wanted to go to her, pull her close, and explain how he wasn't who she thought he was. But the more she spoke, the more he realized…yeah, he was exactly the person she'd been describing. And while Eric and Carys had forgiven him for his stupidity without so much as an afterthought, Ruben could see now how protecting Carys was second nature to Vinny. Now that she was married to Eric and they had the kids, they were included by default.

Vinny quietly tallied every perceived abuse—intentional or not—in her quest to keep her family safe. Understanding that trait went a long way in clarifying her aggression toward him. Ruben had been on thin ice *before* he scared the shit out of her their first meeting, because of his careless—sometimes reckless—behavior toward their shared family.

He just hadn't known it.

"Jenny Moore," Carys mused, sitting down beside Eric, across from Ruben. "Haven't heard that name in a *loooong* time."

"What did she do to Lavender?" Ruben asked quietly.

"It isn't what she did, it's what she *didn't do,*" Carys corrected. "Do you know anything about Vin's mom?"

Ruben shook his head. "I don't know much of anything about the people in her life outside of the ones under this roof. She hasn't exactly been forthcoming, even when I've tried to engage with her."

"You seriously spent *five days* in a car with her and learned *nothing?"* Slow said with surprise.

"Nothing notable," he said. *Accept that she's driving around in* my *mother's car.*

Carys rolled her eyes. "Typical. Look, she got the way she is honestly. Jenny Moore was the first, but she wasn't the last."

"Okay."

"When we were little, our moms were friends. Not best buds, but friendly enough that Vinny spent a lot of time at our house. It never occurred to me how different she looked until we started school, and by then it didn't matter. She was my sister in my heart.

"Albinism can make things hard on kids, not only because

they look different, but because they tend to be clumsy. It's the bad vision. She was smart, but most kids saw a girl with massively thick glasses who still stumbled around all day. They drew childish conclusions and teased her accordingly.

"Vinny took it in stride, for the most part. Eventually she grew out of the worst of it, although she'll always need her vision corrected with contacts or glasses. Things got better for her at school over time. But *before* it did, we met Jenny. Jennifer Moore was a sweet girl the same age as us. She moved into the district at the end of fourth grade, and by the time we started fifth grade, it was like she'd been with us always. The three of us just clicked, in the way only inno-cence can create lasting friendship.

"Then Vinny's mother was diagnosed with cancer. It came out of nowhere. Three months later, she was gone. It was a really aggressive tumor, and she didn't even try fighting it. It was more important to her to savor her last days with Vin and Q than to be in agony from the treatments.

"The week after she was laid to rest, Vinny went back to school. Two days after that, I came down with strep. So there she was, all alone except for Jenny Moore. Jenny wasn't prepared for what the school bully had to say that day, and instead of coming to Vinny's defense, she just stood there and bore witness."

"What did she say to her?" Ruben asked.

"I don't know. Vinny and Jenny both refused to repeat it, but whatever it was had to have been pretty nasty, because she was still suspended for it when I returned to school three days later," Carys said. "The point is, without me there to take charge, Jenny didn't take Vinny's side. Worse, she let the bully convince her to walk away, leaving Vinny completely alone on the playground."

Fuck. Ten years old, alone against the meanest kid at

school, weeks after losing her mother. No wonder she's so angry. A heavy weight settled in the pit of Ruben's stomach. He needed to understand what it all had to do with *him.*

"Why didn't she get angry at the bully? Why take it out on her friend?" he asked.

"Because bullies bully. That's what they do. It wasn't the first time that particular kid got nasty with another kid, much less with Vinny. But Jenny failed to do the one thing Vinny needed. She didn't step in," Carys explained. "She *let* the bully go on and on, until Vinny was a blubbering mess. Then she left Vinny all alone, persuaded by the bully to walk away. And I only know how badly it ended because I overheard her dad telling my mother a few days later."

"That's awful," Slow said beside her, taking Carys's hand over the table.

"It was," she said, giving her husband a sad smile before turning back to Ruben. "When I got back, Jenny tried to hang out with us again. Vinny stared her down so coldly even the California sun couldn't cut the chill on the blacktop. Jenny never tried again, and afterward it was just the two of us, more or less. She still doesn't let a lot of people in, much less closely."

It wasn't the obvious problem; it was the person who had the ability to do something about it and failed to take the responsibility. Ruben closed his eyes, shaking his head. "I fucked up so badly with her, Carys. What do I do?" When he opened his eyes again, she was smiling.

"Don't be like Jenny. Own it. Don't give up on her, even when she's hellbent on pushing you away." Carys laughed softly. "I think it's a margarita night," she said, standing. She kissed Slow goodbye before turning toward the backdoor. "Night, Ruben."

"Night," he called back before the door closed behind her.

"I knew you liked her," Slow said smugly.

"Yeah, nobody likes a guy who gloats, man." Ruben shook his head and smiled softly across the table at his friend. Stolen moments over the summer, glimpses of Vinny while they pointedly ignored each other all summer before she left for Nashville flickered though his mind. He'd always been curious about her, from the first time Slow had described Vinny to him. He wouldn't have admitted it to anyone much less himself before he sent Carla packing. It felt dishonest for a man in a relationship, even if he meant it in a friendly way at the time. But now... "It might be worse than that. I think I caught feelings."

Eric rolled his eyes. "Obviously. You never listen to me when women are involved. I could have saved you a lot of trouble," he continued at Ruben's expense—teasing, as only brothers can do.

"Yeah, yeah."

———

"CAN I ASK YOU SOMETHING?" Ruben said as his dad came into the kitchen where he was making a heart healthy breakfast for them.

Abe eyed him wearily. "I suppose."

"When you met mom, how did you know?"

His dad laughed as he took a seat at the dining room table. "How did I know what?"

"You know *what,*" he said, rolling his eyes over the stove where he couldn't get caught. "You two were inseparable. You didn't even fight and—"

He was cut off by the sound of Abe's laughter. "You sure remember it differently than I do," he hooted. "We fought plenty. Usually about *you,* and the bills. And there were plenty of nights I stuck my foot in it and voluntarily slept on the couch where my breathing wouldn't annoy her into remembering the *death do us part* section of our wedding vows."

Ruben stared at his father slack jawed. "I don't remember any of that!"

"Of course you don't. We put aside our disagreements in front of you like adults *should*. You can't raise a child in a divided household, son. That's how kids figure out they can pit their parents against each other. It was bad enough you knew your mother would likely splurge if you asked her first. Little boys don't have any concept of having the power on *or* having a new baseball mitt." He let out a nostalgic sigh. "Seemed like we were constantly falling into arears because you had asked for something and instead of telling you no or talking it over with me first, she decided we could afford to delay a payment."

"Huh," Ruben said. "Guess I really have no idea."

"I blame myself," Abe said quietly. "I didn't set a good example in that way. All you ever saw was a Yes Man. That ain't good for a child. Instead of hiding our struggles and disagreements from you, I should have *taught* you the importance of setting boundaries and sticking to them. Maybe then…"

"Dad," Ruben said gently as he placed his father's plate in front of him and took his place opposite at the table with his own meal. "You were a great father. I couldn't have asked for better."

"No, son. I had faults enough. I kept telling myself the good stuff would outshine my failings. That you'd remember how strong your mother and I were as a team and emulate our strengths. I never meant to teach you how to be a door mat," he said quietly.

Well, shit.

"What happened with Carla wasn't your fault," he said cautiously. "It was on me. None of my friends got mean about it, but it was clear they didn't like her. Hell, the guys and I celebrated twice as hard when we'd split than when we got back together."

"All the same," he said. "I played my part."

"I think I loved her spirit. Mom had a lot of spirit," Ruben said with a big grin. "I'll never forget when she got her car. I watched her face in the rearview mirror the whole time we were cruising around. She was positively glowing."

"She was," Abe agreed. "Which was a good thing, since the headlights didn't work and it was getting dark out. It's a miracle she didn't get pulled over on the way home, but she still stretched out that drive as long as she could."

They both chuckled over the memory. The next day she'd been in so much pain, she couldn't hide it from Ruben. Same with every day after, and he watched her suffer through mostly bad days right up until she died. But that first and only ride in her car…

"Lavender," he murmured.

"I'm on *her* side of whatever you did wrong," Abe huffed with a laugh.

Ruben didn't hide his eyes as they rolled this time. "Of course you are. Back to my question, how did you know?"

"I didn't. Joy was lovely and smart—and thought I was dirt under her feet when we met," he mused. "Took me a good year to convince her otherwise. I was working at the bowling alley, and she had some cocky idiot she was dating at the time. He came in with another girl, and they were using each other as life support. I called up your mother and told her she should come on down to the lanes."

"Oh, shit! That was brave."

"*Very.* Joy came in right as the idiot locked lips with the other girl, didn't even see her coming. Made the slap she delivered soon as their faces parted all the more gratifying. She caught him off guard and he fell back on his ass," Abe said, laughing.

"Then what?"

"She shouted at him. Made one hell of a show. As she was passing the counter on her way out, she looked at me with new eyes. For the first time, I saw respect. And then she said, 'give me a week to stop being mad before you call me up again, Abner.' And the rest, as they say, is history."

"How come I've never heard this story before?"

"You never asked. After she died, you would get so angry when I brought her up." Abe shrugged. "I stopped trying. Didn't stop arguing with her in my head at night about what the hell to do with you though."

"Was I really that bad?"

"You weren't bad at all, just sad. For a while, I thought I'd have to bury you next to her, your heart was so broken."

"Sorry, Dad."

"Don't be sorry, Ruben. Move on. Live your life the way *she* did. That's how you honor your mother."

Ruben thought about his father's words as they shoveled down breakfast. He cleared their plates at the end and came back to sit with his second cup of coffee. "Carla," he began. Abe growled. Ruben laughed lightly. "I know, just listen."

"Go on," Abe said.

"She didn't just steamroll *me.* I made a lot of excuses for her along the way. I played a part in the chaos she infused into the lives of the people that matter most to me." Ruben thought back to what Carys had told him last night before wandering off to presumably scrape Vinny off the garage floor where Ruben had left her. "She's been through a lot, starting with losing her mom."

"Cancer," Abe piped up. Ruben looked at him with surprise. "Why do you think I sold the car to Quincy Blume to begin with, boy?" he asked with amusement. "The poor girl had been through hell already, at such a young age. She was sleeping when her father pulled up. Out cold the whole time. But even asleep, I could tell she had some spirit. Blume had the means to restore the car, and he was going to teach his daughter as he did it."

"A lot of people came by with the means," Ruben pointed out. "Why were they different?"

"For months, collectors came and drooled over it," Abe said with disgust. "But the Blumes were going to *love* her. She wasn't a trophy; she was one of the family. Your mother would have approved of her car going with them, and I have zero regrets."

Ruben silently agreed with his father. He couldn't see it through his grief back then, but his father was right.

His mother would have adored Vinny.

"Ah. Turns out Lavender doesn't take kindly to anyone she perceives as an enabler, including willful idiots like me. I did a lot of stupid shit—tolerated and excused a lot too— because Carla was my girl, and then my wife."

"And she's holding it against you because you should have known better," Abe finished for him.

"Yeah."

"Does she have a cheating boyfriend you can humiliate down at the bowling alley?" Abe asked humorously.

Chapter Thirty-Three

VINNY

"Ugnhpf," Vinny moaned—or something along those lines. It wasn't a real word. "José, you are *no* friend of mine."

Freaking Carys and her double whammy margaritas. How much did I drink last night?

"That's not what you sang while I was making them," Carys whisper yelled groggily from somewhere close by. It was followed by a snort and a whimper. *"Owe."*

"Sssservvvves you right," Vinny tried to say smugly, but mostly she sounded like she was still drunk. *Shit, am I still drunk? That's a first. Never woken up the next day still blitzed before.*

She finally braved cracking an eyelid. They were in Vinny's living room, the couch made up as a bed. The coffee table was still covered in the remnants of what was apparently too much fun so close to thirty. She opened her second eye and was able to focus on the bottle of pain killers and two glasses of water sitting next to the empty margarita glasses.

Thank you, Eric.

Cautiously, Vinny pushed up on one elbow. The room

didn't exactly spin, but it was a bit fish bowl-*y*. It was going to be a slow start, but anything was better than puking.

"Oh, god. Eric. I love him so much," Carys said from beside her. She was reaching for the water and meds.

"Awe," Vinny said as she focused on the island they'd used as a mixology station last night. "He cleaned the kitchen."

Her bladder protested, and she finally got to her feet. As she wobbled over to the half bath, she saw some electrolyte packets on the counter next to a note informing her he'd put some food in her fridge. *Ooof. Pee first, read second.*

By the time she came out of the bathroom, Carys was on her way across the room. "Oh! Good. I thought I'd have to stumble to the back to pee."

Vinny quirked a smile as her bestie did the same *I waited too long and now I'm about to pee my pants* dance she'd done since they were tots. It was still adorable, watching Carys shift her weight while attempting to simultaneously cross her legs and walk. "All yours," she said, getting out of the way.

By the time Carys was out, Vinny had a couple slices of dry toast ready for each of them and the electrolytes Eric had left mixed up. If she had to guess, he'd converted her couch down and tucked them in too. They sat quietly at the eat in bar, slowly sipping and chewing until a few neurons kicked back on, signaling a system reboot—memories from last night flooding back like a tsunami making landfall.

Vinny abruptly stopped mid chew, nearly choking on her toast with the following gasp. "Oh, fuck." She had yelled at Ruben. Not just *yelled* at him, she'd allowed herself to get worked up enough to break down in front of him. "I told him stuff," she said dumbly, turning her head toward Carys.

She was smiling. Vinny scowled. "You sure did," Carys

said softly out of necessity—she was still looking all kinds of smug despite her matching boozy complexion.

"How did you know I was messed up last night?" she asked warily.

"Ruben came inside—through the *back* door—finally asking the right questions."

"What did you tell him?"

"Not to be like Jenny."

"Carys. He's never going to leave me alone now. Why would you do that?" she whined.

Carys's face softened. It wasn't quite pity, but Vinny still didn't like it. "Vin. I know you don't want to hear it, but he's a good guy. How is he supposed to show you he's changed if you won't give him the time of day?"

Vinny began to shake her head but thought better of it when her toast threatened to come back up. "People like that don't change, Carys."

"Anyone can change if they have the motivation to. I thought you were the type to welcome change too, but it must have been wishful thinking," she said casually.

"I *live* in a world full of change," Vinny said, an edge to her voice. "Here now, in Oceanside with you, is the least change I've had my whole life. Not just my adult life, my *entire* life. You know that, Carys."

"Moving about all the time, going on tour. That's the epitome of living the dream, Vin. You're a musician. Every day a new challenge, a new venue. Dry running to figure out how to use the acoustics and ambiance of each location to best advantage before doing it all over again the next day. A rotating array of other musicians. That's an exciting *challenge,* but it isn't *change."*

"He…he…" *Damn it. He's an idiot, but he's not a bad person.* "I'm not a fan of beating my head against a brick wall and expecting the headache to lessen. There are too many strikes against him, Carys. Too much damage already done. I can't… I'm not letting Ben under my skin."

"Hmmm. Sounds to me like *Ben* is already under your skin," she said, before hopping down off her stool and letting herself out.

That's one way to get the last word.

————

VINNY KILLED THE LIVE FEED. She was exhausted, but happy. Nearly four months away from her studio had proved too long, and she'd been in it nearly every minute she wasn't playing with the kids since she returned two days ago.

"That was fucking *killer,"* Tripp said. "What's next?"

"I don't know."

"You always know," he teased.

"Not this time. I've got another four weeks of content, tops. Then…I don't know," she said with a shrug.

"That's not like you at all, Vin. What's going on?"

"Nothing for you to worry about. It'll come to me when it does, like always. I just drove across the entire country in my car. I have a right to rest up, Tripp."

"I'm worried about you," he pressed. "You've skimped by, but there was always *something* in the wings. Do you want to set up some stuff together? Get the juices flowing? Maybe call Silla and Jae?"

"I don't think so," she said softly. Whatever they did together would end up down at Groove's, and she wasn't in the mood to ignore his puppy eyes. Tyler had still been pining when she left, and she still wasn't interested in anything serious with him. Vinny hoped if she gave him space, they could resume their friendship with time.

"I'm here if you need me," Tripp said as he gathered up his equipment.

"Thanks. I'll walk you out."

Vinny listened quietly while Tripp filled her in on the local music scene drama while she'd been away with amusement. He'd at least stopped pining over Silla and Jae and was now open to finding someone serious—or at least that's what he said. Vinny had never known Tripp to "commit" for more than six months. She suspected that was partly why their mutual friends had both shot him down soundly.

Well, that and they were *cousins*. He should have picked one and stuck with it.

After a longer than usual goodbye hug, Tripp drove off. She'd missed his easy banter and how effortlessly they tuned into one another when they played. He was a good guy to know, and if he ever did pick a partner, Vinny thought he'd be the type to worship the ground they walked on. The thought made her smile widen as Tripp's car disappeared around a corner.

And then her easy peace came crashing down around her.

"Hey, baby."

Vinny's whole body tensed as she turned to face the one person she'd hoped never to talk to again. "Jake. What are you doing here?"

Despite her closed off demeanor, he smiled. *Idiot.* "I missed you, baby. Thought I'd come down and see you."

She took a moment to scan the street around them. There were no cars out of the usual. He'd either gotten a ride from a friend or used a ride share to get here from LA. He could have moved, but she doubted it. Jake loved LA and rarely left town unless he was touring. No car meant he expected to stay.

Not a chance in hell.

"I'm not your baby," she said quietly. "And given I haven't seen or heard from you in over a year now, it was rather ballsy of you to show up uninvited. What do you want, Jake?"

"Just to visit," he said too quickly. "Catch up."

"Okay. Hello, Jake. *Goodbye, Jake.*"

"See, this is what your problem is, Vin. You think you're funny," he said, his voice dropping low as he slowly stalked closer. *Like a predator.* "But I'm not laughing. I sure as hell wasn't laughing when I got *evicted* last year after my girlfriend bailed on me and stopped paying our bills."

"Sounds like a *you* problem to me." Her whole body was strung tight, and she regretted not having her piece strapped on. Jake was already too close. "I came home to find my *committed* boyfriend having a hell of a naked party on *our* bed. I was there a good twenty minutes—maybe longer—grabbing my essentials while you were fucking who knows how many people, completely oblivious. You made your choice, and I made mine. And now, you need to leave."

"I don't think so, baby. You're going to give me another chance." He stopped toe to toe with her. Vinny was already squared up, refusing to show the fear inside. He leaned in, rounding down enough to say into her ear, "You owe me you selfish bitch."

"Lavender," came a voice from close by. She'd been so busy staring Jake down, she hadn't heard or seen Ruben approaching. "You ready to leave? Or I can come back if you prefer."

"Hey, Ben," she said, keeping her eyes locked on Jake. With a syrupy sweet smile she said, "This is Jake. He's my Carla."

Ruben came to a stop behind her. He was a good two

inches taller than Jake, forcing him to lean away from Vinny in order to assess the new player on the field. "That so?"

"Jake," he said, stiffly introducing himself. He awkwardly extended a hand around Vinny toward Ruben. "Ben is it?"

"Nah, man. Lavender calls me Ben. *Only Lavender.*" She could hear the threat through the smile. "You can call me Mister Holt."

Vinny watched Jake wince as Ruben won the hand crushing competition—er, handshake—with a sense of unfettered glee. *Impudent jackass.*

"I was just talking to Vin about our future," he said as he attempted to shake out his crushed hand without drawing attention.

"The lady made herself pretty clear from where I was sitting on my front porch. Can't imagine it was any less clear from where you were standing directly in front of her. What do you say, Lavender?"

"If you have any self-preservation at all, Jake, walk away. You aren't welcome here," she said softly.

"This isn't over, Vinny," Jake snarled at her before shifting his gaze over her head. "Not by a long shot."

Jake spun on his heels and stomped off, comically mimicking Maya at bedtime. He walked a few blocks up before turning the corner, glaring back at Vinny and Ruben before disappearing down the block. The moment he was gone, Vinny's body relaxed.

"The nerve of him," she spat out.

"Your Carla, huh? How far should I read into that?"

"I came back from my last tour to find the same thing you came home to from yours—but with more people in my bed. So, pretty damn far, Ben. He's a fucking prick." Her words flowed easily, her distain evident.

Ruben stepped around her and turned, leaving a few

respectful feet between them as he did so. "Will you be okay now? Do you need anything?"

She scowled up at him. "I'm not some southern bell in need of rescuing, Ben," she snapped.

He looked at her with mild humor. She felt her scowl deepen, and he quickly neutralized his expression. "No, you aren't. But all the same, I'd like to know. Are you okay, Lavender?"

Vinny's frustration came out as a feral growl before she managed to string words together. "Thanks for the solid. We're still not friends…and I still hate you."

At that, Ruben cracked a shit eating grin. "If you say so, Lavender. Glad you're okay."

She turned and stomped off, back up her driveway and away from Ruben, muttering along the way about pigheaded men and false chivalry and peeing on hydrants to mark their territory like wild dogs. She didn't care if he heard her one bit.

"Hold up!" he called, and she heard the shuffle of him gimping after her in his boot. Vinny briefly wondered where his crutches were, but then she remembered that she didn't care.

"What do you want *now?"* she snapped.

"I need to give you something," he said, shoving a hand into the front pocket of his jeans. He yanked out a key and extended his hand. Vinny stared at him without making a move to take it. "It's a key to the house. For Dad."

"If it's for Abner, shouldn't you give it to *him?"*

"It's so you can see him whenever. Mostly it's so you can get in if there is an emergency. He doesn't know Carys, and Slow is gone the same hours as me," he said. "He insisted I give you a house key. He also asked you join him for lunch sometime this week."

She narrowed her eyes at him for a moment longer before swiping the key from his outstretched hand. "For Abner, I'll take your stupid key. You done?"

"Yes'sum," he drawled.

"Good. Go away."

Ruben laughed heartily as he turned to walk back to his own property. "See you around, Lavender."

"I still hate you!" she shouted after him.

"So you say."

I preferred yesterday's hangover to this.

Chapter Thirty-Four

RUBEN

"You look awfully smug, son," Abner said with inquisitive amusement as Ruben gimped across the kitchen as smoothly as possible. The boot on his broken foot was killing his swagger. He tried anyway.

"Saw Lavender," he said.

"I'm guessing by the dopey smile on your face it went well?"

"Nope. She was saying goodbye to one of her collaborators when an ex rolled up on her." Ruben barked out a sharp laugh, mirth pulling his face into a broader smile than he'd had in months. Maybe longer. "What a piece of shit."

Ruben told his father about what he'd seen, sitting on the front porch. He hadn't planned to jump in like he had, but he wouldn't have done it any different if he could either. Something about the way Jake strolled up behind her, clearly expecting something out of her, had put him on edge immediately. Neither had noticed him until he approached, which had made it easier on him—it's hard to be formidable hobbling on a broken foot.

"Sounds serious," Abner said contemplatively. "Not something to smile over."

"That's not why I'm smiling." Ruben sat down at the table across from his dad. "She relaxed into me, Dad. And while *she* didn't notice, he sure as hell did."

"Is he going to be a problem, you think?"

"Probably. She introduced him as *her Carla.*" Abner let out a huff. "That was my thought. I gave her the key before she chased me off though, like you asked."

"What did she say?"

"Said she was only taking it for you."

"And you have hope from this altercation?" Abe didn't bother hiding his doubt.

"Yup. She told me she hated me. *Twice.*"

"No wonder you have such a bad track record with women, son. You can't read them at all."

Ruben threw his head back and laughed. "You'd think. But I've learned something about Lavender. If she doesn't think someone is worth it, she ignores them. Maybe she's vaguely polite. When she's afraid she turns nasty."

"You don't want her to fear you, boy."

"It's not me she's truly afraid of, it's the situation. She's afraid of what will happen if she *doesn't* hate me. She can't control *me,* so she's doing the next best thing. She's controlling her reaction to me and trying to dissuade me from changing her mind about the kind of person I am."

"Sounds complicated. Is she coming to lunch?"

"Text her and find out," Ruben teased. Abner scowled. "Go on. I put her number in your new phone, Dad."

"This isn't a phone," he said disdainfully. "It's a torture devise."

"It's how all the young guys talk to chicks these days.

Once you get the hang of it, we should build you a few dating profiles. Get you back in the game."

"They are *ladies,* son. Not poultry."

———

"WHY ARE YOU SCOWLING?" Slow asked as Ruben stepped into the doorway of his office.

"Everybody wants to run their mouths around here, man."

"Same old, same old."

"About *me.*"

Slow gave him a sardonic look. "And that's different how?"

"This year has been *shit,* man. Coming home to an episode of *Housewives Gone Wild* was bad enough. Since then, I've had the divorce, got my foot broken…and word is going around I have a new woman."

"Well…"

"Are you kidding me, man? It's not like that!"

"Not officially." Eric grinned. Ruben glared at his best friend. "What are you doing over here, anyway? I was packing up to come get you."

"I got the job," he said, hooking his thumb at the closed office door behind him. "My predecessor wanted to have a meet up, so I made one of the grunts drive me over here."

Ruben still wasn't driving much. Between grocery delivery and Slow chauffeuring him to work every day, there wasn't much point in aggravating his foot in rush hour traffic. Using his left foot to drive was too weird and unnatural.

"Congratulations," Slow said diplomatically.

"You knew, didn't you?" Ruben accused. Slow smiled. "Fucker." All the shit they shot to and from work, and he hadn't mentioned it once. "Can we go home now?"

"Sure thing, slugger."

"You put me through the paces when I'm officially here, and I'll be *Carys's* best friend from here on out."

"Vinny won't allow that. I'll take my chances."

It was the first time her name had come up between them in the past week, since Ruben had stumbled into the kitchen and asked who Jenny Moore was. It caught him off guard and he faltered a step. Slow noticed but didn't say anything until they were cruising out the gate on their way to the freeway.

"What's wrong?" he finally asked.

"I'm not used to hearing her name at work, I guess."

"Bullshit. I know she's been over to see Abe every day since you gave her a key. What's going on?"

"Slow…" He was tired of thinking about this exact thing.

"Got a full tank, Ruben. I can take the long way home," Slow said with humor.

"I don't know, man. We go to work, and when I get home, I can smell her in my house. My dad is pleased as fucking punch, telling me all about his day with *Ms. Blume,* and the things she's teaching him about having a healthy heart. She's got him walking every day too. But by the time I get home, she's long gone."

"She doesn't really hate you, Ruben."

"I know, but she thinks she does. I can't get through to her being the same simpering idiot I've been in the past, man. I have to step up. Especially after that piss ant showed up and tried pushing her around."

"What piss ant?" Slow demanded. "Greer?"

"No, her ex. Jake."

"Huh. Funny how she didn't tell *us* about that. What happened?"

"He got in her face. I backed her up. It'll be on the security footage, so long as she didn't delete it." Which he wouldn't put past her. "It happened on the sidewalk in front of your garage. I gave her the key afterward."

"Great. I'm putting Carys on this one."

"Pansy."

"Bet your ass. Think I want to replace you at the top of Vinny's shit list?"

"What else is happening? You mentioned Greer?" Ruben watched Slow's jaw work as he thought over his next words.

"I don't know. I have a lot of strong suspicions, but no evidence. I'll tell you when I know something substantial." His words came out slowly, weighed and precise like he was worried he'd be overheard, and the conversation would be used against him.

"You know I got your six," Ruben said firmly.

After a few minutes of contemplative silence, Slow asked, "How is Abe doing? I haven't seen him yet."

"He's good. Actually, it's the first time we've gotten along this well since—" *since Mom died.* "A long time, man. I didn't realize how much I missed it being easy between us."

"That's good to hear. Especially since we're having a cookout tomorrow and Carys expects you to bring him."

"Eh. I forgot about that."

"Carys didn't, and she told Maya. So don't go screwing it up," he teased.

"Funcle Ruben *never* screws it up," he said firmly.

When Slow came to a stop in Ruben's driveway some minutes later, he hopped out with thanks for the ride and waited for his buddy to back down his drive and directly into his own garage before going up the walkway. It was a stall tactic. He wasn't ready to smell her in his home or hear his father talk ceaselessly about what they had done together all day.

But as the Blackwood's garage door shuddered to a halt,

Ruben knew he was out of time. He made his way up the walk and let himself inside. It was silent. "Dad?"

When the only response was his own voice echoing down the hall, Ruben's heart squeezed with apprehension. He hobbled on his throbbing foot—he'd been lazy about elevating it today and was paying for it—beelining his way to Abe's door. He lifted his hand to knock but was startled into stillness by the sound of laughter.

Lavender's laughter.

"Abner! You're cheating!" She laughed again, pure and easy.

She was in his house. Happy. Ruben's new goal in life was to be the reason she was in his house, happy and laughing the way she was now, instead of his father. *On the bright side, at least they get along.*

He forced himself to knock softly before slowly opening the door far enough to poke his head around it. "Everything good, Dad?"

Abe's face was full of mischief and joy. "I'm just teaching Ms. Blume how to lose at Spades."

"By cheating!" she insisted. When she looked up at Ruben, her smile dulled considerably, and he detested the change.

"Probably," he said congenially. "Mom always said he was a cheat at cards."

"She said nothing of the sort," Abe insisted.

"A *gentleman* doesn't cheat, Abe!"

"Then you have to play Cribbage," Ruben said, grinning ear to ear. He was standing back far enough to watch them both easily so she wouldn't feel like he was staring at her— which he absolutely was doing right now. "Cribbage is a gentleman's game, so Dad says. But *Spades,* now that he'll fudge all day."

"What other games keep him from turning into a card shark?" she quipped.

"If I find another, I'll tell you," he promised.

It set Lavender pealing with laughter. Ruben's grin went wide, pulling into a full smile before he caught the same bug and began laughing with her. Meanwhile, his father sat in his chair, managing to look cool as a cucumber and indignant at the same time, before saying, "Bless your hearts."

"I'll see you lose at Spades one day, Abner," she pledged.

"Oh, that can be arranged," Ruben said, hobbling close enough to drop into the third chair. The pounding in his foot skyrocketed now his weight was off it. He ignored it. "Deal me in, Dad."

"You think you can beat me, boy?"

Ruben smirked. "Hell, yes. Now deal up. Or are you chicken?"

"Don't get cocky now," Abe warned coyly.

Ruben crowed like a rooster. *Obnoxiously.* Lavender laughed again; her head thrown back as she clapped her hands, her feet stomping out a gleeful beat beneath the table.

Oh, yeah. That's my new favorite sound.

"Good thing it's pizza night. I'll drop the order while Lavender here makes sure there are still fifty-two cards in the deck," he teased.

Chapter Thirty-Five

VINNY

Vinny sat nervously, trying to keep her leg from bouncing so hard the table wobbled. She failed. Luckily, Eddie wasn't one to keep her waiting. He'd been kind enough to drive up to Oceanside for a luncheon—the first time she'd missed lunch with Abner in weeks—and not to tell his shitty daughter where and with whom he'd be spending his time.

"Vinny," he said kindly when the hostess brought him to her. "I'm so glad you called, blossom."

"Couldn't stay away, Mister Vedder," she teased. She'd met the man most commonly known as "the admiral" while touring with the USO years ago. He happened to be a huge Eddie Vedder fan, and they had bonded over their equal appreciation for all things Pearl Jam. She didn't know his actual name, but after a night of air guitar and laughing, she began calling him Eddie. It stuck, and they had kept in touch over the years.

Eddie was the one who first encouraged Vinny to learn firearms and basic self-defense. He was also the one she'd gone to when Eric had asked what she thought about adding cameras around his property after a gang initiation had nearly taken Carys and Brendon from them for good. Eddie was good people.

Which was why she'd asked him here today. Also, why she was sweating like a sinner in church. Eddie was amazing, and Vinny still couldn't understand how Carla was his daughter. If she hadn't arrived home shortly after Eddie and Carla had pulled up across the street, Vinny probably would have thought the security cameras were completely fucked later on.

But no.

Her Eddie was the father of Cunty Carla.

Mind. Blown.

Even months after the fact.

They chatted over the menus, bantering casually as they decided what to order. When their server had come and gone, Eddie cleared his throat and began the dreaded conversation with a casual, "Go on, Vinny. Tell me what's got you so nervous. This isn't like you."

She blew out a heavy breath that transitioned into a painfully nervous little laugh. "Am I that obvious?"

"No, but we're good friends."

"And you worked in Naval Intelligence."

"That too," he grinned, before his features softened into gentle concern. "I can take it, blossom."

"I know *you* can. I'm the one who has waited months to tell you the truth," she said, pausing to sip her water. "I don't want to be the reason you are embarrassed."

"Let me worry about that."

"Okay," she began, pushing through her hesitation and desire to protect a friend at all costs. "You taught me a lot, Eddie. I wouldn't be so capable of protecting myself without your guidance and recommendations. I did most of what you suggested, short of taking up martial arts, which is how we got here today. After what happened to my friend, I wired the ever loving shit out of the Blackwood's house. It was…*illuminating.*"

"This is about Carla, isn't it?" he asked quietly.

"Yeah," Vinny choked out, her eyes welling up. "I'm sorry, Eddie. It *looks* like a beautiful day in the neighborhood, but she was the opposite of Mister Rogers. Cleaning up means drawing light to what she's really been doing in Oceanside. It's going to draw a lot of attention, if I do what I *should* do—what you *taught* me to do."

She'd gotten further information from Tripp a few days ago. His friend had kept digging in the background, and between his cyber skills and her security footage, it did not paint a flattering picture. Vinny was scared.

"I wasn't a good dad, Vinny. I love my daughter, but she's a brat. When I was young and incredibly naïve, I thought I'd fallen in love. We were docked in the Philippines. Her mother charmed me. I asked her to marry me, she said yes, and after only three months we were a family. Carla was born before our first wedding anniversary. And for the following two decades, I was gone more than I was home," he said. "Too career driven to realize what I was missing out on. If I'd been home more, my daughter might not be such a mess." He shrugged. "Now she is what she is, more her mother's daughter than mine. I did this to myself, Vinny."

The waitress set down their food, filled their waters, and left again.

Vinny spilled all the tea. While they slowly consumed their food, she told her friend absolutely everything. It was hard to get started, but once she opened her mouth, she couldn't stop. Vinny had desperately needed a safe outlet for too long, and she knew Eddie would give it to her straight. He had bristled when she mentioned Greer, which wasn't a good sign.

"My daughter is involved with *him?* It was bad enough her ex was under his command, but if what you are saying is accurate…"

"I know."

"Does he know?"

"Who, Ben?"

Eddie quirked an inquisitive brow. "Ben?"

"Ruben, I mean." She flushed. *Damn it. He does not need to know I have a nickname for his daughter's ex-husband.*

"Yes, Ruben." She didn't like the way he was smiling at her. "Are you friends now?"

She snorted. "No. I adore his father though. Abner moved out from Georgia after he had a heart attack. He's living with Ruben now and I spend a lot of time keeping him company and making him exercise while the guys are at work."

"This isn't going to reflect well on Holt, either."

"I know. It's going to shred his dad too." Vinny had thought long and hard about her stubbornness since she sat playing cards and eating pizza with the Holts. She wasn't ready to drop her guard, but she begrudgingly had admitted to herself a week ago—as her insomnia and creative block ruled the night—she might have been a tiny bit hard on him.

He still deserved it, but maybe…

For *Abner,* she'd consider a temporary ceasefire.

Maybe.

"Nobody is going to come out of this smelling fresh, Vinny. Reporting someone to a military court is different than a civilian court too. Are you sure you are ready?"

"No, but I won't let that bastard hurt my family."

"I understand. You have my support."

"But what about—"

Eddie shook his head. "I'm retired, honey. They can't take what I've earned away from me because of my daughter's stupidity. Thank you for the warning. Now, unless there is something else dire you need to tell me, what do you say we order a few desserts to split?"

They did just that, a habit of his she rather enjoyed. Vinny didn't think Eddie had taken many chances to be indulgent in his life. He had been ruled by the strict code he was sworn to uphold and model to his subordinates. She like this new, relaxed side of him.

"Retirement looks good on you," she said before moaning over a bit of chocolate mousse. "This is Heaven. Sinful... actually, you know what? If I can't have chocolate mousse in Heaven, send me to the rung of Hell reserved for dirty books and decadent deserts. I can take the heat."

Eddie laughed.

"Before we say goodbye," he said twenty minutes later as she was unlocking her car out front. "I need to tell you something."

"Okay," she said.

"Holt isn't to blame, Vinny. It took me a long time to come to terms with what was really happening between him and my daughter. If it weren't for you, I probably would still be slinging it out over the terms of their divorce on her behalf. He sent her home in bad shape."

"I know," she said. "I was there." She shook her head. "I will deny this if you repeat it to *anyone,* but he was far kinder to her than I would have been. I mean, he ordered a car to take her back to you. I probably would have sent her off with a nine mil slug in her ass and a quarter to call someone who cares if I'd been in his shoes."

Yeah, okay. I've been reconsidering my stance on Ruben more than a teensy bit. Ugh.

"I understand it now. I don't like it—she's still my

daughter—but I accept she isn't the innocent victim I wanted her to be in all this."

Vinny threw her arms around Eddie, squeezing him tight. "I'm sorry I had to be the one to rip off the blindfold."

"I'm not." She looked up at him quizzically. "I'm not, blossom. You were as gentle as a father could hope for when forced to realize his daughter is a trollop."

"He wouldn't have told you, Eddie. He'd have thrown the hand he was delt, knowing it was a winner, before hurting someone he respected."

"That's the second time in as many minutes you have defended him to me. You should think about what that means," Eddie said sadly. "Considering you have been dogging him for going on three years."

Nope. I still hate him, she told herself.

"Thanks for coming, Eddie. Next time, I buy."

"Not a chance, young lady."

She laughed, gave him a final squeeze before releasing him, and then headed home. She was drained from the severity of the conversation, and she still had to sit down with Eric tonight to hash it out all over again.

————

BOTH THE KIDS had hand foot and mouth. Vinny had been more than happy to delay her meeting with Eric in favor of spending time with Abner—who brought her an immense amount of peace and happiness—and combing over the more recent feeds from their security cameras.

Which was both a blessing and a curse.

The latest footage showed erratic behavior between Sonja and Greer. Something was not going his way next door. Sonja hesitated when she opened the door to him now, her body language exposing her reluctance. The information Sloth—Vinny's nickname for Tripp's slow moving tech friend—had provided was compounding by the moment. The guy had fixated on the request and kept digging. She was having a hard time keeping up with the influx of information.

What had her hackles up most were the number of times she'd caught sight of Jake creeping around. He either hadn't seen the cameras, hadn't anticipated their range and quality, or didn't give a flying fuck they were there. While none of those options were attractive, the last one scared the hell out of Vinny.

A man who didn't care was the most dangerous. Regardless of what had set him off after over a year apart, she had felt the malevolent energy he emanated when he'd stopped by. Jake was out for blood. *Her* blood. Why was irrelevant.

"You okay, there?" Abner asked carefully.

It was two days after her lunch with Eddie, and they were taking their daily walk around the block. She shrugged sheepishly before saying, "I honestly don't know, Abner. I can hear the whooshing of a second shoe dropping, and it's got me wound up."

"What was the first shoe?"

"Ah…well. I guess multiple second shoes all at once, then?"

Abner chuckled. "I hate it when that happens."

She let out a heavy sigh. "Why are people so *selfish?"*

"I suppose they can't help themselves. Altruism and empathy are natural in children, but if they aren't nurtured, they are easily displaced with greed and apathy."

Vinny stopped dead in her tracks, turning to Abner. "Why Abner Holt. I *knew* you were a cleverer man than you let on through your southern charms. What a speech!"

He laughed heartily as Vinny continued to stare at him

slack jawed from under the wide brim of her sun hat. "Want to know a secret?" She nodded. "When Ruben went to college, I was afraid I wouldn't know what he was talking about when he came home. I took a few community college classes for personal enrichment."

Vinny's heart swelled painfully. "Abner. *You* are nothing but altruism. All so you could keep up with your smarty pants son?"

"Well…"

"How many classes did you take?" she asked softly.

"I finished an associate's degree. Took a part time janitorial job at the school so I could get a reduced tuition rate," he said humbly, but she could hear the pride in his voice.

"That's not just a few classes," she said. "Why didn't you tell him?"

"I don't need my son pitying me," he harumphed.

"Abner. Tell me the truth. You were hoping if you were more educated, you'd be able to beat him at Spades again, weren't you?" she said with mock seriousness.

"You found me out, Miss Blume," he said wryly, his eyes twinkling with mirth.

"Your secret is safe with me."

Chapter Thirty-Six

RUBEN

It had been a long day, and Ruben was glad he'd been able to cut out of work early for a medical appointment. His foot was healing up nicely, but all the poking and pointing and *flexing* had made it sore. Instead of fighting traffic back to and from base for the last hour of the day, he'd called in.

Driving in light traffic wasn't too bad but stop and go was not something his foot could handle yet. Not when it already throbbed from use. He backed his truck into his garage with relief, cutting the engine and closing the garage door. Once inside the house, he poked his head into Abe's apartment. He was napping in front of one of those small claims court shows.

Ruben rolled his eyes. *That's my dad.*

He went out to his living room and grinned at his old set of couches. Carla had convinced him to get rid of them, and last week the people he'd sold them to had put them back on the base yard sale page. They had been in the husband's man cave and didn't look or feel any more worn then when he'd begrudgingly parted with them.

Of all the things to happen since his marriage ended,

getting his couches back felt like the biggest step toward reclaiming his life and home. An upholstered middle finger. Best of all, he no longer woke feeling older than his dad if he fell asleep watching TV. The leather ones had been nice, but didn't always pass the crick test when he woke up.

A shadow across the street distracted Ruben from his love affair with comfort. Through his front window, he could see a familiar man lithely stalking around, coiled to pounce. *What the hell is that fuckwad doing back here?*

He watched as Jake leisurely made his way up the steps to Vinny's front door. It was late afternoon. He knew the kids had been sick, which meant Carys was exhausted. Slow wouldn't be home for a couple more hours, and he knew Vinny wouldn't trouble Carys when the household was recovering. Ruben's body broke out in tingles.

Fuck.

He didn't think. Ruben silently slipped out his front door and across the street where he wouldn't be seen by Jake, and up onto the Blackwood's porch. He let himself in, turning to find Carys on the couch watching him with curiosity through her exhaustion.

"Vinny has an unwanted visitor. How do I get in through her back door?" he said quietly.

Carys was in the kitchen in a heartbeat, pulling keys down off the rack in the mudroom. "Yellow is the garage side door; blue lets you inside her back hallway."

"Thanks," he said, barely keeping the keys from tumbling to the floor in his haste.

"I'm calling the cops!" she whisper yelled from behind him as he opened the back door.

He nodded before making his way across the deck toward the second garage. From around the corner, he could already hear Jake pounding on the door. "Open up, baby."

Not fucking happening, Ruben thought as he closed and locked the garage door behind him and went directly to the stairs, taking them up two at a time. He shoved the key in the door and dropped to a squat before knocking softly and slowly opening the door enough to poke his head in. Vinny was standing in perfect position to watch both doors, her firearm aimed where his torso would have been if he'd been standing.

Glad I thought to duck.

"I saw him approach," he said low and carefully. "Carys gave me the keys. Can I come in?"

Vinny's shoulders dropped somewhat, and she nodded before turning back toward the front door, retaking up her shooting stance. Ruben could tell she'd trained a long time and knew what she was doing. He stood back up, let himself in and locked up before heading her way.

"How long has he been creeping around, Lavender?" he asked quietly from beside her.

"A few weeks. I started isolating him on the feed a few days ago, but this feels different." She nodded toward her gigantic TV, which was showing a split of three different security feeds outside plus her front door from the inside. "I think he's high, Ben."

Double fuck. Drugs did crazy things to people. He understood her distance from the door and the firearm now, but depending on what Jake was on, it might not be enough if he got through the door somehow. Some drugs made you feel super human, impervious to bullets even when half a dozen of them were lodged inside the body and causing the user to bleed out. Short of a kill shot, some drugs were too strong to override with good old-fashioned pain.

"Carys called the cops. I'll text her he's high and possibly violent," Ruben said, pulling out his phone.

She nodded, but kept her eyes trained on her front door, where Jake was currently pounding away. He'd graduated from calling Vinny *baby* to telling her what a dumb bitch she was. Ruben's skin crawled, watching the feed.

"Can I do anything else?" he asked.

"Don't leave me," she whimpered.

He stepped up behind her, placing one arm around her waist and pulling her shaking body against his solid frame, careful not to impede her ability to shoot. "I'm staying right here, Lavender. Lean on me. I've got you."

To his surprise, she began to hum softly. As she did, the tremor in her body settled. He recognized the song as a duet he remembered his parents singing in the kitchen when he was a little boy. His mind filled with light, his memories following in violent Technicolor.

Daddy snaps a dish towel against Momma's bottom, and she jumps in surprise.

"Abner!" she chastises. "We have an audience."

"Can't help it, woman," he says in a low growl, turning his frame to face hers where she is washing dishes. "He's my pride, and you *are my Joy."*

"And that earned me a towel snap?"

"I wouldn't have either without you, darlin'," Daddy drawls before kissing her cheek. Momma softens beside him. "Thinking of life without you hurts me everywhere. Worse than a little love snap with a dish rag."

"Dry the dishes, Abner."

He goes back to his own sink where she's piled up dishes for him to rinse and dry, but he still bumps her hip with his and grins at her in the weird way Daddy only looks at Momma. Ruben wrinkles his nose and acts like it's gross when they notice him watching, but secretly he loves it.

Daddy and Momma are in love.

Nobody ever said so, he just knows it. It makes his heart happy.

Momma starts humming, and Daddy joins in. It's an old song. Momma said it's by a man who makes things wither. Ruben is still confused about that...isn't he making *music? She'd laughed when he asked, her whole face lighting up like their Christmas tree in the living room.*

In his low timbre, Ruben hums along with Vinny. It was a simple tune full of meaning, "Lean On Me." He hadn't heard it since his mother died, but he still remembered it well, if not perfectly. Vinny hummed the melody, and he did his best to keep up with the harmony.

The feel of her body pressing deeper into his own was grounding, like a live wire finally drawn with purpose through its proper conduit. Lavender. She was Ruben's medium, the director of the symphony of his emotions. She could command anything right now, and he would be power-less to do otherwise.

And not because of the whacko standing on her porch.

Or because she relentlessly kept his father in high spirits.

The room was brighter with her in it. The air always the perfect temperature. And even though she set his emotions tumbling every which way the moment she came near, she also brought him contentment. Stasis. *Peace.* What you see is what you get with Lavender. Ruben hated it sometimes, but he loved it too. She was...mysteriously predictable.

Ruben already knew he'd shove her down the hall and take on Jake if he made it through the reinforced steel door. He wouldn't, but if he did, the fucker would learn firsthand what it means to be on the other end of Ruben's combat train-ing. He would *never* get close enough to touch Lavender again.

The sound of voices outside pulled Vinny out of the tune,

her head swiveling to the TV as the police joined the scene outside. Jake banged harder, and she jumped slightly against him. "I've got you," he said, pulling her in tight. She calmed somewhat, but her firearm was still trained on the door as they watch the screen.

It was likely only a few minutes, but when you are the one in danger, it feels much longer. Hours. *Weeks,* even. Waiting for the danger to pass. Ruben found it reassuring to be able to see it on the TV, at least. Jake didn't go down easily or cooperate in any way. They had to taser him in order to get close enough to cuff him.

Once Jake was removed from the deck, Vinny wilted. Ruben snatched the firearm from her hands and set it on the kitchen island before scooping her up and taking her to the couch. He sat down in the corner, cradling her in his arms.

"You're okay, beautiful. He's gone." Ruben stroked her long wavy strands, occasionally kissing the top of her head. He'd seen a lot on his deployments and recognized Lavender was going into shock.

There was a soft knock on the front door he'd know anywhere. *Slow.*

"Ruben! Is it safe to unlock the door?"

"Yeah," he called back. "She's okay."

"She's not…" *armed,* Ruben's mind filled in.

"Nah, man. We're on the couch cooling off."

"Thank you," she murmured into his chest. "For staying."

"You're welcome," Ruben said roughly. What else would he have done? Watched from his window across the street while she was left alone, terrified? Not a chance in Hell. Vinny could handle herself, but she shouldn't have to. Nobody should be left to do the hard stuff alone.

When Ruben's past mistakes had caught up to him, Vinny had been there. It was the least he could do to return the favor. Carla couldn't hurt him physically the way Jake could Lavender if given the chance, but she'd done more than enough damage in other ways. She'd have done far worse to Ruben if Vinny hadn't put her foot down between them. It was a privilege to be there for her now, as she'd stepped in when he was floundering himself.

Slow cautiously opened the door and poked his head in. "Vinny, is it okay if the police come inside?"

She nodded against Ruben's shoulder, where she'd tucked herself. "She says it's okay," he interpreted.

The door opened and he came in with two officers on his heels. Now that he wasn't standing with the sun at his back, Ruben could see all the worry he'd heard in his friend's voice a moment ago.

Vinny tipped her head up but didn't move from her current position in Ruben's lap, her head tucked under his chin. "Hi, Tuck."

"Hey, Vinny," one of the officers said kindly. Ruben glanced at his name tag. It read Tucker. She obviously knew the guy. "Do you need us to come back?"

She shook her head. "No, I know how it goes."

Why the fuck does she know *how this goes? Jesus.*

"Okay. This is my partner, Mack." Ruben read MacKenzie on the guy's tag. "He's all right."

"It's okay, Tuck. He's with you, so it's okay." She jolted in Ruben's lap, tipping her head back to meet his eyes. "Where is my—"

"Easy. It's on the counter. I made sure the safety is on," he said. She relaxed back against him.

"Okay. I'm ready."

Chapter Thirty-Seven

I shouldn't be sitting in Ruben's lap. She was probably sending the wrong message. But every time Vinny thought about moving away from him, she shuddered. Every time she shuddered, he gave her a comforting squeeze, and she realized she probably wouldn't make it through this without his warmth surrounding her.

Because on the inside, Vinny was *freezing.* She'd understood what paralyzing fear meant in theory, but she hadn't experienced it before today. Not even when the tweaker had tried taking her car in Georgia. The man outside her door pounding and screaming in a Jake meat suit was just that. He wasn't *her* Jake. He wasn't the guy who'd approached her outside a month ago either.

Aside from weed, Vinny hadn't known Jake to use drugs. Not even the party drugs freely flowing out on tour. The contrast between the fun loving, cuddly, tender guitarist she'd spent years laughing with on the road and the beast that had been tased on her doorstep and hauled away by the cops was staggering.

"Okay. I'm ready," she said hoarsely. Before she had time

to gather her thoughts, Eric was handing her a cold water from the fridge. She took it gratefully, slowly sipping down half the bottle as she prepared her mind. "Go."

"Has this happened before?" Tuck began, all business except for the softness in his eyes.

"No," she said, and Ruben cleared his throat. She squeezed his forearm where her hand was resting and kept going. "Not like he was today. He came around about a month ago."

"Can you tell me about that incident?"

Vinny related the whole of Jake's first visit outside, and Ruben collaborated his side before they moved on.

"Is this the first time he's been around since then?" Tuck asked.

"It's the first time he's approached," Vinny admitted. She looked up into Ruben's rich, dark eyes, pleading with her own to be kind and understanding. "I've been busy lately, helping my friend recover. I wasn't watching the security feeds as closely as I should have been when alerts came in. Jake has been creeping around in the periphery since about a week after his first visit, as far as I can tell."

"What was he doing?"

Vinny turned back to Tuck and Mack. "Watching mostly. Most of the time he stayed back from the property line. I didn't realize how often he was around until a few days ago, when I did a full scan of all the motion alerts I'd been missing or ignoring. On my phone, it was too small to see him at a glance. I dismissed most of them. But on the big screen," she said, flicking her gaze behind her to the TV, "I can see a lot more detail."

"Why didn't you say something?" Eric asked from the other end of the couch.

"I was going to, but the kids have been sick, so I figured

we could have a sit down after they stopped being contagious. I should have at least texted you. Sorry, Eric."

"I understand. Let's do it differently the next time there is a risk, okay?" Eric smiled gently when Vinny nodded in agreement.

"Do you have footage of all his comings and goings?" Mack clarified.

"Yes. Well, so long as he got close enough to trigger the cameras."

"What about today?" Tuck asked.

"I was coming back from a jam with Silla and Tripp. I parked in the garage like usual and came upstairs to change. I was home maybe five minutes when he started banging on my door," she said. "Something in the tone of his voice was so menacing, I knew to leave the door locked. I turned on the security feed so I could see what he was doing, grabbed my handgun—oh, it's legal. Registered and everything," she said.

"I know, Vinny. I taught your safety class," Tuck said with a smile.

"Right." She let out a tense laugh. "I stood back from the door just in case, so I could see it and the screen. He knew the cameras were there. More than once, he looked straight into the lens while he was shouting at me."

Vinny felt Ruben stiffen around her before coiling his arms more firmly around her body. Tuck noticed too but didn't say anything. Instead, he nodded for Vinny to continue.

"I forgot my phone in my car. All I could do was hope Eric didn't skimp on the safety door and prepare for it failing. Then Ruben came in." *Smart enough to knock and duck this time.* "He relayed to Carys what was happening by text—she was already on the line with emergency services—and he stayed with me."

He stayed with me.

He stayed.

With.

Me.

Oh my god. He could have been hurt.

Vinny knew in her core if Jake had managed to breach the door, Ruben would have acted to protect her. Her body began to tremble again, and *again* Ruben held her impossibly tighter, yet not too tight.

"We were standing over by the back hall, toward the end of the kitchen island, holding position. Then you guys arrived."

Tuck looked to Ruben. "What's your side of the story?"

"I came home from work early after a medical appointment. I must have made it right before or after Lavender, because I didn't see her or her car when I backed into my garage. I was headed to the living room when I saw Jake crossing the street, headed straight to Lavender's door."

"Did you try to engage with him at all?" Tuck asked.

"No, getting inside was my priority. I knew there was a second set of keys in the house, so I used my key to quietly enter the main residence. Carys gave me the keys and called 911 while I snuck up the back way to get to Lavender."

To get to me. Not my house, not his best friend's property. Me.

Vinny's mind tilted on its axis, spinning out with all the grace of a bent bicycle wheel while Ruben answered more of Tuck's questions in the background. She'd been terrified. The cameras had kept her in the know of Jake's movements, she'd had her firearm for protection, and she was locked neatly behind a solid safety door.

But the only thing that had kept her sane was the solid mass of Ruben's body behind her.

"Anything else you can think of?" Tuck asked, breaking Vinny out of her downward spiral.

"He's not prone to being violent, Tuck," she blurted out. "What will happen to him? I could tell he's high from the video feed."

Mack and Tuck shared a look before Tuck nodded at Mack, giving him the floor. "He has a history of recreational drug use and violence, Miss Blume."

"What?" The word came out a strangled squeak.

"He's hasn't escalated to this level before, but he has become violent while high. Bar fights, things of that nature."

"But...but I've known him for years. We used to share an apartment! Oh god...*we used to share an apartment.*"

"Do you have a card?" Ruben asked briskly, placing Vinny back into the corner of couch and using his body like a shield from their words. "We can call when she's in a better place, get you all the footage."

"Sure," Mack said.

The buzz around her continued to grow, but Vinny didn't hear or see a thing. She buried her face into Ruben's backside, reassured by the presence of his body pinning her into the back of the couch, and allowed herself to let go. Her mind whirled through all the horrible what ifs. Had she missed a sign? There must have been signs. But Jake had been so normal and easy going on tour, and even at home. What had changed?

———

Ruben

"You sure you want me to go?" Slow asked.

"Yeah, man. She won't like you seeing her like this," Ruben answered.

"She won't like *you* seeing her like this either."

"The difference is, she's literally got her claws in me. Even if I wanted to go, *look at her.*" Vinny was hiding in the couch with Ruben's body as her shield, humming a low monotone to herself. Her hands were flexed stiffly into his shoulders, her fingertips digging in hard enough he knew there would be bruises tomorrow.

He didn't give a damn. Ruben wasn't going anywhere.

"Can you take some dinner to my dad and tell him where I'm at?" he asked.

"Yeah, I can do that. Are you sure about this?" Slow asked one last time. He looked nervous, which was rare for Slow.

"I can handle her, man. Please." Slow nodded reluctantly before he walked away, letting himself out the front door. Ruben heard the deadbolt slot into place before the sound of his footsteps descended to the ground and disappeared down the driveway.

After a few more minutes, Vinny's humming slowed into a gentle purr before stopping altogether. She'd fallen asleep. As relieved as Ruben was she was getting a reset, he was barely keeping himself on the edge of the couch. He gave her a good once over before sliding away from her body, shifting smoothly to a crouch in front of her. Vinny whimpered softly, her fingers still gripping his shoulders.

"Shhh. It's okay, Lavender. I've got you. We're going to the bedroom." She didn't stir, but she must have subconsciously recognized he'd spoken, because her body relaxed enough for him to scoop her up and carefully walk her back to her bedroom. He arranged her limp body over his shoulder same as he would one of the kids, allowing Ruben to pull back her blankets before tucking her in.

"Ben," she whispered in her sleep.

"I'm here."

"Don't leave me."

If only she was this easy to comfort when she was coherent, he thought.

Ruben gazed at the heavy blankets on her bed. He'd broil in there, but he couldn't hold her the way she needed him to on top of the covers. He took off his jeans and tee and climbed in with her, only his boxer briefs on. He was still hot as fuck—especially after she wrapped her body around him—but it was better than nothing.

He kicked a leg out to let off some body heat and relaxed into his role as Vinny's human body pillow. All in all, he'd had worse gigs. Besides, he loved the smell of her hair. The sweet lavender scent must have lulled him into a doze, because his eyes snapped wide open what must have been a good while later, given the last light of dusk was filtering through her bedroom window.

Lavender was still wrapped around him, but something was...different. She was undulating her body against his, grinding her most sensitive area against his hip bone.

And her pants were off. *When did she take her pants off? In her sleep?*

Ruben froze, watching her body move lithely over him. *Shit.* This wasn't how he wanted her at all, and he knew for a fact this wasn't really what Lavender wanted. He attempted to wiggle away from her, but she gripped him tightly with the leg thrown over his torso, her nails digging temptingly into his chest. *Jesus. I have to wake her up before she—holy fuck.*

Vinny's hand ran down his body and gripped his hard

length over the fabric of his underwear. *Nope. This is not happening like this.*

"Lavender," he said huskily—because she was still stroking his hard on, damn it. He moved his body, rolling toward her and pushing away at the same time, trying to create space between them. "Lavender, wake up."

She moaned his name, her voice laced with need.

Fuck, fuck, fuck…

"Come on beautiful, open your eyes for me. Time to wake up." She whimpered as he carefully removed her hand from his family jewels. "Lavender!"

Her eyes fluttered slightly, her gaze hazy at best. "Ben."

"There you are," he said, trying to ignore the sexy way she kept calling to him. "You gotta let go of me now."

"Don't want to," she said, her eyes falling closed again. "You stayed."

"Of course I did. You scared the hell out of me earlier."

This time her eyes opened all the way. "You care about me," she said with wonder. They both stilled, eyes locked… until she lunged toward him, plastering her mouth over his. As far as kisses go, it was one for the books. Surprise melted into unyielding lust. Ruben responded to her every nip and pillowy touch, the sensual swipe of her tongue.

Ruben gave in to the feeling of her and his own need. They fought for dominance with their mouths, a battle he'd happily die for. Her taste, the feel of her body against his. She was exquisite. What he'd give to press inside her.

"Ben. Touch me." The command sent a chill down Ruben's spine—not the good kind. He stilled, pulling away from her. He held her face in his hands and stared into her violet orbs, looking for a sign this was more than a trauma response and not finding it.

"Not like this, Lavender."

"Ben," she began to argue, shimmying her body against him.

"No. Not like this. You don't want *me;* you need the release."

"I'm sure we could both use the release after today," she purred, cupping him again.

"No," he said firmly, but gently. Ruben pulled away, sliding to the edge of the bed with his back turned to her. "I won't let you use me, Lavender."

He felt her weight shift on the bed and sprung up before she could reach him. Ruben began to stuff his legs back into his jeans, yanking them up quickly before reaching for his shirt.

"You're going to *leave me?"*

Ruben turned back to the bed, taking her in. Her hair was spread all around her, her makeup smudged from sleep. And her eyes…were venom.

"I didn't leave you, Lavender. Not after they took him away, or after you went catatonic on us from the shock. You are better now, and I have to go. I will not be your broken toy."

"What the hell does that mean?" she snarled.

He went to the other side of the bed and bent down over her, his fingers sliding into her soft locks at her nape and gripping hard. Vinny gasped, her eyes widening with desire.

And Ruben took.

For the first time in his life, he dominated a woman with the nonnegotiable ferocity of a man who was used to getting what he wanted. Ruben kissed Lavender with all the pent-up frustration she'd poured into him, hoping she could feel how desperate and insane she'd made him as he devoured her mouth. He took from her until he could feel her body begin to tremble with a need as painful as his own.

Then he let her go.

Vinny fell back onto the bed as Ruben straightened up. Confusion quickly morphed into fury, and he knew he was giving her a smug look of his own. "That's how you make me feel, *Lavender*. Every second of every damn day. You drive me *crazy* with need. So yes, I'm going to leave you now. There is no way in hell I will let you fuck me and forget me, which is what you are trying to do."

"I'm not—"

"Damn it, Lavender! Don't lie to yourself. You think if you can push me into it now, you can justify pushing me away later by claiming it was a moment of weakness. You were in a state of duress. Sorry, beautiful. It's not happening. Not like this."

"I hate you," she spat out. And he might have believed her on some level if she wasn't eye fucking the bulge in his jeans like a dying man looks at a mirage, believing he's been saved. But she was, and he'd finally learned. Let her look at what she was missing out on.

Ruben wasn't interested in giving up his self-respect for a woman again. Not even Lavender.

"Keep telling yourself that. I *will* have you, Lavender, but on *my* terms. Not yours."

"You'll never touch me again!"

"Soon as you pull that stick out of your ass and admit you want me too," he continued, as if she hadn't spoken. "You better be ready for me when it happens, beautiful. I won't go easy when I claim you."

He grabbed his shoes off the floor before walking out her back door barefoot.

He didn't trust himself to stay, no matter what he'd just told her.

Chapter Thirty-Eight

"Are you okay?" Abner asked.

"I will be," she said with a gentle smile. Vinny *really* did not want to talk to Ruben's dad about yesterday. She was sure he knew more than he was letting on anyway. His son had been in the middle of something straight out of an episode of *Cops*.

No way Ruben hadn't told his father all the juicy details.

Ruben.

Damn it. She looked away as they strolled down the sidewalk. She had her biggest sunglasses and floppy sun hat on, but they wouldn't hide the way her chin quivered as she fought back tears. She'd ruined everything last night, and to make matters worse, he'd been right for calling her out.

Using Ruben's body to release her own tension would have been amazing if his lifechanging goodbye kiss said anything about him. Unfortunately, he was also correct about everything else. Claiming it was in the heat of the moment is exactly what she would have done this morning.

It would have been a lie, but she would have done it.

Admitting to herself she'd been unnecessarily clinging to

her past malice toward Ruben and working toward letting it go was different from fucking his brains out. It was the *opposite* in fact. The second she came down from the high, she'd have turned tail and hid behind her old walls. She would have poured out her own blood to further reinforce those walls with another layer of granite, coagulated into place with the iron of her own faulty convictions.

Vinny had called Tuck soon as his shift started this morning. He and Mack had already stopped back over to review all the footage of Jake being a creeper, starting with the first visit.

"That boyfriend of yours is damn loyal," Tuck had said. Vinny was too embarrassed by her own stubborn idiocy to correct him like she usually would.

Because if she was honest with herself, knowing one person on this earth thought Lavender Blume belonged to Ruben Holt made her a little bit happy. It gave her a sliver of hope.

She had sat patiently with them, explaining the entirety of her relationship with Jake. From the tour they first met on to the way she'd found him at their apartment the night she moved out, Vinny spared no detail. Mack had been more forthcoming than Tuck, but not by much.

"The gaps between match up with his many stints in court mandated rehab," he'd told her kindly.

"No wonder he always seemed on the up and up," she'd said with a shake of her head. "He was only on tour when he was clean. Sex, drugs, and rock 'n' roll…it's a cliché for a reason."

"You did nothing wrong, Vin," Tuck said.

"I know. It's still hard to accept though. I mean, what if he'd been on a violent bender when I'd come home, instead of an orgy? He might have killed me. I was exhausted from months on the road, Tuck. I wouldn't have been prepared to take him on." The realization had stunned her with the magnitude of possibilities, of what she'd likely escaped.

Tuck had given her a hug and promised he'd keep her in the loop. Then he and Mack disappeared back to their car with the thumb drive full of evidence she'd made them and that was that. Vinny had managed a hot shower before forcing herself to take Abner on their daily walk.

"Let's go for a drive," she said out of the blue. "What do you think, Abner? I could use a stroll on the beach, some new scenery."

"I'm always ready to ride in the Camaro," he said jovially. "Let's do it."

Half an hour later, they pulled into a parking spot at one of Vinny's favorite public beaches. She put the engine in park just as her play list changed to Bill Withers.

"Mm! I love this song," Abner said.

"Me too," she agreed, sitting back in her seat. They sat together listening to Bill croon about borrowed strength. Halfway through, Abner began to sing along. His voice cracked from lack of practice at first, but he quickly got his stride. It made Vinny happy to see *him* so happy.

When the song ended and they finally made their way down to the sand, Vinny let out a sigh of relief.

"It's cold," Abner groused. "Ain't cold like this on the beaches in Georgia."

"You love it," she teased.

After a beat, he caught her off guard with a confession. "I do love it."

"Really?"

"I was being stubborn," he said.

"You?" Vinny gasped dramatically. "Never. I refuse to believe it."

"I wasn't ready to leave my Joy behind," he continued, his eyes focused out across the water as they went. "The house, my old neighborhood. I could still hear the sound of Ruben calling back to me at the diamonds, 'watch this one, Dad!' right before he split the stitches off the ball. Every time I walked by the old broken back stop, I saw my boy. I saw the way things used to be, instead of accepting how bad they had become."

"Abner," she said softly, giving his hand a squeeze. "I'm glad you had a heart attack and Ruben made you leave."

He chuckled. "He didn't make me do anything." She looked over at him. His eyes were sparkling with mischief, and he was staring right back at her. "I was still stuck on dying right there where my heart was buried, until you pulled up in that beautiful car of yours."

"Because your wife had one too?"

"Something like that. I decided it was her way of putting a boot up my ass from the other side, so to speak."

It was Vinny's turn to laugh. "But what if I'd pulled up in a Mustang instead?"

Abner wrinkled his nose. "Then I'd have died shortly after you pulled away with Ruben from a home invasion gone wrong, because there is no way she'd keep waiting for me at the gates of Heaven if I even considered riding in a Ford."

"Can't say I blame her," Vinny mused.

They walked along side by side in companionable silence. Vinny breathed in deeply, loving the salty grit in the air hitting the back of her throat.

"What's that you're humming?" Abner asked as they turned to head back toward the car.

"Huh?" Vinny wasn't humming…was she? She'd been blocked for so long, completely incapable of finding anything to draw out a random tune from deep inside. Her well of inspiration was bone dry.

"Is it a new tune I don't know?" he pressed.

"I don't know. Was I *really* humming?" she asked.

"You were," he said, then did his best to mimic whatever she'd been unconsciously creating. She began to hum along with him. By the time they reached the car, she was twitchy as all get out and itching to pick up her guitar.

Her 1972 Stratocaster.

"It's gone!" she cried, laughing manically. "Abner, it's gone! Oh my god, I have to get back to my studio!"

"Well then, you should probably unlock the car."

Touché.

———

Ruben

"I thought we were having a meeting?"

"We are," Slow said.

Ruben closed the back door behind him and joined his best friend on his back deck. He could faintly hear the sound of a guitar building chord progressions from inside the garage. Or rather the mostly soundproofed studio located at the back of the garage. *Lavender.*

"Is there a reason we're standing out here instead?"

"Vinny called the meeting."

"And?"

"She's composing."

"And?"

Slow turned to face him. "She's been blocked for a year, Ruben. She plays, but I haven't heard her compose a single new thing since she moved in."

That wasn't at all what he'd expected to hear, and it stole whatever comeback he'd been formulating clean out of his mind. A year was a long damn time for a person to be incapable of doing something as essential to them as breathing is to the rest of the world. Anytime Ruben got curmudgeonly, he'd go down to the batting cages. Even if he couldn't hit for shit that day, he still felt the cathartic release he craved. What would he do without it?

"What do we do now?" he finally asked.

"I don't know. Wait a few minutes, I guess."

They waited an hour. Twice Carys came out to check on them. The first time she told them to go sit down. The second time she brought them water.

"Is that *shave and a haircut?*" Ruben laughed.

"Yup, she's done."

"How do you know?"

"That's what she plays when she's done."

"Oh." Ruben got up to follow Slow—who was already halfway across the yard—through the side door into Vinny's garage. She was locking up the door to her studio as he came in.

"Hey," she said. "Sorry about that. I lost track of the time."

"I'm just happy to hear you *creating* again," Slow said with a smile.

Vinny blushed. "Yeah, it's been a long time. Let's go up."

Ruben tried not to stare at her perfectly displayed denim wrapped ass as she went up the stairs, but it was impossible. To make matters worse, he'd seen the naked desire she harbored for him yesterday. He'd felt her trust in the way she'd chosen to stay with him for comfort.

And there was no denying her arousal as she dry humped

him while half asleep. She'd been soaked, and her scent had transferred onto his body during the act. Had he driven himself mad last night thinking about it? Absolutely. Had he jerked off to the memory of her body sliding across his? Hell fucking yes, he had.

Slow cleared his throat behind Ruben on the stairs. When he looked back, he was smirking. *Fuck off,* Ruben mouthed. Slow shook his head knowingly. Ruben had already told him where he stood. It wasn't his fault Lavender Blume was as slow moving getting her shit together as a damn glacier.

And about as warm as one too.

"Okay," Vinny began as they settled into her living room. "Here is where we are at as of four days ago. And before you get mad Eric, I'm sorry for the delay."

"We covered that earlier. Proceed," he said with humor.

Vinny turned her head and locked onto Ruben's gaze. "I'm sorry."

"For what?" Something deep flickered across her face before she could bury it behind a façade of indifference. *Interesting.*

"This is going to be hard on you more than any of us," she murmured.

"Rip off the Band-Aid, Lavender."

She nodded before turning to her laptop, which was already connected to her TV. "It wasn't just Carla being a slut. There are a lot of players in this, and I think we need to be careful."

The giant screen exploded with windows as soon as her desktop unlocked. Ruben sat in stunned silence as he took it all in. File after file, videos created in his own damn house, browser windows open to exclusive content…

He wanted to ask her to give him back his Band-Aid.

Maybe call V12 and ask him to come by with a tourniquet.

"Greer isn't seducing wives," Vinny said softly. "He's recruiting them and has been for years. The website hits a certain capacity and he shuts it down, relaunching under a different branding. Then he notifies his previous clientele and keeps right on going. You have to be given the link to find it, and even then the homepage looks benign and incomplete... unless you know where to click to open the login."

"That *fucker,"* Slow snarled.

"I'm going to paraphrase here, but I have correspondence between him and Sonja Perez talking about everything from the website's current version to how they planned on separating you and Carys. Greer didn't want her for his website, he wanted her as a trophy. Something he took from the 'nice guy' everyone thinks is so great. Your last deployment was orchestrated so he could find a way to get to Carys while he believed she was susceptible from her trauma and your absence. The texts all came from Perez's computer. They were tag teaming you, Eric."

The darkness radiating off his best friend was a living entity, a starved beast ready to swallow the world whole. Slow *was* a nice guy, but only an idiot would fuck with his family. "And fucking each other senseless while they waited to claim their prizes," he spat.

"Something like that. Except she's been pushing him off. Not opening her door as readily to him and not answering his messages as eagerly. But yeah, she and Greer were fucking like coked out chimps for who knows how long, and they weren't always alone."

"Who was with them?" Eric asked. Ruben could hear in his tone how hard Eric was working to keep a lid on his rage.

Vinny blew out a breath before turning her violet orbs to Ruben. "Carla mostly. And that's just the tip of the iceberg where she's concerned."

He nodded, knowing if he tried telling her he was ready to hear it all he'd likely do the opposite and run home in avoidance.

"From what I can tell, Carla has been his right hand for a long time."

"How long?" he asked.

"Maybe from the very beginning. At least the last eight to ten years. Some of those *affairs* were there getting paid," she said.

Getting paid. I married a fucking prostitute who was running a sex site with my commander. Out of my goddamn house.

His vision blurred. Ruben closed his eyes and tried to focus on his breathing. Warm hands with calloused pads gripped his face. He opened his eyes to find her stubbornly holding together his pieces for him, her own orbs dancing with determination.

"You were always too good for Cunty Carla, Ben. It's not your fault she was a user."

Ruben couldn't help busting up. "I'm sorry, *Cunty Carla?*"

"That's what I call her in my head," she said nonchalantly, shrugging one shoulder. She released his face and pushed her body back into her chair, leaving Ruben chilled. Lavender had comforted him without hesitation.

"How deep does it go?" Slow asked.

"Deep. Deeper than I can dig, but if we take this to JAG…"

There was no need to finish her sentence. The government would shred Greer and Perez, not to mention anyone else involved.

"She married me to be closer to him, didn't she?" Ruben asked.

"Looks like it. I'm sorry, Ben."

Chapter Thirty-Nine

RUBEN

The thing about grief is it has no proper course or timeline. Ruben had meticulously erased his home of any trace of his ex. Professional cleaners had come through. He'd had painters freshen up most of the house.

He'd gotten his beloved set of couches back. The universe had delivered for him on that day.

Ruben had added a suite for his father. There was a small playset in the backyard for when his godchildren were over.

But as anyone who has mourned before can tell you, grief comes in waves. Finding out he'd put his heart in the hands of a woman who was using him to be close to her lover and business partner was a tsunami grade catastrophe ripping the sandy California beach right out from underneath Ruben's boots.

He was drowning.

There wasn't a paint color that could soothe what she'd done. The breadth of her deception and manipulation was all encompassing. Carla had a business degree…and this was what she'd chosen to do with it. He'd applaud her success if she hadn't been such a vicious, conniving *cunt* to get there. Lavender was right, the word fit Carla flawlessly.

Cunt, cunt, cunt.

He'd found it vulgar before, but now he understood it had a descriptive power he'd been unable to grasp. Now he had the proper context to use the word without cringing.

Ruben had skipped over anger—like a girl determined to win a double Dutch competition at recess—choosing instead to create something better for himself. It had worked for a while. He'd counted himself lucky Carla was someone he could ultimately have a clean break from.

There was no clean break from a scandal of this magnitude. He was the idiot who'd been sucked into a marriage of convenience by an online madame, a sexual starlet. To torture himself a little more, he'd watched some of the videos. Carla had never indicated she enjoyed sex the way she clearly did with others, or even by herself.

Ruben had joined Slow for a meeting with a friend from the legal office two days after Lavender's big reveal. They had thrown around a lot of hypotheticals like foul balls. Hitting one out of the park was daunting, but walking on a difficult turn at bat was easy enough. Greer had friends everywhere, and they had to be covert about going after him so he wasn't tipped off—to get their players in place for a triple header without the defense catching on.

Slow and Ruben had gone ahead and turned over all the information Vinny had collected. Since she hadn't obtained it through *legal* channels, none of it could be used. They could use the current web address and begin building a case moving forward. When they had enough evidence amassed, it would be enough to seize the tech of everyone involved with a warrant and, with any luck, grant them proper access to the files Vinny had unturned. They hoped their posse of culprits continued to neglect wiping evidence off their hard drives in the meantime.

"She asked about you again," Abe said slyly over dinner. "You should call her."

"I can't just call her up Dad." He ignored the way his father's gaze burned into the center of his skull, opting to keep his head lowered while he shoveled down his meal without tasting it. "She doesn't need me snapping at her."

"Why would you snap at her?"

"I wouldn't do it on purpose. Shit just comes out when I'm around her. It's like the off switch to my mouth short circuits anytime she's near."

"Fine, do it your way," he said casually. "Seems a waste to me. She's never asked about you before, and now she does it daily."

Meddling old man.

Abe's words still had their desired effect. Ruben stewed over the idea of Lavender openly inquiring about him during her daily visits with his father. It even distracted him from his aggressive need to burn Carla at the stake like the witch she was.

When his father retired to his own space, Ruben continued to stew, pacing back and forth in his bedroom. He needed to touch her. No. *She wouldn't want that.* Could he find contentment from looking at her? *Maybe. Sure.* He could look in on her, see how she was doing since the thing with her crazy junkie ex. *Fuck, we both have horrible taste in partners.*

After the mental back and forth with himself, he made his mind made up. Ruben yanked on a clean tee, shoved his feet into a pair of sneakers, and headed downstairs. There was no harm if he checked in on her. When he reached her driveway, he could hear music in the back. *Studio it is, then.*

Ruben hadn't been inside the studio since he helped Slow finish building it. He knew Vinny had made some upgrades while moving in. Maybe that could be his in. He could mention he'd like to see what she'd done with the place. The sight of a car parked around back froze Ruben mid-step. He'd seen it before.

Vinny's friend was here. *Fuck. They like to work together,* he remembered.

The sound of laughter broke him out of his daze, and Ruben slowly continued his walk toward the garage door. It opened as he approached.

"Oh, hey! Vin, you got company," he called back, waggling his eyebrows.

"Shut up, Tripp," she said from inside.

"You want me to escort him away?" Tripp said playfully.

"Huh?" Vinny's head popped around the doorframe. She must have thought he was teasing about a visitor. "Oh. Hey, Ben. Everything okay? Abner good?"

"If by 'good' you mean driving me up the wall, he's great. Fantastic, even."

She let off a snort before saying, "Sounds about right."

Ruben stuck his hands in his pockets and leaned against the wall of the garage between the regular door and the roll up. "I can come back later, if you're busy," he said quietly.

"Tripp is leaving. You can stick around a bit."

He watched as she said goodbye to her friend, giving him a platonic hug Ruben suspected Tripp was trying to make look like more to get under his skin. It didn't work. He might not know Tripp, but he knew Lavender.

"Okay," she said after the tail lights faded down her drive-way. "I'm all yours."

I'm all yours.

Ruben closed his eyes and grit his jaw. She wasn't, but

she would be. Assuming he could keep himself under control. It didn't look good, given what those three words were doing to his resolve already.

"Ben?"

He looked up to find her directly in front of him, near enough to pull her against him without extending his arm entirely to do it. "Can we go inside?" he rasped.

"Sure." She cocked her head toward the door, and he took the hint.

Ruben strode inside and planted it on the same step he'd occupied the night she'd yelled at him. When she came to a stop in front of him, he stared at her strappy brown sandals and asked, "How have you been?"

She didn't answer.

"You know, with the whole Jake thing. Carys said you turned over evidence. I haven't actually seen you since you uh…" *Why the fuck am I acting like this? It's Lavender. I don't get nervous around her.*

"I'm up here, Ben," she said with amusement. "Why are you looking at my feet?"

Ruben lifted his head, drinking in every inch of her as his gaze traveled up. "Are you okay, Lavender?"

"Yeah," she croaked out. If he had to guess, she was uncomfortable now too. "Why wouldn't I be?"

He watched as her pupils blew wide, her breathing turning to shallow pants as she continued to stare back at him. She bit down into her plush bottom lip, and he was a goner.

"Lavender," he said huskily, shooting to his feet and yanking her into him. "What are you doing to me?"

She inhaled sharply but didn't fight him off. "I don't know."

"Don't you?" It was a rhetorical question, which he made clear when he sealed his mouth over hers. She moaned as his tongue caressed hers for the first time. He pulled away, drinking in her flushed face and reddened pout. "Fucking hell. Your mouth is perfect."

"Then why did you stop?" There was a challenge in her eyes as she spoke, one he intended on winning.

Ruben backed her up against her Camaro roughly. "So I could enjoy looking at you, beautiful."

He could feel her scissoring her thighs together, pressed between him and the rear fender of the car. Ruben quickly dropped his eyes and flicked them back to hers, lifting one brow in question. "Ben."

Again. What is with this woman moaning my name?

"Come here, Lavender," he said as he scooped her up by the globes of her ass and walked her to the back of the car.

"What are you doing?"

"Giving you what you want." *Taking what we both need,* he finished in his head.

She fisted his shirt and planted her heels on the bumper, lifting her ass up enough for him to easily yank her jeans down. Her creamy skin was pure as freshly fallen snow, but what he intended to do to her sure as fuck wasn't.

"You drive me insane, Lavender." He ran his hands up her bare thighs, stepping close so she couldn't close them, then drug the pad of one thumb through her juices, moving it along to her clit. She hissed as he repeated the motion over and over, until she was slippery where he needed her to be. "Is this for your *friend,* Lavender?"

She shook her head.

"Lay back. That's a good girl." He began circling her nub faster, smiling down at her as she fought to close her legs and couldn't. "Are you ready?"

"F-for whaaaaaat?" she cried. He'd inserted a finger as she spoke.

"To admit what we both already know, beautiful."

"I t-tell you all the time how much I h-haaate you!" He added another finger inside her, adjusting his grip so he could better work his fingers inside with his thumb over her clit.

"Your body doesn't seem to hate me, Lavender." He curled his fingers inside her where he knew she needed it most and her hips came off the trunk with a moan. He pushed her back down with his other hand and held her in place while doubling his speed. He felt her walls swelling around his fingers, her hips attempting to grind down harder on his digits though he held her in place. He plunged in deeper before pulling his fingers out, gently stroking her sex as she cried out with rage.

"What the hell, Ben!"

"Isn't that what you expected?"

"No, damn it! Finish the job!"

He leaned forward over her quivering body—with rage or arousal, either worked for him at this point—until his chest was flush with hers and whispered low and sultry into her ear, "Why would you expect someone you hate to give you pleasure, beautiful?"

Between their bodies, he began circling her clit again. Vinny moaned. "That's right, Lavender. Tell the truth."

"Make me," she grit out, then bit down sharply on his ear lobe.

The pain zinged right down to his groin, where his erection was already struggling against his shorts. "Fuck, woman."

In retaliation, he removed his hand completely from her sex. Vinny cried out again. Ruben stared her down while he licked his fingers clean. He leaned down over her, his hands laced with hers and keeping them firmly against the cool metal where she couldn't gouge his eyes out with her claws.

"I want to give you everything," he murmured softly. "But I cannot make you accept me."

Gently this time, he caught her lower lip between his teeth, sucking it firmly while swiping his tongue across before slowly releasing it. "I cannot make you need me."

He placed tender kisses along her jawline before slowly dragging his mouth to worship her entire face. "I cannot make you love me."

Ruben leaned down to her ear again, gently nipping her lobe before whispering, "But I will never stop showing you I'm no Jenny Moore."

He placed one last kiss on the pulse point at her throat before carefully pushing away from her.

"I hate you, Ben," she said hoarsely.

He took her in, the sexual frustration radiating off her as her sex wept for fulfillment. "Right this moment, I believe you."

"Why?"

"I told you, beautiful. I will not be your broken toy."

"I don't want to break you," she murmured.

"But you also don't believe I won't abandon you. Not yet at least." He saw the words land, and he ached with the acceptance he found on her face. Because it was true, and she knew it.

"Ben." A single tear slid down her face.

"It's okay, Lavender. Goodnight."

Ruben turned slowly and walked out of the garage, closing the door behind him. *Fuck.* He'd hoped if he pushed her, she'd open up to him a little more. Hell, he'd have been happy to have a conversation where she didn't storm off at the end. But she wasn't ready, and they both deserved better.

So tonight he had another date with Rosie Palm and her five friends, while Lavender's scent and tang lingered.

Chapter Forty

VINNY

Vinny slowly dropped her heels from the rear bumper of her baby and stood on shaky legs. She picked up her jeans and staggered to the stairs like a newborn pony. *Damn it, Ben.*

Why did he have to be right?

It was easier to hate him. Her internal metronome was swinging out of control, unable to find a steady rhythm. When he was away, she could admit parts of her animosity were unwarranted and she needed to give him a shot. If nothing else, to accept Ben as a friend. They shared a family and godchildren.

But then he'd get within a few feet of her, and she would panic. How could she let him in? It wasn't so bad when there were others around to focus on. Vinny had enjoyed playing Spades with Ben and Abner together, but the idea of him walking her across the street afterward had done strange things to her.

The act of pushing someone away while simultaneously pulling them close was simply *shaking* them. Push, pull. Push, pull. One or both of them was going to end up with brain trauma if she didn't get herself under control. He was right to refuse a physical relationship without something in return.

He was like Tyler in that way. Ben wanted more from her. But unlike with Tyler, Vinny didn't want to walk away from Ben. She'd had the strength to recognize she and Tyler had both been used in the past and a quick fuck wouldn't have been fair to either of them—for her ability to walk the following day as much as for his feelings which she hadn't reciprocated—but she didn't know how to do the same with Ben.

Vinny didn't know how to give him what he needed and deserved, point blank. At the same time, she knew both of them needed and deserved more from a partner than they had settled on in the past. Ruben didn't want a rebound. Vinny didn't want to spend the rest of her life having empty sex to gloss over the hollowness she'd accepted as her fate long ago.

And yet.

The moment they were alone together, she wanted to strip Ben down and memorize every inch of his body. First with her hands, and then with her eyes and mouth. She wanted everything about him so engrained in her it would be impossible to lose him, even in death. What she couldn't do was give *him* the same openness she craved for herself.

If Ben were to touch her the way she craved, he'd embed himself deeper under her skin than he already had. There was no way he'd like what he saw there. And as she collapsed onto her mattress with the phantom tingles of his touch lingering exactly where she desired him, she unequivocally knew he was right.

She would lure him in.

She would take her pleasure.

She would freak out and shove him away.

Ben didn't deserve to be broken the way Vinny was. She

would have to keep her distance until she could figure out how to be around him without dire consequences for them both. *Right after I finish what he started.*

Vinny reached for her Taco Tickler and favorite tingly lube, only to find she'd forgotten to charge it.

———

"WHAT ARE YOU WRITING?" Carys asked from the doorway.

"Words."

"Vinny."

"Lyrics."

"To *what?"* she let out with obvious exasperation.

"A song, Carys," Vinny answered with false cheer.

"Can I see what you've got?"

"No." She'd never turned Carys down before, and she knew without looking up from her notebook doing so had caught her friend by surprise.

"I'm glad your block is gone, at least."

Vinny let out a sigh, set aside her notebook and pencil and looked up to her best friend. "What can I do for you?"

"We haven't talked in over a week."

"We text every day."

"That's not what I mean. Are you okay? I know you talked to Eric and Ruben about it, but I'm your best friend and...did I upset you?"

"What? Carys, no." Vinny smacked the couch cushion next to her and waited for her bestie to plant her tush before continuing. "What happened with Jake was wild, and I admit it was a traumatic event. But I'm honestly okay with it. He symbolizes a lot of choices I've made over and over in my life to the same result. Not the showing up high threatening me if I don't take him back part—more the jumping into bed with guys without considering the long-term consequences of…well, anything."

"Okay," Carys said with uncertainty.

"I also came to realize while I was in Nashville that I don't want to keep touring. It's exhausting. Eventually I won't want to keep up with my ArtBeat, which is also unnerving. I have built my entire existence around touring and my online presence. I've done well and made great investments, but not enough to retire on my thirtieth birthday and live comfortably forever."

"Oh, Vinny," she squealed. "You're growing up!"

Vinny snorted, rolling her eyes. "Hardly."

"Growing up doesn't mean you have to be boring, Vin," Carys scolded.

"Lies," she said, not because she believed it but because it was more comfortable to cling to her old ways by covering her disease with sarcasm. "I'm at a crossroads, Carys. I don't want to do what I've been doing forever, but I don't know where to go next. Music is still all I know and what drives me. But if I'm not touring, and I'm not continuing my music channels online…" Her speech dropped off as her uncertainties crept in again.

"You'll figure it out," Carys said confidently. "Thank you for telling me what's going on in that head of yours. I've been worried."

"I know, and I'm sorry for putting you through it. I don't really know how to talk about whatever this is. It feels heavy, and *scary.*" Vinny closed her eyes against the pressure building before her tears took an unwanted tumble down her face.

"Lavender Blume, who do you think you are talking to?" Carys laughed and Vinny focused back on her. "I thought I was going to be a brilliant career woman. It was going to be me and my millions, living the life in some expensive beach house my mother didn't know how to find.

"But then *you* drug me off to Mexico. You think allowing myself a week with a stranger was easy? Or going back to meet him later five months pregnant with his baby? I was *terrified.* The only thing that kept me going was knowing if Eric wasn't the guy I thought he was, I had my best friend.

"Change is hard, Vin. I know firsthand. But it's also inevitable. The question is, are you going to make the changes *you* want—accepting you might fail along the way— or are you going to let the world force you into change that will make you miserable? Either way, you will have a place in this family to fall back on. *That* will always be your constant."

"Unless I start doing lines on your roof," Vinny dead-panned, referencing their conversation from the year prior. It had become an inside joke.

Carys laughed. "Right. I forgot about your tar habit."

Vinny didn't bother telling Carys black tar *was* the street name of an illicit drug. She liked her pure of heart bestie just the way she was...somewhat ignorant, in this case. Instead, she pulled her in close and squeezed. "Thank you," she murmured.

"That's what best friends are for," Carys said. When she pulled away, there was a glimmer of spunk in her eyes. "Now can I see your new song?"

"No."

"Fine. Will you tell me why Ruben left your garage last night in a huff?"

Of fucking course, she saw him leave.

"Get out." Vinny gave Carys her best stink eye.

Carys pealed with laughter, undeterred by Vinny's

refusals. "Fine. I'll ask Eric to get it out of Ruben," she said as she sauntered toward the door.

"Out, woman! I'm working!"

It was hard to pretend to be menacing when you were laughing along with your tormentor.

———

BEN CAME BACK THAT NIGHT. He came back *every* night. Sometimes he brought a deck of cards and refused to leave until she played Spades with him, best out of three. Other times he had a movie and popcorn with him.

Every night he left her with a toe-curling kiss as a reminder of what she could have if she gave him the chance —if she gave *herself* the chance. She'd learned her lesson the first night though and made sure she was ready to take care of the ache his goodbyes left throbbing in her core. While she desperately wanted Ben's fingers inside her again, she knew he wouldn't let his control slip until they were both ready.

Her walks with Abner were less comfortable. He wasn't subtle about knowing where Ben went every night after dinner. He would needle her for details until she distracted him with a ride in the Camaro. Abner knew what she was doing. In fact, she was pretty sure there were days he laid it on extra heavy with the Ben and Vinny inquiries because he *wanted* her to take him on a ride.

Seriously. All he had to do was ask.

Ornery old man.

"You still haven't fully explained why you named your car *Lavender's Joy,*" he said one afternoon, his fingers trailing over the script on her dash.

"Technically, you never asked," she responded. They

were on their way back from a beach walk, and she was feeling pretty relaxed.

"Miss Blume," he said with all his formal southern aplomb, "May I know the story behind the name of your car?"

Damn. Who could say no to such a chivalrous request?

"My middle name is Joy, but there was a woman...I don't know her story, actually. I've always wondered. Sometimes when I'm working on her, I like to imagine her previous owner. She died, and her name was Joy. That's all I know about her, other than her love for our baby," Vinny said, giving the dashboard a loving pat. "It feels like our shared love for the car and the name Joy was meant to be so I call our baby Joy, for both the women who have loved her."

Abner was still and silent beside her as she parked back in her garage. When she turned off the engine and looked over at him, he was smiling and had tears streaming down his cheeks from reddened eyes. "That's beautiful."

Vinny blushed. "You don't think its idealistic nonsense?"

He shook his head. "We are only gone once everyone has forgotten us. Every time you think of her, you are keeping a stranger alive a little longer."

"Oh. I hadn't thought of it like that," Vinny said with tenderness. "It's rather poetic. Like a love song."

"Because it *is* a love song, Vinny. Restoring this old car was a labor of love. Over the years I'm sure you and your father put far more money into the car than its selling value, but you also put something much more powerful into it— memories. *Love.*"

"Damn it, Abner." She sniffled. "Now you've got me crying too."

"Come on," he said, unbuckling his seat belt. "I have a secret stash of ice cream in my freezer Ruben doesn't know about. Let's go back across the street and I will make it up to you with rocky road."

"How did you know I like rocky road ice cream?" she asked once they were strolling along.

"I didn't. It was my wife's favorite, and I still like to indulge on occasion."

"Then what is *your* favorite?"

He laughed as they made their way across the street. "Vanilla."

"Vanilla?" she said with surprise.

"I like a blank slate," he said with a little extra pep. "You can do anything with vanilla. Add chocolate, caramel, fruit, nuts…anything."

"So it isn't so much vanilla as the *potential* of vanilla."

"More or less. But sometimes what we really need is something simple too. Something unmarred by the excessively enticing sweetness we tend to be surrounded with."

Why did she feel like he wasn't talking about ice cream anymore?

"Honestly, Abner. *Unmarred?* I don't know how Ben hasn't realized you are a college educated man."

Chapter Forty-One

RUBEN

Greer was still working. Ruben knew it was because they were still deep diving to build the biggest case they could against him before they court marshaled him right into the inner sanctum of Hell. For a man like Greer who enjoyed power, being stripped of rank and thrown in a military prison was as good as an assignment cleaning out Lucifer's chamber pot after he'd suffered a particularly pungent and lasting case of food poisoning.

Nothing could make it easy for him to grin like an idiot every time he ran into the man, which seemed to be unusually often given he had fully transitioned to his new job far, far away from Greer's domain. The man was like a damn tumor. No matter how hard Ruben tried to cut him away, he kept on popping up. Eric was in no better mood over the frequency Greer found his way toward their offices.

Worst of all, he was far too...*nice.* As if they were his beer drinking buddies and not lower ranking officers.

"He still want's my wife," Slow said before angrily sinking his teeth into a sub sandwich. They were holed up in his office for their lunch break with the door locked after

Ruben had seen Greer striding across the parking lot. Ruben had a perfect view out his office window across the hall from Slow and warned him when he could.

"He makes me sick. I mean for real sick, man. Finding out how deep he was in with Carla was more than a little nauseating." Ruben had hurled over the toilet when he got home from the meeting at Vinny's. Realizing his ex-boss and his ex-wife had likely fucked all over *his* house while he was out of town infuriated him.

"How is Operation Lavender?" Slow asked.

Ruben scowled. "Fuck you."

Slow laughed. "You know I'm on your side. It's been what? Two weeks now? Are you getting anywhere with her? Other than blue balls."

"More like purple," he mumbled. "That woman drives me crazy. I know she's cracking on the inside, but she's too stubborn to let me in. What else can I do? After everything that happened with Jake, how can she think I won't run to her defense when she needs me?"

"Maybe it's deeper than that. Jenny Moore was a long time ago. There have been a lot of others to add to and compound her insecurities over the years. You should ask Q this weekend," he suggested.

"Her dad? He's coming down?"

"Yeah, Carys decided we need to have a potluck."

"She does know Thanksgiving and Christmas are coming up, right?"

"I think that may be why. Get everyone together before it gets too crazy."

"The kids were pretty cute on Halloween," Ruben said with a smile. Maya had decided to go as all her favorite princesses. He'd been so proud, even if it did make things frustrating for her when nobody recognized her creative genius. "And it's supposed to be dry, so we can let the kids wear themselves out in your back yard."

"That's the idea."

Ruben balled up his sandwich wrapper and tossed it toward Slow's trash. He missed. "Well, I've got a report to finish," he said as he went after his makeshift ball and put it in the wastebasket. "I'll see you later."

"Yeah, on your way to kiss Vinny goodnight and leave her hanging."

"I'm not the one clinging to their insecurities. She'll figure it out," he said with a shrug of resignation.

"Sure. In the meantime, I meant what I said. You should talk to her dad."

Not a chance in Hell.

"I'll think about it."

———

SATURDAY DAWNED CHEERFULLY, as any weekend in southern California did so long as it wasn't raining or foggy. Ruben woke far less radiant. He probably wouldn't get to kiss Vinny goodnight while her dad was here. Carys had already warned him days ago what he'd assumed for himself; Q stayed with Vinny. Having slept on her couch himself, Ruben knew it wasn't a bad deal.

On the other hand, he was curious to see what would happen when their fathers sat down together. Would they recognize each other? Or would they have to piece it together? Ruben had come home that fateful day to an empty garage, so he hadn't met Quincy Blume the day he'd bought the car off Abner.

Part of him wanted to ask his dad not to draw attention to their connection. Vinny still didn't know, and Ruben wasn't sure it was wise to tell her. *My luck she'll think I'm after her for the damn car.*

On the other hand, maybe she'd think it was destiny. It was anyone's guess, except for maybe Carys. Ruben would not be asking Carys her opinion because it would mean *telling her.* Carys was many things, but good at keeping secrets from Vinny wasn't one of them. One pitcher of her damn margaritas and she'd sing like a canary.

"You're moping," Abe said at the breakfast table.

"I didn't sleep well," he lied.

Abe let out an amused grunt. "I think you're *chicken.*"

Ruben's head snapped up from his plate. "What?"

"Either that or you are already pining over sneaking across the street to see Miss Blume this evening." Ruben scowled. "I see."

"See *what?*"

"It's both," Abe said.

"Oh, for fucks sakes, Dad."

"You better work on something more convincing if you are going to sway her, son."

"Did you miss the way I went to her when her ex showed up high?" he threw back sarcastically.

Abe cocked a brow at him.

"Wasn't that *bowling alley* enough?" he added in frustration.

"Ruben, every woman needs something different. You've shown your dedication, and I think your devotion to these evening meet ups *is* wearing her down further, but she needs something else. It's your job to figure out what it is."

As much as he wanted to remain cross with his father, Abner was right. And despite Ruben's attitude, Abe hadn't risen to the challenge. He saw Vinny daily and was far more accepted by her than Ruben was. Yeah, she kissed him back

—hell, last night she'd anticipated him—but she didn't trust him with her secrets. The Holt man wearing that badge of honor was Abe, not Ruben.

"You'll get there," Abe said, standing from the table. He walked his plate to the sink to rinse before wandering back to his room, clapping his warm hand on Ruben's shoulder as he passed in solidarity.

"What am I missing?" Ruben asked the empty room.

————

Vinny

"There's my girl," Q said, pulling his daughter in for a hug. "Why haven't you been by to see your old man since I got back with *your* van?"

"Hi, Dad." Vinny soaked in the familiarity of her father. "It's been a little crazy lately."

"You okay? I would have come down sooner—"

"No, Dad. I'm not upset about the thing with Jake. It was scary as hell in the moment, but now I feel…indifferent? I'm not even sure." She let him go and stepped back so she could give him a genuine smile.

"Then what's been eating you? Even in Nashville, you were going through the motions," he said with concern.

Of course he picked up on that.

"How did you know?"

"You weren't trying to sneak around with dipshits like usual."

"Dad!"

Quincy laughed. "What, you think I don't know? Where do you think you get the itch?"

"We're not talking about your hound dogging around

before you met Mom," Vinny said with humor. "I know you were once a young man. I've seen the pictures. That's more than enough, thanks."

He laughed. "Fine. But don't think I'm not aware you've been stuck." Q's brows came together as he studied her face. "Well, you *were* blocked. What happened?"

"I don't know," she said with a shrug. "One day it just came back."

Vinny didn't know how to explain to her dad the sledge-hammer appeared to be Jake's dramatic visit. For one thing, it didn't make sense. Why would something so awful break her creative block? Vinny was stumped enough without her father insisting they go over her memory of the events with a fine-toothed comb.

Her block was gone. She was too grateful to require a clear *why.*

To keep him from dwelling on it, she encouraged him to come inside and settle in.

"Oh, I'm not staying with you this time. I told Carys I wanted more time with the kids and she offered her guest room in the house," he said.

Vinny's jaw dropped. "I *am* your kid!"

"Ah, but you are not *a* kid. Maya and Brendon have missed out on Grandpa Q time."

"But," she sputtered. *He's seriously choosing them over me?*

"Sorry, Vinny. You have to share me."

"Fine," she said flatly, turning back from her garage door. She waved her hand toward the back door to the main house. "After you, *Grandpa Q."*

"Jealousy is rather amusing on you, Vin."

"It's your own fault I'm an only child and never learned to share my things."

"Oh, please. You had Carys. The two of you shared everything, including your parents. Sometimes even your underwear."

That's different.

She quietly carried her father's duffle over her shoulder behind him, ignoring the way everyone greeted him along the way and the boisterous giggles from the kids at seeing him. *He's going to see them all day. Why can't he stay with me? We won't have any time alone if he's staying here.*

She was still harumphing when they returned downstairs from the guestroom. While her father stopped to pick up Brendon, Vinny sulked into the kitchen to see what she could do to help Carys ready for her guests.

"You're terrible with sharing your dad," she said with a giggle.

"Well…he's *mine.*" It was lame, she knew. But her father was an integral part of Vinny and she didn't feel sorry about wanting to keep him for herself at least some of the time.

"Oh, please. We both know you weren't so clingy before your mother passed. And I'm not trying to push your buttons, Vin. It is what it is, and there is nothing wrong with it. But to be jealous of your godchildren is a touch ridiculous, even for you," she teased.

Vinny let out a long, overly dramatic sigh before picking up a peeler and a bag of carrots. "I'll start your veggie tray."

"Thank you."

She hummed as she worked, not so much dawdling but certainly not rushing through her task. By the time she was finished, she turned around to find Ben standing in the kitchen doorway, grinning like a lune at her.

"Hi, Lavender."

"Hello, Ben," she said as she walked by him. She set the platter down on the dining room table before turning to dig out the ranch dip Carys had made earlier from the fridge. Carys was obsessed with giving it a day for the flavors to *meld,* whatever that meant. Ranch was ranch to Vinny.

"What's that you were humming?" he asked as she went by again.

"Bill Withers," she said. "It's been stuck in my head for weeks and I can't get it out."

He stepped up next to her as she scooped a healthy glob into the built-in dip bowl in the middle of Carys's fancy tray. "Really? I'm a fan."

"Of ranch?" she asked with confusion, turning to face him. He was still smiling at her like she was the most amusing thing he'd ever seen.

"As delicious as Carys's ranch dip is, I meant the song."

"Oh. It's one of the first things I learned to play on every instrument." *Why did I volunteer that information?* "It's… catchy."

"Seems like it, if you've been humming it for weeks."

"It was my mother's favorite."

"You don't say?" His Georgian accent slipped in enough to make her hesitate.

"Are you mocking me, Ben?" The question somewhat sobered his expression. He was still wearing a goofy smile though.

"I wouldn't do that to you."

"You sound like you're teasing me."

"Not teasing you, but I do find the coincidence amusing."

"What?" *He's maddening today. Spit it out, Ben.*

"Your mother shared musical tastes with *my* mother."

"Oh. It was a popular tune," she said. "'Lean on Me' was the first single off Withers' second album, Still Bill, and was number one on two different Billboard music charts when it was released in '72."

Oh my god, I'm blathering like Carys!

Vinny promptly shut her mouth, but couldn't help adding a whole second later, "My dad taught it to me," before truly locking her jaws shut.

"Maybe I should tell *my* dad so they can talk about something else they have in common," Ben mused.

"Oh, is Abner here?" she asked, perking right up.

"He's in the living room reminiscing about Motown with Quincy." Ben let out a chuckle. "They are two peas in a pod."

"Really?"

"Why do you sound so surprised? After the way Dad praised your playlists the entire drive here?"

"That's true," Vinny conceded. "I think I better go say hello."

Vinny dodged around Ben before he could remark, hot footing it into the living room, only to pull up short as her father and Abner broke into raucous laughter. *Of course, the two of them get along.*

Her stomach curdled.

This wasn't fair.

She spun back on her heel and marched back through the kitchen.

"Where are you going?" Ben asked as she hurried by.

"I just…I'll be in my studio for a bit."

Some time later—having purged her feelings into a recording and uploading it to her profile—she shut down her recording equipment and lighting and tucked away her Strat before realizing with abject horror she'd just poured her everything into a dramatic version of Chris Isaak's song, "Wicked game."

And it was already trending on her ArtBeat.

What were the chances her family would miss it?

Chapter Forty-Two

RUBEN

"What crawled up her ass?" Carys asked from the sink.

"I think she's upset our fathers are getting along so well," he said with amusement.

"Why would *that* upset her? You know what, don't answer. I know exactly why," she huffed.

"Care to share with the class?"

"She's jealous."

"Of my dad?"

"Of anyone who takes Q's attention off *her.*"

Speaking of the man himself, Quincy came through the door with Abe on his heels. "Is she off pouting again?" he asked.

"Of course," Carys chortled.

Quincy rolled his eyes. "That girl. Every time we spend more than a few weeks apart she gets like this. Be glad you have a son, Abe," he said.

"Boys are a different kind of trouble," Abe piped up.

"Hey!" Ruben cried while everyone else had a chuckle at his expense.

"What did I miss?" Slow asked, squeezing into the

kitchen behind the others, who had crowded just inside the doorway.

"Vinny," several voices chorused.

"Ah. Say no more. Do you need any help, sweetheart?" he asked his wife.

"No, we're ready for Zeke to show. I kept it small today."

"While we're waiting, do you play Spades, Q?" Abe asked.

Thus began an afternoon and evening of mostly card games. When Zeke arrived, They pulled out another deck and a folding table and chairs, passing the kids around to "help" from whichever lap they desired. By the time Vinny decided to rejoin them, Zeke was getting swept under the rug by Abe and Q.

"This again," Vinny huffed teasingly. "Careful, Zeke. Abner cheats."

"Why didn't you tell me that an hour ago? Whose side are you on, Vin?" he said.

"You'll never know," she said lightly.

"That's because Vinny also cheats," Ruben said as he took his turn.

"I do not!"

"Prove it." The room *oohed* with Ruben's call out.

"You aren't going to let him talk to you like that, are you?" Carys goaded her.

"I hate you," Vinny muttered under her breath as she dropped into the chair beside him as the next round of Spades began.

"You certainly haven't proven your supposed hatred either. I hope you bring more energy to cards," he parried, keeping his words low as well. "I'm not sure you have the follow through for either."

"Are you saying I can't win without cheating?"

"I'm saying you only hate me because you have to cheat to beat me."

"Oie!" Zeke yelled from across the table. "Flirt on your own time. Deal the cards, brother."

"We—"

"Don't deny you're a flirt, Vin. Then we'll all know you're a liar as well," Carys cut her off.

The rest of the evening was filled with cheap shots and irrational bets. They laughed and cajoled each other long after the kids were tucked into bed, at which point they'd taken a break for dessert.

"You made your cake," Quincy said as he rubbed his hands together. "Still use your mother's recipe?"

"Of course," Vinny said.

"You know," he began, but Vinny was too quick for him to finish whatever he was going to say.

"Nobody wants to hear about how Mom won you over with cake, Dad. Please, if you love me at all, spare everyone your double intenders on frosting."

The men all snickered while Carys and Vinny rolled their eyes.

"At least tell them what it's called," Carys said as everyone was hefting forkfuls into their mouths.

"Better Than Sex Cake!" she yelled with gusto.

Zeke and Ruben both choked as they attempted to swallow, laugh, and breath at the same time.

"Warn a man, Vin," Zeke heckled her when he'd cleared his airway.

Ruben could tell by the smirk on her face, she'd timed her words precisely for the reaction she wanted. Ruben made his decision. *Fuck it. I'm getting my kiss tonight.*

"At the very least, don't kill the only medic," Ruben said.

Zeke headed out after he lost yet another round of Spades

to Abner after dessert. "You're right, Vinny. He cheats. I don't know how, but he's definitely cheating." Zeke said playfully.

"Experience trumps cockiness, son," Abe jabbed back. Ruben could tell his dad liked Zeke, and given his banter all evening, Zeke felt the same about Abe. It made Ruben wish he'd been able to get him out here sooner.

Abe and Quincy walked out with Zeke, waving him off before the older men settled down on the front stoop and continued to gossip like a couple old peahens. Ruben shook his head and went back into the kitchen to help the women clear the remaining mess. Slow insisted on doing the dishes so Carys could enjoy a hot shower. Once the extra table and chairs were stowed away in the garage, there wasn't anything else to do.

Ruben said his goodbyes to Slow and trailed after Vinny out the back door.

"Hold up there, Lavender," he called. She was nearly through her garage door, which he knew she'd bolt once it was closed.

"You need something?"

"You know what I need," he said coyly.

She blushed crimson. "Ben. Someone might hear you."

"Carys is in the shower, the kids are in bed, Zeke's long gone, and our fathers are out front on the stoop most likely throwing us both under the bus."

"You forgot Eric."

Ruben looked back toward the kitchen window, where it was now dark. "He's probably already in the shower with his wife."

"Ben…"

"Can I come in, beautiful?" he tried again.

In answer, she stood back, holding the door open for him.

"Thank you." He took a moment to appreciate her car while he waited for her to close and lock the door. "It really is a gorgeous machine," he said as she came up beside him. "You did an amazing job bringing her back to life."

"She was already alive. We returned her sparkle," Vinny said wistfully as she stared at her Camaro.

"May I walk you up?"

"You just want to stare at my ass," she retorted.

"Who wouldn't," he said casually, not fool enough to deny it.

She shook her head as she turned toward the stairs. "Fine." Once she was on the upper landing, she turned to him and said, "That was a terrible plan. Now I have to walk back down to lock the lower door again when you leave."

"Hmm. Guess you better let me go out your front door then," he said with a smirk. He was two steps down and landed a few inches shorter than her from his position.

"What do you want, Ben?" she whispered as she nervously fiddled with her keys.

"Same thing I want every night, beautiful. For you to let me in." He leaned forward and ran the end of his nose up her jawbone before placing a tender kiss behind her ear. "Unlock the door, Lavender."

He could see her nipples poking through her tee and smiled to himself once her back was turned. Ruben had learned she could be as easily turned on by a gentle caress as she was when he damn near took possession of her. But his favorite was when she dueled him for control of their kisses.

While she'd eventually warmed up, she'd spent most of the day pouting one way or another, like a spoiled little brat— all because her father wouldn't let her monopolize his time. Ruben was highly amused by the display. Especially when he realized Quincy was staying in Carys's guest room, instead of with Vinny.

He followed her inside, closing and locking the door behind him for her. The last time he'd come up the back stairs had been under different circumstances, and he hadn't paid much attention. Now he let his eyes wander around. Vinny's bedside table lamp was on, and he smiled at the *illuminating* collection on display beneath the soft glow.

"What do you do with these, Lavender?" he asked as he gestured through the doorway.

"Oh, fuck," she muttered, her face flushing.

"Of course, but I was hoping for more detail," he teased.

"You want a demonstration?" she snarked.

Ruben grinned down at her wickedly. "If you insist."

"Get your kiss and go, Ben." She tried to lean in, but he stilled her with a hand on her shoulder.

"But you've offered me so much more, beautiful. No man alive could turn down such a generous offer."

"You know it was in jest."

Watching her get all flustered and heated was making Ruben heat up too. "What if we made it a joint effort?"

"Ha! Last time you left me on the edge and all alone!"

"This time you'll have your fully charged collection of toys ready for your use."

"And what will you be doing?"

"What do you want me to be doing?"

"Leaving."

"Liar." The accusation came out with enough heat to make her swallow hard. He watched the motion in the dim light of the hallway with fascination.

"You're growling," she whimpered.

"I'm standing in front of a temptress and being told I can't have her. Of course I'm growling."

"How is it you are so carefree and easy around everyone else, but when we are alone, you look like you want to eat me alive? It's like you are two separate people."

"Because I *do* want to eat you alive, Lavender. I've seen you, smelled you, *tasted* you. You consume me day and night, but especially when I'm alone." He gently pulled her into his side, locking gazes with her. He loved this part. The way her lips parted with anticipation, the feel of her warmth against his larger frame. "I'm not a selfish man, Lavender. But you make me desperate for you. Every kiss adds to the blaze you've set inside me. It's enough to make me want to take for a change."

"Then why don't you?" she asked huskily.

"Because I won't take what needs to be given freely. And I'm not talking about the paradise between your legs, beautiful. I want—*need*—what you keep caged."

She stared up at him with doe eyes, unblinking. For the first time, he could see a change. No longer was she hellbent on denying him. Now she was unsure how to go about giving in. She'd been afraid for so long; she'd forgotten how to trust another with the tempestuous organ beating out the rhythm to which she lived her life.

But she wanted to.

He could see it swirling in her mind.

It gave him hope.

"I'm going to touch you, beautiful. No, not like that," he said when she tensed against him. His eyes wandered over to her sex toys and back. "You will touch *yourself* there."

If he kissed her properly, he'd have what he'd been coming for night after night. Instead, he trailed his lips tenderly across her face, pulling away when she lunged for his mouth with her own. "Not yet." A whine escaped her pouty lips, but she didn't try again.

Ruben led Vinny to her bed, where he gently tugged her top off over her head before sitting down beside her and scooting back to her headboard. "Between my legs, beautiful. I'm going to hold you while you make yourself come."

Without direction, she toed off her sneakers, dropped her jeans and panties together, and then climbed up onto the bed with her back to his chest. He tucked her in against him, wrapping his arms around her while his fingertips began to gently roam over her bare flesh. Ruben watched with fascination as goosebumps erupted wherever he explored.

He left her bra alone, sensing she wasn't ready to expose the rest of herself to him. He watched her peaks pebble through the fabric as he stroked around her breasts. "Choose a toy and tell me about it."

Without hesitation, she reached for an oddly shaped teal vibrator and a bottle of tingling lube. "This is my favorite," she murmured, her eyes focused on the toy. "I like that I can control the stimulation to my clit and my G-spot separately."

"Why tingling lube?" he prompted.

"More sensation, I guess," she said as more of a question, like she hadn't put any thought into it before. She knew what she liked, and that's what she used. Why didn't seem to matter.

"Show me, beautiful." She looked up over her shoulder at him, searching for something. He knew she'd found whatever it was when she turned back around and popped the top of the lube open, dripping a generous amount onto the toy before smearing it around. The excess on her fingers she worked over her sex, her breath catching as she stroked herself. "Ben," she whimpered.

"I'm here." He slid one hand down over her soft stomach, spreading his fingers wide. The other played with her long silvery white locks. "Show me."

Ruben's cock ached, but he fought the impulse to grind it against her backside. He had a feeling he'd embarrass himself if he did, blowing his load in his pants like the sexually starved man he absolutely was. He needn't have worried overly much in the end. Once Vinny began teasing her core with the toy, her hips began working in a steady motion, increasing her own pleasure—and his.

The feel of her body arching and grinding down onto his cock was pure torture. "Jesus, Lavender. Fucking hell."

Emboldened by the arousal plain in his voice, she worked herself harder while he watched. He could hear the faint humming of the toy changing as she switched through the settings, until the moans coming out of the O her mouth was formed into were too loud for him to notice anything else.

"That's it, beautiful. You're so damn sexy."

She arched herself further up his body before dropping back against his cock, oblivious to the torture she delivered in doing so. Ruben pressed his hand down more firmly, keeping her steadier against him.

"Ben."

"Come for me, Lavender. I need you."

Her abs tightened beneath his palm as she began jerking against her vibrator with more desperation than finesse. Her body coiled tight against is, and he slid his hand up her hair until he was cradling the base of her head, his firm grip in her silky strands sending her over the edge.

Ruben directed her head with his grip, giving himself full access to her smart mouth, swallowing her moans of ecstasy as he devoured her, his tongue dominating hers. He teased, alternating nipping with his teeth and gently soothing her lips with his own before sliding his tongue inside for another taste. He drew it out, kissing her long and hard—enough for a second wave of pleasure to tighten her body against his before she relaxed into his embrace.

Ruben slowed when he could sense she was spent, allowing her heart rate to calm as he traded the passion driven ravaging fed by her orgasm for a more languorous exploration. By the time he released her, she was too exerted and relaxed to move off him.

He looked down at her hand, lying limp on her bed next to her favorite vibrator, which was coated in her cream and still pulsing. Vinny let out a satisfied sigh in his arms. If he stayed much longer, he wouldn't be able to leave her at all.

Lavender wasn't ready for a night of spooning.

Carefully, Ruben managed to scoop Vinny up enough to guide her body onto the bed beside him so he could stand up. It took some doing, but he managed to get her limp, sated body tucked in. He even took her vibrator into the bathroom and washed it for her after turning it off.

Next, he switched off her lamp and bent over to gently kiss her forehead before he headed home.

"Ben…"

"Shhh. Sleep, Lavender. Thank you for trusting me tonight."

Chapter Forty-Three

RUBEN

He didn't make it far. Ruben locked up Vinny's front door and slowly headed down the stairs toward the driveway. As he came around the corner of the house, he heard a voice call out to him from the front stoop.

"I suppose this is where I ask what your intentions are with my daughter." It was said with humor, but it was so unexpected Ruben still jumped like a startled alley cat.

"Man, you scared the shit out of me," Ruben said with relief once he'd figured out where Quincy's voice was coming from. "My dad go home?"

"He called it quits after the first twenty minutes waiting on you." He chuckled softly.

"Ah. You two seemed to get along like old friends this evening," Ruben deflected.

"We are old friends, of a sort. It took a good hour for me to convince your father to sell me the Camaro."

"He didn't want to do it."

"He did not. But he was *right* to do it. You're a good man, Ruben. I've often wondered about the boy who needed book money."

"When did you figure it out?"

"Oh, about halfway through the first rant she went on, shortly after Maya was born." Ruben had taken a seat beside him while they spoke and could see Quincy's mirth bubbling over by the way his eyes shined in the dim light of suburbia.

"Why didn't you tell her?"

"I didn't tell her anything about your family."

"I know, I just don't know why."

He shrugged slightly, saying, "It wasn't my tale to tell. You should tell her."

"Nah, man. That will get me banned for life. She'll decide I'm only trying so hard to get to her *baby,* and I'll be ousted before the whole story is out. Besides, she's been to the house I was raised in. She knows my origins." *The humble beginnings I fought to overcome so the future love of my life wouldn't suffer the way Mom did,* he finished in his head.

"And Vinny?"

"What about her?"

Quincy cleared his throat before saying, "Carys said you saw Jake coming."

A wave of dread passed over Ruben as the memory gripped his chest tightly. "Yeah. That was messed up. He didn't look right."

"Why didn't you try going after him?"

"I'd just been cleared for normal activities after breaking my right foot. Going after him would have been stupid."

"Did you consider it?"

"Not for a second. I didn't have a weapon, and no clue as to what he was carrying. I bolted straight through the house and out the back with the spare key."

"Carys said that too."

"Sounds like the queen has been entertaining at the jester's expense," Ruben said.

"I held the baby for ransom."

"It's a good thing I know you're joking," Ruben said, clicking his tongue. "Brendon's got my love for ball already. You should see his accuracy when he throws them at Maya's head."

Quincy chuckled. "He's a toddler."

"Don't care. That's my boy, sleeping up there," he said with an upward jerk of his head.

"Vinny would argue he's *hers.*"

"Lavender needs to learn to *share.*"

"She does, which is why I'm waiting out here to talk to you. My daughter won't give me the nitty gritty details I need, Ruben. You were there."

They both fell silent while Ruben contemplated his response. "I'll do what I can. Depends on what you want to know." The last thing he wanted to do was violate her trust, but he also understood her father needed assurances she wasn't sweeping something serious under the rug.

"Did he get anywhere near her?"

"No. He never set eyes on her, much less a hand."

"Was she…scared?"

"Of course she was, but you know Lavender. She had the security feeds up on the TV so she could see what he was doing and her firearm ready. I personally helped Slow install her front door. It's solid as you can get. She was shaking, but in the moment, she was in control."

"What did you do when you got inside?" he asked after he'd absorbed Ruben's previous answer.

"I supported her."

"How?"

"With my body."

"You mean you shielded her?"

"Hell, no. I've been on the wrong side of her firearm

when she's amped up." Quincy eyed him suspiciously. "Long story, and I did it to myself. The point is, she didn't need shielding. She needed to feel like she was in control. I stood behind her and steadied her against my body while she kept her gun level. That's it."

"You just *held* her?"

"Held her up, yeah. Until the cops came. Then I got her settled on the couch before the adrenaline rush dropped her to the floor."

"My sources say you stayed with her for several hours after the fact."

"I did." He wasn't going to tell Quincy anything else about the hours after the cops left. Especially the last hour before he had to force himself to walk away from her. "She was wiped. I made sure she was steady before I headed out."

He cocked a brow at Ruben's less than forthcoming explanation, but Ruben held firm. "Fine," he conceded when the stare-off didn't make Ruben squirm. "One more thing, and then I'm going to bed. Did she say anything?"

"While we were waiting for the police to arrive?"

"At all."

"I established who I was so she didn't accidentally shoot me." *Lessons learned and all that. Identify yourself when entering another's home.* "When I got to her, she pointed to the screen and said she thought Jake was high. I texted the info to Carys, who was already on the phone with EMS. After that, nothing. Well…" Ruben hesitated. She hadn't spoken, but her dad would probably appreciate it. "She hummed."

"Same song she's been humming all day?"

"That's the one. She said earlier it's been stuck in her head for weeks," Ruben offered.

Quincy let out a deep, honest laugh. "I like you, Ruben. Thanks for stopping to set a father's mind at ease."

Ruben puzzled over what was so funny as he walked home alone.

Am I missing something?

———

THREE DAYS LATER, Ruben watched as Quincy drove off and Tripp pulled in shortly after. He knew Vinny and Abe would both miss him, but Ruben was starting to get a weird vibe from Q. He kept catching the man grinning at him. It was fucking weird.

Tripp on the other hand he now had a rapport with. They'd bump fists outside the garage as he was leaving, snickering over the way Vinny rolled her eyes when Tripp called back something like, "Pucker up, Vin," or "She's all yours," before he climbed into his car to leave. Short of Carys —who already loved Ruben—Tripp was Vinny's next closest friend. Having the gold star from him felt important.

"Hey, beautiful." Ruben grinned at his girl while the sound of Tripp's car disappeared into the night. "Let's get you out of the winter night air."

She snorted. "It's not cold out."

"It is for California. Don't want that pert little nose of yours bulbous and red from a cold for Thanksgiving," he said, crowding her in the doorway until she stepped back. He walked to the stairs and began climbing them as she locked the back door.

"What are you doing, Ben?"

"Going inside."

"We *are* inside!"

"Inside the garage. Not *inside* inside. Come on, Lavender. You know you want to." He looked down on her as he continued to climb. The flush spreading across her like wildfire had his cock jerking against the back of his zipper. With a halfhearted huff, she followed him up, shoving him aside at the landing to unlock the door.

"Don't bother looking. I tucked all my toys away," she said.

"That's a shame. Hand's down, that was the best good-night kiss of my life."

"I don't understand when you got so damn cocky," she groused. "Carys always swore you were sweet as a Georgia peach."

"I am." *If you'd stop making me completely feral, I might lighten up on occasion.*

"Not when we're alone. Only around everyone else. Why is that?"

"That's a trap." He chuckled. "Let's see if you can figure it out on your own."

"Or you could tell me."

"Nah, where's the fun in that?"

He was already striding toward her sofa, so he couldn't make out whatever she was growling under her breath as she locked her rear entry. Ruben took heart in knowing it was about him and decided to take it as a compliment.

"You're too comfortable. Get off my couch."

He'd barely settled in when she snarled at him, her hands on her hips and a wicked scowl on her face—Elphaba wicked, not the sexy kind. "Lavender. That was rude," he deadpanned.

"You don't need to get cozy for your obligatory kiss," she hissed out.

"Obligatory," he repeated, a hand over his heart. "I'm attempting to woo you, beautiful. But if you aren't enjoying out little moments, I can stop."

She shifted her stance, trying to subtly rub her thighs together. Ruben smirked. *That's what I thought.*

"I really hate you," she said in a dead tone.

"Uh huh." He patted the empty cushion beside him. "Come on, Lavender. Where are your manners?"

"As dead as you would be if I had laser vision," she snarked as she planted her sweet ass as far from him as possible on the couch.

He tsked at her. "I think you're grumpy because your dad left."

"Am not," she said with the animation of a rock.

"Did you really hate sharing him with the kids that much? They call him *Grandpa,* Lavender," he teased.

"Shut up. *Please,"* she added as an afterthought.

"What movie are we going to watch?"

Her expression morphed into one of absolute horror. "No."

"Never heard of it. Romantic comedy?"

"No, we are not watching a movie. Get your kiss and get out!"

"That's not what you need, beautiful."

"Don't tell me what I need!" He'd be dust twice over by now if she truly had lethal vision. Unfortunately for Vinny, her ire turned him on, not off. Ruben didn't bother hiding the fact he was adjusting himself. "Are you *serious* right now? Why are you turned on?"

"How do you feel about brat pack movies?"

She stared at him incredulously, her jaw dropping. "Ben."

"Or we could go more modern. Nothing too long, I have to be up early for work. Takes the entire Marvel Universe out of the running, sadly."

"I. Hate you."

"Sure, beautiful. I'll pick," Ruben said, reaching for her

remote. "You seem tense. I'm going back to the romantic comedy idea."

He logged into his streaming account while she continued to will his heart into seizing—he was pretty sure that's what she was attempting with her stern glare. It was only a matter of time before she beaned him with one of the guitars displayed over their heads, so he needed to defuse the situation before she too remembered her collection of makeshift murder weapons. Ruben swiped through his saved list—he'd had the forethought to throw some options in there like a good little Marine, always prepared—and clicked on America's Sweethearts.

"Why this?"

"Are you kidding? Billy Crystal is the man. Great casting, clever puns, and did I mention Billy Crystal?" She glared at him. "You're right. He's worth mentioning twice."

Ruben wasn't sure if he should congratulate himself she was still beside him or back slowly out of the room for his own safety. When she settled down into the cushion halfway through the intro, he decided he was mostly safe. Probably.

Hopefully.

There were a lot of potential weapons hanging over their heads, disguised as guitars.

Chapter Forty-Four

VINNY

Every girl had there go-to movie. It didn't have to be mushy, but for Vinny, it was. Funny and cheesy at times, and oh so sweet with a great soundtrack. *How the fuck did he guess my movie? If Carys told him America's Sweethearts is my comfort movie, I will never make my cake for her again.*

She knew every line and still laughed in all the right places. Ben was right. Billy Crystal was a damn legend. Catherine Zeta-Jones made the debutante roll look easy. Seth Green took a golf ball to the head like nobody's business.

Who could watch without rooting for Eddie and Kiki? Vinny still swooned over the smooching through the bedsheet scene. It didn't get much more genuine than morning breath paralysis. And the way Kiki dumped his breakfast in his lap later…classic. *You go, girl. Make him earn you.*

Ben pulled her closer, and she let him. By the time Eddie publicly renounced Gwen for Kiki, they were a tangled mess of limbs, curled up together under the blanket she kept on the back of her couch. *How did that happen?*

He pulled her closer while the credits rolled, kissing her crown before tenderly trailing kisses down to her mouth. His kisses were different from day to day, always a different goodnight parting from the day before. Tonight was soft and sweet.

Ben's lips caressed her mouth, giving her assurances her needs came before his own. Soft, confident gestures wrapping her in warmth. His kiss was patient, even when she attempted to rush. He was making love to her mouth.

When he pulled away to go, she missed him immediately. Her favorite blanket felt like a meat locker without him sharing it. "Thanks, beautiful. I'll see you tomorrow."

He left. She watched him go, nodding dumbly as he reminded her to get the deadbolt on her way to bed. With every kiss, he'd left enough of himself behind she no longer felt like he was ever gone. He still hadn't taken a single liberty outside those kisses for himself—hadn't even suggested it. Vinny knew he was constantly in a state of arousal around her. She could see the evidence, when it wasn't prodding into whatever part of her he'd pulled close while he held her.

For going on three weeks, Ben had infused her with his intentions every evening. It was by far the most intimate and erotic thing to ever happen to her. Vinny was used to guys who took. The kind of guy who thought getting in her pants was the only end game.

Ben wasn't exclusively after her body.

What he wanted was far more dangerous.

With trepidation, she realized she'd given him all of her along the way without realizing it was done. She was his. But she couldn't let him know it. No matter how she felt about him, the risk still outweighed the reward in Vinny's estimation.

————

"HOW LONG ARE you going to make Ruben suffer?" Carys asked before casually sipping her coffee.

"Ha. I'm the one subjected to his presence every night against my will," Vinny snipped.

Carys rolled her eyes. "Whatever."

"I've got a gig next Tuesday," she said. Talking about Ben wasn't happening. "Tripp had a genius idea for a mash up. We're overlapping some crazy tunes. It's going to be wild."

"Down at Groove's club?"

"Yeah."

"Are you ready for that?"

"It's been over six months since I saw Tyler," she said with a shrug. "I can't avoid him forever, and I don't want to. He's my friend."

"You aren't going to…" Carys blushed.

"What, fuck him?"

"Always so blunt."

"If I was going to get involved with Tyler, I would have done it before, instead of walking out. I told you, he wants more than I can give him. He's a good person, Carys. I can't hurt him like that."

"You are a good person, but you hurt yourself like that."

"Meaning?"

"You push away the good ones for stupid guys who only use their micro heads."

"I'm not in a relationship with him, Carys." Vinny figured she better shut down whatever slop Carys was mentally doodling inside little hearts before the pipe dream could further propagate.

"Not officially."

"Not at *all.*"

"Do you remember when we talked about finding a keeper?"

"Which time?" she quipped.

"I was messed up about Eric, and you told me my guydar was better than yours."

"Yeah. You said it was because I have *guy*dar instead of *man*dar, and implied I needed a recalibration if I wanted a keeper."

"Good. I'm glad you remember. You should get on that recalibration pronto." Carys stood to place her mug in the kitchen sink. "I'm taking a shower now. Would you like me to go to your thing next Tuesday?"

"No, I just wanted you to know. I mean, you can come. I won't have you blacklisted," she said, trying to infuse a bit of humor.

"Okay. You want me to tell Ruben when he shows up Tuesday night wondering why you aren't there to suck face with?" she asked innocently.

"Carys!"

"It's only a question."

"I didn't want *you* to worry."

"Oh. Well, thanks for coming down for coffee this morning," she said as she walked away. "I've missed it."

Has it really been that long since I came down for coffee with her? Vinny thought it over as Carys's steps echoed up the staircase before disappearing altogether. *Huh.*

Ever since her creative block had disintegrated, she'd skipped her happy self straight down to the studio most mornings without coffee at all. Half the time she forgot breakfast until it qualified as a late lunch. She was so excited about the mash up Tripp had suggested, she wasn't doing much else other than fine tuning the set. They were calling it their Dreams Medley, and today was the first run at the club with Silla and Jae. They'd asked a few other friends to jump in as well.

Vinny was over the moon.

It had been a long time since she was this excited about performing. She swept it out of her mind for now as she placed her own mug in the dishwasher and headed out to the studio. There was something else she needed to work on, something that wasn't coming together quite right. She'd been working on it for weeks to no avail, but Vinny wasn't worried.

It would come to her eventually.

———

Ruben

"Better you than me," Slow teased.

"It's not a sure thing."

"Hope you're packed anyway. Surefire way to *make* a TDY a sure thing is to deny it's a possibility at all."

"Why do I eat lunch with you?"

"Because I'm your only friend."

"Low, man."

Slow laughed. "Where are they sending you?"

"They don't know when or where yet."

"Virginia."

"Why do you think that?"

"I'm guessing."

"I don't want to go to Virginia," he whined—in a manly way. Not like a kid.

"Don't you listen? It's set in stone now. They'll send you to Virginia."

"Maybe I should start bitching about how badly I don't want to go to Bora Bora."

"You can't pack Vinny in your luggage, Ruben."

He snorted. "If only. She'd claw my eyes out if I tried."

"How are things going with her?"

"She hasn't refused me entrance yet."

"Still stuck on goodnight kisses?" he asked with amusement.

"Not everyone elopes after a week in Mexico, asshole."

"They would have readily believed it had it been *you* doing the eloping," Slow said, his signature grin climbing up his face.

If I'd stayed long enough to meet Lavender, it might have been me. Ruben's brain went down this particular trail of what ifs often. If he hadn't left Mexico. If he had met her before he proposed to Carla. If, if, if.

What if I'm going about this all wrong, and I never graduate from tucking her in at night?

"You still there, Ruben?"

"Yeah, man. Just got lost for a second."

"You okay?"

He shook his head. "It's been almost a month. Some nights I drag it out with cards or a movie, but most nights I kiss her until I'm on the verge of taking it too far. Then I have to back off and let myself out."

"Have you tried asking her out on a real date?"

"Eh. No."

"Why not?"

"She's gone on plenty of dates. What she needs is someone who shows up for *her.*"

"It hurts when you 'catch feelings'," Slow said, quoting Ruben from the night he came in asking about Jenny Moore. "Even when you know she's yours, shit happens. Life changes. Sometimes you have to step back before you drown yourself in worry."

"I'm not worried she doesn't care," he said. "I'm worried

she won't admit to herself she already does. I'm an idiot about a lot of things, but I've seen real love. When Lavender thinks nobody is paying attention, I catch her staring at me the way Mom used to ogle Dad."

"You don't think she knows?"

"She still manages to tell me she hates me at least once a day. Fuck if I know."

One thing he did know, wooing Vinny was far more rewarding than chasing Carla had been. It was also infinitely more frustrating.

"She's got a show tonight," Slow said.

"I know," Ruben said cockily. "Tripp slipped me his number a few weeks ago. He's been low key threatening my balls if I don't show."

"You're going then, I presume?"

"Hell yes, I'm going. I'm not above stealing my kiss in public."

"You mean claiming her," Slow taunted.

"That too." He smiled to himself. "I don't think Tripp will mind. He stopped trying to make me jealous when he gave me his number."

"Either that or he's batting for the other team," Eric said.

"Man, you suck." He shook his head as Eric laughed at his expense.

Ruben went back to his desk, suffering through the last four hours of work best he could. He and Abe had been catching up on Vinny's ArtBeat account. It was like taking a crash course in all things her, Lavender 101. He could tell she had no clue how gorgeous she was when she was performing. It didn't matter if she was rasping out a tender ballad or wailing over her Strat, she was mesmerizing.

Then the music died and she retreated back into herself. He'd never experienced anything like it. While he and his dad watched one of the lives from the club she'd done last year as a promo, it struck him she only ever did covers and remixes. Ruben knew Vinny composed constantly.

Or had, before she'd been blocked. According to Carys and Tripp, she was working on her first new something since her creative side got with the program again. Unlike the past, she wasn't sharing with either of them. Carys seemed amused by it, but Tripp came off more affronted. Ruben speculated he was used to being Vinny's musical sounding board.

"You're going down to watch Vinny perform," Abe said as he cleared the plates after dinner.

"Yeah, bossy." Ruben chuckled. "I already told you I was surprising her. She hasn't been on stage since Nashville. Tripp said they haven't *collabed* in nearly eight months for a live show." He emphasized Tripp's word the same way Tripp had yesterday when he called instead of texting.

Like Ruben needed a thinly veiled threat to understand her first gig back at Groove's was a big deal.

"Good. Showing up at her door every night to make out is one thing. Showing up for something important to her is another."

Ruben rolled his eyes. "We don't…I gotta go or I'll miss her set." There was no way he'd convince his father he was prioritizing time with her too, not just getting frisky.

"What if there is a line at the door? I wouldn't let the likes of you in," Abe hurled at him while he rinsed the dishes.

"Tripp put me on the doorman's list. Catch you later," he called back as he hurried toward the garage. If he didn't leave now, he'd be trapped as fodder for his father's amusement.

Chapter Forty-Five

VINNY

After several days of fine tuning their set, Vinny was pumped. She'd forgotten how homey the club was. Not because Tyler lived over it, but because these people were her professional family. The lifers behind the bar had welcomed her back with open arms.

Then there was the man himself. Tyler looked as delicious as ever, but Vinny no longer had a second thought to dedicate toward him outside of friendship. Her mind was otherwise occupied.

Will he be upset I'm not home? I should have told him. No, this is better. A night without him inviting himself in just to leave me hanging is a good thing. Space is a good thing.

"Vin," Silla said, shaking her shoulders. "Let's go. Space camp is over."

"Huh?"

"Are you sick?"

She snorted. "Yeah, right."

"You've been staring up at the light rigging for a solid half hour."

She glanced at her watch and winced. *Oh. Shit.* "Damn it. Sorry, Silla. I've got a lot on my mind."

"We know. Tripp told us you are composing again!"

"Bastard," she mumbled.

"Awe! He's excited for you, Vinny. Plus, you know he can't keep secrets," she said as they walked toward the back hall. There was a lounge across from Tyler's office where live acts could warm up.

"It's not a secret I'm composing. Tripp's hung up he hasn't seen what I'm working on," she said with a smirk. "He probably thought if he told you, the pressure would finally get to me, and I'd share."

"Yeah, well…it's Tripp," Silla said.

The following hours were spent going over there set one more time and hydrating. The lights were hot, and the crowd didn't help. If you didn't drink plenty of water before you went up, you were setting yourself up to do something really embarrassing, like pass out. Vinny had seen it happen more times than she could count.

Fifteen minutes before they were set to go on, Tyler came in. "Your fan club is waiting," he teased her.

"I didn't mention performing tonight. How—" Vinny turned her attention to Tripp who was conveniently sitting in the opposite corner, out of reach. *"Tripp!* What did you do?"

"Here," Tyler said, offering up his phone. It was open to Tripp's ArtBeat page, where he had hinted in a post that morning she'd be joining him tonight.

"Platonic *wife?* What the fuck does that mean?" She scowled at Tripp.

"Married through art, of course."

"Of course," Silla said with a giggle. She was obviously enjoying the drama.

"One of these days," Vinny said, leaving the threat open.

"But not today, baby." He winked at her, and she threw her half full water bottle at his head. "Hey!"

"I'm trying to knock some sense into you!" she hollered. "And don't call me that."

"As amusing as this is, I'm going to need you to settle your domestic issues later," Tyler cut in. "It's time to go."

"Domestic issues," she muttered under her breath as she followed Tyler out. "I'll give you domestic issues. Next time he calls me *baby* it's on."

She glared at the back of Tyler's head as his shoulders shook with suppressed laughter. *Asshole.*

They stood off to the side while Tyler went through the familiar intro. It felt amazing being back here. She could feel her blood pumping, her skin breaking out in a light sheen preemptively. The heat of the audience was intense tonight.

She didn't hear Tyler welcoming them back to the Groove stage so much as felt it in the surge of the crowd. They were a living vortex of anticipation that honestly caught Vinny by surprise.

"That's for you, Vin. They don't make that kind of ruckus when you're gone," Tripp said loudly in her ear from behind. She looked over her shoulder at him quizzically. "Ask Groove if you don't believe me."

I will, she mouthed back before facing forward and running up the steps onto the stage. She strutted up to her mic with a smile she couldn't suppress if she tried. It felt good to be back. Sometimes the room was tense and uneasy, but tonight it was the feel good high of a sugar rush before the crash.

"Well, hello there, music aficionados," she purred into her mic. "Are you ready?"

The response bordered on mayhem. Vinny took a required step back from the mic as the sound struck her, looking over toward Tripp in disbelief. *Told you,* he mouthed. Off to the side, Silla gave her a playful wink. Jae was beside her, shaking her head with a smile.

It was an indescribable feeling. Vinny loved sharing it with her friends.

"I told you we didn't bump her off," Tripp said when they had settled down as much as a room that packed could. "Lavender Blume, ladies and gentlemen! In the flesh!"

Vinny laughed as her fingers began picking their way across the guitar she'd brought tonight. "I feel your love. Thanks, guys. I missed you too." She strummed a few more chords before fully focusing on the set.

As she strummed and picked her way through a complex intro she'd been practicing all month, she scanned the room for familiar faces. Occasionally she would lean forward into the mic and give a shout out, creating intimacy. Toward the back of the room, she saw an unmistakable man propped up against a pole. She hadn't expected him. Without hesitation, she said, "Hi, Ben." The smile he gifted her was perfection.

The audience fell away. Ben was the only tangible being left as she led her friends into Tripp's aptly named Dream Medley. From "Dream a Little Dream of Me," to Metallica's "Enter Sandman," they had meticulously pieced together twenty-five minutes of musical history. Mariah Carey's "Fantasy," The Eurethmics' "Sweet Dreams," and The Barenaked Ladies' "When You Dream" swept through. They delicately built their house of cards, layering lyrics with precision and expertise. By the time Tripp rolled into "Sleep" by My Chemical Romance, Vinny was so high she couldn't feel the stage beneath her feet.

The room crackled with power and emotion she had no basis of comparison for—it was too raw, too *new.* Jae and Silla were harmonizing through The Cranberries. Tripp overlapped and the girls faded out before Vinny slowed her fingers down to a whispering lullaby against her guitar strings, ending where they had begun with Ella Fitzgerald.

The set had blurred by as she greedily consumed all of Ben's reactions. The roar of the crowd abruptly catapulted Vinny back into reality. She was still on stage, drenched in sweat and wearing a confident smile. They thanked the crowd and announced a break between acts. Vinny handed her guitar off to Tripp, ignoring his satisfied smirk, and ran to the edge of the stage where Tyler was waiting.

"That was amazing!" he shouted.

"Help me down?" She was too impatient to go around and too tired to stick a landing off the stage.

He held his arms up and she leaned in, laughing as he spun her around before allowing her feet to slowly glide down to the floor. "I mean it, Vin. I know it was Tripp's concept, but the whole set screamed Lavender Blume. One of these days, you are going to be too big to play here. The place is packed."

It was a bigger compliment than she could handle with her emotions so high. "Guess you better be building the new location more spacious. I only want to perform with all of you," she said earnestly. Vinny had been thinking about it for months, but now she knew.

She didn't want to be a touring musician anymore. Groove's club was more than enough for her. Small local gigs gave a feeling you couldn't get with strangers. These people were *her* people.

She pulled Tyler in for a hug, hoping he would feel her gratitude and appreciation for his friendship through their embrace.

"I gotta go," she said as she pulled away. "See you tomorrow?"

Tyler nodded. "Yeah."

Vinny pushed through the crowd as politely as she could, moving in Ben's direction. By the time she reached the pole he'd been standing against, he was gone. She stood on one of the bar top chairs for a better view, scanning over the throng.

She found him as he disappeared into the night without so much as a backward glance in her direction.

————

FOUR DAYS. All of them she spent surrounded by Ben. She was in his home, playing and mostly losing at Spades with Ben's father. Vinny's time with Abner was bittersweet. She loved his company and looked forward to their walks and talks. But the more she knew Abner, the more she saw the more nuanced and endearing characteristics of Ben he'd inherited from the man.

Patience. God, his patience. Ben had patience and persistence in spades—ha, even in her melancholy she had puns—with the way he showed up for his "goodnight kiss." They both knew it was more than that. Every moment he'd spent with her reminded Vinny of his dedication to both his own needs and boundaries with her need to decide whether she could meet them someday, while also remaining steadfast in his attention.

Ben didn't push. He also didn't let go.

Thursday night had been the high of Vinny's life, as well as the cruelest crash. Watching him disappear out the front door of the club had confused and *hurt* her. She hadn't imagined his reaction to her performance. Ben had been as lost in her as she had been in him during the set. Why had he left?

She first thought it was how Tyler had spun her down from the stage before leaning in to talk to her, which must have looked intimate from afar. Had Ben been triggered into thinking about all the men Carla had been with? A slow scroll through the home security footage—yes, damn it, she'd looked like a grade A stalker—showed he hadn't been home since.

For four days.

She could ask Abner or Eric, but her pride prickled. Why hadn't he told her himself? Ben had her number. Nobody seemed concerned with his absence but her, which hinted they knew where he was.

It was her, then. She'd done something wrong.

Every second she wasn't with Abner or the Blackwoods she spent locked up in her studio, hashing out her time spent with Ben, beginning with their unfortunate first meeting. *I was such a bitch to him.* Then there was the way she'd largely ignored him for twenty-three hundred miles of road. Yeah, Vinny had made sure he was as physically comfortable as possible in the backseat, but she hadn't included him. Shame washed over her, remembering the way she'd tried to ditch him at the airport in Albuquerque under the guise of *his* comfort.

Days before, he had followed her across the Target parking lot on crutches to make sure she wasn't alone when her adrenaline crashed after the attempted carjacking outside his childhood home minutes earlier. She'd repaid him with aversion and indifference.

The Jake thing. *Fucking hell.* Ben had been steadfast, and what had she done? Threw herself at him. Tried to use him. She was a horrible person, a realization which smacked of hypocrisy given her shady reasons for treating him like shit to begin with. Ruben had allowed Carla to dictate his life for years, but Vinny had let the *memories* of past abusers control her.

She was no better.

In fact, she was quite sure she was worse.

And she missed his goodnight kisses, damn it.

Vinny's mind spun out, fixating over all the things she'd taken for granted. She should have given Ben a clean break the day he unceremoniously stuffed Cunty Carla in a rideshare. She'd seen it then—the appreciation and respect in his eyes, coupled with curiosity and vulnerability—and it had freaked her out. All she wanted now was to tell him the truth.

She hadn't meant the horrible things she'd said.

She hadn't meant any of it from that moment on, all the hostility and hatred she'd thrown his way like daggers. Vinny had selfishly hoped if she wounded him, he'd be too busy tending to his own survival to see the way she was bleeding out behind her walls of insecurity and hatred.

Hatred toward *herself.* She couldn't hate Ben, no matter how much she tried. As the sun set on the fourth day—the fifth without his lips pressed to hers—Vinny made peace with what she needed to do.

Grovel.

Chapter Forty-Six

VINNY

"Are you sure about this?" Tripp asked nervously. "Couldn't you try *calling* him or something? You've never done this before."

"Exactly," Vinny said with determination.

"I'm with Tripp, even if this stunt did pack the house," Tyler said. The three of them were in his office, waiting for her mic time. "Wouldn't it be better if you did this in person? One on one?"

She shook her head. "Where is the boldness in that?"

"Intimacy is its own form of boldness," Tyler said.

Yeah, but intimacy isn't where I struggle. Or it is, but only with him. I get flustered and fall back on bad habits. It's time I bust through my own walls and show him my scars. I need him to love me for all of me.

"I'll be there playing, so if you change your mind, give me the usual signal. We can play something else we've been rehearsing. Or do a challenge," Tripp suggested.

"No, but thanks for the offer. It's time, guys. I can't break through doing the same things I've always done."

"And what *exactly* are you trying to break through, Vin?" Tyler asked playfully.

She scowled at him. *Pot stirrer.*

"When our girl makes a statement, she is certainly cutthroat about it. I dare *Ben* to miss her intentions in tonight's live." Tripp smirked. "Assuming somebody tells him to watch it. You seriously don't know anything after a week?"

"Nope." The guys shared a look Vinny couldn't interpret. "What?"

"We hope he deserves you, Vin," Tyler said softly as he stood from his desk chair. There was a hint of acceptance in his tone. They hadn't broached the subject of their *almost* tryst, but it seemed they were on the same page and Vinny was relieved.

These knuckleheads were *her* knuckleheads. And she loved them. In the end, it didn't surprise her she'd been persuaded by a man outside of music. Tonight, she was going to use her art to tell him she was ready—more than ready—scared shitless, but all in.

"Who are you texting to make you smile so deviously?" she asked Tripp as she looked back at him. They needed to get ready.

"A friend."

"I'm your friend."

"I do have more than one, Vin."

"Liar," she teased.

"Children," Tyler scolded in his boss voice.

"Yeah, we're going," Vinny said sweetly. "Thanks for letting me do this short notice, Tyler."

"Stop thanking me. You packed the audience in on your own, Miss ArtBeat." Tyler hadn't called her that in a long time. It felt like reverting to a simpler, more comfortable time.

Chapter Forty-Seven

RUBEN

He hated TDYs. Especially ones that landed you in the middle of bumfuck nowhere with no cell service. One minute Ruben was watching Lavender in her element, completely blown away by her passion and soul. The next, he was on a short clock, hightailing it in to work.

He'd thought he was prepared after watching her videos, but nothing compared to Lavender Blume performing live. Everything about her was sex and seduction. The way her voice flowed from a soft rasp to a full powered wail. How her hips seemed to gyrate against her guitar as she played it, plucking and strumming the strings as she made love to the room.

She was fucking beautiful.

The set had ended, and Ruben had waited patiently where he'd propped himself up for her to find him. He knew she would. She was talking to the tall guy who had introduced them on stage. Ruben was pretty sure he owned the club. Like with Tripp, Ruben could tell it was a friendly conversation. He had no trouble waiting.

Until his phone vibrated in his pocket.

Ruben's instincts told him what he didn't want to know. It was go time. Ruben had an hour to get where he needed to be, and he'd need every second to get there. He listened to the message with a heavy heart before turning back to find her. She wasn't by the stage anymore. He looked for her wild shock of silvery white hair but still couldn't see her in the crowd.

Fuck. I have to leave! Where are you, beautiful?

He gave the room one last scan before turning away miserably. No goodnight kiss tonight. As he strode to the door, he sent off messages to Eric and his dad, letting them know he'd gotten the call. Once he was in his truck, he opened a new message to Lavender.

Ruben: You were stunning tonight, beautiful. I have to go do Marine shit. I'm going to miss you.

He wanted to write *I love you,* and hoped it was implied in his simple words. Ruben wanted to take her home and pamper the fuck out of her. Instead, he was going on a damn assignment he would have been stoked for a year ago. Now it got in the way of his personal mission to conquer this woman's heart.

Ruben sent the message and stopped stalling. Work was work, and he'd brought his gear along knowing it was possible he'd get tapped in. So was life.

The entire week since had been miserable. Not because of the work. Ruben genuinely loved his job and was enjoying his new role immensely—from *home.* Where he could ambush Lavender for his nightly demonstration of his intentions. Now he looked at his dead cell phone and practically growled.

The job was over, and he was flying home. His first task was to plug in his phone and see if she had replied. The moment the seat belt sign winked out upon landing, Ruben was moving.

Maybe a heavy make out session will help move past the week I didn't get to see her. I miss her taste. I even miss the way she tells me she hates me.

Ruben made it to his truck and hastily chucked his stuff in before hopping in and firing up the engine. Almost as soon as his phone came to life, it was ringing.

"Tripp, what's happening!" he answered jovially.

"Fuck, dude. *Where have you been?"*

"I literally just got back from a week in hell, man. I can't tell you where I was though, it was work related. What's up? You sound worried." *Which was probably about...* "Didn't Lavender tell you I was out of town?"

"Pfft. When it comes to you, she's a vault. So, no. And frankly, I don't think she *knew."*

"I sent her a text telling her I had work," Ruben insisted. *Not to mention Dad and Eric would tell her. I know she's seen at least my dad in the past week.*

"Then she didn't get it. How far away are you?"

"Why?"

"She's about to do a live at the club, and you need to see it," Tripp said firmly.

"Shit. I won't make it in time. I'm too far out. Like I said, I *just* got back."

"Then you should stream it."

"I will. Thanks, Tripp."

They signed off and Ruben immediately opened up the ArtBeat app, clicking into Lavender's feed and placing the phone in his dash mount. She wasn't live yet, so he reversed the truck out of his parking spot and headed toward Ocean-side, grateful he had a fast charge unit for his phone.

Halfway to the club, the live activated. Ruben opened the stream and waited. Groove was doing a quick version of last week's introduction, and there she was. Behind her, Tripp moved in the background, plugging in a different guitar than he'd used the previous week. He recognized a few others from last week's show too.

"Well, well," Lavender crooned into her mic. "We meet again, aficionados. Welcome."

There was a pause while the crowd hooted in excitement. "We're live tonight, so whatever you do, *don't* behave."

"Reverse psychology won't work on them," Tripp said with a laugh. "Hey, listen. Be idiots and her account will get revoked. You wouldn't want that, would you?"

The crowd went wild.

"All right now, settle down. We are going to work through a few tunes we are feeling this week, and then we have a special surprise at the end," she taunted. "How does that sound?"

Again, the crowd grew rowdy with anticipation before she cut them off with a wave of her hand, as if she was a magician with a mute button in her palm. Immediately, she pushed into a popular 90's ballad. It was angsty, passionate, and allowed her to balance the wispiness she managed so smoothly with her stronger voice as well.

Ruben struggled to keep his eyes on the road instead of the screen. If he got pulled over, it would be a hefty fine. He didn't give a fuck. The only thing that mattered was Lavender.

He listened intently as she worked through a few songs, getting the audience warmed up and in good spirits. Like the week before, they adored her. Everything she did, her people ate it up with satisfaction. And while they *did* behave a bit lower key given it was being broadcast, even through the feed, Ruben could feel the vibe and energy as if he was there.

She was intoxicating in every way. Her sass. Her kiss.

Especially the way she held her '72 Strat like she came into the world knowing exactly what to do with it. The pull to be near her was impossible to ignore.

And he didn't.

Ruben drove like he had everything to lose, glancing at Lavender as often as he safely could on the screen. *Does she know she's sex personified when she's performing? That she steps behind her microphone and makes love to the room? To the world? Tens of thousands of people are watching her right now, and she is living in this moment like it is her last. As if she would cease breathing if she didn't do this thing she was clearly born to do.*

He was broken out of his mystified awe by the change on the feed. Tripp and the other's faded back, shrouded in darkness. The only thing left was Lavender and her guitar, poised on the edge of a stool in front of her mic. The camera had moved in. There was a blaring spot on her. She looked pale—and yeah, she had albinism, but this was more so than usual. Especially given her stage makeup.

And nervous. Lavender *never* looked nervous. Angry, sure. Determined, absolutely. Ruben had only recently rejoiced when his presence stopped triggering a wave of loathing from her general direction. He couldn't get to the club before the end of her set, and he needed to focus on her. The club was only five minutes out now, but that was five minutes longer than he had, given Tripp's speech.

He pulled over and put the truck in park so he could put all his attention on her. Lavender strummed gently, fidgeting with the peg thingies at the head of her guitar. *Are her fingers trembling?*

"Now for the surprise," she cooed softly. "For the first time—the *very first time*—I am going to share with you all something personal. Everyone knows I have a passion for rearranging songs. What I don't advertise, is the amount of time I spend composing.

"There was a family emergency last year, and I was completely blocked afterward. Couldn't write a thing. I told myself it was temporary, something that would break as our family healed. The opposite was true. I had to come face to face with the consequences of my own past choices to break free. Since then, I can't seem to stop writing.

"And to celebrate both the dissolution of my creative block and the *true* reason behind it, I'm going to share with you all my latest song. I hope you enjoy it."

She sucked in the back of her bottom lip and bit the flesh. If he hadn't seen her do it before, he wouldn't have recognized the moment of vulnerability for what it was. It was too subtle for most people to notice, which was the point. Another plate in her armor. If she pulled in her bottom lip fully, people would know; they would *see her.*

Ruben smiled, nodding encouragement he hoped she could sense since she couldn't see him. Lavender took a deep breath on the screen and softly began to build her story.

It's easier to blame the puppet
To see the tip of the blade
Instead of the hand holding the hilt in your back
A bloody handle controlling their victim

When life lessons are hard earned
Fear becomes a sharp motivator
We blame the messenger of bad tidings
Instead of their orchestrator

And it's so easy
So fucking easy

But if it were true
I could look at you
In the backseat of my '72
And Camaro means friend
But that's not what I am
For you

We should go for a drive
So it can end badly
When you say all the right words
And I say we aren't anything

I'm down under the peer
In my hand crafted cement shoes
Waiting for the tide of my grief
To consume what's left of me

Then you show up to free me
And I cling to my fears instead

I'm the one driving
And I can't look at you
In the backseat of my '72
Camaro means friend
But that's not what I am
around you

Don't look at me with those dark soulful eyes
It scares me to know you see right through my walls
Breaking all of my doubts back down into their lies
The things I tell myself to protect what's left inside

Because if you knew
What it means to be seen by you
In the backseat of my '72
Camaro means friend
But I have so much more
To give you

What if this goodnight kiss
Is really a last kiss goodbye
I'll never know if I don't give this a try
Just swallow my pride and admit my own truth

It was never you and that's why it hurt
When did I stop trying and begin victimizing
Insisting I'll hate you forever as punishment
When I hate myself for fearing your honesty

'Cause I knew I loved you
The first time I saw you
In the backseat of my '72
And Camaro means friend
But I'm asking for everything
With you

Chapter Forty-Eight

VINNY

As she slowly picked out the first verse, Vinny could feel the tears building. By the time the band joined in for the middle, tears were slowly tracking down her cheeks. Every lyric triggered a picture gallery of Ben in her mind. as the song slowed into the closing lines, just her under the spotlight again, she knew without a mirror she'd dramatically sobbed black streaks down her cheeks.

And for once, she didn't care.

She was raw and desperate.

Why shouldn't all those things show?

For the first time, she showed her deepest emotions. Not what someone else's work triggered in her, but what bubbled up from the wellspring of her own life and emotional mêlées. She'd been a hypocrite, and a problem. Vinny had never intended to become so jaded, but her week without Ben had been eye opening.

The chips had fallen. The roulette wheel spun. All that was left was to see if her gamble had paid off. As foolish as it was, she *swore* Ben was there. Not in the room, but with her. She looked into the camera and poured everything out to him same as she had last week, when he was propped up against a pole toward the back of the room.

The song ended with a fade to black as the last note reverberated, only to be drowned out by the crowd's approval before the red light went out and she knew the live was off. She took a deep breath as the stage lights slowly came back up and pasted on a smile. Tripp said something into his mic that brought out the audience's rowdy side.

Vinny floated through it all.

She thanked the crowd, credited her friends, and then allowed Tripp to lead her off the stage to where Groove stood waiting. His face was a mask, all smiles and pride. Underneath, the real Tyler shone through his concerned gaze before he tucked her exhausted body under his arm and led her back to his office, Tripp on their heels.

"You okay?" Tyler asked soon as Tripp closed the door. He guided her to sit on the couch.

"No," she choked out with a self-depreciating laugh. "But I will be."

"That was brilliant, Vin. Painful to watch, but *fuck,*" Tripp murmured as he plopped down on her other side, sandwiching her between them.

"Do you want to go upstairs and use my bathroom?" Tyler suggested kindly, nodding toward the back stairway up to his apartment.

She shook her head. "No. I know I'm a mess, but I can't bring myself to care. I appreciate the offer for a quiet moment though. Thanks."

Tyler reached beside him and pulled out water bottles for all of them from the mini fridge and passed them out. The cold water did more to revive Vinny than she expected it to. She'd forgotten to properly hydrate today while she apprehensively paced around her living room.

"You know, even if he wasn't here tonight, it's out there," Tripp says. "How do you feel about knowing the whole world knows you fell?"

"Fell?" Vinny snorted. "I didn't fall."

"No? What would you call it?" Tyler asked genuinely.

"Flying," she answered without hesitation. "When I'm with him, I fly… If only I wasn't afraid of heights."

"Try a blindfold," Tyler teased.

"Kinky," Tripp added, wiggling his brows and grinning like an idiot.

There was a knock at the door, and Vinny didn't miss the quick glance between the two before Tripp hopped up to open the door without asking who it was first.

Because he knows, she realized.

"Hey. 'Bout time," he chided.

"Man, I'm lucky I didn't get a damn ticket," Ben said as he came into the room.

"You're here," Vinny rasped.

"Of course, I am."

"Why?"

"Because *you* are here."

Her brows drew in, her lips pursing. "You left without telling me!"

"What? No. I sent you a message."

"Did not."

"Did too."

She held up her phone. "See for yourself! No messages from *Get Bent."*

Ruben let out a laugh, startling Vinny into remembering they weren't alone when Tyler and Tripp joined in. "You saved my phone number as *Get Bent,* Lavender?"

"Because I hate you."

"You don't."

"I absolutely do."

"Yeah? Can you prove it, beautiful?" He was toying with her.

"Yes, as a matter of fact. That's why I blo…oh, fuck." She felt her face blush scarlet. With the smeared makeup, she probably resembled a fright night extra.

"What was that, beautiful? You did what?" He was smirking at her. Ben knew *exactly* what she'd been about to say. Vinny sighed dramatically.

"I blocked you," she mumbled.

"So, you *wouldn't* have gotten the message I sent you," he stated. "That's okay. We'll fix your lapse in judgment in a minute. Here." He handed her his phone, the message thread open to *Beautiful Hellion*.

Ruben: You were stunning tonight, beautiful. I have to go do Marine shit. I'm going to miss you.

"Oh. You were working?"

"That's all you want to take from the message you didn't get? Because you are, *in fact,* a beautiful hellion. That I was working. Not that I missed you or loved your performance," he deadpanned. "You are impossible, woman."

"Agreed," Tripp piped up. "And that is our cue to give up your office, Groove. Vin, I'll make sure your guitar is stored for when you are ready to go. Nice to see you, Ruben."

They left; the soft sound of the door snicking closed behind them echoing in a manner that made Vinny feel like she'd been put in a prison cell. With Ben. Alone. *Oh, fuck.*

"Lavender Blume," he said, shaking his head. She was nervous, but he was still grinning as he knelt before her where she sat on the couch and took her hands in his. "Only you would write a song like that, put your heart on the line *live* for fucks sake, and then chew my ass out the second you laid eyes on me again."

"You—" He silenced her snarky comeback with a gentle kiss.

"You are a pain in the ass, Lavender. Irredeemable as you are gorgeous. Stubborn as you are talented. The bane of my damn existence and the reason I lie awake at night."

"That's not—"

"I love you." His confession whispered across her skin, a gentle caress that left her aching for more. "And I know you love me. You know I'm not like the others. You aren't a trophy or a challenge. You are unapologetically Lavender Blume. My *beautiful hellion,* who can write a song confessing her truths and perform it to the masses but somehow can't be open when it's just me in the room. If you need to keep up the ruse of a fight when face to face a little longer, I understand. I only need to know one thing, beautiful."

"What's that?" she asked breathlessly.

"Am I still a toy for you to break or do you see me as a person now?"

"You…" she leaned forward, throwing her arms around his neck and burying her face in the crook of his shoulder, her eyes squeezed tightly shut as his addictive scent encased her. If she didn't look at him, she could say it. "You weren't a toy, Ben. I was afraid *I* was. That I'd let *you* break *me.* "

Ben's arms came up around her, firm yet gentle. He held her while she word dumped all her insecurities on him, one hand gently stroking up and down her spine, encouraging her to relax into him. To let it all out at last.

"You needed proof I was going to be different with you. I didn't get so deep as to marry Jake, but I still needed to see how ugly he could be for myself, to realize how low I had set the bar. He was fun, but ultimately he wasn't a safe bet. Not for my heart, and not in any other way. I don't know why I tolerated it. And I don't know why I was so cruel about *your* ex, when I had put myself in the same situation."

"It was and it wasn't," he murmured into her hair. "Looking back, there were plenty of red flags. I'm not an idiot, but I chased her like one. We all have our own journey, Lavender. Things we have to overcome. Boundaries we have to learn to set."

"You aren't Jenny Moore," she blurted. She could feel his chuckle envelope her as his body vibrated around her with the sound.

"Glad we're on the same page."

"And I should have told you a lot sooner why I…I'm sorry I took the safety off, Ben. I was so scared after the accident. I let fear get in the way of safety when I had a firearm in hand, which is never acceptable."

"You need to forgive yourself, beautiful. I forgave you a long time ago."

"You did?"

"Yup."

She pulled back, her hands still clasped behind his neck, and studied his face for any sign of deceit. "When?"

"When you turned it on someone who meant to do harm, keeping my dad safe."

"I took a bunch of extra safety classes after we met so I wouldn't panic again," she admitted. "I could have hurt you."

"You didn't."

"But—"

"No. It's in the past. Although I have to say, I have never known a woman who needed to draw a firearm so much as you have since we met. Maybe this is a mistake. What if you change your mind and shoot my anyway?" he teased.

"You already know better than to eat all my cashew chicken," she said. "You're safe."

"From your trigger finger maybe," he said, his hands coming back up to cup her face again. His relief was a tangible thing, joined with his desire and tenderness. "You could still bean me in the head with one of those guitars you have dangerously hanging over your couch within arm's reach."

A relieved giggle burst out of her, the last of her apprehension releasing with it. She dropped her gaze from his, her eyes focusing on his pillow soft lips as she bit down on her own. "Ben…"

"Yeah, it's time for another kiss," he said, reading her like a love song.

This time, she leaned in before he could, crashing her mouth down on his and tightening her arms around his neck with zealous consent. She took Ben by surprise, but he quickly recovered, tightening one arm around her lower back and yanking her into his lap while his second hand threaded into her hair. He commanded control of the kiss, taking over with a finesse that drew a throaty moan from her. It had originated deep, right from her needy core, and he swallowed it down like a man starved.

Starved for *her.*

Which they both were; starved for each other.

Vinny had had many revelations during his week away, but for now, this was what they both needed. Everything else could wait. This kiss? One where she didn't feel like she had to pull away and push him out of her bubble…she could live here forever.

Knock. Knock.

"Vin? Did you kill him? Please tell me you didn't leave blood all over my new couch," Tyler teased through his door.

Ben pulled back slightly, placing a few firm and decidedly spicy kisses on her pout before turning his face toward the door and shouting, "What makes you think I wasn't the axe wielder?"

Tyler's laugh boomed from the hallway. "I need my office back."

Asshole, Vinny thought, even though she was grinning.

Ben leaned in for one last tender peck before reluctantly scooting Vinny off his lap. "That's two, beautiful. Let's go home and work on the other six."

Chapter Forty-Nine

RUBEN

"I'm glad Tripp drove you tonight," he said, squeezing Vinny's hand across the console of his truck. "I would not have liked you riding home any other way than with me tonight."

"I was too nervous to drive," she admitted.

"Nervous? You? *Pshh.* I don't believe it."

"Calling me a liar?" she teased.

He lifted their joined hands to kiss the back of hers without taking his eyes off the road. "You were perfection, beautiful. I'm so fucking proud of you."

Ruben backed into his garage before taking Vinny's guitar from the backseat as she climbed down from the cab. They converged at the front of the truck, linking their hands again as they walked down his driveway and toward her apartment. After looking back to make sure his garage door had closed, Ruben followed Vinny up to her front door.

She was nervous again. Her hand was trembling in his as she locked the door behind them. Ruben set down her guitar case carefully and pulled her into him, placing a kiss on her forehead. Vinny's face was still smeared from where she'd swiped at the tears on her cheeks. Ruben thought he had never seen her more beautiful.

He had imagined finally having her many times. Now that he stood before her, Ruben realized all the crazy, sexy things he'd envisioned were nothing like what he wanted to give her in the moment.

What she *needed* him to give her.

He could spread her open on the hood of her car and finish what they'd started months ago another time. The sparks they had hurled at each other had caught up into an intense smolder—not a wildfire. Tonight, he would worship her until that smolder grew into a steady, controlled burn. Something she could rely on to keep her warm without blistering her heart.

"I'm going to take my time on you, beautiful. Are you ready?" His voice was pure masculine desire, low and raspy.

She opened her mouth, then closed it again. Whatever smartass comment had popped into her head—and he knew it had been something snarky, given the source—Vinny had decided to let it go this time. Instead, she met his gaze and firmly nodded her head one time. Ruben backed her up to the kitchen island. When they reached the end, he lifted her up to sit on the edge.

Beginning at her collar bone, he trailed open kisses up her neck, groaning over the salty taste of her. Vinny tipped her head to the side as he moved up her throat, nibbled on her ear, and then moved across her jawline. Ruben took her mouth again, one hand gliding up her top to caress her bare skin while the other firmly gripped the hair at her nape again. His hips settled perfectly between her spread thighs, and he ground his erection against her core.

Too many clothes. He'd get to that soon.

Ruben didn't pull back until Vinny had wrapped her legs

around him, grinding her hips as hard as he was, desperate mewling sounds vibrating across his tongue as he led her own through a sumptuous dance. *Delicious.* He met her sweet sounds with a deep groan of approval. *"Three,"* he said when he finally pulled back.

He released her hair while she caught her breath, smirking with pride as he took in his handiwork. Vinny's pupils were blown wide with lust, her lips red and swollen from his attention. Her chest rose and fell shallowly as she panted, her hard nipples poking through her shirt. Without losing eye contact, he slowly lifted the hem of her shirt up, ghosting his hands over her ribs as he did. She shuddered, and her breath hitched.

"Ben." It was a whispered plea for more.

"I think it's only fair a few of these kisses I owe you tend to other needy parts of your body, beautiful. Don't you think?"

She nodded. Ruben quickly removed her top, careful not to yank her hair in the process. Her bra came next, rosy, pink tips begging for their share of attention now they were free. He leaned her back, taking one nipple in his mouth greedily. Ruben nipped and sucked before soothing her flesh with his tongue. As he moved to the other breast, she tightened her legs around him, her core pressing and grinding into him hard enough to draw a hiss.

"Fuck, Lavender," he moaned into her chest. *"Four."*

"Ben," she groaned out. This time, guttural and desperate for him. He unbuttoned her jeans and stepped back enough to tug them down. Vinny immediately wrapped her legs around him again. "God. *Fuck.* Just…*ahhhhh."*

Her voice cut off as his thumb trailed down her wet slit, dipping in and taking her juices back up to circle her clit. "I have dreamed of your taste," he said. "Of what it would be like to sample your wares whenever I want. Fucking Heaven, Lavender. That's what you are."

Ruben tapped her leg gently with his free hand so she would release his waist. "Lay back, feet on my shoulders. That's it. Nice and wide, beautiful." He dropped to his knees, her sopping core glistening at the edge of the counter for him. He began slowly, kissing her inner thighs as his thumb continued to tease her clit. Her arousal was heady, her scent going straight to his cock. He let out another groan as he breathed her in and popped the front of his own jeans open to relieve the strain.

"Hold the edge of the counter." It was the only warning he gave before diving in tongue first. Vinny gasped and her back arched up, forcing her hips harder into his face. Ruben swirled his tongue at her entrance, collecting her flavor with satisfaction before teasing her lips with little nips, then going back to tongue fucking her. Her toes curled into his shoulders. He moved his lips over her clit, pressing a sensuous kiss over her nub before taking it in his mouth and sucking down hard.

Vinny bucked her hips into his face as she cried out something unintelligible. He kept at it, alternating sucking and nipping with gentle laves of us tongue until she screamed his name. He slid two fingers inside of her and curled them against her G-spot until her body convulsed with pleasure, gripping his fingers painfully as her orgasm hit. *"Five,"* he groaned against her flesh. "Fuck, you're addictive."

He moved her feet down from his shoulders and slowly stood back up, placing her legs back around his waist before removing his shirt. *God damn, she's gorgeous. Panting in the dim light, spread across the counter like a fucking buffet.* Ruben carefully scooped her up against his chest, skin to skin.

"I'm taking you to your bed while you taste yourself,

Lavender. Give me your mouth." He expected her to kiss him. Instead, she leaned forward and slowly ran her tongue across his chin where her juices were, dragging it through her essence with a greedy moan before sucking his lower lip into her mouth and biting down. "Good girl. Now kiss me."

He slid his hands under her ass as she wrapped her arms around his neck and began absolutely devouring his face. Ruben lifted her lithe frame up easily and walked down the hall to her bedroom. Her kiss was possessive and sexy as fuck, her dripping core rubbing against his crown where it peaked out of his boxers. He sat down on the end of her bed, her weight sliding down perfectly against him. *"Six,"* he said over her lips. "Christ, woman. Your mouth has endless talents."

"Why are you still wearing pants?" she whined, shimmying her hips.

"Patience," he teased.

"Off."

He chuckled and leaned back on the bed, lifting his hips. She took the hint and planted her knees so he could push his pants down and kick them off. "There. Greedy little thing."

Vinny defiantly sat down on his dick and ground her hips in a slow circle, his head notching perfectly into her opening. She smirked as he let out a groan. "Gimme."

"Gladly." He grabbed hold of her and rolled over, then used his own torso to slide her body up the bed farther. She squeaked with surprise. "Tell me you need me as desperately as I need you, Lavender. Say it."

She leaned up and gave him a tender kiss before murmuring, "I need you too."

"About fucking time."

Ruben pushed inside her, groaning as she let out a gasp. He stopped twice to adjust to her tightness and give her a chance to adjust to his size. On the third thrust, he bottomed out inside her. She was exquisite. A wave of affection and pride washed over him, knowing he'd earned his way into her kingdom. Vinny had finally chosen *him.* Now he would pay homage to her; prove she'd made the right choice letting down her walls.

He began to move. *Slowly.* As they settled into a rhythm together, he tenderly kissed her, loving the way her arousal mixed with the taste of her tongue in his mouth. Ruben rolled up against her clit with every thrust, loving the way she matched him by grinding back. As her walls began clenching harder around him, he gently bit down on her lower lip and grabbed her hip, changing the angle he stroked her inside enough to send her over the edge again.

"Seven," he said as her second orgasm began to wane. He was still thrusting, fighting off his own climax to prolong her pleasure. "I could watch you come all night."

Vinny let out a happy sigh. "What about you?"

"I'm not ready for this to end."

"We can do it again," she suggested as she sunk her nails into his ass and pulled him harder into her with his next thrust. She was going to kill him. The bite of her fingers was fantastic. If only she would…

Vinny's nails dug in, her hands slowly scratching up his back. *"Fuck!* Lavender! God damn, woman."

She tittered drunkenly, her voice the embodiment of sin. *"Bennnnnnn,"* she groaned out.

He nipped her throat as her claws sunk into his shoulders, the zing of pain going straight to his cock. He ran his lips over her pulse point, thrilling at the feel of it racing against his mouth. *Bet I can make her heart pound harder.*

Ruben slid out of her completely, pausing with his crown resting at the gates of her paradise. She looked up at him, wide eyed and desperate. He pressed her hips down into the mattress as she attempted to thrust up. Vinny whined at her failed attempt to take him back inside her. "Stay," he commanded. When she didn't fight, he slowly released her hips and leaned down over her, putting his weight on his forearms.

He took her mouth again, languorously. This kiss was one of slow torture. *Perfect hell, for my beautiful hellion.* His hips gently undulated, his crown mercilessly teasing her clit same as his mouth did her tongue. Ruben drug it out, teasing them both past the point of madness. Then he moved his cock to her entrance again, slowly teasing her with no more than the tip while she whimpered helplessly into his mouth.

But she didn't try to take over again. He had told her to stay, and against her own desires, she did. To the best of her ability, Vinny managed not to grind her hips upward or otherwise try to force him deeper inside her.

Ruben slowly moved one hand between them, pressing his thumb firmly against her mound and circling. Vinny's body began to shake beneath him. He paused his kiss to murmur, "Not until I say, beautiful. You stay on the edge." She mewled out desperately but nodded her head and leaned back into their kiss.

Her arms came around his waist restlessly before falling back to her sides, where they wouldn't be tempted to pull him down.

He could feel her legs begin to shake, and bet her toes were curled again.

Vinny arched her back on impulse, rubbing her peaks against the hard plane of his body in search any relief she could find.

The feel of her beneath him, coiling tighter as he continued to test her limits, was about to send *him* over the edge and he wasn't even inside her. Vinny felt *that good* against his body. Finally, Ruben snapped. He plunged all the way into her heat as his thumb circled faster against her clit. Vinny too lost control, her arms coming up around him and holding on tight. Her nails bit into his back again.

"Eight," he groaned out as he pulled back far enough to see her entire face. "Now, beautiful."

He watched as she screamed herself hoarse through her third climax, her gaze locked on his face as she did. Ruben's hips began to jerk unsteadily as pleasure hurtled through his body. He felt his abs contract hard, his cock squeezed tightly in her channel as she soaked him with her release. He unloaded into her with a heavy groan, pushing himself into her as deep as he could.

Vinny's arms and legs pulled him down onto her, fusing them together as he continued to pulse inside her, still rocking his hips as they came down from their high. In the dim light, he could still make out the flush covering her body.

"That's how a man who respects you takes you to bed, Lavender," he said gently. "He doesn't just fuck you. He loves you. *I love you.*"

Chapter Fifty

VINNY

Vinny lay in Ruben's arms, her body curled around him, their bodies still intimately joined, and allowed his words to sink in. *I love you.* She wasn't afraid. Not of his passion or his affections. Certainly not afraid of the way he'd taken over her body and made love to her. Ruben had taken her to bed and chipped away the last of her defenses one thrust at a time.

Lavender Blume belonged to Ruben Holt.

"Ben." She didn't know how to verbalize all the emotions coursing along her body right now. She hoped it was implied in the way she said his name. "I'm a lava lamp," she murmured.

"A *what?*" He quirked a brow at her, grinning.

"You know. A lava lamp."

"I know what it is."

"That's how a feel."

"Like you are on an acid trip?" he mused.

"Maybe. I've never dropped acid," she said with a shrug. "I don't know. Like I found the perfect cord progression."

He kissed her tenderly before gently rolling to the side. "You feel good, then?"

"Warm and tingly and perfect. Better than good." *Like an astronaut who finally landed on the damn moon. How was everything so…* "Don't leave me," she whispered.

"You're stuck with me now, beautiful."

"I know your job is a challenge. You won't be able to *never* leave me, but…"

"But that's not what you mean. It's okay. I understand."

"How?"

He smiled at her crookedly; his mouth quirked up on one side. She used to *loathe* when he looked at her like that. Now it made her clench down on his slowly receding erection. He groaned. "Oh, I like this reaction way better than the glares I used to get for smiling at you."

Vinny giggled. "Sorry."

"Don't be. We got here in the end, and you were worth the wait."

"I don't think… I've never felt…"

"Felt what, Lavender?" he encouraged, planting a tender kiss on her lips.

"So seen." *So loved.*

"Good."

"Good?"

"Hell, yes. As much as I have craved your body, it's your willingness to let me in I need most. *You.* All of you. That's the real gift. The insane sexual connection is a bonus," he added with a waggle of his brows.

She smiled wide before leaning in to kiss him. "I'm probably going to be a bitch. This is all new and scary."

"I expect nothing less, so long as you talk to me. I can handle the attitude. I can't handle the push and pull shit."

"I can respect that," she said with a sigh. "Will you stay with me tonight?"

"I don't think I could leave if I wanted to. I meant what I said, beautiful. I need you."

"I need you too." *I think I love you too.*

Ruben eventually helped Vinny to the bathroom on wobbly legs, where he took her into the shower. He gently went over her entirely, until she was drenched in suds, even massaging her face soap in around her eyes until the last remnants of her makeup was gone. She ran her hands over his body, exploring every toned inch.

"What was it like, when you were a kid. I bet you had a lot of friends," she said as she examined his palms.

"Not really," he said with a shrug. "I was a scrawny nerd. Outside of baseball, I didn't have many friends. Down at the diamond, everyone was in it for the love of the game. Those same kids generally ignored me at school."

"That's awful." Vinny knew. She had been ignored too, unless she had a guitar strapped on. She won all the talent shows in high school, but the moment it ended, she went right back to being the weird girl.

"What about you? After Jenny ditched you, was it ever better at school?"

"No. The only time I felt equal was on stage. A little makeup and a cute outfit went a long way, but my guitar is still the ultimate accessory."

"Were you in the school band?"

"Fuck, no." She snorted. "The only instrument in the school band I would have wanted to touch was the drums, and even then, I wanted to *rock.* None of that marching around the football field or sitting in the bleachers bullshit. I started gigging with my dad when I was fifteen. Left on my first professional tour with him at eighteen."

"A total badass. *Sexy.*"

She laughed softly. "Was it hard? When your vitiligo started?" The question came out with more timidity than she had wanted, but she knew he didn't talk about it often and didn't know how it would affect him. "I can't believe what *she* said…"

"She is a bitch. The water is getting cold." He turned off the shower and reached out for her towel, carefully drying her before rapidly rubbing the damp towel over himself and dragging her back to bed.

Vinny allowed him to fuss over her, enjoying his attention more than she thought she was capable of. She'd always felt stifled in the past when a guy tried to tuck her in, but with Ben, she felt eager. She wanted him to stay, to hold her while they slept.

"The vitiligo was a shock," he finally said, surprising her by answering her earlier question. "And yeah, it was shit at first. I didn't want to look in the mirror. When classes started back up, I would try to keep covered as much as I could. I didn't like the stares. Eventually I decided I wasn't going to let it bother me anymore. Why worry over something you have no control over?"

"Easier said than done," she said as she ran her hand over his chest. Vinny pressed a kiss over one of his marks. "At least you know what you look like *with* melanin. I've always wondered what I would look like. I've seen makeovers, you know? Before and afters of people with albinism who let a makeup artist give them pigment and freckles, even a wig."

"Is that something you would like to do?" he asked curiously.

"I don't know. I don't think so. It *sounds* good, but this is who I am. Besides, I take after my mom. I think I would look like her. So really, I can admire Mom's pictures to satisfy myself."

"What was your mother like?"

"Warm. Fun. So pretty," she said with a wistful sigh. "Even if they had caught her cancer super early, she would have had a slim chance of survival because it was in her brain. She would have liked you."

"Why do you think she would like me?"

"Because you aren't a musician," she said bluntly.

Ruben let out a sharp laugh, making Vinny smile. "Low standards. Especially from a woman who married a musician. Seems a bit hypocritical."

"My mom tamed my dad. It's no secret. I'm sure he's had partners since she passed, but not an actual girlfriend. At least not anyone he deemed worth introducing to me. She used to tell me Dad was the exception to the rule, and not to expect to find a keeper on the scene."

"What did she look like?" he asked.

"Oh, mocha brown hair. Her eyes were like tiger's eye in color, golden and warm and shimmery. Olive skin. And her nose was slightly crooked from when it got broken."

"How did it break?" he asked immediately, as she expected.

"A roadie tried taking my dad from her. They were pretty hot and heavy by then, enough so she agreed to go on tour with him. This 'bleach blonde tramp' as my mother called her slithered right up and would not take a hint. Mom got up in her face, and she *punched* her. Told her she needed to share instead of being a greedy whore. Dad was *livid.* There was blood everywhere. Before he could step between them, Mom one-two'd her face real good." Vinny laughed. It had been a long time since she thought about this story. "Dad said Mom came out all the better. The roadie had two black eyes and one of her giant hoop earrings was ripped out. Like, *split her earlobe in half,* kind of ripped out."

"Your mom sounds like a bruiser," he said affectionately. "Guess I know where you got your spunk."

She snorted. "Yeah. *Spunk.* There's a new word for pigheadedness."

"Your word, not mine."

"What about your mom? I know her loss was preventable, but Eric and Abner have never said anything more," she asked gently.

"Yeah, Eric isn't one to blab. Dad is just…*Dad.* Instead of thinking about the end, he focuses on all the good times. I envy him that. All I seem to focus on are the doctors lying to her as she sobbed in pain, doubled over." He took in a deep breath, letting it out slowly. "She had endometriosis. They kept telling her it was in her head and her pain wasn't *that bad,"* he said bitterly.

"Endo? That's what Carys has. Well, and a few other similar issues… She died of *Endo.* I'm so sorry, Ben."

"Poor black woman in the south," he said. "Just another fatality statistic on how shitty the healthcare is. That's why I couldn't leave Dad there. They kept fucking up his paperwork—"

She placed her fingers gently over his mouth. He kissed them tenderly and pulled her closer, until she was nearly laying across his body. "You don't have to explain. I understand. And Abner was worth saving from a system that had already failed your family once. I'd have done the same thing, Ben. My mom was going to die. Yours didn't have to. It's shitty, no matter how you look at it. Endometriosis is treatable, manageable. The *system* took your mother."

He clung to her, his body tightening. She could feel his tension building beneath her chest, the sob he was holding back. "How do you do it?" he asked roughly.

"Do what?"

"Have so much *compassion?* You didn't know her at all."

"That's not true. I have seen the way your dad struggles to keep her memory alive. The way *you* have tried to be okay when you clearly are not."

His body shuddered as the emotion became too much. Vinny looked up to see Ben staring at the ceiling as tears ran down his face. "Come here, Ben." She rolled to the side, encouraging him to scoot down the bed and turn into her. Vinny pulled Ben close, cradling his head against her chest while he quietly cried. She cried too. "You are allowed to miss your mother. I miss mine too," she murmured. "We can miss them together."

They held on to each other until the gentle strokes of Vinny's hands on his body and her fingers against his scalp brought him back. His hold on her became possessive, his mouth seeking her skin. He was gentle at first. When his mouth wrapped around one of her pebbled tips, she groaned in pleasure. Vinny scissored her thighs as his teeth gently tugged her nipple, his hand encircling her breast and massaging, bumping against his steel hard length.

Vinny threw a leg over his torso and coaxed him into a sitting position, one hand holding his head firmly against her breast so he wouldn't stop. She straddled him, reaching down with her second hand and grasping his cock, giving him a few gentle tugs before bringing herself down on his tip. She swiveled her hips until he was coated with her arousal, grinding her clit on his length until his shaft was ready.

She was swollen from before but more than ready to return the gift Ben had given her. *Love.* She wasn't ready to say it, but she could show it. Vinny sank down onto him, relaxing her muscles best she could until she'd taken him all the way. "Hold on to me," she whispered into his hair. She swiveled her hips, slowly undulating and gripping him with her walls until he moaned against her flesh. Beneath her hands, she felt his muscles ripple as his body clung to hers, the need to release building within him.

You are safe. She rolled her hips.

You are strong. She arched her back.

You are needed. She called his name.

You are loved. They detonated together.

Vinny tipped Ben's face up and kissed him, infusing all her emotions for him while her hips continued to move over his hard cock until the aftershocks subsided. *"Nine,"* she whispered when she pulled away. He quirked a brow over glassy, sex doped eyes. "For tonight. Now we're all caught up."

Ben's grin set butterflies loose in her ribcage. "How could I forget a kiss for *tonight."*

She pushed him back onto the pillows. "I can't take it," she said.

"Take what?"

"The thought of you leaving my bed. Promise me sex in the morning?"

"Promise. Now let me hold you."

Chapter Fifty-One

RUBEN

Ruben gently ran his fingers through Lavender's hair as she slept curled up against him. He thought about what had happened. He had cried. No. Ruben had *grieved*. She had done the impossible and made him feel safe enough to properly miss his mother.

Maybe he should feel less manly, but he didn't. Lavender had held him, and it had felt right. Being vulnerable around her was easy—which was why he'd waited so long for this. Ruben needed to be his whole self with her, and she hadn't been ready before. He thought about the words they had whispered in the dark. The pain they had shared. Yes, it had been easy.

Nothing had ever been easy with Carla. Ruben thought back to the way she'd spoken to him the day he sent her packing. *I could have anyone, but I took pity on you. Even after you came home that summer from your boy time messed up, I still fucked you.* Lavender didn't "pity" him. She understood him, and she *cared* about him.

Maybe she always had.

That was the lesson, right? He pulled her close, breathing in her lavender shampoo. At least he had her now. Ruben didn't think he deserved her, but he would damn well try. And given the amount of time she'd spent running her hands over his body last night, Ruben was confident his vitiligo was a non-issue for her. He'd never struggled so much with it in his life as he had after Carla had thrown it in his face.

But Lavender…*Lavender….*

Ruben's eyes sprung open in the morning from the sensation of Vinny grinding her hot, wet sex against his thigh and whimpering his name. His morning wood was ready to bat, to deliver on the promise she'd extracted before they had passed out last night.

"Good morning, beautiful," he said, his voice rough with sleep. She moaned his name again. As much as he wanted to dive right in dick first, he wanted to be sure she was ready.

Ruben reached down and cupped her sex, sliding his middle finger through her slickness. "Fucking soaked for me. Did you have naughty dreams of me, beautiful?"

"Mmmm." She ground herself onto his hand, and he let his finger slide inside her channel. Her eyes lazily popped open, a soft smile accompanied by a sigh gifted to him as a greeting. "Ben."

"I promised. Fuck, you are so tight this morning. Ride my hand, beautiful. Come on my fingers before you come on my cock."

"Oh, fuck." She sped up her hips. "It's really hot when you say dirty things, Ben."

"Only for you." And he meant it. Ruben had never spoken to a woman like that before. With Lavender, he couldn't help it. "Now do as I said, beautiful. Come on my fingers," he repeated, adding another finger and curling them up inside her until he hit the right spot.

"Ben."

"Now, Lavender."

She fell apart, her arousal dripping down his palm as she rode his hand through her release. As soon as she began to come down, he removed his fingers and flipped her onto her back, filling her with his cock instead. He looked down at her with a smirk before pressing the fingers she'd rode to her lips. Without hesitation, she opened up and wrapped her mouth around his digits, her tongue wrapping around them as her nostrils flared.

"Fuck, that's sexy. Damn, woman." She moaned around his fingers, sucking harder as she locked eyes with him. His hips immediately thrust harder, his cock throbbing painfully as he bottomed out over and over.

She bit down before releasing his fingers and demanding, *"Harder."*

Vinny opened her hips wider, pulling her knees up, and immediately keened over the shift in position. Ruben pounded into her, fighting to hold steady as she swelled around him. She was strangling his dick inside her channel and it hurt so fucking good. Vinny's breath hitched, her body clenched, and then her release triggered his own as she screamed his name.

Good.

Fucking.

Morning.

———

Vinny

Abner looked exceptionally smug when Vinny arrived for their afternoon walk. As much as she'd wanted to keep Ben in bed all day, he had to go to work. It was business as usual for any Friday, so she was going about her day as well. Which meant a later than usual walk with Abner, since she'd slept in too late for lunch after Ben had sent her blissfully back to sleep in a sex haze.

"You know, my son stumbled in this morning looking equally pleased," he greeted her.

She snorted. "He should."

"Loved your performance last night," he mused. "That original song was powerful. Did you plan all that stuff," he said, gesturing with an open paw around his own face, "to do the running. Really dramatic, Miss Blume."

"Stop teasing, Abner," she said primly.

He did, but his smile. They took a longer stroll than usual. Vinny told Abner it was a good idea since the weather was rather fine for late fall, but really, she liked the ache between her legs with every step. The reminder of what he'd done to her made her impatient for Ben to come home.

She stayed all afternoon, agreeing to play Spades as an excuse. Abner knew she was staying for Ben. Vinny knew she was staying for Ben. Neither of them said a word as she lost hand after hand, her mind lost to the game.

Late in the afternoon, her phone buzzed against the table beside her, the vibration making it jitter across the top. Vinny flipped it over and checked the caller ID. It was a private number. Her first instinct was to send it to voicemail, but instead, she excused herself as she answered it, walking away from Abner's room and out to the main dining room.

"This is Lavender," she said pleasantly.

"Vinny! It's Hal."

"Oh, hey! Wow, it's been a few years. What's up, Hal?"

"The song you sang last night, the original. Does it have a name?"

"Yeah, I call it '72," she said. "You saw it?"

"Well, that's why I'm calling." *Huh?* "Look, Vinny. I know you tend to keep your privacy and you don't want to be a main act *despite clearly having the talent,"* he said. "But Presley has been calling me nonstop since the live went dead—"

"Whoa, whoa, whoa... *Presley Harlow* watched my live?"

"She's a huge fan."

"I knew she followed me; I had no idea she watched my lives," Vinny said in awe. Presley Harlow was hot right now. She'd won the Grammy for Best New Artist last year, and rumors were circling she'd be this year's Woman of the Year.

"Well, she wants your song."

The sound of the door opening in the kitchen alerted Vinny that Ben was home. She turned and looked at him, pointing to her phone. His grin was infectious, and even though she was genuinely interested in what Hal was saying, Ben's obvious pleasure in finding her here momentarily distracted her.

"Sorry, did you just say *Presley Harlow wants my song?"* Ben's eyebrows shot up as he mouthed back at her *Presley Harlow.* She nodded.

"Yeah. Her first album was a hard hitting rebel yell. She's wanting to go deeper for her sophomore, and she wants her first single to be your new original," Hal said.

"What are we talking about here, Hal? Talk to me like I'm new on the scene," she said.

Hal laughed. "You're a gifted musician, Vinny. Have you ever thought about being a professional songwriter?"

Was he kidding? *Only every day of my life since I learned to hold a six string!* It was *the* dream, to be the Diane Warren of her generation. "Do you already have terms?" she asked.

"You know I do." She could hear the smile in Hal's voice.

"Good. I'm glad you are on top of it. It's not good *enough* though. Redraft a better offer and send it to my lawyer, Hal."

He laughed loudly, a bark of surprise that percussed her ear, her hand immediately pulling the handset away from her head until he settled down. "Quincy Blume didn't raise a fool. Okay, Vinny. I'll go sweeten the deal and send the *second* draft over to your lawyer."

They said their goodbyes and Vinny hung up, setting her phone on the table. "Presley Harlow wants my song," she said in stunned disbelief. *"Ben. Presley Harlow wants my song!"*

"Of course she does," he said, pulling her into him. "It's brilliant, just like you."

"Oh! Do you mind?"

"Mind what?" he asked with confusion.

"It's *your* song. I wrote it as a gift for you."

"Lavender, I have *you*. The song is amazing, but *you* are the gift. Keep it. Sell it. It's already taken out the ArtBeat servers. Can't blame Presley for wanting in on the action," he said.

"I'm sorry, it *what?"*

"You didn't know? Shit, Vinny! There was a news clip on it. The replay was so popular, it crashed the ArtBeat server for almost half an hour this morning. I thought you would already know," he said.

"I disabled the alarms on my account before we went live. I've been here since I dressed, getting my ass handed to me by your resident card shark after our walk," she snarked. "I had no idea. I can't believe Tripp didn't text me! Or Tyler…"

"Or *me,"* he added with humor. "We should go out tonight."

"Why?"

"This is it, Lavender. I saw your face. This Hal guy is

handing you the keys to your kingdom of dreams. Pretty soon you're going to be too famous and recognizable to take to dinner."

She snorted. "Yeah, sure."

"I mean it," he said. "Glad I locked you down *before* this happened. Now you will be *my* sugar mama, instead of some idiot drummer like Mick."

"Hey!" Vinny giggled at Ben's gest, rolling her eyes at him. *If he only knew. I don't need this to pan out to be his sugar mama.*

Ben's smile turned predatory as he leaned down toward her. "I'm proud of you."

"I'm a sure thing, Ben. No need to flatter me," she teased.

"Mmm. Uncomfortable with praise outside the bedroom. We'll have to work on that."

"What does that mean?"

"It means when I called you a *good girl* last night you damn near made me come with your kiss afterward. It turned you on," he said low against her ear.

Vinny felt her face heat. *What woman doesn't want to be told she's a good girl in bed?*

"It was sexy, beautiful. Expect to hear it often." He pulled away from her ear before continuing. "Now, letting me praise you *outside* of the bedroom, you are going to have to get used to that too. You deserve to celebrate your accomplishments with someone who is proud of you, Lavender. That's me."

Fuck. I think my ovaries just exploded. Why is this so damn attractive? She knew the answer to her own question. A man who would treat his woman like a queen would do the same for their children. One night of hot sex did not make her ready for motherhood by any stretch, but she *did* realize…

Ben made her yearn for the possibility of a family; the

one she'd all but given up on a year ago. Not today or tomorrow, but *someday,* with someone like Ben.

No. With Ben. Nobody else.

I can see it.

"Okay," she said. "Take me on a date. *Tomorrow.* Tonight, I want to eat pizza with you and Abner and then go tell Carys and Eric after the kids go to bed. Then I want you to take me home and forget to leave until sometime after lunch tomorrow—and only then because I will need time to make myself presentable for our first date."

"Wait, are we telling Slow and Carys you finally gave in to my charms, or the fact you *broke* ArtBeat, or that *Presley fucking Harlow* wants to sing one of your original songs," he rattled off, his eyes teasing as much as his smirk was. "Just so we're clear on the plan."

"All of it, Ben. Now shut up and kiss me."

Chapter Fifty-Two

VINNY

Carys's eyes went wide with glee when Ben let himself in with Vinny in tow, their fingers laced together. *"Really?"* she squealed. Beside her, Eric gave one of his signature grins. He looked far less surprised.

"I knew it," he said.

"You did not," Ben countered.

"Man, you have been strutting around like the cat who got the canary all day at work. I fucking *knew."* Eric laughed jovially, though careful not to wake the kids. "Your boots didn't touch the ground all day."

"Whatever, man. Lavender has other news too," he said, changing the subject before turning to smile at her encouragingly.

"Uh…" *Smooth, Vinny.* "I broke ArtBeat today."

"Ooooh! With last night's live? I haven't had a chance to watch it yet," Carys rushed out. "But I will. Promise."

"I performed my new song," she said.

"Wait, *your* song? The one you haven't let anyone so much as touch?" Carys's jaw hung open comically. "Well, that's bullshit."

"Don't be jelly," Ben teased her.

"Yes," she pressed on. "The song I've been writing. I finished it and taught it to the set band. Carys…"

"Oh my god," she whispered, taking in Vinny's face, and Vinny *knew* she didn't need to say any more. "Who?"

"Presley Harlow," she murmured.

Carys gawked a full minute before jumping up off the couch and running toward Vinny screaming. Vinny found herself ripped away from Ben as Carys tugged her in for a hug that was more like a one sided happy dance on Carys's part. *She's going to give me brain damage. Am I too old for shaken baby syndrome?*

Brendon's cry echoed from both the top of the stairs and the baby monitor on the side table. "Carys," Eric scolded without any bite.

She immediately settled, releasing Vinny. "Sorry! My fault. Shit, Vin! Have you told your dad?"

"No, I'll call him tomorrow. He's got a gig tonight."

"Okay. Wow. Wowie. We need to call the crew! *Oooooh!* Have another margarita sleepover! We could do it tomorrow—"

"Nope. I've waited long enough. Tomorrow is date night," Ben said before Carys could verbally plan a menu and shopping list. She deflated instantly, scowling at him. "Don't give me that look."

"I'm the *Queen of Oceanside,* remember? I can look at you any way I want," she pouted.

"You know, once upon a time, I could call up my best friend at any time of the day or night, and he would come running. Hell, I didn't even need a reason. Then he got *married,"* Ben teased affectionately. "You don't see *me* mean mugging *you."*

"Come on, Carys," Eric said, standing from the couch and

walking to her side. "You always wanted double dates with them. You win in the end, don't you think?"

Carys turned to her husband, positively beaming.

"Ugh. Four fucking years of this shit," Vinny teased. "Come on, Ben. I need to go brush my teeth before the honeymooner sweetness rots them all out of my jaw."

"My pleasure," he murmured wickedly into her ear. "After you."

———

"WHY AM I SO NERVOUS?" It was a rhetorical question, but Vinny was unsurprised when Carys answered her anyway.

"Because it's Ruben, and he's amazing." She sighed wistfully. "You know, if he'd stayed in Mexico, we might not even be here. Eric and me, I mean. Since I moved into their room after Ruben left. At the same time, maybe we would have, and *you* would have tempted him to stay, and you'd have married him by now."

It was something Ben had mentioned once too. *If we'd met in Mexico, would he have wasted two years married to someone else?* It was wishful thinking at best, but it brought her a sense of comfort. Even if he'd still chased after his ex for a time, would meeting in Mexico have made it more likely for them to cross paths again or keep in touch?

There was no way to know. That was the reality of *what ifs.* Vinny wasn't convinced it would have been better another way. What if she'd skipped out on Nashville? She wouldn't have gone to Georgia to help bring Abner home otherwise. Like it or not, it was her pivot point. Vinny loved Abner and was well aware their friendship had made her more susceptible to giving his son a chance.

"I don't know what we're doing, Carys! Am I dressed okay?"

"Perfect," she insisted. "He told me the game plan earlier."

Vinny wiped her sweaty palms on her jean clad thighs. *I've never been this...ugh,* jittery *over a man before. I don't think I like it.* Kissing Ben until her clothes fell off was remarkably easy. Going out as a couple, making their budding relationship public knowledge, that was a whole different thing—like a strong green tea when she was expecting something light and fruity. Hot when she was accustomed to iced. Not bad, but inherently *different,* when she'd spent years rolling from bum to bum in an attempt to keep things comfortably the same with the impression of different.

This was more. It was *change.*

Change made Vinny want to throw up.

Change gave her butterflies.

It drove home her fear it would all end tragically while simultaneously stoking her desire to see how long she could stand in the flames without getting torched. Change—when related to Ben—made Vinny ache all over, in ways she hadn't experienced before.

Change made her wish for her mother. Was this what it was like, when her parents met? Had her father looked at her mother and immediately known? *Pivot.* He hadn't quit or forced her mother to live on the road. No, her father had *pivoted,* taken the thing he knew better than anything and used it as a means to support his wife and daughter. Quincy Blume hadn't given up his identity, but he *had* adjusted his boundaries when he became a faithful and doting husband.

Lavender Blume had felt herself finally open up to love, poured it into her song, and now the hottest rocker in the country wanted her track. Her declaration of love was facilitating her own pivot, allowing her to stay active in the world she loved while still being able to be home with the Marine who had broken her cursed creative block and protective walls one determined moment at a time.

One kiss at a time.

"You might want a jacket or sweater," Carys suggested. "And good, thick socks."

"Yeah, okay. It's practically winter, so it makes sense." Ben had said it would be a casual date. "I don't think I've been this mentally fucked since your accident. Scratch that, *nothing* could mess with my head as much as the accident and the months after it. This is a different thing, but I feel sort of the same. Does that even make sense?"

"Yes," Carys said simply.

"This is why we are forever friends."

"Well, Tripp already claimed you as his—what was it— oh, his *platonic wife.*" Carys chortled. "So, I better scoop up 'forever friend' before it gets claimed too."

Vinny opened her mouth to reply but was interrupted by the doorbell. "That's for me," she said awkwardly.

"I'll let myself out the back and lock up," Carys said. "You look lovely, Vin. I hope you have a great time tonight."

Vinny nodded awkwardly, her nerves spiking again as she headed out of her bedroom and toward the front door. She wiped her hands again, hating how clammy they felt. But when she opened the door, she forgot to be nervous...mostly because Ben looked worse off than she was, and her first instinct was to reassure him.

"Hi," she said softly.

"Hey," he offered back gently. "You look beautiful."

"Thanks. Do I need anything more than my wallet?"

"Nah, I got you covered."

She nodded her head and gave him her best reassuring

smile. She hoped it said, *I've got you covered too.* "So, where are we going?"

"It's a surprise."

"I'm sure it will be great."

"Carys told me you aren't a fan of surprises," he blurted.

Vinny laughed. "Not usually, no. They are too often unpleasant. But this is from you so it's different."

Ben stepped into her house and pulled her in close, wrapping an arm behind her and tipping her head back with his second hand before sending her head spinning with a sensual kiss. There was no tongue, just his lips paying homage to hers with tender, pillowy touches that flushed her body with heat and desire. "I needed that," he murmured when he pulled back.

Vinny nodded her head dumbly. "Uh huh."

He leaned back down, placing a series of kisses on her lips without taking it deeper. "Okay, let's go. I think that will tide me over."

"I hope it's a short drive, because I'm not sure it will tide *me* over. I could kiss you all day."

Ben groaned. "Let's go before I take you to bed instead."

He'd pulled his truck across the street, parking so her door was at the base of the staircase. Ben opened her door and helped her into his truck, going so far as to buckle her seatbelt. It was ridiculous, but it made her feel valued. Like she was precious to him, worth protecting. Instead of over-thinking it, she simply allowed herself to feel.

It felt good.

They rolled out of town, down a road Vinny didn't recognize. She tended to head *into* town, not *away* from it. Her curiosity was getting the better of her, and Vinny squeezed Ben's hand over the console as she watched their surroundings change with an unprecedented eagerness.

"I'm glad you are excited," he said.

"I can't help it," she admitted. "Even if I am another true crime horror story in the making."

"A what?"

"You know… Carys listens to all these creepy true crime podcasts while she's cleaning or whatever, and it's always some weird Ted Bundy shit. Women disappearing into the wilderness, never to be heard from again."

"You're almost famous, so rest assured. I wouldn't get away with it anyway," he teased.

"Almost famous? I have the most combined followers and subscribers on ArtBeat for independent music, and the third most on the entire platform."

"Wow. That's the first time I've heard you boast. Good on you."

She felt herself blushing. It was true. Vinny was proud of all she had accomplished, but she didn't often talk in depth about herself. Music she'd talk about until she passed out. Herself? *Meh.* "I'm still in shock Presley Harlow wants our song. And breaking the platform…it hasn't been done since it first exploded onto the scene. They had to buy up more servers or whatever they're called because ArtBeat kind of plunked along at first, but when it took off, the exponential growth caught them off guard. So being the reason it crashed is wild."

"As wild as you, Lavender. Anyway, I hope you like what I have planned. Give it a few years, and this may be the only way I get privacy with you. I can handle sharing you to an extent, but I'm greedy, beautiful. When you're with me, I don't want any distractions or interruptions."

She snorted. "You say it like I'm going to be hounded by paparazzi without a moment's rest. It's only one song, Ben.

And fame is fleeting. I'll enjoy my fifteen minutes, but in the end, I'm just a girl who can strum a guitar."

"Go back to bragging. It was more accurate. *Just a girl who can strum a guitar.* Pfft. Not even close." He turned down a gravel road. "You're not *just* anything."

"Where are we?" she changed the subject.

"Almost there," he said coyly. Vinny rolled her eyes at him. "Trust me."

And she did.

Ben had earned her trust.

Chapter Fifty-Three

RUBEN

Was it normal to want to tell someone how you felt about them constantly? Ruben didn't think so, but when it came to Lavender, all he wanted to do was tell her she meant everything to him. All. The. Time.

"I love you, Lavender." She squeezed his hand, which bolstered his resolve. He didn't dare glance over at her. "I…" He let out a heavy sigh. *How do I even put this into words?*

Beside him, Vinny began humming Bill Withers. Ruben began to relax. When she reached the chorus, he joined along in singing "Lean On Me." Sometimes it felt like his parents had meticulously selected this woman just for him with a helping hand from fate. She understood him, a gift he intended to cherish.

When they pulled up outside the cabin, Ruben was feeling more grounded. They were going to have an amazing evening. There was no reason to be this anxious. She was too good to be true and too good for him—but then Vinny would stop his heart with her smile, the affection in her eyes making quick work at sending his pulse racing again.

When Vinny went in, she went *all* in. He knew better than

to put all his second chance hopes and dreams in their basket too soon, but earning the opportunity felt like winning the lotto. As if he had misinterpreted a three dollar scratch it ticket, expecting to cash in for what he bought in at, only to find out he was a jackpot winner instead.

"This is beautiful," she murmured. "What's the plan? Can I help?"

"Only one thing to do," he said as he opened the back window on the cab. "And that's plug in the air compressor."

"Huh?"

"For the air mattress in the bed of the truck. We're having a sunset dinner over on the porch, then stargazing. Not as many meteor showers in the late fall, but this far away from the city, we should see plenty."

"I've never been stargazing before," she said.

Ruben puffed up. "Yeah? Well, all right. You are in for a treat, beautiful." He grinned at her, feeling boyish but no less excited. "Camping was one of the few things we could afford growing up. Real rough, just a sleeping bag under the stars. Hell of a way to grow up, watching the heavens shift above with the last of the fire crackling beside you and your belly full of hotdogs and potato chips."

"It sounds amazing. Are we staying the night?" she asked, nodding toward the cabin.

"Not tonight, but if it's something you are interested in, I can ask Zeke. It's his cabin."

"Really? I didn't know Zeke had a cabin."

"I think he and his cousin Enzo share the property. They grew up nearby."

"I adore Zeke. He's a good man," she said. "Really, most of you are."

Her face soured for a moment, and he knew she was thinking of Greer. Things were still up in the air on his old commander. They had gotten legal involved, and Ruben knew an investigation was quietly being done. But that wasn't date night material, so he shoved it to the back of his mind.

"What was it like for you? Growing up on the California coastline," he asked.

"You would get a better answer from Carys. While you were out stargazing in Georgia, I often spent my school vacations on a bus with my dad. All the stars I gazed upon were under bright lights on a big stage, rocking out," she said with a smile and a laugh. "Especially once Mom died. I went where Dad went."

"And after? How did it work with Q still touring?" he asked curiously.

"He took tours that paid well enough for him to gig around town during the school year, more or less. Mom inherited the house from somebody or other, so we didn't have a mortgage to worry about. Honestly, I think that's the only reason he could do it. We were fortunate."

"And he still has the house?"

"He does. He's renting it out to some friends right now and living between here and LA, but he would never sell our house. Dad promised he'd make sure it was always there for me if I wanted it. Selling will be my decision."

"Do you want that? To move back to your home town someday?"

"Eh. Not unless Carys's mom moves. She still owns the house next door. Maybe someday, though," she said. "We'll see."

Ruben finished filling up the airbed, unrolled his heavy sleeping bags, and chucked the pillows in before leading Vinny to the porch. "I hope you like scalloped potatoes."

"I like *all* potatoes. Scalloped, chipped, wedged, fried… maybe not vodka."

"Vodka isn't my thing either. It gives me the worst hangovers," he said.

"Same."

"I also brought garlic green beans and this chicken stuff—I don't know what it's called, but it's baked—and a few bottles of local hard cider," he said.

"Wow. Did you order for pickup?" she asked as she settled into the chair he'd pulled out for her.

"Nah, it's all me," he said with pride. The scalloped potatoes were his mom's recipe, and one of his favorite comfort foods. Everyone in the south was born knowing how to cook vegetables in butter, so the beans were no secret.

"I didn't know you could cook," she said, her tone captivated. "Well, let me rephrase. Obviously you can cook, but I wouldn't have expected something of this caliber. I'm impressed, Ben."

"Eh. You should probably save your accolades for *after* you've tried my cooking." Because honestly, he'd been so nervous while he was cooking, Ruben wasn't sure he hadn't over salted the whole kibosh and made it inedible. At least he had the cider and S'mores as a backup.

He pulled out the containers he'd had in a warming tote in the truck, relieved they were still good and hot. Ruben made a big to do about serving her before dishing up himself. By the time he sat, she'd opened the growler he'd brought and poured their beverages. He pushed his food around with his fork to look busy while he watched her from under his brows across the table.

"Oh, god," she moaned. "Please tell me there are more potatoes."

He grinned ear to ear, relief and pride flowing across his nerves like a soothing tonic. "Plenty."

"Good, because I'm obsessed already," she said with a sigh.

Ruben finally allowed himself to shovel up a forkful and settle in. They didn't speak much over dinner. The sounds of her satisfaction bordered on indecent, especially when Vinny was scooping up her third helping of potatoes. It struck Ruben how good it felt to eat with a woman who actually *ate*. Carla had rarely eaten what he prepared because it didn't fit whatever ridiculous fad diet she was on at the time.

It brought Ruben a deeply settling contentment to feed Vinny and know she enjoyed it. As they washed down their meal with the last of the cider, he found himself completely at ease. They cleared away their dishes and trash, Ruben stashing it in the backseat of the truck, before he gave her a helping hand into the bed.

"Now, it is vitally important you experience stargazing from the bed of a pickup, beautiful," he teased. "Otherwise, you haven't done it properly."

"I thought you watched from your sleeping bag on the ground, next to a campfire."

"Yeah, when I was a boy. But this isn't child's play. We are talking serious *adult* stargazing here," he said, pulling back the top layer of the sleeping bags he'd zipped together. He waited until she'd kicked her shoes off and climbed in before following her example and hunkering down with her. "Good, but you are too far away."

"I'm right next to you on my own pillow, Ben."

"Yeah, but that pillow is more a suggestion. Think of it as décor, really."

"Then where am I supposed to lay my head?" she asked with mock confusion.

Ruben lifted his arm from between them. "Right here. Scoot your perfect body right on over."

She giggled as she followed his command. "Am I stargazing correctly yet?"

"Almost." With her head resting on his peck, he wrapped his arm around her and reached across his body with his other arm, snagging her hand and placing it on the other side of his chest. "Getting warmer," he said, his hand roving down her body and around her hip, catching her thigh behind her knee and dragging her leg over his torso. "Perfect."

"You're right. This is much better. The whole experience would have been ruined all alone with that gapping inch of space between us."

"You're welcome, beautiful. I aim to please." He squeezed her, his hand settling over her hip. "Won't be long now. Better get a wish or two ready."

"Wishing on a shooting star?"

"Only if you want to stargaze correctly."

"What if my wish already came true?"

Ruben took in a sudden breath as her leg shifted down, brushing the bulge behind the zipper of his jeans. He'd already been at half-mast from her presence alone, but the extra attention had him straining for a full salute. "Was your wish to sexually torture me?" he managed to huff out with a groan.

"Mmmm."

"That wasn't a *no,* Lavender."

"It wasn't a *yes* either, Ben." Her hand slid down his body to his fly. When her thumb brushed the head of his cock as she swept it below his waistband, he nearly bucked away. *"Mmmm, "* she repeated as a moan this time.

"You are playing with fire, woman," he warned. "I don't have self-control with you."

"I'm counting on it," she murmured against his ear before trailing kisses down his throat. Her hand made quick work yanking his fly open and gripping him with a firm stroke from base to crown, her thumb circling his tip and dragging the bead of pre-cum with it. "Since we're a thing now, I'm pretty sure I saw in a few dozen coming of age movies that you are supposed to take me tenderly."

Her lips were moving over his Adam's apple as she spoke, and he could feel the ghost of her smile against his skin. "Ah, but we already *are* of age," he rasped. "Remember, this is *adult* stargazing."

She pushed herself up enough to meet his gaze while her hand continued to wreak havoc on his cock. "Then take me the way a man takes a woman, Ben."

"So much for a proper first date," he said as he moved his hands down to the hemline of her shirt and began tugging it up her body. "Burrow down so you don't freeze, beautiful."

"It's a perfect first date, Ben. I love everything about it. Now show me *all* the stars. The ones in the sky and in my mind. The ones you are going to drag out of me while I beg you not to stop." Her voice was sultry and needy.

"Your wish is my command," he said, peeling off her bra next. "Fuck, your tits are perfect."

They stripped each other inside the joined sleeping bags as the night sky deepened above them. It was slow; their hands wandering across each other languidly, stopping whenever they liked. Ruben drug open mouth kisses across her chest, ducking under the sleeping bag so she was still warm while he sucked and laved her breasts as his thumb circled her clit. She had one hand gripping the back of his head and the other over his, helping him maintain the right pressure as she ground her hips up against his hand and arched her body into his mouth.

"Ben! *Aaaaaah,"* she cried out, her body tensing beneath

him as her first orgasm hit. He kept up the pace until she relaxed beneath him again.

"That's my girl," he said before taking her mouth in as unhurried a manner as he had her nipple. Her hand clasped him again, drawing a grunt from his chest. Vinny's touch was exquisite. She knew how to drag out his pleasure, changing her pace and pressure in a way that had Ruben achingly hard. His hips bucked into her hand, prompting her to squeeze him firmly base to tip each time. "You're going to make me come too soon," he said between kisses.

"I want to ride you."

"It's too cold," he said. "Let me love you, Lavender. You can ride me at home where you won't catch hypothermia."

She nodded her consent, and he shifted his body above her, settling his hips between her legs with his torso pressed into her form to keep her warm. Her hands trailed over his body; her eyes locked with his. "I can't believe you're mine," she murmured with awe, her words ending on a groan he matched as he pushed inside her.

Me either, beautiful.

He moved above her, maintaining the slow, dedicated tempo they had set from the start. Ruben murmured words of praise and affection to Vinny, watching her reactions and learning what she liked most to hear. He made love to her under the stars, knowing she was right there with him all the while. As she began to crest, she said, "a star."

"Make a wish while you come for me, beautiful." Ruben watched as her eyes glazed, the reflection of the night sky taking over her orbs, and through them, he too wished on a shooting star as it passed above them, their orgasms meeting in a tidal wave of ecstasy.

I wish for a life with you, Lavender.

Chapter Fifty-Four

VINNY

After a few hours of stargazing in the bed of Ruben's truck with their naked bodies tangled together, they had giggled like fools while they attempted to sort whose clothing was whose underneath the cover; awkwardly dressing best they could without leaving the warmth they had generated together. Vinny had exploded around Ben's cock while her first shooting star streaked across the sky over his shoulder.

I wish for all the things I thought I was too late for with you, Ben.

She had insisted on riding him to a second orgasm once they made it back to her apartment. It had been more than satisfying to watch his eyes roll into the back of his head below her as she milked every drop out of him. Enough so, she came all over him again.

Afterward, she collapsed against his chest while they both waited for their breathing to even out. He stroked her hair away from her face, dragging his fingers through the long silken strands until she could feel it fanned out behind her on the bed. They fell asleep wrapped up in the "perfect way to stargaze."

"Come home with me," Ruben said after they both woke the next morning. "Have breakfast with me and Dad."

"I don't know," she said nervously.

"Why not?"

"I don't know. Don't you think it's weird to wander over together for breakfast, all sex mussed and satisfied."

"He knows we have sex, beautiful," Ben teased.

"I know, but...I don't know!" she huffed. "I don't want him to see me differently."

"My dad has loved you from the moment he laid eyes on your car—*ooof,*" he grunted as she playfully elbowed him. "I mean *you,* first laid eyes on *you.*"

"Liar."

"Never. If I ever tell you a falsehood, it will be because I believed it true at the time, Lavender," he said more seriously. "I'll never intentionally mislead or outright lie to you. We've both been through enough."

"Okay."

"Okay you believe me, or *okay* you'll go home with me for breakfast?"

"Yes."

"Well...*okay.*"

"Hey, Ben?"

"Yes, Lavender?"

"Happy Birthday."

"Who said it was my birthday?"

"You're kidding me, right? I spend more time with Abner than you do. But even so, I've known your birthday since Carys moved in here," she admitted.

Vinny rolled away to the side of the mattress and reached into the gap between her bed and nightstand, rolling back with a gift. She'd put a lot of thought into it, but right now she was second guessing her choice.

"You got me a present," he said with surprise. "You didn't have to do that."

"I wanted to," she said. "I hope it's okay. I'll understand if you don't like it."

He placed his hands over hers, where her clammy palms were wrinkling the shiny green paper she had carefully wrapped it in. "I'm going to love it because it's from you."

She nodded and released the box. Ruben began to carefully peel up the corner of the paper but quickly switched to shredding it away, a boyish grin emphasizing his excitement. Paper off, box opened, he removed the frame and pulled back the white tissue paper protecting it. Vinny watched with her heart in her throat as his face shifted from innocent glee to one of contemplative awe.

"How…"

"I always knew the owner of my car was a woman named Joy," she murmured. "Your dad left the expired vehicle registration in the car when he sold it to us. I thought it was kismet we shared a name. About a month ago, I was going through my car, cleaning it out and trying not to think about how long it would be before you showed up to kiss me." She smiled wide at the memory, cautiously peeking up at him through her lashes. She felt exposed, which brought out a smidge of shyness.

"And you found it," he said.

"Yeah. It was in the glove box. Joy Holt. Abner Holt. And the address Eric texted me when he asked me to drive you guys home."

"It's why he ran out the door the moment he laid eyes on you," Ben said with a smile, still staring at the gift. "He knew immediately. Took me a few days to notice the name on the dash, but I got there."

"Do you like it?" she asked hesitantly.

Ben looked over at her, his rich, dark eyes full of happiness and gratitude. "It's perfect. How did you get the pictures?"

"Your dad fell asleep watching one of his shows after a particularly long walk on the beach and I snuck his photo album over here. I'd seen him going through it before, but he'd flip around the pages, only showing me certain images." She laughed. "I was so afraid he'd wake up and catch me sneaking it back into place."

She looked down at her handiwork, where Ben's hand roamed over the frame. Vinny had gone down to a local shop and paid for a custom, professional job shortly after she'd snuck several pictures and scanned them. There was Ben in the backseat of the Camaro giving the camera a thumbs up with a big smile. Ben, Abner, and Joy in front of the car before her maiden—and Vinny now knew *only*—voyage. One of Joy behind the wheel, her face filled with pride and…well, *joy.* Another of Abner looking at his wife like his world revolved around her. They were laid out with the registration card, ready for display.

"I don't have a single photo of my mother. It hurt too much, and by the time I realized I wanted one, I was too conflicted over everything to ask Dad about it. Thank you, Lavender. It's the best gift I've ever been given." His voice was a soft rasp, full of emotion and love. He kissed her tenderly, complaining when she pulled away.

Vinny giggled. "I have one more thing,' she said.

"How can you top this?" he asked, waving his hand over the frame.

"I don't think I can, but I wanted to tell you first."

"Okay, I'm listening." Ben lowered the frame back into the box and gave her his full attention.

"My lawyer and I came to terms we both felt are fair.

Presley Harlow is going to record our song," she said. Ben's face lit up, and she put her hand up to keep him from speaking yet. "She wants me to play an instrument on the track as well. I'm not sure which one. *And* she wants to explore my library for other tracks, plus have me help co-write at least part of her next album."

"That's amazing, Lavender."

"There is more," she said, laughing when his eyebrows shot up and his jaw dropped. "The label is connecting me with other clients who liked the song as well. Several of them want me to work with them on composing. I'm a songwriter now, Ben. No more touring, and if I decide to step away from ArtBeat permanently, the kind of royalties I have the potential to make is more than I ever dreamed of."

"You were wrong. That is way better than the photo frame," he said, capturing her face in his hands and her lips with his own mouth. Vinny's body warmed all over as she leaned into their kiss.

"Ben." His name came out muffled between them.

"Yes?" He pulled back, clearly not happy with the inter-ruption.

"I'm not leaving Oceanside. I want this. I want *you.* And if you get orders in a few years, well…"

"You'd go with me?" The hope in his voice brought tears to her eyes.

"Yeah. If you'll have me, I want to be with you."

"You'll say yes when I ask the big question?"

"Most likely, yes," she said nervously. She didn't want to kill the mood, but there needed to be a firm boundary on that particular question. "But not too soon, okay?"

"I know you aren't ready, beautiful. I'm happy to go at whatever pace we naturally move at."

"Thank you."

He pulled her in close, shifting down the bed and tugging her down with him. Ben ran his nose up her neck, stopping behind her ear where she was pretty sure he was smelling her hair. She'd noticed him doing it when they cuddled on the couch and he thought she wasn't paying attention. Vinny loved it.

"Do you want kids, Lavender?"

"I think I want *your* kids. I've never imagined having a family with anyone before and felt excited about it," she confessed. "Making that sort of commitment should be with someone you feel confident will be there no matter what, not fill you with dread and uncertainty."

"Fuck, I can't wait." He let out a sexy groan and Vinny clenched her thighs. "I mean, I can. But you are going to be gorgeous with my baby in you and *fuck,* do not tell Eric I said that."

Vinny laughed. "Why not?"

"It's a whole conversation we had after Maya was born," he said, waving his hand like it was no big deal when clearly it was. "I don't need him giving me shit."

"Mmmm. Tell you what, I won't tell him until after this month, assuming I remember at all. Don't want to ruin your birthday month," she teased.

"Lavender, *you* are the best birthday gift I have ever had," he said adamantly as he reached out to pull her closer again.

"Oh. Well, then. I guess you don't need the other thing I had in mind for your birthday before we go to your place for breakfast."

"What was that?" He hissed as she grasped his morning wood.

"Don't the best days start out with an orgasm?" she teased.

Ben rolled her over and preceded to devour her, his mouth

as fervent against hers as her hand was on his eager cock. When he slid home, she screamed his name as he bottomed out, his pelvis rubbing her clit as he took control. *"Fuck,"* he bit out as his hips began pounding erratically. They were both so close. "You. Are. The. Gift." Each word was punctuated with his hips slamming into her, his cock hitting just the right spot. They came undone together, Vinny jabbering incoherently as she gave over to the pleasure.

"One more thing," she gasped once the haze began to fade. She could still feel him pulsing inside her. "I'm taking you for a ride later."

"You just did," he said playfully, grinding his hips into hers.

"I meant in the Camaro," she said with a laugh. "It's about time you rode in the front seat."

Ruben

As if she wasn't already amazing, Vinny had given Ruben the best birthday since his mother died. He was thirty-four. She would be thirty in a few months. He had begun letting go of the *what ifs* as she cruised down the highway later that afternoon, the passenger seat of her Camaro a million times more comfortable than the backseat.

Vinny pulled over at a bluff new to Ruben; a deserted area down a bit of road which had been precarious to navigate, despite being paved. Throw in a Sunday in November, he figured it was safe to make a birthday demand. Ruben made her come on his fingers and tongue before allowing her to recover well enough to drive home.

Home, where he threw her over his shoulder like a damn

cave man and carried her across the street to his house for the night. As much as he loved crashing with her, Ruben wanted to spend the rest of his day making love to her in his new bed. It was time he erased the last of the ghosts Carla had left behind and replaced them with new and better memories.

Memories of Vinny moaning his name while he bent her over his new bed and brought her to orgasm. Memories of the way her hair felt fisted between his fingers as he denied her last orgasm until she was a begging, whimpering mess in his arms. There would be nights they would have to be apart, but now he knew exactly what she looked like spread out for him in his room. It would be agony when he was alone.

How had he ever fooled himself into believing she was anything short of perfection? Aside from in her song, she hadn't said she loved him. It was okay. Ruben knew Vinny loved him, and she would say it when she was ready. He decided that was how he would know she was ready to consider the next step.

Maybe it's time to plan another trip to Mexico.

Chapter Fifty-Five

RUBEN

There were some messages you didn't want to get. This was one of them.

Ruben stared at his friend's bloodshot eyes and knew Zeke Vorderstrasse would never be the same.

"You want to talk about it? I'm here to listen." In all reality, Ruben didn't want the details on how something so horrible came to pass, but it was the least he could do for his bereft friend. They settled down on the couch in V12's house.

"He was just doing a normal shift. We were at his mom's house the day before, you know? Eating and laughing. Enzo was talking about buying a new house now he has Iris to consider—"

"Sorry, Iris?"

"Yeah," he choked out. "You know Enzo and his hero complex. He saved this woman from a bad situation. She was homeless and pregnant. Really fucked up mess. He told me last Sunday he'd picked out a ring." His voice was completely void of emotion now.

Ruben wondered if Zeke wasn't fond of this Iris woman. He hadn't mentioned his cousin having a woman before, either. While he was a private guy, Ruben had tagged along to more cookouts than he could count with Zeke's family and considered Enzo a friend.

A couple weeks ago, Ruben had been high on the way Vinny's face looks when she comes, enjoying his birthday immensely. Now he was trying to keep his shit together after Enzo Ramirez died the day after Thanksgiving, thanks to a domestic disturbance turned deadly. Enzo had always been passionate about working in the worst districts. *Being the light,* he would say. Ruben hadn't been best buds with him, but he knew Enzo pretty well—*had known*—and had been shocked to hear he'd died in route to the hospital in his own ambulance, bleeding out from a gunshot wound to the chest.

But Zeke? He and his cousin were more like brothers. They had been raised side by side, born only a few weeks apart. Zeke without Enzo wasn't a reality. Period.

Until now.

Because Enzo was dead.

And he'd taken a huge chunk of Zeke with him.

The funeral had been packed with EMS and military, the family having little choice but to switch to the largest church they could find. It had still been standing room only. The bulk of the crowd was wearing some sort of service dress, all turned out in their best to honor the life of a good man cut short. In the front, standing between his mother and aunt, Zeke had stood tall.

Ruben and Slow had forced their way forward, refusing to leave their friend's side. They took up posts on either side of the women, lending them their strength and in turn taking a nip off the burden settled squarely onto Zeke's broad shoulders. Off to the side, a woman with a baby sat looking conspicuously alone for such a crowded room.

Iris, Ruben had realized. What must she be feeling? Enzo

had been ready to make a life with her. And though Enzo was not the father of her baby, he had been there the entirety of her short life. *They must be in agony.*

But more surprising was the way Enzo's mother kept side eyeing the woman, as if she was miffed she'd had the nerve to show up. Ruben had offered Yesenia gentle words of condolence and strength, drawing her ire away from the poor alienated woman. It was bad enough she was completely alone in such a crowded room, without having Enzo and Zeke's mothers glowering at her.

On the way home, Slow and Ruben both let out a sigh as soon as they hit the highway. "That was fucking intense," Slow said. "I'm glad Carys stayed home with the kids."

"Yeah, man. Wild. What was with the family and Enzo's woman?"

"I have no clue. Zeke barely mentioned her when he told us what happened."

"I know. I didn't even know Enzo *had* a lady. I hadn't seen him since before our last stint down range, but usually Zeke keeps us in the loop."

"Something isn't right," Slow said carefully. "I hope he confides in us eventually. Iris is going to need compassion, and she won't get any from Yesenia and Marisol."

Not a chance in hell, Ruben mentally agreed. "They are forever on the guys to get married and give them grandbabies. I don't understand why they wouldn't love her. She was pretty shook up, but I said hello and introduced myself. Iris seemed kind to me."

"Same. The only bad vibes I got were off the sinister sisters. It's a shit show. I told Zeke she's welcome over anytime. We'd love to have her around, and it seems like she could use a few friends since the family isn't exactly embracing her," Eric added.

"For sure. Lavender loves babies too, so it's not like your house wouldn't be an ideal place for her to take a load off," Ruben said.

Things with Vinny were better and better, but things in the neighborhood were plain odd. Perez had left. Not only the Brown's income suite, but Camp Pendleton. When Ruben asked Zeke if he knew anything, he declined to say a word. Then there were the Browns. They had packed up nearly as fast as Perez had.

Ruben and Slow couldn't make sense of it. Christmas was ten days away, and there they were, emptying their home of nearly thirty years with the efficiency of a seasoned military family. They had quietly sold their home and were moving closer to where their children had settled.

Yet there hadn't been a for sale sign in the yard. *Fucking weird.*

In every other way, Ruben felt like his life was one long sigh of relief. His father was safe under his roof. Abe loved his new woman—always a bonus when your father likes your girlfriend—and she lived across the street. He was highly unlikely to be deployed in his new position.

The bliss and ease of having his personal life sorted was humbling after what he'd been through to get it.

And then Christmas Eve came.

They were all gathered at the Blackwood's house. Q had come down from his place. Ruben had made scalloped potatoes at Vinny's insistence and walked them across the street with his dad. The two men had settled down together happily, same as they had the first time everyone had gathered, while Ruben had busied himself making up bullshit reasons to be in the kitchen with Vinny until Carys chased them both out.

While they were all clustered in the living room waiting for the last of the food to warm in the oven, laughing and joking while Maya and Brendon competed for attention, Zeke arrived. They had expected him to drop by, but *not* with Iris and her daughter in tow. It was a welcome surprise, Carys and Vinny immediately going all out to make them feel welcome. Soon as he saw she was settled, Zeke nodded toward the back deck. Ruben and Slow followed him out, settling down around the seating area farthest from the door.

"I need your help," Zeke said right out the gate.

"Of course, man." Ruben would do anything for Zeke.

"Anytime," Eric joined.

"I bought the house next door," Zeke said.

"Hold up. Is that why Perez had orders out on such short notice?" Eric asked the question on Ruben's mind.

Zeke shrugged, but his eyes gave him away. *Affirmative.* "The Browns had told her she was the only reason they hadn't moved yet. She mentioned it to me, and I asked her to give them my information as a potential buyer highly motivated to close soon."

"Okay. Why now?" Ruben asked. "It's a dream having you on the street, but the timing is…" *Fucking weird.*

"It's Enzo's will, and Iris. And Jesus *fuck,* my damn family," Zeke spit out with frustration. "They treat her like she's an enemy. You would think she was the one who shot Enzo, the way *tía* and mom go on."

"Your mom was less than happy to see her at the funeral," Ruben commiserated. "What's with that?"

"They think she's some sort of golden boy stealing gold digger. Honestly, they seemed fine with her until Enzo…" Zeke sucked in a stuttered breath, his eyes squeezing tightly closed. They waited patiently while he slowly let it back out, doing his best not to lose it. "I fucking miss him."

"And you should," Ruben said softly. "Enzo was a hell of a guy, Zeke. Irreplaceable."

"He left his benefits to her. That's why my family is being so *stupid*. Enzo told his mom he was serious about her before he died. Before he spoke up, they all thought it was more of a roommate situation. Now he's gone, she's got his life insurance, and everyone is losing their damn minds over her, assuming the worst."

"Shit," Eric said. "Is she living alone at Enzo's place?"

Zeke shook his head. "No. He was renting, so she had to leave."

"Ouch. It must have been hard finding a place so close to Christmas," Ruben said. Zeke looked him dead in the eyes. "Oh, fuck."

"You moved her in with you," Eric said, catching on quickly.

Zeke nodded. "In my one bedroom condo."

"Oh, *fuck.*" Ruben repeated. "So, you need to move ASAP."

"Yeah. My couch is not as comfortable as yours, buddy. My neck is killing me." He rubbed his hands over his face, trying to work through what to say next. Zeke had been that way as long as Ruben had known him. "I just... I can't force her out on her own. She isn't ready."

"Especially if it was getting serious between her and Enzo," Ruben said. "She's probably grieving pretty hard. And since your family is being the way they are, she's suffering alone."

The anguish on Zeke's face said more than his next words. "You know Enzo...always the white knight."

Shiiiiit. It was one sided. "So, your family is attacking her because they know?"

"No, they think she ensnared him with some kind of act. That she doesn't care at all about him or that he died, except now she's lost her meal ticket. And now she has his life insurance, they are threatening to hire a lawyer and fight the will."

They sat in silence, Zeke's words thickening the cool winter air. It was a mess. No doubt about it.

"She doesn't deserve their cruelty," he said some minutes later. "The shit they have said to her... Iris is a *good person.* Enzo maybe jumped the gun with his intentions—hell, maybe she *is* in love with him, I don't know—but she's a wonderful woman and a good mom. Kind. Sweet. *Smart.* She has nobody else, and what they are doing to her is not right. It's not what Enzo would want. I approached the Browns and bought their house so Iris and the baby can have the income suite until she's on her feet. And I told my family where to go."

"Christ," Ruben said, shaking his head. "I'm sorry, man. I know you love your family. This must be eating you from the inside out."

"It is, but what can I do? Throw her out? Drop her at a shelter? She isn't who they've made her out to be, and I can't let Enzo down like that. She needs stability and community. I can give her that, at least. She's got a lot to learn about a lot of things, but I can give her *time.* All she needs is time. What I need to know is, can you guys help me help her?"

"Like you had to ask," Eric said, clasping a hand over Zeke's shoulder. "We *are* family. Whatever you need; whatever they need."

"At any time of the day or night," Ruben added. "We're brothers, man. Enzo was a brother too. We will help you honor him in any way we can."

"Thanks. You were the only two who didn't hesitate to approach her at his funeral. That meant a lot. Even Enzo's colleagues were standoffish. I mean, *tía* has fed them enough to earn loyalty. And they know how she came into his life. I just thought they would have more compassion, you know? It's not a war. Nobody needs to choose a side in this shit." Zeke shook his head. "My family thinks I chose *her* when I didn't shun her. When I did what Enzo clearly wanted when he changed his shit to benefit her if he wasn't around. I don't know if they will ever come around, you know? And I don't know how to help Iris and her daughter. The money is hers, but under my control until certain conditions are met per his will. He set her up to succeed, and I can handle it financially, but the real day to day shit…it's out of my league."

"That's why you are a medic and not a long-term care provider," Ruben jested. "You are great at getting those in need to the right place, but you've never been responsible past drop off. There is no shame in that, man. We got you."

Ruben thought about all the shit he'd had to pull back in Georgia before his dad finally moved to California with him. Yeah, he knew how to make some noise. He could teach Zeke how to approach some of the bullshit. But he didn't think Zeke was giving himself enough credit, either. Maybe he wasn't "long-term" in his day to day crisis management skills, but the man was steadfast to his people—blood or no. Enzo had known what he was doing when he made Zeke his executor.

Chapter Fifty-Six

VINNY

"How is Zeke?" she asked. Vinny and Carys had been happy to pull Iris into the fold and allow the guys time to sort their shit outside, but she wasn't used to being separated from those conversations. She knew Zeke. The familiar is easier than trying to get a read on someone new who is both under duress and clearly scared shitless.

"He's doing better than he thinks he is. His family is being shitty, but Zeke has a plan and is making solid choices. We all know how tight he and Enzo were. Essentially taking on responsibility for another's family *while grieving* is a hell of an undertaking," Ben said thoughtfully. "I think he'll get through it, especially here on the block. Iris won't be alone. Having other women around, another mother, will be good for her too."

"I agree. She's a sweet woman, but I get the sense she's survived more than the rest of us put together. There is a shadow in her eyes," Vinny said.

"Yeah. But the way she handles the kid? You can't fake that. She loves her baby."

"You should have seen how nervous she was to let Maya sit with her," Vinny mused. "I think the scuff marks all over her doll were like a sinister warning to Iris."

Ben let out a chuckle. "We all had the same feeling when Brendon was born. Princess is hell on her toys, but a natural with babies."

It was completely true. Maya was something else. It had Vinny thinking…

"And you want kids? Not tomorrow," she added quickly, in case he got the wrong idea. Ben was the first man she felt she could genuinely *talk* to, and it surprised her how easy it was. Though it would take time for her to trust his openness wasn't a front, and she didn't want to give him the wrong impression when her mouth ran away with her in the interim. "But…someday? I know we talked about it on your birthday, but if it was a heat of the moment thing, I need to know."

"Yeah. It's not something I'll likely change my mind on, given I've always thought I'd be a dad someday. Are you okay with that?" The hope in his eyes about did her in.

"Yeah, Ben. I could be persuaded to have babies with you. Someday."

"And the rest of it?"

"Rest of it?"

"You know," he said sheepishly.

She did, but she wasn't giving in that easily. Sometimes Ben was still skittish over his divorce, understandably so. But if she had to move past her hangups, so did Ruben. Putting on her finest innocent expression, Vinny looked up at him and said, "No."

"Fuck." He was so adorable when he was flustered. "Just…maybe not go straight to babies. Be a family you and me first."

She continued to look at him with doe eyes. "Well, sure.

We *are* a family, Ben. Us, our dads, the Blackwoods. Hell, I'd even add Zeke."

"Ah, yeah. I meant…" She finally cracked a smile, the joining giggle drawing him out of his head, his gaze locking with hers. "Lavender Blume, you are a pain in my ass."

She slid her body up his, pressing her bare flesh against him as she stole a kiss. "I'm not ready for *that* tomorrow either. I want to explore the pivot I'm taking my career on first. Plus, once I'm your wife, I don't think I'll want to wait long for babies."

"Mmm. I'm not ready yet either, but I'm glad we're talking about it. What do you say we practice while we wait for Santa to bring our gifts?" He pulled her over his body, notching his erection at her opening.

"He won't come until we're all asleep. You heard the same Christmas poem I did five times at Maya's insistence," she teased.

"As long as *we* come, I don't give a shit about the fat fucker. I got what I want, right here," he said, nudging his head inside her.

"Tease," she said with a groan. "Maybe I don't want to lose out on *my* gifts."

"Our stockings are all meticulously hung over Carys's fireplace, not here." He pressed the rest of his length into her in one smooth motion. "Now ride me, Lavender."

She sat up, shifting her hips over his in a slow, ruinous dance she knew he didn't have the patience for tonight. As Lavender's pleasure pooled in her core, Ben tried to move things along beneath her. She tsked him playfully, stilling in warning. *I'm in control,* she said with her smirk.

"Lavender." His husky plea had her core spasming around him as she continued to move, grinding harder.

"Hold it," she teased. "I'm going to draw it out."

Ben flexed his core and rolled her beneath him in one smooth move. "You've been teasing me all night with your fuck me eyes. You know it. I know it." He emphasized his words with his thrusts. "I'm not waiting to paint your canvas while you sing my name, Lavender."

"Fuck, that's beautiful." She groaned as he settled in right over her sweet spot and began pumping into her. *"Beeennnn."*

"Exactly like that," he said, pinching one of her tender tips. She clenched around him again, the zing from his touch pushing her closer to the edge. She rolled her hips, grinding her desperate clit against him every time he bottomed out. "Touch yourself," he commanded.

One of her hands went between them, the other digging into his ass. She clung to him as she swept her arousal off his pistoning cock with her fingers and moved it up to her nub. Ben's praise as he watched her touch them both was all she needed. Her first orgasm broke, crested, and rolled right into her second when he took a toy she'd hadn't seen before and pressed it to her nipple before slowly dragging it down to where they were joined.

Ben held it there, rolling the textured tip between them in firm strokes until she was panting and pleading for just a little more. "Fuck, I'm close. Please, Ben. Please! *Ooohhhhh!"* He sent her into her brutally passionate third orgasm as he increased the vibration and pinched her second nipple, giving it a sharp tug before taking her breast into his palm and squeezing. Vinny's hips bucked hard into him, her core refusing to release him as she felt him do exactly what he wanted to, leaving his mark inside her while she wailed his name.

"I'm going to have your fingerprints on my tit," she

rasped with a smile. Vinny loved when Ben marked her. Seeing and feeling reminders of him on and in her body kept her libido purring along on high octane.

"At least you don't have to sit on them," he said, leaning down for a kiss. "Like the ones you just left on my ass cheek."

She spanked said ass cheek playfully. "You love it."

"I love *you,* beautiful."

———

THEY SPENT most of New Years Eve helping Zeke move into the house next door. Ben and Eric picked up the heavy lifting duties with Zeke, while Vinny and Carys assisted Iris in unpacking the income suit and setting it up for her and her daughter before shifting toward the rest of the house. Zeke's condo had sold immediately, and they had no time to spare.

Truth be told, their friend group was more than a little eager to have them closer. Many hands make light work, especially with the resident grandpas keeping an eye on the littles. Vinny was still surprised how fast they were in and done, including most of the furniture arranging and unpacking. Zeke was a bachelor, but he was a bachelor with good taste and nice furnishings.

Afterward, they ordered pizza, drank too many of Carys's blasted double margaritas, and then all stumbled to bed around ten. They were fucking exhausted. And if anyone wanted to get snarky, the ball *technically* had already dropped in Time Square on the other side of the country.

So there.

A few weeks later, Carys co-hosted a welcome party. Marcy, Hailey, Bella, and Lexi—along with their husbands and children—gave Iris a beautiful greeting, offering anything she needed for her baby and adding her to the group chat. She was properly overwhelmed by the community that had so easily embraced her, and Vinny overheard Zeke telling the guys he hoped it made up some for the horrid way his family was treating both of them.

The following week, Presley Harlow asked Vinny to join her in Los Angeles. Not only was she releasing "'72" as the first single off her album dropping in the coming Spring, but Presley had also asked Vinny to help co-write a few other tracks with her, as well as join in as a studio musician. She was having the time of her life and getting paid handsomely for it. Despite years of covering her favorites on her ArtBeat, this was ultimately the direction Vinny wanted to take her life.

And the timing couldn't be more perfect. Vinny didn't want to leave Ben for a second longer than she had to, and since he wasn't deploying, the idea of leaving on tour was the worst. She loved her regular time with Abner. Her dad had been coming around more often, finally slowing down a bit himself. While Q claimed he was getting old, Vinny knew he loved having a family again.

It was wild, looking back at where they had come in four years. The trip to Mexico Vinny had forced Carys on—or *voluntold,* as Eric tells it from his side given Ben had strong armed him as well—had given Vinny more than she had ever dreamed of. When Carys became a Blackwood, it started a chain reaction. She cherished her extended musical family, but the military family she'd pseudo inherited with her bestie was something else.

Something she was hoping to write a song about soon.

They were still building their case against Greer. There wasn't much they were privy to outside the information they had provided, but nobody was sad when it was confirmed Cunty Carla was in deep and going down with him. Vinny was still combing through the security footage for anything she missed on the rare occasion she wasn't curled up with Ben.

Ben, who she loved in a way she didn't know a person *could* love. She still hadn't told him outside of their song back when she thought she'd blown it with him, but she knew he felt her affection and was giving her all the time she needed to be ready to say those three little words.

With March came the culmination of Vinny's work with Presley. She had chosen three singles to pre-release before the album, all of them with Vinny's mark. The first time it aired on the radio, she'd been helping Carys in the kitchen ready for dinner. They were screaming so loud, they didn't hear the guys come in until their excitement added to the general chaos.

"I'm so fucking proud of you, beautiful," Ben had said, scooping her up and spinning her around before kissing her stupid.

"I can't believe our song is the first single!" Vinny squealed.

"Funcle, *yuck,*" Maya had said as she came in from the back yard. "Auntie isn't your princess, *I am.*"

"You're right, princess. But you know, if you ever want cousins, wouldn't it be nice if Lavender and I made them together? You have to share me with her sometimes," he tried.

"No," Maya deadpanned. "We have enough babies. No more. They take *sooooo* long to be any fun."

After she left the room, Carys blew out a nervous breath from where she was leaning against the sink. Eric was rubbing her back. "Shit. This is going to be a disaster."

"She'll be fine. It's not a baby; it's another big girl. Maya could use some exposure to older kids before she starts elementary school this fall," he reassured her.

"I'm sorry, *what?*" Vinny looked back and forth between the pair, her jaw hanging and hands on her hips. "What's going on?"

"Yeah, man. What she said," Ben said with a tip of his head in Vinny's direction.

"They have a girl for us to foster, possibly adopt. She's been fully surrendered to the state." Eric took point, explaining what Carys couldn't and still nervously chew her lips off her face at the same time.

"Wow! How old?" Ben asked.

"Six, or thereabouts. We don't have great details yet. She was living with her older brother after her mom got incarcerated. No father in the picture or other relatives," Eric rattled off.

From the look of Carys though, Vinny knew there was so much more to the story they were withholding. She looked at Ben and thought of how patient he was with her. *That's what Carys needs.* Vinny kissed Ben's cheek with gratitude before walking across the room and yanking her bestie into a hug that didn't end until Carys let go.

"I'm so nervous, Vin," she murmured.

"Because you care, Carys. That's not a bad thing." Carys nodded her head but didn't verbally respond to Vinny's words.

Time would tell.

A new girlie in the Blackwood household, whatever weird shit was happening next door between Zeke and Iris, Vinny's *blooming* career—ha! Plus the rest of their friend group. Not to mention Ben. They rarely spent a night apart, and Vinny was more than happy to spoon with him every night.

"This family can do *anything,* Carys." Vinny's smile made her cheeks hurt.

"That's right," Ben said, surprising Vinny by tossing her over his shoulder. "Like right now. I'm going to go show this woman how amazing I think she is."

They laughed all the way up to her bedroom.

Epilogue

VINNY

The following winter…

"How are you not leaving pit stains all over your Versace?" Vinny said in a panic as she dug for her emergency stick of deodorant. "Seriously, Presley. *How?"*

"I don't know why you are so out of sorts, Vin. And it's not Versace, it's Dior," Presley teased.

"Oh, yeah. That's totally different," she mumbled under her breath. "Ha!" She uncapped her deodorant and went to liberally apply as much as possible when Presley caught her arm.

"Don't. You think you are self-conscious now, imagine going out there with white smears clearly visible on your clothes while you are playing," she warned.

Holy shit, she's right. "I never feel this way down at the club with my friends."

"It's not televised. I mean, aside from your lives. But it still isn't the same as performing at the Grammy's. You're going to be *amazing,* my friend. We are going to perform the song we are *both* nominated for in twenty minutes, and it is going to be so fucking great. Like, deliriously high afterward.

You know, so long as you don't lock your knees and faint on stage."

"Thanks," Vinny said dryly. "What would I do without you?"

Finding out last fall her song was up for a songwriting Grammy had been the most soul shocking moment of Vinny's life. Then Presley had asked her to join her in performing it live at the ceremony as well. She'd had three months to freak out about what it would mean to be up there. Ultimately, showing other artists with albinism not to hide was too good an opportunity to skip.

Vinny was going to do this.

Thankfully her stage outfit wasn't as fussy as the one Presley had convinced her to wear on the red carpet and while they were in the audience. Also…Ben had cut through her nerves somewhat on the limo ride over with his fingers. Vinny had insisted she was too tense to orgasm her stress away, so he proved her wrong three times. The man in his uniform was sinful. Ben in a tuxedo had her wanting to let out a siren's call and go home instead.

Alas, she'd dreamed of this moment for as long as she could remember. And while Vinny was a little manic over performing, she hoped Presley won because she knew her new friend was secretly worried she'd flop on her sopho-more album and disappear before her time. It wouldn't happen, but Vinny understood her need for validation. Plus…yeah. Vinny could use a dose of *hell yes; you were absolutely made for this* herself via a standing ovation. Even if that ovation was just one man shouting her name over the room—her man.

Somewhere behind them, a soundstage tech informed them they had curtain in five, disappearing before she even saw the face attached to the warning. "I have to go over with the others now. See you after," Vinny murmured to Presley before heading to her position.

"I'm so glad you agreed to come, Vinny! See you after!"

Yup. From the bottom of my coffin, because I am going to have an aneurysm the second we get out there.

She picked up her '72 Stratocaster and did another quick check. It was still in tune from when she did the same fifteen minutes ago. *Here goes nothing.*

———

Ruben

The Grammys were nothing like Ruben had imagined it would be. He was sitting alone next to Vinny's empty seat, trying not to appear rude to the people around him as he anxiously waited for her to take her place on stage. Even Q had been surprised by the level of intensity this opportunity had set Vinny on edge.

She was gorgeous and talented. There was nothing to fear. He'd been telling her so for weeks.

Finally, the last award was given before her slot, and it was time. Presley Harlow was announced, and all attention went to one of the side stages used for the performances. She stood in front of everyone, the giant spot setting her gown shimmering. Beside her and a few feet back in a more subtle lighting, sat Vinny on a stool with her Strat. She looked like she was bored already, having done everyone the great favor of showing up for this shindig.

Hell, she'd even cleaned the grease out from under her nails after tuning up her baby. Lavender didn't shimmer the way Presley did, but it wasn't who Vinny was. She *could* be, on talent alone. Ruben knew Vinny had leading lady power.

But you can't force something on faith alone. The ethereal creature on stage with fishnets showing though her ripped jeans?

That's my woman.

For obvious reasons, Ruben preferred Vinny's version of the song. But Presley still gave him goosebumps. She had talent and was surprisingly kind. When Vinny had introduced him as the man who inspired the song, Presley had been elated.

Now Ruben got to be full of awe for them. Well, mostly Vinny. Shortly after saying *I love you* became comfortable for her, Ruben had driven out to Quincy's house while she was at the studio in LA with Presley. He didn't need Q's blessing, but he respected the hell out of the man for raising Vinny so well. Ruben *wanted* the blessing of his future father-in-law.

And he got it.

Right now? Ruben was in the moment. While the majority of onlookers were staring at Presley, Ruben only had eyes for the rocker chick beside her. Vinny had no idea how effortless she made this look. Her whole body was in the song, the beat keeping her bouncing along in step with her guitar. When she returned to her seat at his side, she'd be back in her fancy rented gown. On stage, she was all Lavender Blume.

'Cause I knew I loved you
The first time I saw you
In the backseat of my '72

Ruben listened as the crowd went wild at the end. He was crying and didn't give a flying fuck who saw how much she affected him. Lavender had leaned in for the last verse and looked right at him while she harmonized those three lines with Presley. Ruben was immediately back in his truck on the side of the road, staring at his phone while she confessed her feelings the only way she knew how.

I'm never letting you go, beautiful.

———

Thank you for reading one of my stories. Find out what happens next in the Devoted Brothers series! Zeke and Iris's journey is the final book, *Zeke.* If you liked *Ruben,* please consider writing a review on Amazon, or wherever you like to review. Even a few short words help small authors find our way to more readers.

Keep in touch! You can find me online, or send an email to sian@sianuptonbooks.com.
Facebook: Siân Upton *and* Siân Upton Reader Group
Facebook Page: Siân Upton Books
Instagram & Threads: @sianuptonauthor
Pinterest: @sianuptonbooks
Bookbub: Siân Upton

You can also join my newsletter and receive a **FREE** bonus novella by going to my website:
https://www.sianuptonbooks.com/
Or scan the QR code below!

Also by Siân Upton

Taste of Love **series**

Salty

Bitter

Sweet

Sour

There Was Only You (A Salty Prequel Novella)

Devoted Brothers **series**

Eric

Ruben

Zeke

Acknowledgments

Thank you for being here! Vinny and Ruben's story was a messy ball of trauma and growing pains. As I wrote Eric, Ruben formed in the back of my twisted mind, clear as day. The bullying, the settling, and the reconciling. We've all experienced a bully at some point, and I think these two have covered a lot of bases between them.

The awkward kid with glasses. The kid who is lauded for their talent one moment and shunned the next. The kid who looks different. The nerdy kid. The kid who grew up in poverty. The kid who was life smart instead of book smart.

Some traumas run deeper than others. Sometimes the part that hurts the most isn't the part people outside the situation perceive as a slight to begin with. Trauma is messy, and so too is healing from the fallout of those experiences.

For many in the military community, joining gave them true connection for the first time in their lives. Those who serve *make* a family, often over and over again when inevitable career and location changes force a tight knit group to separate. Now, add on how many joined to escape home (enter personal reasons here), and you are going to have some interesting challenges, to say the least.

After Eric and Carys's rare connection, it was time to showcase and celebrate the ones who read the room wrong the first go around. So, shout out to those who never gave up, military and civilian alike. Love is its own battleground but well worth the fight.